THE BEST
PARANORMAL
CRIME STORIES
EVER TOLD

THE BEST
PARANORMAL
CRIME STORIES
EVER TOLD

EDITED BY
MARTIN H. GREENBERG

INTRODUCTION BY
JOHN HELFERS

SKYHORSE PUBLISHING
A HERMAN GRAF BOOK

Skyhorse Publishing books may be purchased in bulk at special discounts for sales promotion, corporate gifts, fund-raising, or educational purposes. Special editions can also be created to specifications. For details, contact the Special Sales Department, Skyhorse Publishing, 555 Eighth Avenue, Suite 903, New York, NY 10018 or info@skyhorsepublishing.com.

www.skyhorsepublishing.com

10 9 8 7 6 5 4 3 2 1

Library of Congress Cataloging-in-Publication Data

The best paranormal crime stories ever told / edited by Martin H. Greenberg.
    p. cm.
  ISBN 978-1-61608-119-5 (pbk. : alk. paper)
  1. Detective and mystery stories, American. 2. Parapsychology in criminal investigation--Fiction. 3. Fantasy fiction, American. 4. Detective and mystery stories, English. 5. Fantasy fiction, English. I. Greenberg, Martin Harry.
  PS648.D4B48 2010
  813'.087208--dc22

                              2010029698

Printed in Canada

Table of Contents

Copyrights

Introduction

JOHN HELFERS

A lot of paranormal fans think that supernatural creatures have all the fun. Vampires have that immortality thing going on, as well as near-invulnerability to all but a few common household items (and one really big environmental one). Werewolves get that super-strength, speed, and senses, not to mention wicked claws, and a nice, thick fur coat (although there is that problem of what to do with your heap of shredded clothes when you change). Witches and warlocks get to wield phenomenal cosmic power (that almost never backfires on them, usually).

But, as a famous uncle from the comics said long ago, "With great power comes great responsibility." Specifically, the responsibility *not* to use those amazing powers for evil. Sadly, many of those creatures of the night don't manage to stay on the side of good. Although the temptation is understandable—after all, they're already outsiders in society, so what's to stop them from breaking the rest of humanity's laws? And whether transgressing or being transgressed against, these creatures will find a way to get away with much more than they should . . .

Of course, for those who try to break the law, there are also those who do their best to bring the perpetrators to justice as well. If the officer of the law is a human, they might be biting off more than they can chew, but if they're also a paranormal, then get ready for all hell to break loose.

The fifteen stories collected here represent both sides of supernatural law and disorder. From best-selling author Kelley Armstrong comes a tale of two shapeshifters on their honeymoon in the big bad city, and how their trip is enlivened by another werewolf who's looking for a fight—and gets much more than he expected. Simon R. Green brings us another story set in his inimitable, shadowy world of Nightside, where nothing and no one is who they first seem to be. Veteran crime writer Max Allan Collins serves up a gritty tale of crime and detection during the Great Depression; and when someone starts killing the down-and-out frequenting a soup kitchen, it takes a very special detective to go undercover and find out who's committing murder. And another best-selling author, Patricia Briggs, brings us a story of an estranged father and daughter who come together while protecting a special boy from a very dangerous predator.

From con artists with a touch of the *fae* to—and I'm not making this up—motorcycle-riding rats wielding ninja swords, these stories will take you on several walks into the wild side of supernatural life, with the good, the bad, and in several instances, the ugly. So take a deep breath, and prepare to break a few laws . . . or chase after the lawbreakers . . . in *The Best Paranormal Crime Stories Ever Told.*

Appetite for Murder

SIMON R. GREEN

I never wanted to be a Detective. But the call went out, and no-one else stood up, so I sold my soul to the company store, for a badge and a gun and a shift that never ends.

The Nightside is London's very own dirty little secret; a hidden realm of gods and monsters, magic and murder, and more sin and temptation than you can shake a wallet at. People come to the Nightside from all over the world, to indulge the pleasures and appetites that might not have a name, but certainly have a price. It's always night in the Nightside, always three o'clock on the morning, the hour that tries men's souls and finds them wanting. The sun has never shone here, probably because it knows it isn't welcome. This is a place to do things that can only be done in the shadows, in the dark.

I'm Sam Warren. I was the first, and for a long time the only, Detective in the Nightside. I worked for the Authorities, those grey and faceless figures who run the Nightside, in as much as anyone does, or can. Even in a place where there is no crime, because everything is permitted, where sin and suffering, death and damnation are just business as usual . . . there are still those who go too far, and have to be taken down hard. And for that, you need a Detective.

We don't get many serial killers in the Nightside. Mostly because amateurs don't tend to last long among so much professional competition. But I was made Detective, more years ago than I care to remember, to hunt down the very first of these human monsters. His name was Shock-Headed Peter. He killed three hundred and forty-seven men, women and children, before I caught him. Though that's just an official estimate; we never found any of his victims' bodies. Just their clothes. Wouldn't surprise me if the real total was closer to a thousand. I caught him and put him away; but the things I saw, and the things I had to do, changed me forever.

Made me the Nightside's Detective, for all my sins, mea culpa.

I'd just finished eating when the call came in. From the H. P. Lovecraft Memorial Library, home to more forbidden tomes under one roof than anywhere else. Browse at your own risk. It appeared the Nightside's latest serial killer had struck again. Only this time he'd been interrupted, and the body was still warm, the blood still wet.

I strode through the Library accompanied by a Mister Pettigrew, a tall stork-like personage with wild eyes and a shock of white hair. He gabbled continuously as we made our way through the tall stacks, wringing his bony hands against his sunken chest. Mister Pettigrew was Chief Librarian, and almost overcome with shame that such a vulgar thing should have happened in his Library.

"It's all such a mess!" he wailed. "And right in the middle of the Anthropology Section. We've only just finished refurbishing!"

"What can you tell me about the victim?" I said patiently.

"Oh, he's dead. Yes. Very dead, in fact. Horribly mutilated,

Detective! I don't know how we're going to get the blood out of the carpets."

"Did you happen to notice if there were any . . . pieces missing, from the body?"

"Pieces? Oh dear," said Mister Pettigrew. "I can feel one of my heads coming on. I think I'm going to have to go and have a little lie down."

He took me as far as the Anthropology Section, and then disappeared at speed. It hadn't been twenty minutes since I got the call, but still someone had beaten me to the body. Crouching beside the bloody mess on the floor was the Nightside's very own superheroine, Ms. Fate. She wore a highly polished black leather outfit, complete with full face mask and cape; but somehow on her it never looked like a costume or some fetish thing. It looked like a uniform. Like work clothes. She even had a utility belt around her narrow waist, all golden clasps and bulging little pouches. I thought the high heels on the boots were a bit much, though. I came up on her from behind, making no noise at all, but she still knew I was there.

"Hello, Detective Warren," she said, in her low smoky voice, not even glancing round. "You got here fast."

"Happened to be in the neighbourhood," I said. "What have you found?"

"All kinds of interesting things. Come and have a look."

Anyone else I would have sent packing, but not her. We'd worked a bunch of cases together, and she knew her stuff. We don't get too many superheroes or vigilantes in the Nightside, mostly because they get killed off so damn quickly. Ms. Fate, that dark avenger of the night, was different. Very focused, very skilled, very professional. Would have made a good detective. She made room for me to crouch down beside her. My knees made loud cracking noises in the Library hush.

"You're looking good, Detective," Ms. Fate said easily. "Have you started dying your hair?"

"Far too much grey," I said. "I was starting to look my age, and I couldn't have that."

"I've questioned the staff," said Ms. Fate. "Knew you wouldn't mind. Noone saw anything, but then noone ever does, in the Nightside. Only one way in to this Section, and only one way out, and he would have had blood all over him, but . . ."

"Any camera surveillance?"

"The kind of people who come here, to read the kind of books they keep here, really don't want to be identified. So, no surveillance of any kind, scientific or mystical. There's major security in place to keep any of the books from going walkabout, but that's it."

"If our killer was interrupted, he may have left some clues behind," I said. "This is his sixth victim. Maybe he got sloppy."

Ms. Fate nodded slowly, her expression unreadable behind her dark mask. Her eyes were very blue, very bright. "This has got to stop, Detective. Five previous victims, all horribly mutilated, all with missing organs. Different organs each time. Interestingly enough, the first victim was killed with a blade, but all the others were torn apart, through brute strength. Why change his MO after the first killing? Most serial killers cling to a pattern, a ritual, that means something significant to them."

"Maybe he decided a blade wasn't personal enough," I said. "Maybe he felt the need to get his hands dirty."

We both looked at the body in silence for a while. This one was different. The victim had been a werewolf, and had been caught in mid-change as he died. His face had elongated into a muzzle, his hands had claws, and patches of silver-grey fur showed clearly on his exposed skin. His clothes were ripped and torn and soaked with blood. He'd been gutted, torn raggedly open from chin to crotch, leaving a great crimson wound. There was blood all around him, and more spattered across the spines of books on the shelves.

"It's never easy to kill a werewolf," Ms. Fate said finally. "But given the state of the wound's edges, he wasn't cut open. That rules out a silver dagger."

"No sign of a silver bullet either," I said.

"Then we can probably rule out the Lone Ranger." She rubbed her bare chin thoughtfully. "You know; the extent of these injuries reminds me a lot of cattle mutilations."

I looked at her. "Are we talking little Grey aliens?"

She smiled briefly, her scarlet lips standing out against the pale skin under the black mask. "Maybe I should check to see if he's been probed?"

"I think that was the least of his worries," I said. "This must have been a really bad way to die. Our victim had his organs ripped out while he was still alive."

Ms. Fate busied herself taking samples from the body and the crime scene, dropping them into sealable plastic bags, and tucking them away in her belt pouches.

"Don't smile," she said, not looking round. "Forensic science catches more killers than deductive thought."

"I never said a word," I said innocently.

"You didn't have to. You only have to look at my utility belt and your mouth starts twitching. I'll have you know the things I store in my belt have saved my life on more than one occasion. Shuriken, smoke bombs, nausea gas capsules, stun grenades . . . A girl has to be prepared for everything." She stood up and looked down at the body. "It's such a mess I can't even tell which organs were taken; can you?"

"The heart, certainly," I said, standing up. "Anything else, we'll have to wait for the autopsy."

"I've already been through the clothing," said Ms. Fate. "If there was any ID, the killer took it with him. But I did find a Press Pass, tucked away in his shoe. Said he worked for the *Night Times.* But no name on the pass, which is odd. Could be an investigative reporter, I suppose, working undercover."

"I'll check with the editor," I said.

"But what was he doing here? Research?"

We both looked around, and Ms. Fate was the first to find a book lying on the floor, just outside the blood pool. She opened the book, and flicked quickly through it.

"Anything interesting?" I said.

"Hard to tell. Some doctoral dissertation, on the cannibal practices of certain South American tribes."

I gestured for the book, and she handed it over. I skimmed quickly through the opening chapter. "Seems to be about the old cannibal myth, that you are what you eat. You know; eat a brave man's heart to become brave, a runner's leg muscles to become fast . . ."

We both looked at the torn open body on the floor, with its missing organs.

"Could that be our murderer's motivation?" said Ms. Fate. "He's taking the organs so he can eat them later, and maybe . . . what? Gain new abilities? Run me through the details of the five previous victims, Detective."

"First was a minor Greek godling," I said. "Supposedly descended from Hercules, at many removes. Very strong. Died of a single knife wound to the heart. Chest and arm muscles were taken."

"Just the one blow, to the heart," said Ms. Fate. "You'd have to get in close for that. Which suggests the victim either knew his killer, or had reason to trust him."

"If the killer has acquired a godling's strength, he wouldn't need a knife any more," I said.

"There's more to it than that." She looked like she might be frowning, behind her mask. "This whole hands-on thing shouts . . . passion. That the killer enjoyed it, or took some satisfaction from it."

"Second victim was a farseer," I said. "What they call a remote viewer these days. Her head was smashed in, and her eyes taken. After that; an immortal who lost his testicles, a teleporter for a messenger service who had his brain ripped right out of his skull, and finally a minor radio chat show host, who lost his tongue and vocal chords."

"Why that last one?" said Ms Fate. "What did the killer hope to gain? The gift of the gab?"

"You'll have to ask him," I said. "Presumably the killer believed that eating the werewolf's missing organs would give him shape-changing abilities, or at least regeneration."

"He's trying to eat himself into a more powerful person . . . Hell, just the godling's strength and the werewolf's abilities will make him really hard to take down. Have you come up with any leads yet, from the previous victims?"

"No," I said. "Nothing."

"Then I suppose we'd better run through the usual suspects, if only to cross them off. How about Mr. Stab, the legendary uncaught immortal serial killer of Old London Town?"

"No," I said. "He always uses a knife, or a scalpel. Always has, ever since 1888."

"All right; how about Arnold Drood, the Bloody Man?"

"His own family tracked him down and killed him, just last year."

"Good. Shock-Headed Peter?"

"Still in prison, where I put him," I said. "And there he'll stay, till the day he dies."

Ms. Fate sniffed. "Don't know why they didn't just execute him."

"Oh, they tried," I said. "Several times, in fact. But it didn't take."

"Wait a minute," said Ms. Fate. She knelt down again suddenly, and leant right over to study the dead man's elongated muzzle. "Take a look at this, Detective. The nose and mouth tissues are eaten away. Right back to the bone in places. I wonder . . . " She produced a chemical kit from her belt, and ran some quick tests. "I thought so. Silver. Definite traces of silver dust, in the nose, mouth and throat. Now that was clever . . . Throw a handful of silver dust into the werewolf's face, he breathes it in, unsuspecting, and his tissues would immediately react to the silver. It had to have been horribly painful; certainly enough to distract the victim and interrupt his shape change . . . while leaving him vulnerable to the killer's exceptional strength."

"Well spotted," I said. "I must be getting old. Was a time I wouldn't have missed something like that."

"You're not that old," Ms. Fate said lightly.

"Old enough that they want to retire me," I said.

"You? You'll never retire! You live for this job."

"Yes," I said. "I've done it so long it's all I've got now. But I am getting old. Slow. Still better than any of these upstart latecomers, like John Taylor and Tommy Oblivion."

"You look fine to me," Ms. Fate said firmly. "In pretty good shape too, for a man of your age. How do you manage it?"

I smiled. "We all have our secrets."

"Of course. This is the Nightside, after all."

"I could have worked out your secret identity," I said. "If I'd wanted to."

"Perhaps. Though it might have surprised you. Why didn't you?"

"I don't know. Professional courtesy? Or maybe I just liked the idea of knowing there was someone else around who wanted to catch murderers as much as I did."

"You can depend on me," said Ms. Fate.

Our next port of call was the Nightside's one and only autopsy room. We do have a CSI, but it only has four people in it. And only one Coroner; Dr. West. Short, stocky fellow with a smiling face and flat straw-yellow hair. I wouldn't leave him alone with the body of anyone I cared about, but he's good enough at his job.

By the time Ms. Fate and I got there, Dr. West already has the werewolf's body laid out in his slab. He was washing the naked body with great thoroughness and crooning a song to it as we entered. He looked round unhurriedly, and waggled the fingers of one podgy hand at us.

"Come in, come in! So nice to have visitors. So nice! Of course, I'm never alone down here, but I do miss good conversation. Take a look at this."

He put down his wet sponge, picked up a long surgical instrument, and started poking around inside the body's massive wound. Ms. Fate and I moved closer, while still maintaining a respectful distance. Dr. West tended to get over-excited with a scalpel in his hand, and we didn't want to get spattered.

Dr. West thrust both his hands into the cavity and started rooting around with quite unnecessary enthusiasm. "The heart is missing," he said cheerfully. "Also, the liver. Yes. Yes . . . Not cut out, torn out . . . Made a real mess of this poor fellow's insides; hard to be sure of anything else . . . Not sure what to put down as actual cause of death; blood loss, trauma, shock . . . Heart attack? Yes. That covers it. So; another victim for our current serial killer. Number six . . . how very industrious. Oh yes. Haven't even got a name for your chart, have we, boy? Just another John Doe . . . But not to worry; I've got a nice little locker waiting for you, nice and cosy, next to your fellow victims."

"You have got to stop talking to the corpses like that," I said sternly. "One of these days someone will catch you at it."

Dr. West stuck out his tongue at me. "Let them. See if I care. See if they can get anyone else to do this job."

"How long have you been Coroner, Dr. West?" said Ms. Fate, tactfully changing the subject.

"Oh, years and years, my dear. I was made Coroner the same year Samuel here was made Detective. Oh yes, we go way back, Samuel and I. All because of that nasty Shock-Headed Peter . . . The Authorities decided that such a successful serial killer was bad for business, and therefore Something Must Be Done. It's all about popular perception, you see . . . There are many things in the Nightside far more dangerous than any human killer could ever hope to be, but the Authorities, bless their grey little hearts, wanted visitors to feel safe, so . . ."

He stopped and looked at me sourly. "You'd never believe he and I were the same age, would you? How do you do it, Samuel?"

"Healthy eating," I said. "And lots of vitamins."

"Why haven't you called in Walker?" Ms. Fate said suddenly. "He speaks for the Authorities, with a Voice everyone has to obey; and I've heard it said he once made a corpse sit up on a slab and answer his questions."

"Oh he did, he did," said Dr. West, pulling his hands out of the body with a nasty sucking sound. "I was there at the time, and very edifying it was too. But unfortunately, all six of our victims had their tongues torn out. After our killer had taken the bits and pieces he wanted. Which suggests our killer had reason to be afraid of Walker."

"Hell," I said. "Everyone's got good reason to be afraid of Walker."

Dr. West shrugged, threw aside his scalpel and slipped off his latex gloves with a deliberate flourish, as though to make clear he'd done all that could reasonably be expected of him.

Ms. Fate stared into the open wound again. "Our killer really does like his work, doesn't he?"

"He's got an appetite for it," I said solemnly.

"Oh please," said Ms. Fate.

I moved in beside her, staring down into the cavity. "Took the heart out first, then the liver. Our killer must believe they hold the secret of the werewolf's abilities. If he is a shape-changer now, he'd be that much harder to take down."

Ms. Fate looked at me thoughtfully, and then turned to Dr. West. "Do you still have all the victims' clothes and belongings?"

"Of course, my dear, of course! Individually bagged and tagged. Help yourself."

She opened every bag, and checked every piece of torn and blood-soaked clothing. It's always good to see a real professional at work. Eventually she ran out of things to check and test, and turned back to me.

"Six victims. Different ages, sexes, occupations. Nothing at all to connect them. Unless you know something, Detective."

"There's nothing in the files," I said.

"So how were the victims chosen? Why these six people?"

"Maybe the people don't matter," I said. "Just their abilities."

"Run me through them again," she said. "Names and abilities, in order, from the beginning."

"First victim was the godling Demetrius Heracles," I said patiently. "Then the farseer, Barbara Moore. The teleporter, Cainy du Brec. The immortal Count Magnus, though I doubt very much that was his real name. The chat show host, Adrian Woss, and finally the werewolf, Christopher Russell."

"This whole business reminds me unpleasantly of Shock- Headed Peter," Ms. Fate said slowly. "Not the MO, but the sheer ruthlessness of the murders. Are you sure he hasn't escaped?"

"Positive," I said. "No-one escapes from Shadow Deep."

She shook her masked head, her heavy cloak rustling loudly. "I'd still feel happier if we checked. Can you get us in?"

"Of course," I said. "I'm the Detective."

So we went down into Shadow Deep, all the way down to the darkest place in the Nightside, sunk far below in the cold bedrock. Constructed . . . no one knows how long ago, to hold the most vicious, evil and dangerous criminals ever stupid enough to prey on the Nightside. The ones we can't, for one reason or another, just execute and be done with. The only way down is by the official transport circle, maintained and operated by three witches from a small room over a really rough bar called The Jolly Cripple. If the people who drank in the bar knew what went on in the room above their heads . . . they'd probably drink a hell of a lot more.

"Why here?" said Ms. Fate, as we ascended the gloomy back stairs. "Secrecy?"

"Partly, I suppose," I said. "More likely because it's cheap."

The three witches were the traditional bent-over hags in tattered cloaks, all clawed hands and hooked noses. The great circle on the floor had been marked in chalk mixed with sulphur and semen. You don't want to know how I found out. Ms. Fate glowered at the three witches.

"You can stop that cackling right now. You don't have to put on an act; we're not tourists."

"Well pardon us for taking pride in our work," said one of the witches, straightening up immediately. "We are professionals, after all. And image is everything, these days. You don't think these warts just happened, do you?"

I gave her my best hard look, and she got the transport operation underway. The three witches did the business with a minimum of chanting and incense, and down Ms. Fate and I went down, to Shadow Deep.

It was dark when we arrived. Completely dark, with not a ghost of a light anywhere. I only knew Ms. Fate was there with me because I could hear her breathing at my side. Footsteps approached, slow and heavy, until finally a pair of night vision goggles were thrust into my hand. I nearly jumped out of my skin, and from the muffled squeak beside me, so did Ms. Fate. I slipped the goggles on, and Shadow Deep appeared around me, all dull green images and fuzzy shadows.

It's always dark in Shadow Deep.

We were standing in an ancient circular stone chamber, with a low roof, curving walls and just the one exit, leading onto a stone tunnel. Standing before us was one of the prison staff; a rough clay golem with simple pre-programmed routines. It had no eyes on its smooth face, because it didn't need to see. It turned abruptly and started off down the tunnel, and Ms. Fate and I hurried after it. The tunnel branched almost immediately, and branched again, and as we moved from tunnel to identical tunnel, I soon lost all track of where I was.

We came at last to the Governor's office, and the golem raised an oversized hand and knocked once on the door. A cheery voice called out for us to enter, and the door swung open before us. A blinding light spilled out, and Ms. Fate and I clawed off our goggles as we stumbled into the office. The door shut itself behind us.

I looked around the Governor's office with watering eyes. It wasn't particularly big, but it had all the comforts. The Governor came out from behind his desk to greet us, a big blocky man with a big friendly smile that didn't touch his eyes at all. He seemed happy to see us, but then, he was probably happy to see anyone. Shadow Deep doesn't get many visitors.

"Welcome, welcome!" he said, taking our goggles and shaking my hand and Ms. Fate's with great gusto. "The great Detective and the famous vigilante; such an honour! Do sit down, make yourselves at home. That's right! Make yourselves comfortable! Can I offer you a drink, cigars . . . ?"

"No," I said.

"Ah, Detective," said the Governor, sitting down again behind his desk. "It's always business with you, isn't it?"

"Ms. Fate is concerned that one of your inmates might have escaped," I said.

"What? Oh no; no, quite impossible!" The Governor turned his full attention and what he likes to think of as his charming smile on Ms. Fate. "No one ever escapes from here. Never, never. It's always dark in Shadow Deep, you see. Light doesn't work here, outside my office. Not any kind of light, scientific or magical. Not even a match . . . Even if a prisoner could get out of his cell, which he can't, there's no way he could find his way through the maze of tunnels to the transfer site. Even a teleporter can't get out of here, because there's no way of knowing how far down we are!"

"Tell her how it works," I said. "Tell her what happens to the scum I bring here."

The Governor blinked rapidly, and tried another ingratiating smile. "Yes, well, the prisoner is put into his cell by one of the golems, and the door is then nailed shut. And sealed forever with pre-prepared, very powerful magics. Once in, a prisoner never leaves his cell. The golems pass food and water through a slot in the door. And that's it."

"What about . . . ?" said Ms. Fate.

"There's a grille in the floor."

"Oh, ick."

"Quite," said the Governor. "You must understand, our prisoners are not here to reform, or repent. Only the very worst individuals ever end up here, and they stay here till they die. However long that takes. No reprieves, and no time off for good behaviour."

"How did you get this job?" said Ms. Fate.

"I think I must have done something really bad in a previous existence," the Governor said grandly. "Cosmic payback can be such a bitch."

"You got this job because you got caught," I said.

The Governor scowled. "Yes, well . . . It's not that I did anything really bad . . ."

"Ms. Fate," I said, "Allow me to introduce to you Charles Peace, villain from a long line of villains. Burglar, thief, and snapper up of anything valuable not actually nailed down. Safes opened while you wait."

"That was my downfall," the Governor admitted. "I opened Walker's safe, you see; just for the challenge of it. And I saw something I really shouldn't have seen. Something no one was ever supposed to see. I ran, of course, but the Detective tracked me down and brought me back, and Walker gave me a choice. On the spot execution, or serve here as Governor until what I know becomes obsolete, and doesn't matter any more. That was seventeen years ago, and there isn't a day goes by where I don't wonder whether I made the right decision."

"Seventeen years?" said Ms. Fate. She always did have a soft spot for a hard-luck story.

"Seventeen years, four months, and three days," said the Governor. "Not that I obsess about it, you understand."

"Is Shock-Headed Peter still here?" I said bluntly. "There's no chance he could have got out?"

"Of course not! I did the rounds only an hour ago, and his cell is still sealed. Come on, Detective; if Shock-Headed Peter was on the loose in the Nightside again, we'd all know about it."

"Who else have you got down here?" said Ms. Fate. "Anyone . . . famous?"

"Oh, quite a few; certainly some names you'd recognise. Let's see; we have the Murder Masques, Sweet Annie Abattoir, Max Maxwell the Voodoo Apostate, Maggie Malign . . . But they're all quite secure, too, I can assure you."

"I just needed to be sure this place is as secure as it's supposed to be," said Ms. Fate. "You'd better prepare a new cell, Governor; because I've brought you a new prisoner."

And she looked at me.

I rose to my feet, and so did she. We stood looking at each other for a long moment.

"I'm sorry, Sam," she said. "But it's you. You're the murderer."

"Have you gone mad?" I said.

"You gave yourself away, Sam," she said, meeting my gaze squarely with her own. "That's why I had you bring me here to Shadow Deep, where you belong. Where even you can't get away."

"What makes you think it was me?" I said.

"You knew things you shouldn't have known. Things only the killer could have known. First, at the Library. That anthropology text was a dry, stuffy and very academic text. Very difficult for a layman to read and understand. But you just skimmed through it and then neatly summed up the whole concept. The only way you could have done that was if you'd known it in advance. That raised my suspicions, but I didn't say anything. I wanted to be wrong about you.

"But you did it again, at the autopsy. First, you knew that the heart had been removed *before* the liver. Dr. West hadn't worked that out yet, because the body's insides were such a mess. Second; when I asked you to name the victims in order, you named them all, including the werewolf. Who hasn't been identified yet. Dr West still had him down as a John Doe.

"So; it had to be you. Why, Sam? Why?"

"Because they were going to make me retire," I said. It was actually a relief, to be able to tell it to someone. "Take away my job, my reason for living, just because I'm not as young as I used to be. All my experience, all my years of service, all the things I've done for them, and the Authorities were going to give me a gold watch and throw me on the scrap heap. Now; when things are worse than they've ever been. When I'm needed more than ever. It wasn't fair. It wasn't right.

"So I decided I would just take what I needed, to make myself the greatest Detective that ever was. With my new abilities, I would be unstoppable. I would go private, like John Taylor and Larry Oblivion; and show those wet behind the ears newcomers how it's done ... I would become rich and famous, and if I looked a little younger, well ... this is the Nightside, after all.

"Shed no tears for my victims. They were all criminals, though I could never prove it. That's why there was no paperwork on them. But I knew. Trust me; they all deserved to die. They were all scum.

"I'd actually finished, you know. The werewolf would have been my last victim. I had all I needed. I teleported in and out of the Library, which is why no one saw me come and go. But then . . . you had to turn up, the second-best detective in the Nightside, and spoil everything. I never should have agreed to train you . . . but I saw in you a passion for justice that matched my own. You could have been my partner, my successor. The things we could have done . . . But now I'm going to have to kill you, and the Governor. I can't let you tell. Can't let you stop me, not after everything I've done. The Nightside needs me.

"You'll just be two more victims of the unknown serial killer."

I surged forward with a werewolf's supernatural speed, and grabbed the front of Ms. Fate's black leather costume with a godling's strength. I closed my hand on her chest and ripped her left breast away. And then I stopped, dumbstruck. The breast was in my hand, but under the torn open leather there was no wound, no spouting blood. Only a very flat, very masculine chest. Ms. Fate smiled coldly.

"And that's why you'd never have guessed my secret identity, Sam. Who would ever have suspected that a man would dress up as a super-heroine, to fight crime? But then, this is the Nightside, and like you said; we all have our secrets." And while I stood there, listening with an open mouth, she palmed a nausea gas capsule from her belt and threw it in my face. I hit the stone floor on my hands and knees, vomiting so hard I couldn't concentrate enough to use any of my abilities. The Governor called for two of his golems, and they came and dragged me away. They threw me into a cell, and then nailed the door shut, and sealed it forever.

No need for a trial. Ms. Fate would have a word with Walker, and that would be that. That's how I always did it.

So here I am, in Shadow Deep, in the dark that never ends. Guess whose cell they put me next to. Just guess.

One of these days they'll open this cell and find nothing here but my clothes.

Star of David

PATRICIA BRIGGS

"I checked them out myself," Myra snapped. "Have you ever just considered that *your boy* isn't the angel you thought he was?"

Stella took off her glasses and set them on her desk. "I think that we both need some perspective. Why don't you take the rest of the afternoon off?" *Before I slap your stupid face.* People like Devonte don't change that fast, not without good reason.

Myra opened her mouth, but after she got a look at Stella's face she shut it again. Mutely she stalked to her desk and retrieved her coat and purse. She slammed the door behind her.

As soon as she was gone, Stella opened the folder and looked at the pictures of the crime scene again. They were duplicates, and doubtless Clive, her brother the detective, had broken a few rules when he sent them to her—not that breaking rules had ever bothered him, not when he was five and not as a grown man nearing fifty and old enough to know better.

She touched the photos lightly, then closed the folder again. There was a yellow sticky with a phone number on it and nothing else: Clive didn't have to put a name on it. Her little brother knew she'd see what he had seen.

She picked up the phone and punched in the numbers fast, not giving herself a chance for second thoughts.

The barracks were empty, leaving David's office silent and bleak. The boys were on furlough with their various families for December.

His mercenaries specialized in live retrieval which tended to be in and out stuff, a couple of weeks per job at the most. He didn't want to get involved in the gray area of unsanctioned combat or out-and-out war—where you killed people because someone told you to. In retrieval there were good guys and bad guys still—and if there weren't, he didn't take the job. Their reputation was such that they had no trouble finding jobs.

And unless all hell really broke loose, they always took December off to be with their families. David never let them know how hard that made it for him.

Werewolves need their packs.

If his pack was human, well, they knew about him and they filled that odd wolf-quirk that demanded he have people to protect, brothers in heart and mind. He couldn't stomach a real pack, he hated what he was too much.

He couldn't bear to live with his own kind, but this worked as a substitute and kept him centered. When his boys were here, when they had a job to do, he had direction and purpose.

His grandsons had invited him for the family dinner, but he'd refused as he always did. He still saw his sons on a regular basis. Both of them had served in his small band of mercenaries for a while, until the life lost its appeal or the risks grew too great for men with growing families. But he stayed away at Christmas.

Restlessness had him pacing: there were no plans to make, no wrongs to right. Finally he unlocked the safe and pulled out a couple of the newer rifles. He needed to put some time in with them anyway.

An hour of shooting staved off the restlessness, but only until he locked the guns up again. He'd have to go for a run. When he emptied his pockets in preparation, he noticed he had missed a call while he'd been shooting. He glanced at the number, frowning when he didn't recognize it. Most of his jobs came through an agent who knew better than to give out his cell number. Before he could decide if he wanted to return the call, his phone rang again, a call from the same number.

"Christiansen," he answered briskly.

There was a long silence. "Papa?"

He closed his eyes and sank back in his chair feeling his heart expand with almost painful intentness as his wolf fought with the man who knew his daughter hated him: didn't want to see him, ever. She had been there when her mother died.

"Stella?" He couldn't imagine what it took to make her break almost forty years of silence. "Are you all right? Is there something wrong?" Someone he could kill for her? A building to blow up? Anything at all.

She swallowed. He could hear it over the line. He waited for her to hang up.

Instead, when she spoke again, her voice was brisk and the wavery pain that colored that first "Papa" was gone as if it had never been. "I was wondering if you would consider doing a favor for me."

"What do you need?" He was proud that came out evenly. Always better to know what you're getting into, he told himself. He wanted to tell her that she could ask him for anything—but he didn't want to scare her.

"I run an agency that places foster kids," she told him, as if he didn't know. As if her brothers hadn't told her how he quizzed them to find out how she was doing and what she was up to. He hoped she never found out about her ex-boyfriend who'd turned stalker. He hadn't killed that one, though his willingness to do so had made it easier to persuade the man that he wanted to take up permanent residence in a different state.

"I know," he said because it seemed like she needed a response.

"There's something—" she hesitated. "Look, this might not have been the best idea."

He was losing her again. He had to breathe deeply to keep the panic from his voice. "Why don't you tell me about it anyway? Do you have something better to do?"

"I remember that," she said. "I remember you doing that with Mom. She'd be hysterical, throwing dishes or books, and you'd sit down and say, 'Why don't you tell me about it?'"

Did she want to talk about her mother now? About the one time he'd needed to be calm and failed? He hadn't known he was a werewolf until it was too late. Until after he'd killed his wife and the lover she'd taken while David had been fighting for God and country, both of whom had forgotten him. She'd been waiting until he came home to tell him that she was leaving—it was a mistake she'd had no time to regret. He, on the other hand, might have forever to regret it for her.

He never spoke of it. Not to anyone. For Stella he'd do it, but she knew the story anyway. She'd been there.

"Do you want to talk about your mother?" he asked, his voice carrying into a lower timbre; as it did when the wolf was close.

"No. Not that," she said hurriedly. "Nothing like that. I'm sorry. This isn't a good idea."

She was going to hang up. He drew on his hard-earned control and thought fast.

Forty years as a hunter and leader of men had given him a lot of practice reading between the lines. If he could put aside the fact that she was his daughter, maybe he could salvage this.

She'd told him she ran a foster agency like it was important to the rest of what she had to say.

"It's about your work?" he asked, trying to figure out what a social worker would need with a werewolf. Oh. "Is there a—" His daughter preferred not to talk about werewolves, Clive had told him. So if there was something supernatural she was going to have to bring it up. "Is there someone bothering you?"

"No," she said. "Nothing like that. It's one of my boys."

Stella had never married, never had children of her own. Her brother said it was because she had all the people to take care of that she could handle.

"One of the foster kids."

"Devonte Parish."

"He one of your special ones?" he asked. His Stella had never seen a stray she hadn't brought home, animal or human. Most she'd dusted off and sent home with a meal and bandages as needed—but some of them she'd kept.

She sighed. "Come and see him, would you? Tomorrow?"

"I'll be there," he promised. It would take him a few hours to set up permission from the packs in her area: travel was complicated for a werewolf. "Probably sometime in the afternoon. This the number I can find you at?"

⁓

Instead of taking a taxi from the airport, he rented a car. It might be harder to park, but it would give them mobility and privacy. If his daughter only needed this, if she didn't want to smoke the peace pipe yet, then he didn't need it witnessed by a cab driver. A witness would make it harder for him to control himself—and his little girl never needed to see him out of control ever again.

He called her before setting out, and he could tell that she'd had second and third thoughts.

"Look," he finally told her. "I'm here now. Maybe we should go and talk to the boy. Where can I meet you?"

⁓

He'd have known her anywhere though he hadn't, by her request, seen her since the night he'd killed his wife. She'd been twelve and now she was a grown woman with silver threads running through her kinky black hair. The last time he'd seen her she'd been still a little rounded and soft as most children are—and now there wasn't an ounce of softness in her. She was muscular and lean— like him.

It had been a long time, but he'd never have mistaken her for anyone else: she had his eyes and her mother's face.

He'd thought you had to be bleeding someplace to hurt this badly. The beast struggled within him, looking for an enemy. But he controlled and subdued it before he pulled the car to the curb and unlocked the automatic door.

She was wearing a brown wool suit that was several shades darker than the milk and coffee skin she'd gotten from her mother. His own skin was dark as the night and kept him safely hidden in the shadows where he and people like him belonged.

She opened the car door and got in. He waited until she'd fastened her seatbelt before pulling out from the curb. Slush splattered out from under his tires, but it was only a token. Once he was in the traffic lane the road was bare.

She didn't say anything for a long time, so he just drove. He had no idea where he was going, but he figured she'd tell him when she was ready. He kept his eyes on traffic to give her time to get a good look at him.

"You look younger than I remember," she said finally. "Younger than me."

"I was thirty-five or thereabouts when I was Changed. Being a werewolf seems to settle physical age about twenty-five for most of us." There it was out in the open and she could do with it as she pleased.

He could smell her fear of him spike and if he'd really been twenty-five, he thought he might have cried. Being this agitated wasn't smart if you were a werewolf. He took a deep breath through his nose and tried to calm down—he'd earned her fear.

"Devonte won't talk to me or anyone else," she said, and then as if those words had been the key to the floodgate she kept going. "I wish you could have seen him when I first met him. He was ten going on forty. He'd just lost his grandmother, who had raised him. He looked me right in the eye, stuck his jaw out and told me that he needed a home where he would be clothed and fed so he could concentrate on school."

"Smart boy?" he asked. She'd started in the middle of the story: he'd forgotten that habit of hers until just now.

"Very smart. Quiet. But funny, too." She made a sad sound, and her sorrow overwhelmed her fear of him. "We screen the homes. We visit. But there's never enough of us—and some of the horrible ones can put on a good show for a long time. It takes a while, too, before you get a feel for the bad ones. If he could have stayed with his first family, everything would have been fine. He stayed with them for six years. But this fall she unexpectedly got pregnant and her husband got a job transfer . . ."

They'd abandoned the boy like he was an old couch that was too awkward to move, David thought. He felt a flash of anger for this boy he'd never met. He swallowed the emotion quickly; he could do that these days. For a while. He was going to have to take that run when he got back home.

"I was tied up in court cases and someone else moved him to his next family," Stella continued, staring at her hands, which were clenched on a manila folder. "It shouldn't have been a problem. This was a family who already has fostered several children—and Devonte was a good kid, not the kind to give anyone problems."

"But something happened?" he suggested.

"His foster mother says that he just went wild, throwing furniture, breaking things. When he threatened her, his foster father stepped in and knocked him out. Devonte's in the hospital with a broken wrist and two broken ribs and he won't talk."

"You don't believe the foster family."

She gave an indignant huff. "The Linnfords look like Mr. and Mrs. Brady. She smiles and nods when he speaks and he is all charm and concern." She huffed again and spoke very precisely,

"I wouldn't believe them if all they were doing was giving me the time of day. And I know Devonte. He just wants to get through school and get a scholarship so he can go to college and take care of himself."

He nodded thoughtfully. "So why did you call me?" He was willing to have a talk with the family, but he suspected if that was all she needed it would have been a cold day in hell before she called him—she had her brothers for that.

"Because of the photos." She held up the folder in invitation.

He had to drive a couple of blocks before he found a convenient parking place and pulled over, leaving the engine running.

He pulled six photos off a clip that attached them to the back of the folder she held and spread them out to look. Interest rose up and he wished he had something more than photos. It certainly looked like more damage than one lone boy could do: ten boys maybe, if they had sledge hammers. The holes in the walls were something anyone could have done. The holes in the ten foot ceiling, the executive desk on its side in three pieces and the antique oak chair broken to splinters and missing a leg were more interesting.

"The last time I saw something like that . . ." Stella whispered.

It was probably a good thing she couldn't bring herself to finish that sentence. He had to admit that all this scene was missing was blood and body parts.

"How old is Devonte?"

"Sixteen."

"Can you get me in to look at the damage?"

"No, they had contractors in to fix it."

His eyebrows raised. "How long has it been?"

"It was the twenty-first. Three days." She waved a hand. "I know.

Contractors are usually a month wait at least, but money talks. This guy has serious money."

That sounded wrong. "Then why are they taking in a foster kid?"

She looked him in the eye for the first time and nodded at him as if he'd gotten something right. "If I'd been the one to vet them I'd have smelled a rat right there. Rich folk don't want mongrel children who've had it rough. Or if they do, they go to China or Romania and adopt babies to coo over. They don't take in foster kids, not without an agenda. But we're desperate for foster homes . . . and it wasn't me who approved them."

"You said the boy wouldn't talk. To you? Or to anybody?"

"To anybody. He hasn't said a word since the incident. Won't communicate at all."

David considered that, running through possibilities. "Was anyone hurt except for the boy?"

"No."

"Would you mind if I went to see him now?"

"Please."

He followed her directions to the hospital. He parked the car, but before he could open the door she grabbed his arm. The first time she touched him.

"Could he be a werewolf?"

"Maybe," he told her. "That kind of damage . . ."

"It looked like our house," she said, not looking at him, but not taking her hand off him either. "Like our house that night."

"If he was a werewolf, I doubt your Mr. Linnford would have been about to knock him out without taking a lot of damage. Maybe Linnford is the werewolf." That would fit, most of the werewolves he knew, if they survived, eventually became wealthy. Children were more difficult. Maybe that was why Linnford and his wife fostered children.

Stella jerked her chin up and down once. "That's what I thought. That's it. Linnford might be a werewolf. Could you tell?"

His chest felt tight. How very brave of her: she'd called the only monster she knew to deal with the other monsters. It reminded him of how she'd stood between him and the boys, protecting them the best that she could.

"Let me talk to Devonte," he said trying to keep the growl out of his voice with only moderate success. "Then I can deal with Linnford."

The hospital corridors were decorated with garland and green and red bulbs. Every year Christmas got more plastic and seemed farther and farther from the Christmases David had known as a child.

His daughter led him to the elevators without hesitation and exchanged nods with a few of the staff members who walked past. He hated the way his children aged every year. Hated the silver in their hair that was a constant reminder that eventually time would take them all away from him.

She kept as much distance between them as she could in the elevator. As if he were a stranger—or a monster. At least she wasn't running from him screaming.

You can't live with bitterness. He knew that. Bitterness, like most unpleasant emotions, made the wolf restless. Restless wolves were dangerous. The nurse at the station just outside the elevator knew Stella, too, and greeted her by name.

"That Mr. Linnford was here asking after Devonte. I told him that he wasn't allowed to visit yet." She gave Stella a disappointed look, clearly blaming her for putting Mr. Linnford to such bother. "What a nice man he is, looking after that boy after what he did to them."

She handed Stella a clipboard and gave David a mildly curious look. He gave her his most harmless smile and she smiled back before glancing down at the clipboard Stella had returned.

David could read it from where he stood. Stella Christiansen and guest. Well, he told himself, she could hardly write down that he was her father when she looked older than he did.

"He may be a nice man," Stella told the nurse with a thread of steel in her voice, "but you just keep him out until we know for sure what happened and why."

She strode off toward a set of doors where a policeman sat in front of a desk, sitting on a wooden chair, and reading a worn paperback copy of Stephen King's *Cujo*. "Jorge," she said.

"Stella," he buzzed the door and let them through.

"He's in the secured wing," she explained under her breath as she walked briskly down the hall. "Not that it's all that secure. Jorge shouldn't have let you through without checking your ID."

Not that anyone would question his Stella, David thought. Even as a little girl, people did what she told them to do. He was careful not to smile at her; she wouldn't understand it.

This part of the hospital smelled like blood, desperation, and disinfectant. Even though most of the scents were old, a new wolf penned up in this environment would cause a lot more excitement that he was seeing: and a sixteen-year-old could only be a new wolf. Any younger than that and they mostly didn't survive the Change. Anyway, he'd have scented a wolf by now: their first conclusion was right—Stella's boy was no werewolf.

"Any cameras in the rooms?" he asked in a low voice.

Her steady footfall paused. "No. That's still on the list of advised improvements for the future."

"All right. No one else here?"

"Not right now," she said. "This hospital isn't near gang territory and they put the adult offenders in a different section." She entered one of the open doorways and he followed her in, shutting the door behind them.

It wasn't a private room, but the first bed was empty. In the second bed was a boy staring at the wall—there were no windows. He was beaten up a bit and had a cast on one hand. The other hand was attached to a sturdy rail that stuck out of the bed on the side nearest the wall with a locking nylon strap—better than handcuffs, he thought, but not much. The boy didn't look up as they came in.

Maybe it was the name, or maybe the image that "foster kid" brought to mind, but he'd expected Devonte to be black. Instead, the boy looked as if someone had taken half a dozen races and shook them up—Eurasian races, though, not from the Dark Continent. There was Native American or Oriental in the corners of his eyes— and he supposed that nose could be Jewish or Italian. His skin looked as if he had a deep suntan, but this time of year it was more likely the color was his own: Mexican, Greek or even Indian.

Not that it mattered. He'd found that the years were slowly completing the job that Vietnam had begun—race or religion mattered very little to him anymore. But even if it had mattered . . . Stella had asked him for help.

Stella glanced at her father. She didn't know him, didn't know if he'd see through Devonte's defiant sullenness to the fear underneath. His expressionless face and upright military bearing gave her no clue. She could read people, but she didn't know her father anymore, hadn't seen him since . . . that night. Watching him made her uncomfortable, so she turned her attention to the other person in the room.

"Hey, kid."

Devonte kept his gaze on the wall.

"I brought someone to see you."

Her father, after a keen look at the boy, lifted his head and sucked in air through his nose hard enough she could hear it.

"Where are the clothes he was wearing when they brought him in?" he asked.

That drew Devonte's attention and satisfaction at his reaction slowed her answer. Her father's eye fell on the locker and he stalked to it and opened the door. He took out the clear plastic bag of clothes and said, with studied casualness, "Linnford was here asking about you today."

Devonte went still as a mouse.

Stella didn't know where this was going, but pitched in to help. "The police informed me that Linnford's decided not press assault charges. They should move you to a room with a view soon. I'm scheduled for a meeting tomorrow morning to decide what happens to you when you get out of here."

Devonte opened his mouth, but then closed it resolutely.

Her father sniffed at the bag, then said softly, "Why do your clothes smell like vampire, boy?"

Devonte jumped, the whites of his eyes showing all the way round his irises. His mouth opened and this time Stella thought it might really be an inability to speak that kept him quiet. She was choking a bit on "vampire" herself. But she wouldn't have believed in werewolves either, she supposed, if her father weren't one.

"I didn't introduce you," she murmured. "Devonte, this is my father, I called him when I saw the crime scene photos. He's a werewolf." If he was having vampire problems, maybe a werewolf would look good.

The sad blue-gray chair with the ripped naughahyde seat that had been sitting next to Devonte's bed zipped past her and flung itself at her father—who caught it and gave the boy a curious half-smile. "Oh I bet you surprised it, didn't you? Wizards aren't exactly common."

"Wizard?" Stella squeaked regrettably.

Her father's smile widened just a little—a smile she remembered from her childhood when she or one of her brothers had done something particularly clever. This one was aimed at Devonte.

He moved the chair gently between his hands. "A witch's power centers on bodies and minds, flesh and blood. A wizard has power over the physical—" The empty bed slammed into the wall with the open locker, bending the door and cracking the drywall. Her father was safely in front of it and belatedly she realized he must have jumped over it.

He still had the chair and his smile had grown to a wide, white grin. "Very nice, boy. But I'm not your enemy." He glanced up at the clock on the wall and shook his head.

"Someone ought to reset that thing. Do you know what time it is?"

No more furniture moved. Her father made a show of taking out his cell phone and looking at it. "Six-thirty. It's dark outside already. How badly did you hurt it with that chair I saw in the photo?"

Devonte was breathing hard, but Stella controlled her urge to go to him. Her father, hopefully, knew what he was doing. She shivered, though she was wearing her favorite wool suit and the hospital was quite warm. How much of the stories she'd heard about vampires was true?

Devonte released a breath. "Not badly enough."

On the tails of Devonte's reply, her father asked, "Who taught you not to talk at all, if you have a secret to keep?"

"My grandmother. Her mother survived Dachau because the American troops came just in time—and because she kept her mouth shut when the Nazis wanted information."

Her father's face softened. "Tough woman. Was she the Gypsy? Most wizards have at least a little Gypsy blood."

Devonte shrugged, rubbed his hands over his face hard. She recognized the gesture from a hundred different kids: he was trying not to cry. "Stella said you're a werewolf."

Her father cocked his head as if he were weighing something. "Stella doesn't lie." Unexpectedly he pinned Stella with his eyes. "I don't know if we'll have a vampire calling tonight—it depends upon how badly Devonte hurt it."

"Her," said Devonte. "It was a her."

Still looking at Stella, her father corrected himself. "Her. She must have been pretty badly injured if she hasn't come here already. And it probably means we're lucky and she is alone. If there were others they'd have come yesterday or the day before—they can't afford to let Devonte live with what he knows about them. Vampires haven't survived as long as they have by leaving witnesses."

"No one would have believed me," Devonte said. "They'd have locked me up forever."

That made her father release her from the grip of his gaze as he focused his attention on Devonte. The boy straightened under the impact—Stella knew exactly how he felt.

"Is that what Linnford told you when his neighbors came running to see why there was so much noise?" her father asked gently. "Upscale apartment dwellers aren't nearly as likely to ignore odd sounds. Is that why you threw around so much furniture? That was smart, boy."

Devonte was nodding his head—and he straightened a little more at her father's praise.

"Next time a vampire attacks you and you don't manage to kill it, though, you shout it to the world. You may end up seeing a psychologist for the rest of your life—but the vampires will stay as far from you as they can. If she doesn't come tonight, you tell your story to the newspapers." Her father glanced at Stella and she nodded.

"I know a couple of reporters," she said. "'Boy Claims He Was Attacked by Vampire' ought to sell enough papers to justify a headline or two."

"All right then," her father returned his attention to her. "I need you to go out and find some wood for us: a chair, a table, something we can make stakes out of."

"Holy water?" asked Devonte. "They might have a chapel here."

"Smart," said her father. "But from what I've heard it doesn't do enough damage to be worth running it down. Go now, Stella—and be careful."

She almost saluted him, but she didn't trust him enough to tease. He saw it, almost smiled and then turned back to Devonte. "And you're going to tell me everything you know about this vampire."

Stella glanced in the room next to Devonte's, but, like his, it was decorated in early naughahyde and metal: no wood to be found. She didn't bother checking any more but hurried to the security door—and read the note on the door.

"No, sir. She lived with them—they told me she was Linnford's sister." Devonte stopped talking when she came back.

"Jorge's been called away, he'll be back in a few minutes."

Her father considered that. "I think the show's on. No wooden chairs?"

"All the rooms in this wing are like this one."

"Without an effective weapon, I'll get a better chance at her as a wolf then as a human. It means I can't talk to you though—and it will take a while to change back, maybe a couple of hours." He looked away, and in an adult version of Devonte's earlier gesture, rubbed his face tiredly. She heard the rasp of whisker on skin. "I control the wolf now—and have for a long time."

He was worried about her.

"It's all right," she told him. He gave her the same kind of keen examination he'd given Devonte earlier and she wondered what information he was drawing from it. Could he tell how scared she was?

His face softened. "You'll do, my star."

She'd forgotten that he used to call her that—hated the way it tightened her throat. "Should I call Clive and Steve?"

"Not for a vampire," he told her. "All that will do is up the body count. To that end, we'll stay here and wait—an isolation ward is as good a place to face her as any. If I'm wrong, and the guard's leaving isn't the beginning of her attack—if she doesn't come tonight, we get all of us into the safety of someone's home, where the vampire can't just waltz in without invitation. Then I'll call in a few favors and my friends and I can take care of her somewhere there aren't any civilians to be hurt."

He looked around with evident dissatisfaction.

"What are you looking for?" Devonte asked so she didn't have to.

"A place to hide." Then he looked up and smiled at the dropped ceiling.

"Those panels won't support your weight," she warned him.

"No, but this is a hospital and this is the old wing. I bet they have a cable ladder for their computer and electric cables . . ." As he spoke, he'd hopped on the empty bed and pushed up a ceiling panel to take a look.

"What's a cable ladder?" Stella asked.

"In this case, it's a sturdy aluminum track attached to the oak beam with stout hardware." He sounded pleased as he replaced the ceiling panel he'd taken out. "I could hide a couple of people up here if I had to."

He was a mercenary, she remembered, and wondered how many times he'd hidden on top of cable ladders.

He moved the empty bed away from the wall and climbed on it again and removed a different panel. "Do you think you can get this panel back where it belongs after I get up here, boy?"

"Sure." Devonte sounded thoroughly pleased. If anyone else had called him "boy" he'd have been bristling. He was already well on the way to a big case of hero worship, just like the one she'd had.

"Stella." Her father took off his red flannel shirt and laid it on the empty bed behind him. "When this is over, you call Clive, tell him everything and he'll arrange a cleanup. He knows who to call for help with it. It's safer for everyone if people don't believe in vampires and werewolves. Leaving bodies makes it kind of hard to deny."

"I'll call him."

Without his shirt to cover him, she could see there was no softness in him. A few scars showed up grey on his dark skin. She'd forgotten how dark he was, like ebony.

As he peeled off his sky-blue undershirt he said, with a touch of humor, "if you don't want to see more of your father than any daughter ever should, you need to turn your back." And she realized she'd been staring at him.

Devonte made an odd noise—he was laughing. There was a tightness to the sound and she knew he was scared and excited to see what it looked like when a man changed into a werewolf. For some reason she felt her own mouth stretch into a nervous grin she let Devonte see just before she did as her father advised her and turned her back.

David didn't like changing in front of anyone. He wasn't exactly vulnerable—but it made the wolf edgy and if someone decided to get brave and approach too closely . . . . well, the wolf would feel threatened, like a snake shedding its skin.

So to the boy he said quietly, "Watching is fine. But wait for a bit if you want to touch . . ." He had a thought. "Stella, if she sends the Linnfords in first, I'll do my best to stay hidden. I can take a vampire . . ." Honesty forced him to continue. "Maybe I can take a vampire, but only with surprise on my side. Her human minions, if they are still human enough to walk in daylight, are still too human to detect me. Don't let them take Devonte out of this room."

He tried to remember everything he knew about vampires. Once he changed, it would be too late to talk. "Don't look in the vampire's eyes, don't let her touch you. Unless you are really a believer, don't plan on crosses helping you out. When I attack, don't try and help, just keep out of it so I don't have to worry about you."

Wishing they had a wooden stake, he knelt on the floor and allowed himself to change. Calling the wolf was easy, it knew there was a fight to be had, blood to be shed, and in its eagerness it rushed the change as if called by the moon herself.

He never remembered exactly how bad it was going to hurt. His mother had once told him that childbirth was like that for women. That if they remembered how bad it was, they'd lack the courage to face the next time.

But he did remember it was always worse than he expected, and that somehow helped him bear it.

The shivery, icy pain slid over his bones while fire threaded through his muscles, reshaping, reorganizing and altering what was there to suit itself. Experience kept him from making noise—it was one of the first things he learned: how to control his instincts and keep the howls, the growls, and the whines inside and bury them in silence. Noise can attract unwanted attention.

His lungs labored to provide oxygen as adrenaline forced his heart to beat too fast. His face ached as teeth became fangs and his jaw extended with cheekbones. His eyesight blurred and then sharpened with a predatory clarity that allowed him to see prey and enemy alike no matter what shadows they tried to hide in.

"Cool," said someone. Devonte. He-who-was-to-be-guarded.

Someone moved and it attracted his attention. Her terror flooded his senses like perfume.

Prey. He liked it when they ran.

Then she lifted her chin and he saw a second image, superimposed over the first. A child standing between him and two smaller children, her chin jutting out as she lifted up a baseball bat in wordless defiance that spoke louder than the her terror and the blood.

Not prey. Not prey. His. His star.

It was all right then. She could see his pain—she had earned that right. And together they would stop the monster from eating the boy.

For the first few minutes after the change, he mostly thought like the wolf, but as the pain subsided he settled back into control. He shook off the last of unpleasant tingles with the same willpower he used to set aside the desire to snarl at the boy who reached out with a hand . . . only to jerk back, caught by the strap on his wrist.

David hopped on to the bed and snapped through the ballistic nylon that attached Devonte's cuff to the rail and waited while the boy petted him tentatively with all the fascination of a person touching a tiger.

"That'll be a little hard to explain," said Stella.

He looked at her and she flinched . . . then jerked up her chin and met his eyes. "What if the Linnfords ask about the restraint?"

It had been the wolf's response to seeing the boy he was supposed to protect tied up like a bad dog, not the man's.

"They haven't been here," said Devonte. "Unless they spend a lot of time in hospital prison, they won't know it was supposed to be there. I'll cover the cuff on my wrist with the blanket."

Stella nodded her head thoughtfully. "All right. And if things get bad, at least this way you can run. He's right, it's better if the restraint is off."

David let them work it out. He launched himself off Devonte's bed and onto the other—forgetting that Devonte was already hurt until he heard the boy's indrawn breath. David was still half-operating on wolf instincts—which wasn't very helpful when fighting vampires. He needed to be thinking.

Maybe it had only been the suddenness of his movement though because the boy made the same sound when David hopped through the almost-too-narrow opening in the ceiling and onto the track in the plenum space between the original fourteen-foot ceiling and false panels fitted into the flimsy hangers that kept them place. The track groaned a little under his sudden weight, but it didn't bend.

"My father always told us that no one ever looks up for their enemy," Stella said after a moment. "Can you replace the panel? If you can't I—"

The panel he'd moved slid back into place with more force than necessary and cracked down the middle.

"Damn it."

"Don't worry, no one will notice. There are a couple of broken panels up there."

***

She couldn't see any sign that her father was hiding in the ceiling except for the bed. She grabbed it by the headboard and tugged it back to its original position, then she did the same with the chair.

She'd forgotten how impressive the wolf was . . . almost beautiful: the perfect killing machine covered with four-inch-deep, red-gold fur. She hadn't remembered the black that tipped his ears and surrounded his eyes like Egyptian kohl.

"If you'll get back, I'll see what I can do with the wall," said Devonte. "Sometimes I can fix things as well as move them."

That gave her a little pause, but she found that wizards weren't as frightening as werewolves and vampires. She considered his offer, then shook her head.

"No. They already know what you are." She gathered her father's clothes from the bedspread and folded them neatly. Then she stashed them—and the plastic bag with Devonte's clothes—into the locker. "Just leave the wall. We only need to hide the werewolf from them, and you might need all the power you've got to help with the vampire."

Devonte nodded.

"Right then." She took a deep breath and picked up her catch-all purse from the floor where she'd set it.

Her brothers had made fun of her purses until she'd used one to take out a mugger. She'd been lucky—it had been laden with a pair of three-pound weights she'd been transporting from home to work—but she'd never admitted that to her brothers. Afterwards they'd given her Mace, karate lessons, and quit bugging her about the size of her purse.

Unearthing a travel-sized game board from its depths she said, "How about some checkers?"

Five hard-won games later she decided the vampire either wasn't coming tonight, or she was waiting for Stella to go away. She jumped three of Devonte's checkers and there was a quiet knock on the door. She turned to look as Jorge, the cop who'd gotten babysitting duty today, stuck his head in.

"Sorry to leave you stuck here."

"No problem. Just beating a poor helpless child at checkers."

She waited for him to respond with something funny—Jorge was quick on his feet. But his face just stayed . . . not blank precisely, but neutral.

"They need you down in pediatrics, now. Looks like a case of child abuse and Doc Gonzales wants you to talk to the little girl."

She couldn't help the instincts that brought her to her feet, but those same instincts were screaming that there was something wrong with Jorge.

Between her job and having a brother on the force, she'd gotten to know some of the cops pretty well. Nothing bothered Jorge like a child who'd been hurt. She'd seen him cry like a baby when he talked about a car wreck where the child hadn't survived. But he'd passed this message along to her with all the passion of a hospital switchboard operator.

In the movies, vampires could make people do what they wanted them to—she couldn't remember if the people were permanently damaged. Mostly, she was afraid, they just died.

She glanced down at her watch and shook her head. "You know my rules," she said. "It's after six and I'm off shift."

Her rules were a standing joke with her brothers and their friends—a serious joke. She'd seen too many people burn out from the stress of her job. So she'd made a list of rules she had to follow, and they'd kept her sane so far. One of her rules was that from eight in the morning until six in the evening she was on the job, outside of those hours she did her best to have a real life. She was breaking it now, with Devonte.

Instead of calling her on it, Jorge just processed her reply and finally nodded. "All right. I'll tell them."

He didn't close the door when he left. She went to the doorway and watched him walk mechanically down the hall and through the security door, which he'd left open. Very unlike him to leave a security door open, but he closed it behind him.

"That was the vampire's doing wasn't it?" she asked, looking up.

The soft growl that eased through the ceiling was somehow reassuring—though she hadn't forgotten his reservations about how well he'd do against a vampire.

She went back to Devonte's bed and made her move on the board. Out in the hall the security door opened again, and someone wearing high heels *click-click*ed briskly down the hall.

Stella took a deep breath, settled back on the end of the bed and told Devonte, "Your turn."

He looked at the board, but she saw his hand shake as whoever it was in the hallway closed in on them.

"King me," he said in a fair approximation of triumph.

The footsteps stopped in the doorway. Devonte looked over her shoulder and his face went slack with fear. Stella inhaled and took her first look.

She'd thought a vampire would be young, like her father. Wasn't that the myth? But this woman had gray hair and wrinkles under her eyes and in the soft, white skin of her neck. She was dressed in a professionally-tailored wine-colored suit. She wore a diamond necklace around her aging neck, and diamond-and-pearl earrings.

"Well," said Stella, "No one is going to think you look like a cuddly grandma."

The woman laughed, her face lighting up with a cheer so genuine that Stella thought she might have liked her if only the laughter didn't showcase her fangs. "The boy talked, did he? I thought for sure he'd hold his tongue, if only to keep his own secrets. Either that or broadcast it to the world, and then you and I wouldn't be in this position."

She gave Stella a kindly smile that showed off a charmingly-mismatched pair of dimples. "I am sorry you had to be involved. I tried to get you out of it."

But Stella had been dealing with people a long time, she could smell a fake a mile away. The laughter had been real, but the kind concern certainly wasn't.

"Separating your prey," Stella said. She needed to get the vampire into the room where her father could drop on top of her, but how?

The vampire displayed her fangs and dimples again. "More convenient and easier to keep the noise down," she allowed. "But not really necessary. Not even if you are a—" she took a deep breath, "—werewolf."

The news didn't seem to bother her. Stella fought off the feeling that her father was going to be over-matched. He'd been a soldier and then a mercenary, training his own sons and then grandsons. Surely he knew what he was doing.

"Hah," sneered Devonte in classic adolescent disdain. "You aren't so tough. I nearly killed you all by myself."

The vampire sneered right back and, on her, the expression made the hair on the back of Stella's neck stand up and take notice. "You were a mistake, boy. One I intend to clear up."

~~~~~~~~

David crouched motionless, waiting for the sound of the vampire's voice to indicate she had moved underneath him.

Patience, patience, he counseled himself, but he should have been counseling someone else.

If the vampire's theatrics scared Stella, they drove Devonte into action. The bed he tried to smash her father with rattled across the floor. He must have tired himself out with his earlier wizardry because it was traveling only half as fast as it had when he'd tried to drive her father through the wall.

The vampire had no trouble grabbing it . . . or throwing it through the plaster wall and into the hallway where it crashed on its side, flinging wheels, bedding, mattress and pieces of the arcana that distinguished it from a normal bed.

She was so busy impressing them with her Incredible Hulk imitation, she didn't see the old blue-gray chair. It hit her squarely in the back, driving her directly under the panel Devonte had cracked.

"Now," whispered Stella diving toward the hole the vampire had made in the wall, hoping that would be out of the way.

Even though Devonte's chair had knocked the vampire to her knees, Stella's motion drew her attention. The thing was fast, and she lunged for Stella in the same motion she used to rise. Then the roof fell on top of her, the roof and a silently snarling red-gold wolf with claws and fangs that made the vampire's look like toys.

For a moment she was twelve again, watching the monster dig those long claws into her mother's lover and she froze in horror. The woman looked frail beneath the huge wolf's bulk—until she pulled her legs under him and threw him into the outer wall, the one made of cinder blocks and not plaster.

With an inhuman howl the vampire leaped upon her father. She looked nothing like the elegant woman who had walked into the room. In the brief glimpse she'd had of her face, Stella saw something terrible . . . evil.

"Stella, behind you!" Devonte yelled, hopping of the bed, his good arm around his ribs.

She hadn't been paying attention to anything except the vampire. Devonte's warning came just a little late and someone grabbed her by the arm and jerked her roughly around—Linnford. Gone was the urban smile and *GQ* posture; his face was lit with fanaticism and madness. He had a knife in the hand that wasn't holding her. She reacted without thinking, twisting so his thrust went past her abdomen, slicing though fabric but not skin.

Something buzzed between them, hitting him in the chest and knocking him back to the floor. He jerked and spasmed like a skewered frog in a film she'd once had to watch in college. The chair sat on top of him, balanced on one bent leg, the other three appearing to hover in the air.

It took a moment for her to properly understand what she was seeing. The bent chair leg was stuck into his ribcage, just to the left of his sternum. Blood began spitting out like a macabre fountain.

"Honey?" Hannah Linnford stood in the doorway. Like Stella, she seemed to be having trouble understanding what she was seeing.

Muttering, "Does no one remember to shut the security doors?" Stella pulled the mini-canister of Mace her youngest brother had given her after the mugging incident out of her pocket and sprayed it in the other woman's face.

If she'd been holding Linnford's knife she could have cheerfully driven it through Hannah's neck: These people had taken one of her kids and tried to feed him to a vampire.

Thinking of her kids made Stella look for Devonte.

He was leaning against the wall a few feet from his bed, staring at Linnford—and his expression centered Stella because he needed her. She ran to him and tugged him to the far corner of the room, away from the fighting monsters, but too close to the Linnfords. Once she had him where she wanted him, she did her best to block his view of Linnford's dying body. If she could get medical help soon enough, Linnford might survive—but she felt no drive to do it. Let him rot.

Mace can in hand, she kept a weather eye on the woman screaming on the floor, but most of her attention was on the fight her father was losing.

They fought like a pair of cats, coming together clawing and biting, almost too fast for her eyes to focus on, then, for no reason she could see, they'd retreat. After a few seconds of staring at each other, they'd go at it again. Unlike cats, they were eerily silent.

The vampire's carefully arranged hair was fallen, covering her face, but not disguising her glittering . . . no, glowing red eyes. Her arm flashed out in a jerky movement that was so quick Stella almost missed it—and the wolf twitched away with another wound that dripped blood: the vampire was still virtually untouched.

The two monsters backed away from each other and the vampire licked her fingers.

"You taste so good, wolf," she said. "I can't wait until I can sink my fangs through your skin and suck that sweetness dry."

Stella sprayed Hannah in the face again. Then she hauled Devonte out the door and away from the vampire, making regrettably little allowance for his broken ribs. Dead was worse than in pain.

It's working, David thought, watching the vampire lick his blood off her fingers. Though he was mostly focused on the vampire, he noticed when Stella took the boy out of the room. Good for her. With the vampire's minions here, one dead and one incapacitated, she shouldn't have trouble getting out. He hoped she took Devonte to her home—or any home—where they'd be safe. Then he put them out of his mind and concentrated on the battle at hand.

He'd met a vampire or two, but never fought one before. He'd heard that some of them had a strange reaction to werewolf blood. She seemed to be one of them.

He could only hope that her blood lust would make her stupid. He'd heard that vampires couldn't feed from the dead. If it wasn't true, he might be in trouble.

He waited for her to come at him again—and this time he stepped into her fist, falling limply at her feet. She hit him hard, he felt the bone in his jaw creak, so the limp fall wasn't hard to fake. He'd wait until she started feeding, and the residual dizziness from her blow left, then he'd take her.

She fell on him and he waited for her fangs to dig in. Instead she jerked a couple of times and then lay still. She wasn't breathing and her heart wasn't beating—but she'd been like that when she walked into the room.

"Papa?"

Stella was supposed to be safely away.

He rose with a roar, making an audible sound for the first time so the vampire would pay attention to him and leave his daughter alone. But the woman's body rolled smoothly off of him and lay on the floor—two wooden chair legs stuck through her back.

"Are you all right? Jorge left the security door open, I knew it when the Linnfords came in. We broke the legs off Jorge's chair and used whatever he used to toss the furniture around to drive them into her back."

The soldier in him insisted on a full and quick survey of the room. Linnford was dead, the abused chair was the obvious cause of death. A woman, presumably his wife, sobbed harshly, her face pressed into Linnford's arm: a possible threat. Stella and Devonte were standing way too close to the vampire.

They'd killed her.

For a moment he felt a surge of pride. Stella didn't have an ounce of quit in her whole body. She and the boy had managed to take advantage of the distraction he'd arranged before he could.

"Everyone was gone, Jorge and everyone." He looked at the triumph in Stella's face, not quite hidden by her worry for her friends.

She thought the vampire was finished, but wood through the heart didn't always keep the undead down.

"Are you all right?" Stella asked. And then when he just stared at her, "Papa?"

He'd come here hoping to play hero, he knew, hoping to mend what couldn't be mended. But the only role for him was that of monster, because that was the only thing he was.

He pulled the sheet off the bed and ripped it with a claw, then tossed it toward Linnford's sobbing woman. Stella took the hint and she and Devonte made a rope of sorts out of it and tied her up.

While they were working at that, he walked slowly up to the vampire. Stella had called him Papa tonight, more than once. He'd try to hold on to that and forget the rest.

He growled at the vampire: her fault that he would lose his daughter a second time. Then he snapped his teeth through her spine. The meat of her was tougher than it should have been, tougher than jerky and bad tasting to boot. His jaw hurt from the hit he'd taken as he set his teeth and put some muscle into separating her head from her body.

When he was finished, the boy was losing his last meal in the corner, an arm wrapped around his ribs. Throwing up with broken ribs sucked: he knew all about that. Linnford's woman was secured. Stella had a hand over her mouth as if to prevent herself from imitating Devonte. When she pulled her eyes away from the vampire's severed head and looked at him, he saw horror.

He felt the blood dripping from his jaws—and couldn't face her any longer. Couldn't stay while horror turned to fear of him. He didn't look at his daughter again as he ran away for the first time in his long life.

When he could, he changed back to human at the home of the local werewolf pack. They let him shower, and gave him a pair of sweats— the universal answer to the common problem of changing back to human and not having clothes to put back on.

He called his oldest son to make sure that Stella had called him and that he had handled the cleanup. She had remembered, and Clive was proceeding with his usual thoroughness.

Linnford was about to have a terrible car wreck. The vampire's body, both parts of it, were scheduled for immediate incineration. The biggest problem was what to do with Linnford's wife. For the moment she seemed to be too traumatized to talk. Maybe the vampire's death had broken her—or maybe she'd come around. Either way, she'd need help, discreet help from people who knew how to tell the difference between the victim of a vampire and a minion and would treat her accordingly.

David made a few calls, and got the number of a very private sanitarium run by a small, very secret government agency. The price wasn't bad—all he had to do was rescue some missionary who was related to a high-level politician. The fool had managed to get kidnapped with his wife and two young children. David's team would still get paid, and he'd probably have taken the assignment anyway.

By the time he called Clive back, his sons had located a few missing hospital personnel and the cop who'd been guarding the door. David heard the relief in Clive's voice: Jorge was apparently a friend. None of the recovered people seemed to be hurt, though they had no idea why they were all in the basement.

David hung up and turned off his cell phone. Accepting the offer of a bedroom from the pack Alpha, David took his tired body to bed and slept.

⌐∽⌐

Christmas day was coming to a close when David drove his rental to his son's house—friends had picked it up from the hospital for him.

Red and green lights covered every bush and railing as well as surrounding all the windows. Knee-high candy canes lined the walk.

There were cars at his son's house. David frowned at them and checked his new watch. He was coming over at the right time. He'd made it clear that he didn't want to intrude—which was understood to mean that he wouldn't come when Stella was likely to be there.

He'd already have been on a flight home, except that he didn't know how to contact Devonte. He tapped the envelope against his leg and wondered why he'd picked up a Christmas card instead of just handing over his business card. Below his contact information he'd made Devonte an open job offer beginning as soon as Devonte was eighteen. David could think of a thousand ways a wizard would be of use to a small group of mercenaries.

Of course, after watching David tear up the vampire's body, Devonte probably wouldn't be interested, so more to the point was the name and phone number on the other side of the card. Both belonged to a wizard who was willing to take on a pupil; the local Alpha had given it to him.

Clive had promised to give it to Devonte.

David had to search under the giant wreath on the door for the bell. As he waited, he noticed that he could hear a lot of people inside, and even through the door he smelled the turkey.

He took a step back, but the door was already opening.

Stella stood in the doorway. Over her shoulder he could see the whole family running around preparing the table for Christmas dinner. Devonte was sitting on the couch reading to one of the toddlers that seemed to be everywhere. Clive leaned against the fireplace and met David's gaze. He lifted a glass of wine and sipped it, smiling slyly.

David took another step back and opened his mouth to apologize to Stella . . . just as her face lit with her mother's smile. She stepped out onto the porch and wrapped her arms around him.

"Merry Christmas, Papa," she said. "I hope you like turkey."

If Vanity Doesn't Kill Me

MICHAEL A. STACKPOLE

For a guy who squeezed into a rubber nun's habit before hanging himself in a dingy motel room closet, Robert Anderson didn't look so bad. Sure, his face was still livid, especially that purple ring right above the noose, and his neck had stretched a bit, but with his eyes closed you couldn't see the burst blood vessels. He looked peaceful.

I glanced back over my shoulder at Cate Chase, the Medical Examiner. "I've seen worse. Is that a good thing?"

"Let's don't start comparing instances." With her red hair, blue eyes, and cream complexion, Cate should have been a heartbreaker. She would have been, save she was built like a legbreaker. One glance convinced most men that she could hurt them badly, and not in a good way. She jerked a thumb at the room's vanity table. "What do you think?"

I shrugged. Dragging it along had tipped over a can of soda, and a half-eaten sandwich had soaked most of it up. The Twinkie had resisted the soda, being stale enough you could have pounded nails with it. "Looks like he unscrewed it from the wall, shifted it so he could watch himself. Auto-erotic asphyxiation?"

She nodded. "Suffocating as you climax is supposed to take the orgasm off the charts. You pass out, you can strangle to death."

"Not my idea of fun."

"There go my plans for the rest of our afternoon." She flicked a finger at Anderson. "Take another *look*."

I caught her emphasis and breathed in. I closed my eyes for a second, then reopened them. I peered at him through magic. He was a silhouette, all black and drippy. Corpses tend to look like that. I'd seen it before.

"Something special I'm supposed to see?" I faced her as I asked the question, and magic rendered her in shades of red gold, much like her hair. It put color into everything, save for that Twinkie. It was neither alive nor dead.

Cate shook her head. "Something, I hoped. Anything."

I waited for her to expand on her comment, but she never got a chance.

Detective Inspector Winston Prout charged into the room and thrust a finger into my chest. "What the hell are you doing here, Molloy?"

"I invited him, Prout."

I smiled. "Coffee date."

He glared at the both of us, about a heartbeat from arresting us for indecent urges. He was one of those skinny guys who'd look better as a corpse. He wouldn't have to keep his parts all puckered and pinched tight. He habitually dressed in white from head to toe, and had exchanged his skimmer for a fedora after his recent promotion to Inspector.

"Civilians aren't allowed in a crime scene, Molloy."

"My prints, my DNA are on record. I haven't touched anything."

"If you don't have a connection to this case, get the hell out of here."

I hesitated just a second too long.

He raised an eyebrow. "You connected?"

"Maybe." I shrugged. "A little."

"Spill it."

"Your vic?" I nodded toward the man in the closet. "He's married to my mother."

❧

That little revelation had Prout's eyes bugging out the way Anderson's must have at the end. I'd have enjoyed poking them back into his face, but he got control of himself pretty quickly. He was torn between wanting to arrest me right that second and fear that I'd already set a trap for him. He'd wanted a piece of me since before his stint in the Internal Affairs division. He saw it as a divine mission and getting me tossed from the force for bribery hadn't been enough.

He punted the two of us, leaving a tech team to do the crime scene. Cate and I retreated through a hallway where painters were trying to cover years of grim in a jaunty yellow, and to a nearby coffee joint. We ordered in java-jerkese, then sat on the patio amid lunch-bunnies catching a post-Pilates, pre-spa jolt.

"You didn't know about Anderson, did you?"

Cate shook her head. "Should I say I'm sorry for your loss?"

"If it will make you feel better."

"I'm sorry."

"Don't be. He was a shit. He and my mother were very Christian, which meant they were usually anti-me."

Cate understood. Prejudice against those who are magically gifted isn't uncommon, especially with Fundies. It's that "thou shalt not suffer a witch to live" thing. Having a talented child is as bad as having a gay kid was late last century. My mom had compounded things by being the society girl who ran off with a working man—my father—then getting pregnant and actually delivering the child. My having talent was the last straw. She ditched my father, the Church got the marriage annulled, and she made a proper society match with Anderson.

I blew on my coffee. "Why *did* you call me?"

Cate leaned forward, resting her forearms on the table. "Anderson's the fifth Brahmin that's died like that in the last two months. Very embarrassing circumstances. The deaths have been swept under the carpet."

She fished in her pocket, produced a PDA and beamed case files into mine. I glanced at the names on each document. I knew them. I dimly recalled that they'd died, but I couldn't remember any details. I'd met three of them, liked one, but only because she didn't like my mother.

"How did Amanda Preakness die?"

"You won't want to look at the photos. She drowned. In her tub. In chocolate syrup."

"What?" She'd been slender enough to make Nancy Reagan look like a sumo-wrestler. Tall and aristocratic, with a shock of white hair and a piercing stare, she could have dropped an enraged rhino with a glance. She always threw lavish parties, but never ate more than a crumb. "Not possible."

"Not only did she drown in the syrup, but her belly was stuffed full of chocolate bars. Junk food everywhere at the scene, all washed down with cheap soda." Cate shook her head. "Nothing to suggest anything but an accidental death. Or suicide."

"Neither of which could be reported, so her society friends wouldn't snigger at her passing." I frowned. "No leads?"

"Plenty. Problem's no investigation. I pester Prout. He hears, but doesn't listen."

"Which is odd since you suspect our killer is talented."

"Has to be. And strong."

Just being born with talent isn't enough. Talent needs a trigger, and not many folks find that trigger. Mine's whiskey—I discovered it when I was four by sucking drops from my old man's shot glass after he passed out. The better the whiskey, the faster the power comes.

Once you find the trigger, you next have to learn your channel. For most folks it's the elements: earth, air, fire, or water. A talented gardener with an earth channel is good; one who works with plants is better. Some channels are a bit more esoteric, like emotions. I even met a guy whose channel was Death.

Not really a fun guy, that one.

If there was a killer, knowing his trigger and channel would be useful. I could guess on the channel being emotional or biological, but that didn't narrow things down much. More importantly, it really did nothing to figure out *why* the murders were taking place. Without a *why*, figuring out *who* was going to be tough.

I set the PDA down. "What's in this for me?"

Cate rocked back. "Stopping a murderer isn't enough?"

"Not like it's my hobby. I work mopping up puke in a strip club. I know where I stand in the world. I don't see this getting me ahead."

"Maybe it won't, Molloy, maybe it won't." Cate's eyes half lidded and she gave me a pretty good Preakness-class glance. "Maybe it'll stop you from sinking any lower."

"Is that possible?"

"You're not there yet." Her expression hardened. "If you were I'd ask if you had an alibi for when Anderson died."

⁓◦⌒◦⁓

I guess being a murderer would be a step down. Not that I minded Anderson being dead. Given the right circumstances I might even have killed him. Or, at least, let him die. A shrink would have said it because he was a surrogate for my mother, and that secretly I was wishing her dead.

There wasn't any "secretly" about it. I knew I had to start with her, so I reluctantly left Cate. The part I was resisting was that seeing her would prove she was still alive.

I tried to look on the bright side.

Maybe she was sick, really, really sick.

And not just in the head this time.

The Anderson Estate up in Union Heights was hard to miss. Fortune 500 companies had smaller corporate headquarters. The fence surrounding it had just enough juice flowing through to stun you, then the dogs would gnaw on you for a good long time.

The gate was already open and a squad car was parked there. The officers waved me past, but it wasn't any blue-brotherhood thing. I'd never known then when I was on the force. I'd just gotten their asses out of trouble at the strip club.

Took me two minutes to reach the front door. Would have been longer, but I cut straight across the lawn. Wilkerson, the chief-of-staff—which is how you now pronounce the word "butler"—opened the door before I'd hit the top step. "It will do no good to say the lady of the house does not wish to see you, correct?"

He didn't even wait for me to reply before he stepped aside. He looked me up and down once. He channeled my mother's mortification, then led the way up the grand staircase to my mother's dressing room. He hesitated for a moment and memorized the location of every item in the room, then reluctantly departed, confident the looting would begin once the door clicked shut.

The room was my mother. Elegant, well-appointed, tasteful, and traditional. I'm sure it was all "revival" something; but I couldn't tell what. Even though she'd made an attempt to "civilize" me in my teens, very little had stuck. I did know that if it looked old, it was *very* old, including some Byzantine icons in the corner with a candle glowing in front of them. In a world where even people were disposable, antiques held a certain charm.

Not so my mother.

She swept into the room wearing a dark-blue dressing gown—clearly Anderson's—and dabbed at her eyes with a monogrammed handkerchief. Her eyes were puffy and rimmed with red. For a moment I believed she might have been crying for him, but grief I could have felt radiating out from her.

My mother doesn't radiate emotions. She sucks them in. Like a black hole. I think that's why her daughter is a nun in Nepal, I'm a waste of flesh, and my half-brother is the Prince of Darkness.

"There's nothing in his will for you, Patrick."

"Good to see you, too, mother. I hope he spent it all on himself."

Her blue eyes tightened. "It's in a trust, all of it, save for a few charitable donations."

I chuckled. "That explains the tears. Hurts to still be on an allowance."

"Yours is done, Patrick. I know he used to give you money." She fingered the diamond-encrusted crucifix at her throat. "He was too soft-hearted."

"He gave me money *once*, and it wasn't Christian charity." I opened my hands. "I came from the crime scene . . ."

Her eyes widened. "You beast! If you breathe a word!" Tears flowed fast. "How much do you want?"

"I don't want anything." I shook my head. "Five people have died in the last two months, your husband included. All of them nasty. Sean Hogan, Amanda Preakness, Percival Kendall Ford, and Dorothy Kent."

"Dottie? They said it was a botox allergy."

"It doesn't matter what they said, mother."

She blinked and quickly made the sign of the cross. "Are you confessing to me, Patrick? Have you done this? Have you come for me?"

"Stop!" I balled my fists and began to mutter. Like most folks, she bought into the Vatican version of the *talented*. She figured I was going sacrifice her to my Satanic Master, or at least turn her into a toad.

Tempting, so tempting.

She paled and then sat hard on a daybed. "I'll do anything you ask, Patrick. You don't want to hurt me, your mother."

I snorted. If she had enough presence of mind to invoke the maternal bond, she wasn't really shocked, just scheming. "How was Anderson hooked up with the others?"

"Hogan did the trust work, damn him. Everyone else we knew socially. The Club, of course, the Opera Society. Various nonprofit boards." She paused, her eyes sharpening. "Yes, this is all your fault."

"My fault?"

"Absolutely. They were all on the board of the Fellowship. All of them." Her accusing finger quivered. "I never wanted him to have anything to do with that place, but he did, because of you. And now he's dead."

"The Fellowship never killed anyone."

"They saved your life, Patrick. I know. He told me." Her eyes became arctic slits. "If they hadn't, if you were dead, my husband wouldn't be. Dear God, I wish it were so."

She burst into a series of sobs which were as piteous as they were fake, so I took my leave. It really hadn't been her best effort at emotional torture. Anderson's death had hurt her. Probably was more than having a leash on her spending. I wondered how long it would be until she realized that herself.

~⌒∽⌒~

From the Heights I descended back into my realm. People in my mother's class acknowledge it exists, but only just barely. It's where they go slumming when cheating at golf has lost its thrill. For the rest of us it's just a waiting room. Prison or death, those are your choices. Sure, you hear stories of someone making good and escaping. Never seems any of us down here knew them when; and they damned sure don't know any of us now.

Reverend Martha Raines could have made it out, but she stayed by choice. She was kind of the "after" picture of Amanda Preakness doing a chocolate diet for a decade or two; but her brown eyes had never narrowed in anger. Not that she couldn't be passionate. She could, and often held forth at City Council meetings or prayer services. She kept her white hair long and wore it in a braid that she tied off with little beaded cords the children in her mission made for her.

She smiled broadly as I stepped through the door and I couldn't help but mirror it. Even before we could speak, she caught me in a hug and held on tight, even when I was ready to let go. She whispered, "You need this, Patrick."

Maybe I did.

Finally she stepped back. "I'm so sorry for your loss."

"No loss."

She gave me a sidelong glance. "I seem to remember things a little bit differently."

"You always think the best of everyone."

"It's a skill you could acquire."

"I don't like being disappointed."

She slipped an arm around my waist and guided me into the mission. The Fellowship has built out through several warehouses and manufacturing buildings which, save for Martha's fiery oratory, would have long since been converted into lofts. The city wanted this end of town gentrified and envisioned galleries and bistros. Martha thought buildings should house people and proved convincing when she addressed the City Council.

Things had changed a lot since I'd done my time in the mission. The first hall still served as church and dining facility, but the stacks of mattresses that used to be piled in the corner had moved deeper into the complex. The far wall had been decorated with a huge mural that looked like a detail piece of da Vinci's *Last Supper*. Thirteen plates, each with a piece of bread on it; but one was already moldy. The style wasn't quite right for da Vinci—some of that stuff my mother had forced into my head was creeping back.

Martha smiled. "Our artist is very talented."

I raised an eyebrow. "Talented? Or *talented*?"

"She's a lot like you, Patrick." Martha just smiled. "You'll like her."

"I need to ask you some questions."

"About Bob Anderson?"

"About all of them."

She studied my face for a moment, then led me over to a table and pulled out two chairs. She sat facing me and took my hands in hers. "They were all lovely people, every one of them. I know many people said bad things about them; but they had seen the work we do here. They wanted to help. They did things for us. Projects. Fundraisers. What they gave wasn't much for them, but it was everything for us."

I nodded. "When they died, they left the mission money."

Martha drew back. "What are you suggesting?"

"There are idiots down here who figure that if you start making money, they want a piece. Criminals aren't bright; and you're a soft touch."

"True on both counts." She smiled. "But your stepfather and Sean Hogan were not stupid. Bequests go into a trust with a board of trustees who vote on capital expenses. I can't really touch that money. More to the point, no one has tried to extort money."

"No rivalries? No animosity on the committee?"

Martha smiled. "The meetings were all very pleasant."

That didn't surprise me. Martha had *talent*, though I wasn't sure she knew it. Somehow her positive nature was infectious. When she gave a sermon, people listened and her words got inside them. She always exhorted folks to be their best selves. It was like a round of applause accompanied by a boot in the ass that left you wanting more of each.

It was her inclination to think the best of folks that had her believing Anderson's death was a loss. She remembered he'd pulled me out of the Mission and had given me money. She thought I'd been rescued. My mother, having taken to Christianity like a drunk to vodka, had tried to save me a couple times before, especially after my father went away. Martha thought this was another instance of maternal concern.

Truth was Anderson had been fed up. He just wanted me to stop embarrassing my mother. He wanted me gone from the city. By giving me money he hoped I'd crawl into some motel room and die anonymously, pretty much the way he did.

What goes around, comes around.

"Who else was on the committee?"

"No one, per se. They'd lined up a number of people to make donations. Let me get you a list."

Martha left her chair, then waved a hand at a petite woman with white blonde hair and a pale complexion. She had freckles, but they were barely visible beneath a spattering of paint. "Leah, come here. I want you to meet Patrick Molloy. He used to live here, too."

Leah smiled at me, all the way up into her blue eyes. I started liking her right then, because a lot of beautiful women would have been mortified to be introduced wearing overalls thick with paint. She wiped her hand on a rag, then offered it to me, bespeckled and smeared. "I've heard a lot about you, Mr. Molloy."

"Trick." She had a firm handshake, warm and dry. My flesh tingled as we touched. It was more than attraction. She truly was *talented*, but I was liking what I was seeing normally so much that I didn't look at her through magic. That would have been an invasion of privacy—the last bastion of privacy in the mission.

I nodded toward the mural. "Nice work."

She smiled and reluctantly released my hand as Martha headed toward her office. "You recognize it as da Vinci, yes?"

"Not his style."

"True. I interpreted it through *vanitas*."

"Uh huh."

Leah laughed delightfully. "Sixteenth- and seventeenth-century painters in Flanders and the Netherlands popularized the style. It's still-life with decay. It's supposed to remind us that everything is fleeting and that we'll die some day. But you knew that."

It was my turn to laugh. "That's maybe the one bit of art knowledge that stuck. I was in my nihilistic teen phase when I was force-fed."

"I'm sorry."

"For?"

"Art is something that everyone should experience because it helps them grow. You got it like you were a veal-calf being fattened up. No wonder you didn't like it."

"I wouldn't say that."

"But you don't go to galleries or museums, do you?" She glanced down. "I used to, all the time. I'd sit and sketch. I'd see the work through the artist's eyes and then I'd endure watching boorish people troop through, or school kids rushed through with only enough time to look at the back of the kid in front of them. They were walking through beauty and saw none of it. Yet the teachers and the parents all thought the kids were getting culture."

"They were, it was just the McRembrant version of it."

She snorted out a little laugh, but didn't look up. "I kind of lost it. Nervous breakdown. That's how I ended up here. Martha's very good at putting puzzles back together."

I nodded, reached up and parted my hair. "You can't even see the joints anymore."

Leah laughed openly, warmly, and looked up again. "She said you could be cold, but I don't get that. And she said you could be trusted."

"She's right on both counts."

"I'm right? I guess my work here is done." Martha handed me a print-out of the recent donors to the mission. "The initials after each name indicates the contact."

"Thanks." I wasn't sure what the list would get me, but if the Fellowship was the connection, it was a vector in. "I guess I have to go to work."

Martha smiled. "You go, but you're going to come back later. We'll be having a big crowd tonight, and I need an extra hand on the soup line."

Leah nodded. "You soup them, I'll bread them."

I studied her face, then smiled pretty much against my will. "I think I'd like that."

◦◦◦

Back in the street, my phone rang.

Cate. "4721 Black Oak Road. You want to be here now."

"Who?"

"E. Theodore Carlson."

I glanced at the printout. "We have a winner."

"I'd hate to see what happened to the loser. Hurry, Trick. It's not pretty, and it isn't going to get any better with time."

Cate wasn't kidding. The corpse was ripe. He'd been dead a couple of days. Carlson had a reputation as a food critic and gourmand who got himself a cooking show and sold a lot of cookbooks and spices. While he liked exotic stuff, his critics claimed he simplified things for the common man. He took folks living hand to mouth and made them think they were mastering *haut cuisine*.

All while using hot dogs, ground chuck and catsup, and the secret ingredient.

Food lay all around in the kitchen, on presentation platters, but it had curdled or dried, crumbled or gotten covered in flies. He even had packaged cupcakes arranged on a set of stacked trays looking festive. They were the only things that hadn't gone bad yet, but that didn't soften the most gruesome aspect of the scene—aside from the corpse, that is.

On the granite countertop of the island, in a roasting pan surrounded by potatoes and carrots and chopped onions, lay a leg.

A human leg.

Carlson's leg.

He'd managed to hack it off at the knee, rub some salt on it, add pepper, before he collapsed and bled out on the floor. The butcher's knife lay half-beneath him, covered in bloody prints. Angle of the cuts and the way the bone was sheered meant he'd taken the leg off with only a couple whacks.

I looked around. "What did Prout say? Carlson slipped?"

Cate shook her head. "He was gone before I got here. Manny said he covered his mouth with a handkerchief, then got that look on his face like he'd gotten an idea."

Manny, who was taking pictures of the scene, grunted. "I said he looked like he'd just dumped a load in his tighty-whities."

"Same thing when his brain has movement." My eyes tightened. "Time of death?"

"Two days, three."

I glanced at my PDA and the listing of case files. "Killer's on a tight cycle, and it's getting faster. Two days between Carlson and Anderson. Someone is going to die in the next twelve hours."

"No, they won't."

I spun. Prout had returned, with handkerchief in place. "We just arrested the murderer."

"What? Who?"

He lowered the handkerchief so I could see his sneer. "Martha Raines."

"Are you out of your mind?"

"Only if you are, Molloy." His beady eyes never wavered. "You followed the money. So did I. The Fellowship's made millions on these deaths. You didn't want to see it because you always were a lousy detective."

"Arresting Raines solves nothing."

"You trying to confess to being an accomplice? How much did she pay you?"

I glanced at Prout through magic. He almost looked as bad as the corpse, all mushroom gray and speckled with black. He had no *talent*—nor talent, for that matter—so one spell, just a tiny one, and his white suit would be sopping up blood as he thrashed on the floor.

Cate grabbed my shoulder. "Don't."

Prout gave her a hard stare. "I think you better escort your friend from my crime scene."

"He's going. He's got a friend in jail who could use a visit." She poked a finger into Prout's chest, leaving a single bloody fingerprint on his tie. It looked like a bullet hole and I wished to God it was. "But this isn't *your* crime scene. It isn't even a crime until I say it is, Inspector. Right now, my running verdict is that he slipped. Death by misadventure, and unless you want to be doing all the paperwork and having all the hearings to change that, you'll be letting me finish this one fast."

Prout snorted. "Take your time."

Cate shook her head. "I don't have any. The killer's next vic will show up in another six hours, so time is not a luxury I enjoy."

∽ ◠ ◡ ◠

I would have stayed, just to bask in the glory of that sour expression on Prout's face, but Manny got a shot of it. He gave me a wink. I'd be seeing it again. I wished he had a shot of the sneer too. I wanted it for reference. Next time I saw it I was going to realign the nose and jaw.

Cate had been right. Martha was in jail, and it wasn't for picketing some city office this time. She needed a friend. I owed her. I didn't think the bulls down in lockup would want to do her any harm, but they'd have to cage her with the hard cases. Still, a visit could get her out of a holding cell at least for a little bit.

I got down to the jail pretty quick. I only made one stop, at a drive-through liquor store. I bought a bottle of twelve- year-old Irish whisky and took a long pull off it. Recorking it, I slid it under my seat. It burned down my throat and out into my veins. It made me feel more alive, and prepped me to use magic just in case.

I didn't need it. Hector Sands was working the desk and he'd always believed I'd been framed for bribery. "You want to see Raines?

Do you have to?"

"What am I not getting?"

Hector took me through into the holding area. Two big cells separated by a tiled corridor. Usually it was awash in profanity, urine, spittle, blood, and any other bodily fluid or solid that could be squirted, hurled, or expelled. People didn't like being caged like animals; so they acted like animals in protest.

Not this time, though. Martha Raines sat on a cot, with all the other inmates sitting on the floor, and the people across the corridor hanging onto the bars. And hanging on to her every word. She just spoke in low tones, so quiet I could barely hear her.

Maybe I couldn't. Maybe I was just remembering her calm voice and soft words. I heard her telling me that drinking myself to death wasn't going to solve problems. She told me I had something to live for. It really didn't matter what. I could change things from day to day. They were out there. I owed it to them and myself to straighten out.

"Been like that since we put her in the population. See why I don't want to take her out?"

"Yeah. You'll call me if there is trouble?"

Hector nodded. "I have to call Prout, too." He glanced up at the security cameras. "I wouldn't, but he wanted to know when you showed up, and he'll go through the tapes."

"Got it. Don't want you jammed up."

"I'll wait to the end of my shift, about an hour, to call, you know, if that will help."

I nodded, even though I didn't care. He'd call Prout. Prout would call me. I wouldn't answer. It didn't matter.

"Thanks." I left the jail armed with two things. The first was the list. The fact that Martha had given it to me without hesitation spoke against her guilt. If she were killing people, there's no reason she would hand me a list of her victims.

Unless she wanted to be stopped.

Serial killers feel compelled to kill, which is why they cycle faster and faster, their need pushing aside anything else. I wanted to dismiss the possibility of Martha's guilt outright, but I didn't know if she had alibis. I only had her word about how nicely things had gone. What if Anderson and Hogan set up the trusts for another reason, to deny her funding and to oust her? What if they were scheming to move the mission and profit from the location, using that project as some cornerstone to gentrify a swath of the city? Would that be enough to make her snap?

I crossed to a little bistro and ordered coffee. Martha was *talented*. She sat in that den of lions and made them into lambs. I'd felt it. I knew her power. I'd benefited from it. But that was the good side of it. Was there a dark side? Could she talk someone into hanging himself or chopping off his own leg?

And if she could do that, could she convince a jury—no matter how overwhelming the evidence—to let her go? If she could, there was no way she could ever be brought to justice. While the Fellowship was a noble undertaking, did its preservation justify murder?

Those were bigger questions than I could answer, so I did what I could do with the meager resources at hand. Starting at the top, I called down the donor list. I left messages—mostly with servants since these sorts of folks like that personal touch—or talked to the donors directly. I told them there was a meeting of donors in the Diamond Room at the Ultra hotel at nine. I told everyone to be there. I didn't so much care that it disrupted their evenings, as much as I hoped it would disrupt the killer's pattern.

It took me two hours to go through the list. I spent a lot of time on hold, or listening to bullshit excuses, so I used it to study those case files. Cate was right, I really didn't want to look at the Preakness photos. There was something there, though, in all of them, but I couldn't put my finger on it.

At the end of those two hours I was no closer to knowing who the next victim would be.

Then it came to me.

Prout.

He'd never called.

I drove to his home as fast as I could. Red lights and a fender-bender let me double-check the full case packages Cate had sent me. I finally saw it. As far as a signature for a serial killer goes, this one was pretty subtle. Maybe there was part of me that didn't want to see it before, but there was no denying it now.

I rolled to a stop on the darkened street in front of the little house with the white picket fence. Figured. He probably owned a poodle. A sign in an upstairs window told firefighters there were two children in that room. I didn't even know he was married.

I fished the whiskey from beneath the seat and drank deep. I brought the bottle. Prout wouldn't have anything there, and if he did, he'd not offer.

That's okay. I don't like to impose.

I crossed the street and vaulted the fence. I could have boosted my leap with magic, but there was no reason to waste it.

And it didn't surprise me that the hand I'd put on the fence-post came away wet with white paint. Had my head not been full of whiskey vapors I'd have smelled it. White footprints led up the steps and across the porch, hurried and urgent. The screen door had shut behind him, but the solid door remained ajar.

Beyond it, darkness and the flickering of candles. That wasn't right for the house. It should have been brightly lit, all Formica and white vinyl, with plastic couch-condoms covering every stick of furniture. Lace doilies, and white leather-bound editions of the Bible scattered about.

I toed the door open.

I got the last thing right. Bibles had been scattered, page by page. They littered the darkened living room. Across from the doorway sat a woman in a modest dress, and a little girl in a matching outfit. Both had been duct taped into spindly chairs, with a strip over their mouths to keep them quiet.

On the wall, where I guess once hung the slashed portrait of Jesus crumpled in the corner, someone had painted a pentagram in sloppy red strokes. A little boy hung upside down at the heart of it, from a hook to which his feet were bound. He'd been muted with duct tape too, and stared in horror at the center of the floor.

His father sat there, naked, in a circle of black candles. Thirteen of them. He'd cut himself on the neck and wrists—nothing life-threatening—and blood had run over his chest and been smeared over his belly. He clutched a long carving knife in two hands. He waved it through the air, closing one eye, measuring his son for strokes that would take him to pieces.

I took another drink, and not because I needed the magic.

Prout looked up at me. "Yes, Father Satan, I have served thee well, and now have this sacrifice for you."

I held a hand out. "Easy, Prout."

He wasn't listening. "You come to me in the shape of my enemy to mock me. I did harm to your pet. That opened my heart to you, didn't it?"

I had no idea what he was going on about, but talking was better than slashing. "You begin to see things, my son."

He nodded and studied his reflection in the blade.

I looked at him through magic. Prout had always been leopard-spotted, just full of weaknesses. That had changed. The spots had become long, oily rivers that ran up and down his body, like circulating currents. I'd never seen its like before, but it wasn't part of Prout. He had no talent.

I closed my fist and opened it again. A blue spark, invisible to Prout and his family, flew from my palm and drilled into his forehead. His stripes went jagged. He tried to rise, then toppled and fell, snuffing two of the candles against his belly.

I looked past him toward the kitchen. "Come on out, Leah. This ends here."

The young artist stepped from the darkened kitchen, glowing silver with magic. She'd streaked paint over her face and in her hair. It had to be her trigger—something in it, or the scent—and the glow made her very powerful. She opened her hands innocently and stared into my eyes.

"You don't know what he did, Trick."

"He arrested Martha for your murders."

"Not that." Her voice came soft and gentle, like a lover's whisper. "Before that, when he was investigating you. He knew you were set up. He had evidence to clear you. He didn't. You know why? Your mother is part of his church. You were an embarrassment for her. He wanted to make you go away."

I stared down at the man and suddenly found the knife in my hand. Prout *had* known I was innocent. He destroyed my life because magic was evil and he couldn't abide it. He got me tossed from the force and hid behind being a good church-going man, an upstanding officer.

I weighed the knife in my hand. "Right. He's a hypocrite."

"Just like the others. They all pledged money, but only in trust, only upon death, for capital expenses, not operations." Leah's eyes narrowed. "They knew how tight things were for the mission. They helped Martha to expand until she couldn't keep the place going. They had their own plans. They'd move her out, revoke their gifts. They had to be stopped."

"You made them pay."

"I made them reveal themselves. They wallowed in their own vanity. They died embracing their inner reality."

"Why the staging? The rotten food, from the *vanitas* paintings?"

"It was all a warning to others. They should have seen death coming."

"And the Twinkie. I saw one at each site."

Leah smiled coldly. "The promise of life everlasting. They never saw it."

"They never could have understood."

"But you do, Trick." Her eyes blazed. "You have to kill Prout. He betrayed you. Let him die here. Let everyone see how black his heart really is."

Argent arcane fire poured over me. Every moment of pain I'd felt exploded within. I'd made a good life. I'd had friends. I'd been respected, and Prout conspired with my mother and with criminals to smear me and destroy me. Leah's magic wrapped me up and bled down into the blade, tracing silver lightning bolts over the metal.

One second. A heartbeat. A quick stroke and Prout's blood would splash hot over me. I could revel in it. Victory, finally.

Then it was over.

I dropped the knife.

She stared at me. "How?"

"I've been where you've been, darlin'. As low as can be." I let blue energy gather in my palm. "No vanity. No illusion. I know exactly what I am."

The azure bolt caught her in the chest and smashed her back against the wall. Plasterboard cracked. She left a bloody smear as she sank to the floor.

In turn I used magic to put Prout's family out and to let them forget. They'd have nightmares, but there was no reason to make them worse.

And it was going to get worse.

I'd been worried that Martha could have turned a jury with her *talent*. There's no juror in the world, much less jurist or lawyer, that isn't a little bit vain. I never figured the way Prout did, that being talented meant one was evil; but I knew better than to rule it out.

I had to deal with it.

I picked up the knife. I wrapped Prout's hand around it.

We went to work.

Cate found me on the hill overlooking Anderson's graveside service. Huge crowd, including Prout. He dressed properly. The only white on him was his shirt and bandages on his face. He stood beside my mother, steadying her, being stoic and heroic.

That was his right, after all, since he'd put an end to the Society Murderess.

"How can you watch this, Trick?"

"Only way I can make sure he's dead." I half-smiled. "Think my mother will throw herself on the casket?"

"Not her. Prout. Preening."

"Why shouldn't he? He's a hero. He killed a sociopath." I nodded toward him. "She put up a hell of a fight before he stabbed her through the heart. I heard his jaw was broken in two places."

"Three. Cracked orbit, busted nose."

"Whoda thunk she could hit that hard?"

"Never met her." Cate shook her head. "How's your hand?"

"Scrapes and bruises. I'll be more careful walking to the bathroom in the dark."

"You know, there were some anomalous fingerprints on the knife."

"Ever match 'em?"

"No. Was I wrong about you, Trick?"

"I don't think so, Cate." I met her stare openly. "They need their heroes. They need someone to fend off the things lurking beyond the firelight. Prout battled to save his family. Its best he never knows how much danger he was in. How much danger they were all in. All their fear and they couldn't even imagine."

"I don't think they really want to."

"You're probably right."

Down below, Martha Raines closed the prayer book and made a final comment. I didn't hear it. I didn't need to.

They did, and they looked peaceful.

Grave-Robbed

P. N. ELROD

Chicago, February 1937

When the girl draped in black stepped in to ask if could help
her with a séance, Hal Kemp's version of "Gloomy Sunday" began to
murmur sadly from the office radio.

Coincidences annoy me. A mournful song for a dead sweetheart put
together with a ceremony that's supposed to help the dead speak with
the living made me uneasy—and I was annoyed it made me uneasy.

I should know better, being dead myself.

"You sure you're in the right place?" I asked, taking in her outfit.
Black overcoat, pocketbook, gloves, heels, and stockings—she was
a walking funeral. Along with the mourning weeds she wore a
brimmed hat with a chin-brushing veil even I couldn't see past.

"*The Escott Agency*—that's what's on the door," she said, sitting
on the client chair in front of the desk without an invitation. "You're
Mr. Escott?"

"I'm Mr. Fleming. I fill in for Mr. Escott when he's elsewhere."
He was visiting his girlfriend tonight. I'd come over to his office to
work on his books since I was better at accounting.

"It was Mr. Escott who was recommended to me."

"By who?"

"A friend."

I waited, but she left it at that. Much of Escott's business as a private agent came by word of mouth. Call him a private eye and you'd get a pained look and perhaps an acerbic declaration that he did not undertake divorce cases. His specialty as an agent was carrying out unpleasant errands for the unable or unwilling, not peeking through keyholes, but did a séance qualify? He was interested in that kind of thing, but mostly from a skeptic's point of view. I had to say *mostly* since he couldn't be a complete skeptic what with his partner—me—being a vampire.

And nice to meet you, too.

Hal Kemp played on in the little office until the girl stood, went to the radio, and shut it off.

"I hate that song," she stated, turning around, the veil swirling lightly. Faceless women annoy me as well, but she had good legs.

"Me, too. You got any particular reason?"

"My sister plays it all the time. It gets on my nerves."

"Does it have to do with this séance?"

"Can't you call Mr. Escott?"

"I could, but you didn't make an appointment for this late or he'd be here."

"My appointment is for tomorrow, but something's happened since I made it, and I need to speak with him tonight. I came by just in case he worked late. The light was on and a car was out front . . . "

I checked his appointment book. In his precise hand he'd written *10 AM, Abigail Saeger*. "Spell that name again?"

She did so, correct for both.

"What's the big emergency?" I asked. "If this is something I can't handle I'll let him know, but otherwise you'll find I'm ready, able, and willing."

"I don't mean to offend, but you look rather young for such work. Over the phone I thought Mr. Escott to be . . . more mature."

Escott and I were the same age but I did look younger by over a decade. On the other hand, if she thought a man in his mid-thirties was old, then she'd be something of a kid herself. Her light voice told me as much, though you couldn't tell by her mannerisms and speech, which bore a finishing school's not so subtle polish.

"Miss Saeger, would you mind raising your blinds? I like to see who's hiring before I take a job."

She went still a moment, then lifted her veil. As I thought, a fresh-faced kid who should be home studying, but her eyes were red-rimmed, her expression serious.

"That's better. What can I do for you?"

"My older sister, Flora, is holding a séance tonight. She's crazy to talk with her dead husband, and there's a medium taking advantage of her. He wants her money, and more."

"A fake medium?"

"Is there any other kind?"

I smiled, liking her. "Give me the whole story, same as you'd have told to Mr. Escott."

"You'll help me?"

"I need to know more first." I said it in a tone to indicate I was interested.

She plunged in, talking fast, but I had good shorthand and scribbled notes.

Miss Saeger and her older sister Flora were alone, their parents long dead. But Flora had money in trust and married into more money after getting hitched to James Weisinger, Jr., who inherited a tidy fortune some years ago. The Depression had little effect on them. Flora became a widow last August when her still-young husband died in a sailing accident on Lake Michigan.

I'd been killed on that lake. "Sure it was an accident?"

"A wind shift caused the boom to swing around. It caught him on the side of the head and over he went. I still have nightmares about the awful thud when it hit him and the splash, but it's worse for Flora—she was at the wheel at the time. She blames herself. No one else does. There were half a dozen people aboard who knew sailing. That kind of thing can happen out of the blue."

I vaguely remembered reading about it in the paper. Nothing like some rich guy getting killed while doing rich-guy stuff to generate copy.

"Poor James never knew what hit him, it was just that fast. Flora was in hysterics and had to be drugged for a week. Then she kept to her bed nearly a month, then she read some stupid article in a magazine about using a Ouija boards to talk to spirits and got it into her head that she had to contact James, to apologize to him."

"That opened the door?"

"James is dead, and if he did things right he's in heaven and should stay there—in peace." Miss Saeger growled in disgust. "I've gotten Flora's pastor to talk to her, but she won't listen to him. I've talked to her until we both end up screaming and crying, and she won't see sense. I'm just her little sister and don't know anything, you see."

"What's so objectionable?"

"Her obsession. It's not healthy. I thought after all this time she'd lose interest, but she's gotten worse. Every week she has a gaggle of those creeps from the Society over, they set up the board, light candles, and ask questions while looking at James' picture. It's pointless and sad and unnatural and—and . . . just plain *disrespectful*."

I was really liking her now. "Society?"

"The Psychical Society of Chicago."

Though briefly tempted to ask her to say it three times fast, I kept my yap shut. The group investigated haunted houses and held sittings—their word for séances—writing their experiences up for their archives. Escott was a member. For a buck a year to cover mailing costs he'd get a pamphlet every month and read the more oddball pieces out to me.

"The odious thing is," said Miss Saeger, "they're absolutely *sincere*. When one has that kind of belief going, then of course it's going to produce results."

"What kind of results?"

"They've spelled out the names of all the people who ever died in the house, which is stupid because the house isn't that old. The man who supervises these sittings says that's because the house was built over the site of another, so the dead people are connected to *it*, you see. There's no way to prove or disprove any of it. He's got an answer for everything and always sounds perfectly reasonable."

"Is he the medium?"

"No, but he brought him in. Alistair Bradford." She put plenty of venom in that name. "He looks like something out of a movie."

"What? Wears a turban like Chandu the Magician?"

Her big dark eyes flashed, then she choked, stifling a sudden laugh. She got things under control after a moment. "Thank you. It's so good to talk with someone who sees things the way I do."

"Tell me about him."

"No turban, but he has piercing eyes, and when he walks into a room everyone turns around. He's handsome . . . for an old guy."

"How old?"

"At least forty."

"That's ancient."

"Please don't make fun of me. I get that all the time from him, from all of them."

"I'm sorry, Miss Saeger. Are you the only one left in the house with any common sense?"

"Yes." She breathed that out, and it almost turned into a sob, but she headed it off. The poor kid looked to be only barely keeping control of a truckload of high emotion. I heard her heart pound fast, then gradually slow. "Even the servants are under his spell. I have friends, but I can't talk to them about this. It's just too embarrassing."

"You've been by yourself on this since August?"

She nodded. "Except for our pastor, but he can't be there every day. He tells me to keep praying for Flora, and I do, and still this goes on and just gets worse. I miss James, too. He was a nice man. He deserves better than this— this—"

"What broke the camel's back to bring you here?"

"Before Alistair Bradford came all they did was play with that stupid Ouija board. I'd burn it but they'd just buy another from the five and dime. After *he* was introduced they began holding real séances. I don't like any of that stuff and don't believe in it, but he made it scary. It's as though he gets taller and broader and his voice changes. With the room almost totally dark it's easy to believe him."

"They let you sit in?"

"Just the once—on sufferance so long as I kept quiet. When I turned the lights on in the middle of things Flora banished me. She said my negative thoughts were preventing the spirits from coming through, and that I was endangering Bradford's life. You're not supposed to startle a medium out of a trance or it could kill him. I wouldn't mind seeing that, but he was faking. While they were all yelling I had my eye on him, and the look he gave me was pure hate . . . and he was *smiling*. He wanted to scare me and it worked. I've kept my door locked and haven't slept much."

"I don't blame you. No one believes you?"

"Of course not. I'm not in their little club and to them I'm just a kid. What do I know?"

"Kid's have instinct, a good thing to follow. Is he living in the house?"

"He mentioned it, but Flora—for once—didn't think that was proper."

"Is he romancing her?"

Miss Saeger's eyes went hard. "Slowly. He's too smart to rush things, but I see the way he struts around, looking at everything. If he lays a finger on Flora I'll—"

I raised one hand. "I get it. You want Flora protected and him discredited."

"Or his legs broken and his big smirking face smashed in."

That was something I could have arranged. I know those kind of people. "It's better if Flora gets rid of him by her own choice, though."

"I don't see how, I may have left it too late. I called here on Saturday to make the appointment, but—" She went red in the face. "I could just *kill* him."

"What'd he do?"

"The last séance—they have one every Sunday and that's just *wrong* having it on a Sunday—something horrible happened. They all gathered in the larger parlor at the table as usual, lighted candles, and put out the lights. Soon as it went dark I slipped in while they were getting settled. There's an old Chinese screen in one corner, and I hide behind it during their séances. Negative feelings, my foot, no one's noticed me yet, not even Bradford, so I saw the whole thing."

"Which was?"

"He put himself in a trance right on time. It usually takes five minutes, and by then everyone's expecting something to happen, you can feel it. He starts out with a low groan and breathing loudly, and in the dark it's spooky, and that's when his spirit guide takes over. His voice gets deeper and he puts on a French accent. Calls himself *Frère* Lèon. He's supposed to have been a monk who traveled with Joan of Arc."

"Who speaks perfect English?"

"Of course. No one's ever thought of talking to him in French. I doubt Bradford knows much more than *mon Dieu* and *sang sacré*."

She'd attended a good finishing school, speaking with the right kind of pronunciation. I'd heard it when I'd been a doughboy in France during the last year of the war, and had picked up enough to get by. Much of that was too rough for Miss Saeger's tender ears, though.

"And the horrible thing that happened?"

"It was at the end. He pretends to have *Frère* Lèon pass on messages from James. He can't have James talk directly to Flora or he'd trip himself up. He doesn't pass too many messages, either, just general stuff about how beautiful it is on the other side. She tries to talk to him and ask him things and she's so desperate and afterwards she always cries and then she goes back for *more*. It's cruel. But this time he said he was giving her a sign of what she should do."

"Do?"

"I didn't know what that meant, until . . . well, Bradford finished just then and pretended to be waking from his trance. That's when they found what he'd snuck on the table. It was James' wedding ring, the one he was buried with."

I gave that the pause it deserved. "Not a duplicate?"

She shook her head, a fast, jerky movement. Her voice was thick. "Inside it's engraved with *To J. from F.—Forever Love.* He never took it off and it had some hard wear: two distinct parallel scratches, and it wasn't a perfect circle. Flora showed it to me as proof that Alistair Bradford was genuine. She didn't want to hear my idea that . . . that he'd dug up and robbed James' grave. I thought she'd slap me. She's gone crazy, Mr.—"

"Fleming. Call me Jack."

"Jack. Flora's never raised a hand to me, even when we were kids and I was being bratty, but this has her all turned around. I thought Mr. Escott could find something out about Bradford that would prove him a fake or come to a séance and do something to break it up, but I don't think she'd listen now. The last thing Bradford said before his trance ended was 'you have his blessing.' Put that with the ring and I know it means if he asks Flora to marry him she'll say yes because she'll think that's what James would want."

"Come on, she can't be that—"

"Stupid? Foolish? Under a spell? She is! That's what's driving *me* crazy. She should be *smarter* than this."

"Grief can make you go right over the edge. Guilt can make it worse, and I bet she's lonely, too. She should have gone to a head-doctor, but picked up a Ouija board instead. Does this Bradford ask for money?"

"*He* calls it a donation. She's given him fifty dollars every time. He gets that much for all his sittings—and he does thirty to forty a month. My sister's not the only dope in town."

My mouth went dry. Fifty a week was a princely income, but that much times forty? I was in the wrong business. I'd gotten twenty-five a week back in New York as a reporter and counted myself lucky. "Well. It beats robbing banks. Your sister can give him more by marriage?"

"Yes, her trust money and the estate from James. Bradford would have it, the house, never have to work again. Please, can you help me stop him?"

I thought of the people I knew who broke bones for a sawbuck and could make a man totally disappear for twice that. "I need to check this, you know. I only have your side of things."

"And I'm just a kid."

"Miss Saeger, I'd say the same thing to Eleanor Roosevelt if she was in that chair. Lemme make a phone call. Anyone going to be worried you're gone?"

"I snuck out and got a taxi. Flora and I had a fight tonight and she thinks I'm sulking in my room. She's busy, anyway—the new séance."

"Uh-huh." I dialed Gordy at the Nightcrawler Club and asked if he had any dirt on an Alistair Bradford, professional medium.

"Medium what?" asked Gordy in his sleepy-sounding voice.

"A swami, you know, séances, fortune-telling. It's for a case. I'm filling in for Charles."

He grunted, and he sounded amused. "You at his office? Ten minutes." He hung up. As the Nightcrawler was a longer than ten-minute drive away I took him to mean he'd phone back, not drop by.

"Ten minutes," I repeated to Miss Saeger. "What's with the black getup? You still in mourning for your brother-in-law?"

"It was the only way I could think of to cover my face. I'm full grown, but soon as anyone looks at me they think I'm fifteen or something."

"And you're really . . . ?"

"Sixteen."

"Miss Saeger, you are one brave and brainy sixteen-year-old, so I'm sure you're aware that this is a school night."

"My sister is more important than that, but thank you for the reminder." There was a dryness in her tone that would have done credit to Escott. A couple years from now and she'd be one formidable young woman.

"What time is this séance?"

"Nine o'clock. Always."

"Not at midnight?"

"Some of the older Society members get too sleepy if things go much past ten."

"Why tonight instead of next Sunday?"

"James' birthday. Bradford said that holding a sitting on the loved one's birthday always means something special."

"Like what?"

"He won't say, he just *smiles*. It makes my skin crawl. I swear, if he's not stopped I'll get one of James' golf clubs and—" She went red in the face again, stood up, and paced. I did that when the pent up energy got to be too much.

I tried to get more from her on tonight's event, but she didn't have anything else to add, though she had plenty of comment about Bradford's antics. Guys like him I'd met before, they're always the first to look you square in the eye and assure you they're honest long before you begin to wonder.

The phone rang in seven minutes. Abigail Saeger halted in mid-word and stride and sat, leaning forward as I put the receiver to my ear. Gordy was like a library for all that was crooked in the great city of Chicago, with good reason: if he wasn't behind it himself, he knew who was and where to find them. He gave me slim pickings about Bradford, but it was enough to confirm that the guy was trouble. He'd done some stage work as a magician, Alistair the Great, until discovering there was more cash to be had conjuring dead relatives from thin air instead of rabbits. He preferred to collect as much money in the shortest time, then make an exit. The wealthy widow Weisinger was too good a temptation to a man looking for an easy way to retire.

"You need help with this bo'?" Gordy asked.

"I'll let you know. Thanks."

"No problem."

"Well?" asked Miss Saeger.

I hung up. "Count me in, ma'am."

"That sounds so old. My name's Abby."

"Fine, you can sign it here." I pulled out one of Escott's standard contracts. It was short and vague, mostly a statement that the Escott Agency was retained for services by, with a blank after that and room for the date.

"How much will this be?"

"Five bucks should do it."

"It has to be more than that. I read detective stories."

"Special sale, tonight only. Anyone walking in here named Abby pays five bucks, no more, no less."

For a second I thought she'd kiss me, and I was prepared to duck out of range. If my girlfriend found out I'd canoodled, however innocently or briefly, with a mere pippin of sixteen I would find myself dead for real and for ever after.

Abby signed, fished a five-dollar bill from her pocketbook, and took my receipt in exchange. I put the money and the contract in Escott's top desk drawer along with my shorthand notes. He'd have a fine time trying to figure things out when he came in tomorrow morning. I harvested my overcoat and fedora from the coat tree in the corner, and ushered my newest client out, locking up. She made it to the bottom of the stairs, then pulled the veil back over her face.

"Afraid someone will recognize you?" I asked. The street was empty.

"No sense in taking chances."

Now I really liked her. I opened my new Studebaker up and handed her in, checking the sky. It had been threatening to sleet since before I got up tonight; I hoped it would hold off.

"Nice car," she said.

The nicest I'd ever owned. My faithful '34 Buick had come to a bad end, but this sporty replacement helped ease the loss. I got the motor purring, remembered to turn the headlights on, and put it in gear, pulling slowly from the curb. "Where's your brother-in-law buried?" As Abby's chin was just visible, I could see her jaw drop.

"Why do you need to know that?"

"I want to pay my respects."

"The cemetery will be closed."

"Which one? And where?"

She told me, finally, and I made a U-turn and got us on our way. Chicago traffic was no worse than usual as we headed toward Lincolnwood. Following Abby's directions we ended up driving slow along North Ravenswood Avenue. A railroad track on our left obscured the view of the cemetery grounds. When a cross street opened, I took the turn under the tracks. A pale stone building with crenellations, Gothic windows, square, two-storied tower with a number of slender, round towers at the corners and along the front wall looked back at us. It had too much dignity to be embarrassed. The gates that blocked its arched central opening were, indeed, closed.

"Told you," said Abby.

"Is Mr. Weisinger anywhere near the front?" This place looked huge. They only put fancy stone buildings like that in front of the really large cemeteries.

"Go back south and turn on Bryn Mawr, I'll tell you when to stop."

What the lady said. It took awhile to find a sufficiently secluded place to park, then Abby provided very specific directions to the grave, which was not too far from the boundary wall.

"What are you going to do?" she asked.

I was about to say she didn't want to know, but decided that would get me an observation about not treating her like an adult. "I'm going to check to see if the grave has been disturbed enough to bring in the law."

"But the police, the papers—"

"A necessary evil. If they show up asking Bradford how he got that wedding ring, how long do you think he'll stick around?"

"Would they put him in jail?" She looked hopeful.

"We'll see. You gonna be warm enough? Good. I'll be quick."

"Don't you want me along?"

"I'll bet you're good at it, but you're not exactly dressed for getting around fences."

She looked relieved.

I slammed the door, opened the trunk, and drew out a crowbar from the tool box I kept there. Since Abby didn't need to see it and try to guess why I'd want one I held it out of sight while approaching the cemetery's boundary. It was made of iron bars with points on top, an easy climb if you were nimble.

I had the agility, but slipped between the bars instead. Literally. One of my happier talents acquired after my death was being able to vanish and float just about anywhere I liked, invisible as air. Since it was dark and there was some distance between me and the car I figured Abby wouldn't see much if I partially vanished, eased through, and went solid again. Blink of an eye and it was done.

The cemetery grounds were covered with a thick layer of mostly undisturbed snow. Trees, bushes, and monuments of all shapes showed black against it. I made my way to one of the wide paths that had been shoveled clear, looking out for the landmark of an especially ornate mausoleum with marble columns in front. Weisinger's grave marker was just behind it. The dates on the substantial granite block told me he'd been born this day and was only a few years younger than I, the poor bastard. Another, identical, block sprouted right next to it with his widow's name and date of birth already in place.

The snow lay differently over his plot, clumped and broken, dirtier than the stuff in the surrounding area. Footprints were all over, but not being an Indian tracker I couldn't make much from them, only that someone had recently been busy here and worn galoshes.

I poked the long end of the crowbar into the soil, and it went in far too easily. Ground that had had seven months to settle and freeze in the winter weather would have put up more resistance. Bradford or someone working for him had dug down, opened the coffin, grabbed the wedding ring, and put the earth back. Then he'd taken the trouble to dump a shovelfuls of snow on top so a casual eye wouldn't notice. He was probably hoping there'd be another fall soon to cover the rest of the evidence.

The ghoulishness of the robbery appalled me, the level of greed behind it disgusted me. I knew some tough customers who worked for Gordy, and even they would have balked at this level of low.

The moment Abigail Saeger told me about Weisinger's death on the lake I'd signed myself onto the job. Something twinged inside me then, connecting that death to my own and to that damned "Gloomy Sunday" song playing on the radio. I didn't want to believe in coincidences of the weird kind; signs and portents were strictly for the fortune-teller's booth at the midway.

But still . . . I got a twinge.

It was different from the goose-flesh creep that means someone's walking over your grave. When it came down to it, I didn't have a grave, just that lake. The people who'd murdered me had also robbed me of a proper burial. Weisinger had gotten one but Bradford had violated it.

That was just *wrong*.

And just as that thought crossed my mind the wind abruptly kicked up, rattling the bare branches as though the trees were waking up around me. They scratched and clacked and I tried not imagine bones making a similar noise, but it was too late.

"All right, keep your shirt on," I said to no one in particular, stepping away from the grave. It sure as hell felt like someone was listening.

I was dead (or undead), surrounded by acres of the truly dead. The wind sent snow dust skittering along the black path. My imagination gave it form and purpose as it swept by. A sizable icicle from high up broke away and dropped like a spear, making a pop as loud as a gun shot when it hit a stone marker and shattered not two yards away. If my heart had been beating it would have stopped then and there.

It's easy to be calm about weird coincidence when one is *not* in a cemetery at night. I decided it was time to leave. That I winked out quick and sped invisibly over the ground toward the fence faster than a scalded cat was my own business. Anyway, I went solid again as soon as I was on the other side.

Abby and I needed to get to her house before nine.

That's what I told myself while quick-marching to the car, consciously not looking over my shoulder.

Rich people live in some damned oddball houses. The Weisinger place started out with Frank Lloyd Wright on the ground floor, lots of glass and native stone, then the rest looked like a Tudor mansion straight from *The Private Life of Henry VIII*. I could almost see Charles Laughton waving cheerily from an upper window, framed by dark wood cross pieces set into the plaster.

"It's awful, but roomy," said Abby as I parked across the street to indulge in a good long stare.

"You okay for going back without getting caught?"

"Yes, but aren't you coming in?"

"This is the part where I do some sneaking around."

"They'll catch you, they'll think you're a burglar!"

"You hired an expert. Look, we can't go through the front so you can introduce me to everyone. It'll put Bradford on his guard, and your sister will be within her rights to kick me out."

"What will you do?"

"Exactly what's needed to get rid of him—and for that *you* need an alibi so they'll know you aren't involved. This means you can't hide behind that screen as usual. You said there're servants? Do they eavesdrop? Perfect. Think you can eavesdrop with them?"

"It wouldn't be the first time."

"Good for you. Whatever happens I want them to truthfully vouch that you were with them the whole time. This keeps you off the hook with Flora. I'm going to do my best to make Bradford look bad, so you have to be completely clear. Can you look innocent? Never mind, you're a natural." I checked my watch: twenty to nine. "I need a sketch of the floor plan."

I pulled a shorthand pad from the glove compartment and gave her a pencil. A street lamp on the corner bled just enough light to work by as she plotted out an irregular shape, dividing it into squares and rectangles, putting a big *X* in to mark the parlor.

"That's the ground floor." She handed the pad over. "Kitchen, dining room, card room, music room, small parlor, large parlor, that's where they have the séances. How will you—"

"Trade secret. You'll get your money's worth and then some, now beat it. Shuck those weeds and keep some witnesses around you. Don't be alone for a minute." She got out of the car quickly, coming around to the driver's side. I rolled the window down. "One more thing . . ."

She bent to be at eye-level. "Yes?"

"When the dust settles, don't give your sister any 'I told you so's,' okay?"

Abby got a funny look, and I thought she'd ask one more time about what I'd be doing, and I'd have to put her off, not being sure myself. Instead, she pecked me a solid one right on the mouth, and honest to God, I did *not* see it coming.

"Good luck!" she whispered, then scampered off.

No point in wiping away the lip color, she wasn't wearing any. Dangerous girl. I felt old.

I took the car around the block once and found a likely place to leave it, close behind another that had just parked along the curb. A line of vehicles of various makes and vintages led to the Weisinger house. Partygoers, I thought. A well-bundled couple emerged and stalked carefully along the damp sidewalk toward the lights. Slouching down, I waited until five to nine, then got out and followed.

Not as many lights showed around the curtains now, but I could hear the noise of a sizable gathering within the walls. The possibility of sneaking in to blend with the crowd occurred, but I decided against it. Groups like the Psychical Society tended to be close-knit and notice outsiders. With his membership card Escott could get away with bluffing himself in (his English accent didn't hurt, either), but I was a ready-made sore thumb. Better that they never see my face at all.

I took the long way around the house to compare it to Abby's sketch. She'd not marked the windows, not that I needed to open any to get inside; they were just easier to go through than lath and plaster. Picking a likely one above the larger parlor, I vanished, floated up the wall, and seeped through by way of the cracks.

Bumbling around in the space on the other side I regretted not getting a sketch of the second story as well. The room was big and I sensed furniture shapes filling it. Though my hearing was muffled I determined no one else was there, and cautiously reformed, taking it slow. An empty, dark bedroom, and laid out on the bed was a man's dressing gown. Neatly together on the floor were his slippers. The rest of the room was in perfect order, personal items set out on a bureau, no dust anywhere, and yet it didn't feel lived-in. No one is ever this tidy when they're actually using such things.

The hair went up on the back of my neck.

This stuff was too high quality to belong to the butler. The *J. W.* engraved into the back of a heavy silver hairbrush confirmed it—the room was a shrine. I concluded that Flora Weisinger was in sore need of real help to deal with her grief and guilt, not well-meaning morons with Ouija boards.

The upstairs seemed to be deserted, but I crept softly along the hall, ready to vanish again if company came. The downstairs noise was loud from several conversations going at once, the same as for any party, but no music, no laughter.

Nosy, I opened doors. The one nearest Weisinger's room led to Flora's, to judge by the furnishings and metaphysical reading matter. I never understood why it was that rich couples sometimes went in for separate bedrooms, even when they really liked each other.

Her closet was stuffed with dark clothing, all the cheerful print dresses and light colors shoved far to either side. Women wore dark things in the winter, but this was too much. There was an out of place-looking portable record player on a table by the bed. The only record on the spindle was Kemp's "Gloomy Sunday."

Enough already, I got out before I had another damn twinge.

One of the hall doors opened to a sizable linen cupboard. I stepped in and put on the light. With my vision the night is like day to me if there's any kind of illumination, but not so much in interior rooms with no windows. This place reminded me of the hidden room under Escott's kitchen where I slept while the sun was up. It seemed safe enough, so I took off my overcoat and hat, putting them out of sight in the back on an upper shelf. I wanted to be able to move around quick, if required.

Sheets and towels filled other shelves, along with some white, filmy material that I figured out were spare curtains. When I was a kid my mom drafted me twice a year to help change the winter to summer curtains and back again. No matter that it was women's work, I was the youngest and available.

I held the fabric up and it was just like what Mom used. In a lighted room you could see through it, but in a dark place with only a candle burning and imaginations at a fever pitch—yeah, I could make good use of it. The widest, longest piece folded up small, and I easily pushed it into the gap between my belt and shirt in the back.

But I wanted something more spectacular than a fun house spook. The items in Weisinger's room would do it.

From his bureau I pocketed the hairbrush, a pipe, comb, some keys, and checked out a bottle of aftershave cologne. Aqua Velva was good enough for me, but rich guys had to be different. I shook some into my hands and gave myself a thorough slapping down, face, neck, hands, and lapels. Fortunately, it smelled pretty nice.

Downstairs, things suddenly went quiet. The séance must be starting.

No time for further refinements, I vanished and sank straight through the floor until I'd cleared its barrier and was sure it was now a ceiling. I hovered high, listening.

They sang "Happy Birthday."

I could have done without that.

The mostly in-key singing ended, then a man gently urged, "Blow them out and make a wish for him, Flora."

The soft applause that followed indicated success, then there was a general shuffling and scraping as they took seats. No one spoke, which was odd. People talked at parties.

Silence now, a long stretch of silence. I took the pause as an opportunity to explore the edges of the room. Certainly I bumped and brushed into people, and they'd shiver in reaction, because in this form I'd feel like a cold draft to them, but the silence held. Without too much trouble I found a corner and determined this was where Abby hid herself. She was absent, so I gradually re-formed.

The Chinese screen—and I didn't have much experience with them—was seven feet tall and wide enough to conceal a sizable serving area. When holding formal receptions you didn't have to see the servants messing with the dishes. There were spaces between the painted panels that I could peer through, though. Each sliver of space provided a different angle on things.

The large parlor was much bigger than I expected. A long table was set up in the middle and seated eight to a side. Each chair had an occupant, and they were a motley group: some wore formal clothes, others were artistically Bohemian.

An older, more polished, more somber version of Abby sat at one end on the side opposite me: Flora Weisinger. Behind her was a framed portrait of a young man in his prime: her late husband. In front of her was a large birthday cake, its candles dead. She clutched a wadded handkerchief in one hand, in the other, pinched between thumb and forefinger and held up like an offering, was a gold ring. I could guess whose. Her posture was tense, expectant, her big dark gaze fixed on the tall man next to her.

At the head of the table, clearly in charge, stood Alistair Bradford. Having seen a few mediums in the course of my checkered life I knew they ran to all types, from self-effacing, lace-clad ladies, to suave young lounge lizards with Vaseline-slicked hair. Bradford was lofty and distinguished, his own too-long hair swept back like that of an orchestra maestro. It suited his serious features. He was handsome, if you liked that brand of it, and his slate-blue eyes did look piercing as they took in the disciples at the table.

"Now, dear friends," he said in startlingly soft, clear, beautiful voice, "please let us bow our heads in sincere prayer for a safe and enlightening spiritual journey on this very, *very* special night."

Such was the influence of that surprising voice that I actually followed through with the rest of them. I had to shake myself and remember he'd been happy to dig up a grave to get to that ring in Flora Weisinger's fingers. The wave of disgust snapped me out of it. The next time he spoke, saying *Amen*, I had my guard up.

Down the whole length of that big, bare table there were only two candles burning, leaving the rest of the room—to their eyes—dark. It was as good as daylight to me.

"And now I ask that everyone remain utterly quiet, and I will attempt to make contact," he said, smiling warmly.

I expected them to hold hands, touch fingers, or something like that. So much for how things were done in the movies.

Bradford sat, composed himself with his palms flat on the table, and shut his eyes. He drew in a deep breath, audibly releasing it. In contrast, no one else seemed able to move. Flora looked at him with an intense and heartbreaking hope that was terrible to see.

His stertorous breathing gradually got louder. The man knew how to play things to raise the suspense.

And I knew how to bust it.

His noises got thicker with more throat behind them, so I could guess he was ready to turn it into a good long groan so *Frère* Lèon could make his entrance.

I went invisible, floated until I was exactly behind his chair, went solid while crouched down, and drew a big breath of my own. During the brief silence between his puffings I cut loose with loudest, juiciest Bronx cheer I could manage, then vanished.

In a tense, emotion-charged room it had a predictable effect. I slipped behind the screen to watch.

His rhythm abruptly shattered, Bradford looked around in confusion, as did the others. Some seemed scandalized, a couple were amused, and one guy suggested that perhaps there was a playful spirit in the room already. A more practical man got up to check my corner, which was the only hiding place, and announced it to be empty.

A few of them noticed the cologne and mentioned it. Much to their delight, Flora finally confirmed that it was James' scent hanging in the air. She sounded awful. Bradford made no comment.

After some excited discussion that didn't go anywhere, they settled down, and Bradford started his breathing routine again. I watched and waited.

Frère Lèon eventually began to speak through Bradford, and to give him credit, it was a damned well-done French accent. His voice was rougher, deeper in pitch, very effective in the dark.

I ventured forth again, keeping low while he gave them a weather report for the Other Side, and went solid just long enough to call out a handy bit of French I'd learned while on leave in Paris. The loose translation was *How much for an hour of love, my little cabbage?*

Or something like that, it had usually been enough to get my face slapped.

Then I clocked him sharp on the back of the noggin with the hairbrush, dropped it, and vanished.

I was back to the screen, going solid in time to see things fall apart. A few in the room had understood what I'd said and were either flabbergasted or trying not to laugh. Bradford's trance was thoroughly broken; he launched from his chair to look behind it, startled as the rest. He remembered himself, though, and flopped down again, apparently in a state of collapse. They fussed over him, and the electric chandelier was switched on.

Somewhere in the middle of it Flora spotted the hairbrush. She froze, screamed, and sat down fast, sheet white and pointing to where it lay on the floor.

It took attention away from Bradford, and I was betting he was none too pleased. The knock he'd taken bothered him—his hand kept rubbing the spot—but I'd hit to hurt, not cause permanent damage. He'd earned it. I kept myself out of sight for the duration, going solid in the next room over, which was empty. Vanishing took it out of me. I'd have to stop at the Stockyards before dawn for some blood or I'd feel like hell tomorrow night.

Some guy who seemed to be the one in charge of the Psychical Society was for canceling the sitting, but Bradford assured everyone that he was fine. Sometimes mischievous spirits delighted in disrupting things—unless, of course there was a more earthly explanation. With Flora's permission the ground floor was searched for uninvited guests. I had to not be there for a few minutes, but didn't mind.

Elsewhere in the house, probably the distant kitchen, I heard strident voices denying any part of the business. Abby's was in that chorus, her outrage genuine. Good girl.

This time it took longer for everyone to settle. Though the hour inched toward ten, none showed signs of being sleepy enough to leave. The entertainment was too interesting.

The hour struck and they assembled in the parlor again. On the long table fresh candles were substituted for the ones that had expired. The chandelier was switched off.

From my vantage point at the screen I tried to get a sense of Flora's reaction to things. She had the silver-backed hairbrush square in front of her and kept looking at it. She had to be the gracious hostess, but her nerves were showing in the way she played with that handkerchief. She'd rip it apart before too long. As she took her seat again close to Bradford she held the wedding ring out as before, but her fingers shook.

Third time's the charm, I thought, and waited.

Bradford did his routine without hitch, and before too long good old *Frère* Lèon was back and in a thick accent offered them greetings and a warning against paying mind to dark spirits who could lead them astray from the True Path.

That's what *he* called it. I just shook my head, assembling my borrowed weapons quietly on the serving table, a napkin scrounged from a stack at one end to nix the noise.

Flora gave *Frère* Lèon a formal greeting and asked if her husband was present.

"He is, *mon petit*. 'E shines like the sun and speaks of 'is love for you."

She released a shaky sigh of relief and it sounded too much like a sob. "What else does he say? James? Are you sure? Tell me what to do!"

Bradford's old monk tortured her a little longer, not answering. He said he could not hear well for the dark spirits trying to come between, then:

"Ah! 'E is clear at last. 'E says 'is love is deep, and 'e wants you to be 'appy on this plane. You are to open your 'eart to new love. Ah—the 'appiness that awaits you is great. 'E smiles! Such joy for you, sweet child, such joy!"

Flora shook her head a little. Some part of her must have known this was all wrong.

Time to confirm it.

I'd pulled out the curtain material and draped it over my head, tying one of the napkins kerchief-like around my neck to keep the stuff from slipping off. It looked phony as hell, I was sure, but the darkness with this crowd it would lay 'em in the aisles.

Picking up Weisinger's things, I eased from behind the screen. Everyone was looking at Bradford. He might have seen me in the shadows beyond the candle glow, but his eyes were shut.

Made to order, I thought, and accurately bounced the keys off his skull. It was a damned good throw, and I followed quickly with the other things. The comb landed square in the cake, the pipe skidded along the table and slid into Flora's lap. She shrieked and jumped up.

If *Frère* Lèon had a good entrance, that was nothing to compare to that of Jack Fleming, fake-ghost for hire.

I vanished and reappeared but only just, holding to a mostly transparent state—standing smack dab in the middle of the table. The top half of my body was visible, beautifully obscured by the pale curtain. The bottom half went right into the wood.

It didn't feel good, but was pretty spectacular. The screaming helped.

With some effort I pressed forward, moving right *through* the table, candles and all, down its remaining length, working steadily toward Bradford. His eyes were now wide open, and it was a treat to see him shed the trance to see some real supernatural trouble. When I raised a pale, covered hand to point at him I thought he'd swallow his tongue.

Then I willed myself higher, rising until I was clear of the table, and floating free. I made one swimming circuit of the room, then dove toward Bradford, letting myself go solid as I dropped.

I took in enough breath to fill the room with a wordless and hopefully terrifying bellow and hit him like bowling ball taking out one last stubborn pin. It was a nasty impact for us both, but I had the advantage of being able to vanish again. So far as I could tell he was sprawled flat and screaming with the rest.

Remaining invisible was uphill work for me now, but necessary. I clung close to Bradford so he could enjoy my unique kind of cold. I'd been told it was like a death's own breath from the Arctic. Through chattering teeth he babbled nonsense about dark spirits being gathered against him and that he had to leave to before they manifested again. He got some argument and a suggestion they all pray to dispel the negative influences, but he was already barreling out the door.

I stuck with him until he got in his car, then slipped into the backseat and went solid. He screeched like a woman when I snaked one arm around his neck in a half nelson. I'm damned strong. He couldn't break free. When he stopped making noise I noticed him staring at the rearview mirror. It was empty, of course.

Leaning in, my mouth close to his ear, in my best imitation of the Shadow, I whispered, "Game's over, Svengali. Digging up that grave pissed off the wrong kind of *things*. We're on to you and we're *hungry*. You want to see another dawn?"

He whimpered, and the sound of his racing heart filled the car. I took that as a yes.

"Get out of town. Get out of the racket. Go back to the stage. Better a live magician than a dead medium. Got that? *Got that?*"

Not waiting for a reply, I vanished, exiting fast. He gunned the motor to life and shot away like Barney Oldfield looking to make a new speed record.

⁂

As the wrecked evening played itself out to the survivors in the parlor I made it back to the linen closet, killed the light, and parked my duff on an overturned bucket, to wait in the dark. I needed the rest.

The house grew quiet. The last guests departed with enough copy from tonight to fill their monthly pamphlets for years to come. Escott would have some interesting reading to share. I got the impression Flora was not planning another sitting, though a few people assured her that tonight's events should be continued.

The residents finished and came upstairs one by one. Flora Weisinger went into James' room and stayed there for a long time, crying. Abby found her, they talked in low voices for a time, and Flora cried some more. I wasn't sorry. Better now than later, married to a leech. Apparently things worked out. The sisters emerged, each going to her own room. Some servant made a last round, checking the windows, then things fell silent.

I'd taken off the spook coverings, folding the curtain and napkin, slipping them in with similar ones on a shelf. Retrieving my coat and hat I was ready to make a quiet exit until catching the faint sound of "Gloomy Sunday" seeped through the walls.

Damn.

This night had been a flying rout for Bradford, but Flora was still stuck in her pit. She might dig it even deeper until it was a match for her husband's grave.

Someone needed to talk sense into her. I felt the least qualified for the job, but soon as I recognized the music I got that twinge again.

I did my vanishing act and went across to Flora's room.

The music grew louder as I floated toward it, just solid enough to check the lay of the land. The lights were out, only a little glow from around her heavy curtains, enough to navigate and not be seen.

Quick as I could I re-formed, flicked the phonograph's needle arm clear, and pulled out the record. It made a hell of a crunch when I broke it to pieces.

There was a feminine gasp from the bed, and she fumbled the light on. By then I was gone, but sensed her coming over. Another gasp, then . . .

"James?" Her voice quavered with that heartbreaking hope, now tinged with anguish. "James? Oh, please, darling, talk to me. I know you're here."

She'd picked up on the cologne.

"James? *Please* . . . ."

This would be tough. I drifted over to a wall and gradually took shape, keeping it slow so she had time to stare, and if not get used to me, then at least not scream.

Hands to her mouth, eyes big, and her skin dead white, she looked ready to faint. This was cruel. A different kind from Bradford's type of torture, but still cruel.

"James sent me," I said, keeping my voice soft. "Please don't be afraid."

She'd frozen in place and I wasn't sure she understood.

I repeated myself and she finally nodded.

"Where is he?" she demanded, matching my soft tone.

"He's with God." It seemed best to keep things as simple as possible. "Everything that man told you was a lie. You know that now, don't you?"

She nodded again, the jerky movement very similar to Abby's mannerism. "Please, let me speak to James."

"He knows already. He said to tell you it wasn't your fault. There's nothing to forgive. It was just his time to go, that's all. *Not* your fault."

"But it *was*."

"Nope." I raised my right hand. "Swear to God. And I should know."

That had her nonplussed. "What . . . who are you?"

"Just a friend."

"That cologne, it's *his*."

"So you'd know he sent me. Flora, he loves you and knows you love him. But this is not the way to honor his memory. He wants you to give it up before it destroys you. He's dead and you're alive. There's a reason you're here."

"What? Tell me!"

"Doesn't work like that, you have to find out for yourself. You won't find answers in a Ouija board, though."

Flora had tentatively moved closer to me. "You look real."

"Thanks, I try my best. I can't stay long. Not allowed. I have to make sure you're clear-headed on this. No more guilt—it wasn't your fault—get rid of this junk, and live your life. James wants you to be happy again. If not now, then someday."

"That's all?"

"Flora . . . that's a lifetime. A good one if you choose it."

"I'll . . . all right. Would you tell James—"

"He knows. Now get some sleep. New day in the morning. Enjoy it." I was set to gradually vanish again, then remembered— "One last thing, Flora. James' wedding band." I held my hand out.

"Oh, no, I couldn't."

"Yes, you can. It belongs with him and you know it. Come on."

Fresh tears ran down her face, but maybe this time there would be healing for her. She had his ring on a gold chain around her neck, and reluctantly took it off. She read the inscription one more time, kissed the ring, and gave it over.

"Everything will be fine," I said. "This is from James." I didn't think he'd mind. I leaned over and kissed her on the forehead, very lightly, and vanished before she could open her eyes.

For the next few hours I drove around Chicago, feeling like a prize idiot and hoping I'd not done even worse damage to Flora than Alistair Bradford. I didn't think so, but the worry stuck.

Eventually I found my way back to that big cemetery and got myself inside, walking quickly along the path to the fancy mausoleum and the grave behind it.

I was damned tired, but had one last job to do to earn Abby Saeger's five bucks.

Pinching the ring in my fingers as Flora had done at the séance, I extended my arm and disappeared once more, this time sinking into the earth. It was the most unpleasant sensation, pushing down through the broken soil, pushing until what had been my hand found a greater resistance.

That would be James Weisinger's coffin.

I'd never attempted anything like this before, but was reasonably sure it was possible. This was a hell of a way to find out for certain.

Pushing just a little more against the resistance, it suddenly ceased to be there. Carefully not thinking what that meant, I focused my concentration on getting just my hand to go solid.

It must have worked, because it hurt like a Fury, felt like my hand was being sawed away at the wrist. Just before the pain got too much I felt the gold ring slip from my grasp.

One instant I was six feet under with my hand in a coffin and the next I was stumbling in the snow, clutching my wrist and trying not to yell too much.

My hand was still attached. That was good news. I worked the fingers until they stopped looking so claw-like, then sagged against a tree.

What a night.

I got back in my car just as the sleet began ticking against the windows, trying to get in. It was creepy I wanted some sound to mask it but hesitated turning on the radio, apprehensive that "Gloomy Sunday" might be playing again.

What the hell. Music was company, proof that there were other people awake somewhere. I could always change the station.

When it warmed up, Bing Crosby sang "Pennies from Heaven." Someone at the radio station had noticed the weather, perhaps, and was having his little joke.

I felt that twinge again, but now it raised a smile.

The Judgement

ANNE PERRY

The court came to order and the Judge entered, not with the shrill call of bugles or the roll of drums, but in silence and alone. His men-at-arms were outside, breastplates under their tunics as always, swords at the ready, and amulets at their necks. Since this was a trial for murder by witchcraft, perhaps this last was the most important.

The Judge took his seat in the high, carved chair, behind the ancient bench with its runes and symbols so dark with use they were almost impossible to read. He was a tall man, but beneath his voluminous robes his body might have been any shape.

The Prosecutor waited as everyone settled in their places. There was a big crowd today, drawn by fear and excitement. He was impatient to begin, and he could see that the Judge was also. It was clear in his hard, clever face, even though he made no move to hasten the ushers. Perhaps he liked seeing them in their black robes, moving like shadows, or reminders of doom.

The Procurator shifted his weight from one foot to the other. He knew he would win. It was a simple case of a woman who had lusted after her brother-in-law. When he had rejected her, forcing her to face the truth of his loyalty to his wife, she had revenged herself by casting a spell which had caused his death. Murder by witch-craft could hardly be clearer. The trial was really just to demonstrate that justice was done. To begin with he had been impatient with the waste of time and the cost of it, until he had appreciated the deter-rent effect on other women who might be tempted to such a thing. This new Judge was right to proceed, and publicly. Regrettably, it was a necessary performance. These days too many people were ignorant of the reality of dark powers. They needed reminding of justice, and where it was breached, of punishment.

At last they were settled, and the Chief Usher read out the charge. The accused denied it. Her voice might normally be pleasant, her diction was beautiful, but now she was strained with fear. Good. So she should be. The Prosecutor looked at her curiously. She was quite tall. And slender. The weight of the chains on her must hurt. She was not beautiful, there was too much passion in her face. It was clever and wilful, perhaps what should be expected in one who turned to sorcery.

He stood up. "My fellow citizens!" His voice rang around the room. He surveyed them. After all, this was for their benefit, or it could have been done secretly. He was interested to see that there were as many women here as men. Some were in fine dresses of rich fabric decorated with embroidery, the heavy girdles around their waists were studded with gems, their hair braided with ribbons. Others wore plain browns and drabs, hair tied back with scarves, as if lately come in from some form of work.

The men too were of every variety, knights-at-arms, clerks in brown jerkins with ink-stained fingers, students and artisans with calloused hands. He saw at least one apothecary—now there was an art which at times verged too close to the sorcerers! And of course there were many farmers and labourers. The dead man had been a farmer, a rich one.

He called his first witness, Stroban, the dead man's father. Stroban moved forward from the front bench and into the Square of Testimony, straightening his shoulders with an effort. Grief had aged him in a few terrible days. His face was bleached of colour, his grey hair seemed thinner, drawn across his skull like an inadequate protection. He looked at the accused just once, and his outrage was naked in his eyes. Then he turned to the Prosecutor. He was here to see justice for his dead son, and he would not let himself down by losing his composure.

The Prosecutor asked his name and circumstances. He answered clearly in a low voice in which pride and sorrow were equally mixed.

The Prosecutor pointed to the accused where she stood, body stiff, face averted as though she found it too difficult to meet his eyes. "And who is she?" he demanded.

"Anaya," Stroban replied. "The widow of my daughter-in-law's brother. She came in her time of need, and we took her in and treated her as our own." His voice cracked. He struggled to control it. "And she repaid us with envy, rage and murder!"

There was a ripple of horror around the room, a mixture of hunger and fear.

The judge leaned forward, his face grave, the lines around his mouth deep and hard. "That is what we are here to test, and to prove, aye or nay."

"Of course, my lord," Stroban acknowledged bleakly. "It is right that judgement should be seen. It is the law, and necessary to a just and civilized life."

The judge nodded. "Justice will be served, I promise you, and great and everlasting justice, deeper than men will easily grasp."

The Prosecutor permitted himself to smile. The Judge was a proud man, even a little arrogant, and he would frequently interrupt where it was not needed, because he liked the sound of his own voice. But he would rule correctly. The Prosecutor would one day be a judge like him, with his strengths, but not his weaknesses, not his pomposity or his conceit. Curious how quickly one could see that.

"You took her in and gave her a home?" he said aloud, just to confirm it for the court.

"Yes," Stroban agreed. "It was no less than our duty."

The Prosecutor flinched. That sounded a little cold and self-righteous. It was not the image he had wished to display of the bereaved family. "How long ago was this?" he said hastily.

"Just under a year."

"And how did she behave?" He must move them on to think about the accused. He glanced at her, and saw no contrition in her face, no respect, only what seemed to be fear.

"At first, with meekness and gratitude," Stroban answered. "All gentleness, modesty and obedience." His face reflected the hurt of her betrayal.

The Prosecutor felt an overwhelming anger rise in him. Of all crimes witchcraft infuriated him the most, it was the culmination of everything evil that deceived and destroyed. It denied honour, and humanity. He looked at the Judge and saw a like anger in his high, thin face, the disgust and revulsion that he felt himself, and the knowledge that he had it within his power, at least this time, to punish it as it should be punished—with death. Witches might have black arts, but they were still mortal, and once they were exposed, they could feel pain like anyone else.

He controlled his face and his voice with difficulty, and only because he was certain of the outcome.

Stroban was less certain. All his life he had known right from wrong. Any man did, if he were honest in heart. And could there be any virtue greater than to know truth and judge rightly? It was the cornerstone of all virtue. Too often evil prevailed. Had it not done so in his own house his beautiful son would not now be lying dead. Bertil, whom he had raised so carefully, taught every detail of honour and righteousness. And then this woman, with her cleverness, her inappropriate laughter, her wild thoughts, had come into their home, taken in by charity, and first betrayed them by trying to seduce Bertil away from his wife, and then when he had rejected her she had threatened to kill him. And when he had still refused, she had cast her spell, an act of deliberate murder.

The Prosecution was speaking again. "How long did she behave this way, feigning love and obedience?"

"She never stopped," Stroban said with disgust for her deceit.

The Prosecutor looked at the Judge's face. Stroban had not been duped because of his own innocence and charity, his inability to imagine such duplicity. The man was self-righteous, too quick to judge and condemn. It was a cold fault, an ugly one.

But the Judge would be shown the truth, and then it would be the time to act. There must be law. Rules must be made and kept, by everyone. Without rules there was chaos, and that was truly terrifying, the gateway to all darkness. Even the Judge must obey the law.

The Prosecutor wanted more details. "Did she work hard around the farm? And the house? Was she truthful, as far as you know? Did she respect you, and your wife? Did she treat you with a courtesy and gratitude that she owed you?"

"Oh yes," Stroban replied. "She was very careful." He knew he must speak the exact truth, whatever it was. He had committed no wrong, so it could not harm him, or his family.

The Prosecutor's eyes widened. "Your choice of words suggests that you think she planned something evil from the beginning. Is that so?"

Stroban hesitated for a moment. He believed that she had, but it was only in the hindsight of what she had done. He had not known it then. He looked at her standing in her chains, and wondered how he could have been so blind. It was his own innocence that had blinded him.

"No," he admitted aloud. "I should not have implied that. I do not know what was in her mind. But she was attracted to poor Bertil from the start, that was plain. At the time I believed it was only recognition of his goodness. Everyone liked Bertil." Emotion overcame him and he was unable to regain control of himself for several minutes. He saw pity in the Judge's eyes, and admiration, but neither would have anything to do with his decisions.

"Please continue," the Prosecutor prompted. "How did the accused show this affection, precisely?"

Stroban forced himself to steady his voice. "She helped him around the farm."

"How?"

"She was clever." He said the word so it was half a curse. "She had ideas for improving things. And she was clever with figures, and measurements." He said the last bitterly. It was measurements she had used to kill Bertil, although he still did not know how.

"She improved your yield?" the Judge interrupted, leaning forward over the ancient bench, his sleeve hiding some of the runes on it. "She made life easier for you, better?"

Stroban felt a surge of anger. He was making her sound good! "For a while," he admitted. "Oh, she was clever!"

The Prosecutor was annoyed. It showed in his expression, and the nervous clenching and unclenching of his fists. This was his territory and the Judge was trespassing. "Were you grateful for this help?" he cut across. "Did you wish it?"

"At the time, of course we were," Stroban said.

"All of you? Your wife, Enella, and your daughter-in-law, Korah, as well?"

"Of course."

"You all trusted the accused?" He pointed to where she stood, her face white, her eyes hollow and frightened even though her head was still high. Did she realize yet that there was no escape for her?

"Yes," Stroban answered. "Why should we not?"

"Indeed. Tell us what happened to change your mind?"

Stroban felt his stomach twisting with the pain of memory, and yet he was on the brink of finding justice. It was up to him, his word, his saying what was right and true. He must be exact.

"There was a quarrel between Korah and Anaya, the accused." He avoided looking at her now. "I didn't know what it was about at the time . . ."

"Korah will tell us," the Prosecutor assured him. "Please go on."

Stroban obeyed. "A few days later there was a more serious quarrel. That same evening Anaya said that if Bertil did not do as she had told him to, then the barn roof would cave in and kill him." He could barely say the words. The scene was carved indelibly in his mind, Anaya standing in the kitchen, her hair wound in a copper-red ribbon, the sun warming her face, the smells of cooking around them, the door open to the yard beyond and the lowing of the cattle in the distance. It was another world from this. They could not then have imagined the horror that awaited them.

The court was silent, faces still with fear.

"And how did Bertil reply to her?" the Prosecutor asked.

"He said she was wrong," Stroban whispered. "My poor son! He had no idea." His voice caught in a sob. "He didn't believe in witchcraft."

There was a shudder around the room. People shifted in their seats, closer to loved ones.

"But you do?" the Prosecutor insisted.

Stroban was angry, and afraid. He looked at the Judge and saw anger in him too, at the stupidity of the question, perhaps? Then he saw something else in the high-boned, curious face, passionate one moment, ascetic the next. It was a long, breathless moment before he understood that it also was fear. He had tasted the power of sorcery, and he knew there was nothing to protect ordinary men except righteousness, and the exact observance of the law.

But if the Judge knew that, really knew it, then there was hope for them. He squared his shoulders and lifted his chin. "Of course I do! But I know that just men, obedient men, can defeat it!"

There was a murmur of admiration around the room, like a swell of the tide. Faces turned to the accused, tight with hatred and fear.

"Had you ever thought before that the barn roof would collapse?" the Prosecutor asked.

"Of course not!" Stroban was angry. "It rests on a great post, thick as a tree trunk!"

"Was anyone in the barn when this happened, apart from your son?"

"No, just Bertil, and one of the oxen."

"I see. Thank you. The Defender may wish to ask you something."

Stroban turned to face the young man who now rose to his feet. He was a complete contrast to the Prosecutor. Far from being arrogant, he looked full of doubt, even confused, as if he had no idea what he was going to say or do.

And indeed he did not have. The whole proceeding was out of his control. When he had spoken with Anaya earlier he had believed her when she had said she was innocent. Now he did not know what to think, nor did he have any faith in himself to achieve a just trial for her. Perhaps the Judge would help him? But when he looked at the Judge, his long, pale face seemed as utterly confused as he was himself.

The Defender turned to Stroban, cleared his throat and began. "We are deeply sorry for your grief." He hesitated. He must say something to the point, but what? "Where was the accused when this tragedy happened?"

Stroban's face was a mask of anger, his voice high-pitched. "You say 'tragedy' as if it were a natural happening! It was witchcraft! She made the roof fall in, exactly as she told him she would, if he did not submit to her lust. But he was a righteous man, and he refused, so she killed him!"

There was a shiver of horror around the room. People reached for amulets.

The Defender turned to the Judge for help, but the Judge did nothing. He seemed just as lost and overwhelmed. The Defender turned back to Stroban. "I asked you where was she?"

"I don't know," Stroban said sullenly. "Out in the fields some-where, she told us."

"Not in the barn?"

"Of course not! She didn't need to be there to make it happen. Don't you know anything about sorcery?"

"No, I don't. Perhaps you would be good enough to instruct me?"

Stroban's cheeks flamed. "I know nothing either! What do you think I am? But it is powerful and wicked, and all good people who love truth and the law must fight against it with every strength they have. We must see that justice is done. It is our only protection."

There were nods of agreement, a mixture of fear and an attempt at assurance.

The Defender knew he would accomplish nothing with Stroban. It would be better to wait for his wife.

But when the Prosecutor called Enella she echoed exactly what her husband had said, almost in the same words. The Prosecutor sat down again, wholly satisfied.

The Defender rose. "You agreed that the accused was very fond of your son," he began, not quite sure where he intended the ques-tion to lead. He glanced at Anaya, and saw a strange kind of peace in her eyes. He turned back to Enella. "In what ways did she show this?"

Enella was confused. "Why . . . the usual ways, I suppose."

"And what are they?" he pressed.

"She . . . she talked with him easily, comfortably. She made him laugh, without telling the rest of us what it was about."

"You felt excluded?"

"No! Of course not!" Now she was confused as well. She had been tricked into saying something she had not meant to.

"Why not?" he asked. "It sounds as if you were excluded."

She looked at Stroban, then away again. "It was exactly as my husband said, she wanted him for herself, in spite of the fact that he was married to her dead husband's sister, whom she should have loved and honoured. It was because of Korah that Bertil took Anaya in in the first place. Only a wicked woman would be so ungrateful!" Enella was afraid of uncertainty. She liked order. It was the only way to be safe.

"It sounds from what you say as if Bertil also liked her," the Defender pointed out. "Are you certain that she was not merely responding to him? After all, he was her host, so to speak. The head of her household."

Enella was afraid. Stroban was not helping her. She looked at the Judge.

The Judge leaned forward over the bench, his face tense and unhappy. He stared at the Defender. "I cannot see where you are leading. Stay on the known path, if you please."

Enella relaxed again. The Judge was a decent man, a fair man. There was no need to be afraid after all.

"I'm sorry, my lord," the Defender apologized. He was confused again. He looked at Anaya where she stood perfectly still. Her face was white, as if exhausted by plunging from hope to despair, and back again. Her shoulders drooped, as if the courage of a few moments ago had slipped from her. He had promised her that he would do his best, and so far he had been pathetic. He must do better.

He took a step towards her, waving his hand. "We have heard that Anaya," he used her name self-consciously, "liked to make Bertil laugh. She helped him in his work, because she was clever, and inventive. Is that true?" He knew that Enella would agree that it was, her husband had already said so, and she would never contradict him.

"Yes," she said unhappily.

"She made new suggestions for efficiency and skill, things that had not been done before?" he pressed, beginning to see a tiny light of hope.

There was only one possible answer, to have denied it would have been ridiculous. "Yes."

"So she was cleverer than Korah, or than any of you?"

"Well . . ."

"Or you would have thought of them for yourselves, before she came?"

"Well . . . yes, I suppose so."

The Defender was beginning to feel better. He looked at the Judge and saw a spark of hope in his eyes also, a slight straightening of his shoulders and easing of the muscles of his jaw. It gave him courage to go on. He felt less alone. "Surely it must be true?"

Enella said nothing.

The Defender was sorry for her, but he could not let her deny it.

The Judge looked at her, his face gentle. "You must answer," he told her.

"Yes," she said very quietly, her face filled with unhappiness.

"Thank you," the Defender acknowledged. "So Korah had to have seen it also?"

"I don't know!" It was a lie, and the scarlet guilt flooded up her face. She must have felt its heat. "I imagine she did."

"Perhaps she was angry? Could that be what the quarrel was about?"

"I don't know!" That was the literal truth, the letter of the law if not the spirit. She hid in the safety of that, looking to the Judge for protection, and from the easing of the rigidity of her body, believing she received it.

The Defender thanked her and gave her leave to go.

The Prosecutor called Korah, handsome, angry, thin-lipped. She walked into the Square knowing exactly what she was going to say. It had been sitting in her heart like a black weight since the first time she had seen Bertil laughing with Anaya and realized that while loyalty would hold him to Korah, but, if not now, then soon, it would be Anaya he loved, Anaya who touched the man within and awoke his heart and his dreams. In that day her hatred was born.

The Prosecutor faced her, arrogant and angry. She faced him squarely meeting his eyes. He would not treat her as he had cowardly, obedient Enella. Korah was not funny or imaginative, or beautiful, but she understood people. She could see right through the façade, the pretences, to the weakness within. And the Judge would help. She had been watching him, the high, thin face, the tight mouth. He was just like her. He understood what it was like to be mocked, to be left out, even in your own home. He could see the need for justice now. It was not revenge, it was what Anaya deserved, not for witchcraft, there was no such thing, but for theft.

"Anaya is your brother's widow, and after his death you took her in and gave her a home?" The Prosecutor was repeating the important facts, just to remind the crowd, and the Judge.

"Yes, I did," Korah answered. Never say more than you need to, that was the way to make mistakes.

"And she repaid you by helping in the house and on the farm?"

"Yes. She was very skilled at it." Be generous. It sounded better than grudging praise. And it was the truth.

"Better than you?"

"In some ways, not in others." Don't let them see the envy. Don't look at Anaya in case your thoughts are there in your face, in spite of all you can do. She looked instead at the Judge. He understood, it was obvious in his expression, the eyes, the lips. Perhaps he too had been betrayed? It must have been long ago. He was dried up now, desiccated, withered inside.

The Prosecutor was talking again. "Was your husband a hand-some man, charming?"

"Yes." Oh yes, that was true. "Everyone liked him. It was far more than looks. It was his manner, his honesty, his warmth, his laughter, his kindness." All that was so painfully true. It hurt to say it now for all these prurient, superstitious people peering at her. Damn Anaya! They should burn her! Let her feel the fire on her body, consume her flesh and destroy it, even if they could not make it burn her soul on the inside.

"So you were not surprised when your sister-in-law was attracted to him?"

In spite of herself Korah's eyes were drawn to Anaya and for an instant they looked at each other. Korah saw faith struggling with fear of pain, of failure, of utter loneliness, and victory was like honey on her tongue.

"No," she answered. "I believed she would honour her place as my sister and my guest. I had no idea she had . . . powers."

The Prosecutor had seen the exchange. "Bertil rejected her?" he asked.

"Yes. He was very distressed by it. He found it grossly dishon-ourable. He was revolted."

"What did Anaya do?"

Korah smiled very slightly, just a tiny movement of the lips. "She said that if he did not change his mind and come to her, then the barn roof would cave in and crush him to death." No one could catch her out in that. They were not the exact words, but the meaning was the same. Timour had heard her say it, and he could testify. He was so transparently honest everyone would believe him.

"And did he change his mind?"

There was a silence in the room as if no one breathed. The sunlight outside seemed a world away.

"Of course not," Korah said. "I don't think he was afraid, but even if he had been, he would rather have died than give in to such a thing."

A hundred voices in the room murmured approval, and sympathy.

Anaya stood with her eyes closed, as if needing to summon all her strength just to remain upright.

"It seems we have lost an exceptionally fine man with his death," the Prosecutor said with relish. "Perhaps evil always seeks to destroy that which is purest and best."

The Judge seemed about to say something. He drew in his breath, then let it out again in a sigh, as if some inner resolution had prevailed.

"Finally, Mistress," the Prosecutor said, "How long had that barn stood with that roof safe and secure?"

"Seventy years."

"Thank you." He looked smug, totally satisfied with himself.

The Defender took his place. He seemed even more confused than before.

"I have nothing to ask you."

She stood down, glancing at the Judge's pinched, unhappy face, and for an instant seeing her own future in it, old and alone, eaten by bitterness and self-disgust. Then she drove it from her mind and returned to her seat beside Enella, but a coldness remained in the pit of her stomach.

The Prosecutor called Timour, who confirmed all that Korah had said. He looked trustingly at the Defender as he approached. He felt sorry for all of them, especially Anaya. He had liked her, as he knew Bertil had. She had seemed funny and kind and brave. He had had no idea that she had any harm in her, still less that she had knowledge of the black arts. He still found it hard to believe. But he did know barns, and he knew oxen. He said as much when the Defender asked him.

"Oh yes. It's my trade," he agreed.

"Did you see this barn after it had fallen in?"

"Yes. I wanted to know what had happened. It's important, in case it should happen again." He looked at the Judge to see if he understood. He seemed to. He had the air of a brave man, not only a strength in his face but a gentleness as well, as if he expected the best in people. He was the sort of man Timour liked, wise without arrogance, kind without sentiment. "I saw it before, you see," he explained. "They had been keeping oxen in it for a long time, my lord. Big beasts, and very heavy, very powerful. They like to lean against the posts and rub their backs, scratch them, as it were. If you don't keep an eye on them, sooner or later they'll dislodge the pole from its base. I warned Bertil about it. He was a good man, and my friend, but he did put things off." He glanced at Stroban an apology. "I'm sorry, but that's true. Anaya saw it, and she warned him too. But he was always going to do it tomorrow. I suppose when tomorrow finally came, it was too late."

There was silence for a moment, a realization, a wakening from a dream both good and bad. It was the Judge who asked the question, not the Defender. "Could the ox have pushed against it while Bertil was there, and knocked it over when it was at the most vulnerable?"

"I suppose it must have done," Timour answered. "It ran out just as the roof buckled and caved in. It got bruised by some of the falling timbers. He should have put it out before he began to work, but he can't have."

"Witchcraft!" Stroban cried out, rising to his feet, his face flushed. "It's still her fault!"

"No!" the Defender said with sudden strength, whirling round, his robe flying, his arm outstretched. "A man delayed mending his barn until the post was seriously weakened. It is a tragedy. It is not a crime." He looked to the Judge, raising his eyes to the high seat, the dark runes carried in the wood. "My lord, I ask that you pronounce Anaya innocent of this poor man's death, free these people of the fear of sorcery, and allow them to grieve for their loss without fear or blame. She did not threaten him, she warned him. And tragically, he did not listen. If he had done, we should not be here today mourning him, seeing witchcraft where there is only jealousy."

Stroban looked desperately at the Judge, and saw a man filtered by the details of the law and unable to see the greater spirit of it, a man who understood loss but not love. He was a small man, who could in the end become a hollow man.

Enella looked at the Judge and saw a man who kept to the safe path, always, wherever it led, upward or down, and there was an emptiness in it that nothing would fill.

Korah saw what she had recognized before, only this time it was not for an instant. It would always be there, whether she looked at it or not.

The Prosecutor was angry. He saw a Judge whose arrogance had allowed him to lose control of the court. He did not know how it had happened, or why victory had inexplicably become defeat.

Timour and the Defender both saw an upsurge of optimism. Hope had come out of nowhere, and vanquished the error and despair.

The Judge pronounced Anaya innocent. The court was dismissed and people poured out into the dark, gulping the sweet air, leaving the room empty except for Anaya and the Judge.

He moved his right hand very slightly, just two fingers from the surface of the bench. The chains fell away. She stood free, rubbing her wrists and stretching her aching shoulders.

"You did well," he said quietly. He was smiling.

"I doubted," she answered. It was a confession.

"Of course you did," he agreed, and as he spoke his face changed, it became wiser, stronger, passion and laughter burned in it, and an indescribable gentleness. "If it were easy, it would be worth little. You have not yet perfected faith. Do not expect so much of yourself. For lessons learned hastily or without pain are worthless."

"Will they understand?" she asked.

"That they were the ones on trial, and that the judgement was your own? Oh yes. In time. Whether they will pay the cost of change is another thing. But there is love, and there is hope. We are far from the end." His cloak shimmered and began to dissolve. She could no longer see his shoulders, only his strong, slender hands and his face. "Now I have another charge for you."

She looked at him, at the white fire around him. All she could distinguish was his smile, and his voice, and a great peace shone within her. "Yes?"

The Angel of the Lord

MELVILLE DAVISSON POST

I always thought my father took a long chance, but somebody had to take it and certainly I was the one least likely to be suspected. It was a wild country. There were no banks. We had to pay for the cattle, and somebody had to carry the money. My father and my uncle were always being watched. My father was right, I think.

"Abner," he said, "I'm going to send Martin. No one will ever suppose that we would trust this money to a child."

My uncle drummed on the table and rapped his heels on the floor. He was a bachelor, stern and silent. But he could talk . . . and when he did, he began at the beginning and you heard him through; and what he said—well, he stood behind it.

"To stop Martin," my father went on, "would be only to lose the money; but to stop you would be to get somebody killed."

I knew what my father meant. He meant that no one would undertake to rob Abner until after he had shot him to death.

I ought to say a word about my Uncle Abner. He was one of those austere, deeply religious men who were the product of the Reformation. He always carried a Bible in his pocket, and he read it where he pleased. Once the crowd at Roy's Tavern tried to make sport of him when he got his book out by the fire; but they never tried it again. When the fight was over Abner paid Roy eighteen silver dollars for the broken chairs and the table—and he was the only man in the tavern who could ride a horse. Abner belonged to the church militant, and his God was a warlord.

So that is how they came to send me. The money was in greenbacks in packages. They wrapped it up in newspaper and put it into a pair of saddlebags, and I set out. I was about nine years old. No, it was not as bad as you think. I could ride a horse all day when I was nine years old—most any kind of a horse. I was tough as whit'-leather, and I knew the country I was going into. You must not picture a little boy rolling a hoop in the park.

It was an afternoon in early autumn. The clay roads froze in the night; they thawed out in the day and they were a bit sticky. I was to stop at Roy's Tavern, south of the river, and go on in the morning. Now and then I passed some cattle driver, but no one overtook me on the road until almost sundown; then I heard a horse behind me and a man came up. I knew him. He was a cattleman named Dix. He had once been a shipper, but he had come in for a good deal of bad luck. His partner, Alkire, had absconded with a big sum of money due the grazers. This had ruined Dix; he had given up his land, which wasn't very much, to the grazers. After that he had gone over the mountain to his people, got together a pretty big sum of money and bought a large tract of grazing land. Foreign claimants had sued him in the courts on some old title, and he had lost the whole tract and the money that he had paid for it. He had married a remote cousin of ours, and he had always lived on her lands, adjoining those of my Uncle Abner.

Dix seemed surprised to see me on the road.

"So it's you, Martin," he said; "I thought Abner would be going into the upcountry."

One gets to be a pretty cunning youngster, even at this age, and I told no one what I was about.

"Father wants the cattle over the river to run a month," I returned easily, "and I'm going up there to give his orders to the grazers."

He looked me over, then he rapped the saddlebags with his knuckles. "You carry a good deal of baggage, my lad."

I laughed. "Horse feed," I said. "You know my father! A horse must be fed at dinnertime, but a man can go till he gets it."

One was always glad of any company on the road, and we fell into an idle talk. Dix said he was going out into the Ten Mile country; and I have always thought that was, in fact, his intention. The road turned south about a mile our side of the tavern. I never liked Dix; he was of an apologetic manner, with a cunning, irresolute face.

A little later a man passed us at a gallop. He was a drover named Marks, who lived beyond my Uncle Abner, and he was riding hard to get in before night. He hailed us, but he did not stop; we got a shower of mud and Dix cursed him. I have never seen a more evil face. I suppose it was because Dix usually had a grin about his mouth, and when that sort of face gets twisted there's nothing like it.

After that he was silent. He rode with his head down and his fingers plucking at his jaw, like a man in some perplexity. At the crossroads he stopped and sat for some time in the saddle, looking before him I left him there, but at the bridge he overtook me. He said he had concluded to get some supper and go on after that.

Roy's Tavern consisted of a single big room, with a loft above it for sleeping quarters. A narrow covered way connected this room with the house in which Roy and his family lived. We used to hang our saddles on wooden pegs in this covered way. I have seen that wall so hung with saddles that you could not find a place for another stirrup. But tonight Dix and I were alone in the tavern. He looked cunningly at me when I took the saddlebags with me into the big room and when I went with them up the ladder into the loft. But he said nothing—in fact, he had scarcely spoken. It was cold; the road had begun to freeze when we got in. Roy had lighted a big fire. I left Dix before it. I did not take off my clothes, because Roy's beds were mattresses of wheat straw covered with heifer skins—good enough for summer but pretty cold on such a night, even with the heavy, hand-woven coverlet in big white and black checks.

I put the saddle-bags under my head and lay down. I went at once to sleep, but I suddenly awaked. I thought there was a candle in the loft, but it was a gleam of light from the fire below, shining through a crack in the floor. I lay and watched it, the coverlet pulled up to my chin. Then I began to wonder why the fire burned so brightly. Dix ought to be on his way some time, and it was a custom for the last man to rake out the fire. There was not a sound. The light streamed steadily through the crack.

Presently it occurred to me that Dix had forgotten the fire and that I ought to go down and rake it out. Roy always warned us about the fire when he went to bed. I got up, wrapped the great coverlet around me, went over to the gleam of light and looked down through the crack in the floor. I had to lie out at full length to get my eye against the board. The hickory logs had turned to great embers and glowed like a furnace of red coals.

Before this fire stood Dix. He was holding out his hands and turning himself about as though he were cold to the marrow; but with all that chill upon him, when the man's face came into the light I saw it covered with a sprinkling of sweat.

I shall carry the memory of that face. The grin was there at the mouth, but it was pulled about; the eyelids were drawn in; the teeth were clamped together. I have seen a dog poisoned with strychnine look like that.

I lay there and watched the thing. It was as though something potent and evil dwelling within the man were in travail to re-form his face upon its image. You cannot realize how the devilish labor held me—the face worked as though it were some plastic stuff, and the sweat oozed through. And all the time the man was cold; and he was crowding into the fire and turning himself about and putting out his hands. And it was as though the heat would no more enter in and warm him than it will enter in and warm the ice.

It seemed to scorch him and leave him cold—and he was fearfully and desperately cold! I could smell the singe of the fire on him, but it had no power against this diabolic chill. I began myself to shiver, although I had the heavy coverlet wrapped around me.

The thing was a fascinating horror; I seemed to be looking down into the chamber of some abominable maternity. The room was filled with the steady red light of the fire. Not a shadow moved in it. And there was silence. The man had taken off his boots and he twisted before the fire without a sound. It was like the shuddering tales of possession or transformation by a drug. I thought the man would burn himself to death. His clothes smoked. How could he be so cold?

Then, finally, the thing was over! I did not see it for his face was in the fire. But suddenly he grew composed and stepped back into the room. I tell you I was afraid to look! I do not know what thing I expected to see there, but I did not think it would be Dix.

Well, it was Dix; but not the Dix that any of us knew. There was a certain apology, a certain indecision, a certain servility in that other Dix, and these things showed about his face. But there was none of these weaknesses in this man.

His face had been pulled into planes of firmness and decision; the slack in his features had been taken up; the furtive moving of the eye was gone. He stood now squarely on his feet and he was full of courage. But I was afraid of him as I have never been afraid of any human creature in this world! Something that had been servile in him, that had skulked behind disguises, that had worn the habiliments of subterfuge, had now come forth; and it had molded the features of the man to its abominable courage.

Presently he began to move swiftly about the room. He looked out at the window and he listened at the door; then he went softly into the covered way. I thought he was going on his journey; but then he could not be going with his boots there beside the fire. In a moment he returned with a saddle blanket in his hand and came softly across the room to the ladder.

Then I understood the thing that he intended, and I was motionless with fear. I tried to get up, but I could not. I could only lie there with my eye strained to the crack in the floor. His foot was on the ladder, and I could already feel his hand on my throat and that blanket on my face, and the suffocation of death in me, when far away on the hard road I heard a horse!

He heard it, too, for he stopped on the ladder and turned his evil face about toward the door. The horse was on the long hill beyond the bridge, and he was coming as though the devil rode in his saddle. It was a hard, dark night. The frozen road was like flint; I could hear the iron of the shoes ring. Whoever rode that horse rode for his life or for something more than his life, or he was mad. I heard the horse strike the bridge and thunder across it. And all the while Dix hung there on the ladder by his hands and listened. Now he sprang softly down, pulled on his boots and stood up before the fire, his face—this new face—gleaming with its evil courage. The next moment the horse stopped.

I could hear him plunge under the bit, his iron shoes ripping the frozen road; then the door leaped back and my Uncle Abner was in the room. I was so glad that my heart almost choked me and for a moment I could hardly see—everything was in a sort of mist.

Abner swept the room in a glance, then he stopped.

"Thank God!" he said; "I'm in time." And he drew his hand down over his face with the fingers hard and close as though he pulled something away.

"In time for what?" said Dix.

Abner looked him over. And I could see the muscles of his big shoulders stiffen as he looked. And again he looked him over. Then he spoke and his voice was strange.

"Dix," he said, "is it you?"

"Who would it be but me?" said Dix.

"It might be the devil," said Abner. "Do you know what your face looks like?"

"No matter what it looks like!" said Dix.

"And so," said Abner, "we have got courage with this new face."

Dix threw up his head.

"Now, look here, Abner," he said, "I've had about enough of your big manner. You ride a horse to death and you come plunging in here; what the devil's wrong with you?"

"There's nothing wrong with me," replied Abner, and his voice was low. "But there's something damnably wrong with you, Dix."

"The devil take you," said Dix, and I saw him measure Abner with his eye. It was not fear that held him back; fear was gone out of the creature; I think it was a kind of prudence.

Abner's eyes kindled, but his voice remained low and steady.

"Those are big words," he said.

"Well," cried Dix, "get out of the door then and let me pass!"

"Not just yet," said Abner; "I have something to say to you."

"Say it then," cried Dix, "and get out of the door."

"Why hurry?" said Abner. "It's a long time until daylight, and I have a good deal to say."

"You'll not say it to me," said Dix. "I've got a trip to make tonight; get out of the door."

Abner did not move. "You've got a longer trip to make tonight than you think, Dix," he said; "but you're going to hear what I have to say before you set out on it."

I saw Dix rise on his toes and I knew what he wished for. He wished for a weapon; and he wished for the bulk of bone and muscle that would have a chance against Abner. But he had neither the one nor the other. And he stood there on his toes and began to curse—low, vicious, withering oaths, that were like the swish of a knife

Abner was looking at the man with a curious interest.

"It is strange," he said, as though speaking to himself, "but it explains the thing. While one is the servant of neither, one has the courage of neither; but when he finally makes his choice he gets what his master has to give him."

Then he spoke to Dix.

"Sit down!" he said; and it was in that deep, level voice that Abner used when he was standing close behind his words. Every man in the hills knew that voice; one had only a moment to decide after he heard it. Dix knew that, and yet for one instant he hung there on his toes, his eyes shimmering like a weasel's, his mouth twisting. He was not afraid! If he had had the ghost of a chance against Abner he would have taken it. But he knew he had not, and with an oath he threw the saddle blanket into a corner and sat down by the fire.

Abner came away from the door then. He took off his great coat. He put a log on the fire, and he sat down across the hearth from Dix. The new hickory sprang crackling into flames. For a good while there was silence; the two men sat at either end of the hearth without a word. Abner seemed to have fallen into a study of the man before him. Finally he spoke:

"Dix," he said, "do you believe in the providence of God?"

Dix flung up his head.

"Abner," he cried, "if you are going to talk nonsense I promise you upon my oath that I will not stay to listen."

Abner did not at once reply. He seemed to begin now at another point.

"Dix," he said, "you've had a good deal of bad luck . . . . Perhaps you wish it put that way."

"Now, Abner," he cried, "you speak the truth; I have had hell's luck."

"Hell's luck you have had," replied Abner. "It is a good word. I accept it. Your partner disappeared with all the money of the grazers on the other side of the river; you lost the land in your lawsuit; and you are tonight without a dollar. That was a big tract of land to lose. Where did you get so great a sum of money?"

"I have told you a hundred times," replied Dix. "I got it from my people over the mountains. You know where I got it."

"Yes," said Abner. "I know where you got it, Dix. And I know another thing. But first I want to show you this," and he took a little penknife out of his pocket. "And I want to tell you that I believe in the providence of God, Dix."

"I don't care a fiddler's damn what you believe in," said Dix.

"But you do care what I know," replied Abner.

"What do you know?" said Dix.

"I know where your partner is," replied Abner.

I was uncertain about what Dix was going to do, but finally he answered with a sneer.

"Then you know something that nobody else knows."

"Yes," replied Abner, "there is another man who knows."

"Who?" said Dix.

"You," said Abner.

Dix leaned over in his chair and looked at Abner closely.

"Abner," he cried, "you are talking nonsense. Nobody knows where Alkire is. If I knew I'd go after him."

"Dix," Abner answered, and it was again in that deep, level voice, "if I had got here five minutes later you would have gone after him. I can promise you that, Dix.

"Now, listen! I was in the upcountry when I got your word about the partnership; and I was on my way back when at Big Run I broke a stirrup-leather. I had no knife and I went into the store and bought this one; then the storekeeper told me that Alkire had gone to see you. I didn't want to interfere with him and I turned back . . . . So I did not become your partner. And so I did not disappear . . . . What was it that prevented? The broken stirrup-leather? The knife? In old times, Dix, men were so blind that God had to open their eyes before they could see His angel in the way before them . . . . They are still blind, but they ought not to be that blind . . . . Well, on the night that Alkire disappeared I met him on his way to your house. It was out there at the bridge. He had broken a stirrup-leather and he was trying to fasten it with a nail. He asked me if I had a knife, and I gave him this one. It was beginning to rain and I went on, leaving him there in the road with the knife in his hand."

Abner paused; the muscles of his great iron jaw contracted.

"God forgive me," he said; "it was His angel again! I never saw Alkire after that."

"Nobody ever saw him after that," said Dix. "He got out of the hills that night."

"No," replied Abner; "it was not in the night when Alkire started on his journey; it was in the day."

"Abner," said Dix, "you talk like a fool. If Alkire had traveled the road in the day somebody would have seen him."

"Nobody could see him on the road he traveled," replied Abner.

"What road?" said Dix.

"Dix," replied Abner, "you will learn that soon enough."

Abner looked hard at the man.

"You saw Alkire when he started on his journey," he continued; "but did you see who it was that went with him?"

"Nobody went with him," replied Dix; "Alkire rode alone."

"Not alone," said Abner; "there was another."

"I didn't see him," said Dix.

"And yet," continued Abner, "you made Alkire go with him."

I saw cunning enter Dix's face. He was puzzled, but he thought Abner off the scent.

"And I made Alkire go with somebody, did I? Well, who was it? Did you see him?"

"Nobody ever saw him."

"He must be a stranger."

"No," replied Abner, "he rode the hills before we came into them."

"Indeed!" said Dix. "And what kind of a horse did he ride?"

"White!" said Abner.

Dix got some inkling of what Abner meant now, and his face grew livid.

"What are you driving at?" he cried. "You sit here beating around the bush. If you know anything, say it out; let's hear it. What is it?"

Abner put out his big sinewy hand as though to thrust Dix back into his chair.

"Listen!" he said. "Two days after that I wanted to get out into the Ten Mile country and I went through your lands; I rode a path through the narrow valley west of your house. At a point on the path where there is an apple tree something caught my eye and I stopped. Five minutes later I knew exactly what had happened under that apple tree . . . . Someone had ridden there; he had stopped under that tree; then something happened and the horse had run away—I knew that by the tracks of a horse on this path. I knew that the horse had a rider and that it had stopped under this tree, because there was a limb cut from the tree at a certain height. I knew the horse had remained there, because the small twigs of the apple limb had been pared off, and they lay in a heap on the path. I knew that something had frightened the horse and that it had run away, because the sod was torn up where it had jumped . . . . Ten minutes later I knew that the rider had not been in the saddle when the horse jumped; I knew what it was that had frightened the horse; and I knew that the thing had occurred the day before. Now, how did I know that?

"Listen! I put my horse into the tracks of that other horse under the tree and studied the ground. Immediately I saw where the weeds beside the path had been crushed, as though some animal had been lying down there, and in the very center of that bed I saw a little heap of fresh earth. That was strange, Dix, that fresh earth where the animal had been lying down! It had come there after the animal had got up, or else it would have been pressed flat. But where had it come from?

"I got off and walked around the apple tree, moving out from it in an ever-widening circle. Finally I found an ant heap, the top of which had been scraped away as though one had taken up the loose earth in his hands. Then I went back and plucked up some of the earth. The under clods of it were colored as with red paint . . . . No, it wasn't paint.

"There was a brush fence some fifty yards away. I went over to it and followed it down.

"Opposite the apple tree the weeds were again crushed as though some animal had lain there. I sat down in that place and drew a line with my eye across a log of the fence to a limb of the apple tree. Then I got on my horse and again put him in the tracks of that other horse under the tree; the imaginary line passed through the pit of my stomach! . . . I am four inches taller than Alkire."

It was then that Dix began to curse. I had seen his face work while Abner was speaking and that spray of sweat had reappeared. But he kept the courage he had got.

"Lord Almighty, man!" he cried. "How prettily you sum it up! We shall presently have Lawyer Abner with his brief. Because my renters have killed a calf; because one of their horses frightened at the blood has bolted, and because they cover the blood with earth so the other horses traveling the path may not do the like; straightway I have shot Alkire out of his saddle . . . . Man! What a mare's nest! And now, Lawyer Abner, with your neat little conclusions, what did I do with Alkire after I had killed him? Did I cause him to vanish into the air with a smell of sulphur, or did I cause the earth to yawn and Alkire to descend into its bowels?"

"Dix," replied Abner, "your words move somewhat near the truth."

"Upon my soul," cried Dix, "you compliment me. If I had that trick of magic, believe me, you would be already some distance down."

Abner remained a moment silent.

"Dix," he said, "what does it mean when one finds a plot of earth resodded?"

"Is that a riddle?" cried Dix. "Well, confound me, if I don't answer it! You charge me with murder and then you fling in this neat conundrum. Now, what could be the answer to that riddle, Abner? If one had done a murder this sod would overlie a grave and Alkire would be in it in his bloody shirt. Do I give the answer?"

"You do not," replied Abner.

"No!" cried Dix. "Your sodded plot no grave, and Alkire not within it waiting for the trump of Gabriel! Why, man, where are your little damned conclusions?"

"Dix," said Abner, "you do not deceive me in the least; Alkire is not sleeping in a grave."

"Then in the air," sneered Dix, "with the smell of sulphur?"

"Nor in the air," said Abner.

"Then consumed with fire, like the priests of Baal?"

"Nor with fire," said Abner.

Dix had got back the quiet of his face; this banter had put him where he was when Abner entered. "This is all fools' talk," he said; "if I had killed Alkire, what could I have done with the body? And the horse! What could I have done with the horse? Remember, no man has ever seen Alkire's horse any more than he has seen Alkire—and for the reason that Alkire rode him out of the hills that night. Now, look here, Abner, you have asked me a good many questions. I will ask you one. Among your little conclusions do you find that I did this thing alone or with the aid of others?"

"Dix," replied Abner, "I will answer that upon my own belief you had no accomplice."

"Then," said Dix, "how could I have carried off the horse? Alkire I might carry; but his horse weighed thirteen hundred pounds!"

"Dix," said Abner, "no man helped you do this thing; but there were men who helped you to conceal it."

"And now," cried Dix, "the man is going mad! Who could I trust with such work, I ask you? Have I a renter that would not tell it when he moved on to another's land, or when he got a quart of cider in him? Where are the men who helped me?"

"Dix," said Abner, "they have been dead these fifty years."

I heard Dix laugh then, and his evil face lighted as though a candle were behind it. And in truth, I thought he had got Abner silenced.

"In the name of Heaven!" he cried. "With such proofs it is a wonder that you did not have me hanged."

"And hanged you should have been," said Abner.

"Well," cried Dix, "go and tell the sheriff, and mind you lay before him those little, neat conclusions: How from a horse track and the place where a calf was butchered you have reasoned on Alkire's murder, and to conceal the body and the horse you have reasoned on the aid of men who were rotting in their graves when I was born; and see how he will receive you!"

Abner gave no attention to the man's flippant speech. He got his great silver watch out of his pocket, pressed the stem and looked. Then he spoke in his deep, even voice.

"Dix," he said, "it is nearly midnight; in an hour you must be on your journey, and I have something more to say. Listen! I knew this thing had been done the previous day because it had rained on the night that I met Alkire, and the earth of this ant heap had been disturbed after that. Moreover, this earth had been frozen, and that showed a night had passed since it had been placed there. And I knew the rider of that horse was Alkire because, beside the path near the severed twigs lay my knife, where it had fallen from his hand. This much I learned in some fifteen minutes; the rest took somewhat longer.

"I followed the track of the horse until it stopped in the little valley below. It was easy to follow while the horse ran, because the sod was torn; but when it ceased to run there was no track that I could follow. There was a little stream threading the valley, and I began at the wood and came slowly up to see if I could find where the horse had crossed. Finally I found a horse track and there was also a man's track, which meant that you had caught the horse and were leading it away. But where?

"On the rising ground above there was an old orchard where there had once been a house. The work about that house had been done a hundred years. It was rotted down now. You had opened this orchard into the pasture. I rode all over the face of this hill and finally I entered this orchard. There was a great, flat, moss-covered stone lying a few steps from where the house had stood. As I looked I noticed that the moss growing from it into the earth had been broken along the edges of the stone, and then I noticed that for a few feet about the stone the ground had been resodded. I got down and lifted up some of this new sod. Under it the earth had been soaked with that ... red paint.

"It was clever of you Dix, to resod the ground; that took only a little time and it effectually concealed the place where you had killed the horse; but it was foolish of you to forget that the broken moss around the edges of the great flat stone could not be mended."

"Abner!" cried Dix. "Stop!" And I saw that spray of sweat, and his face working like kneaded bread, and the shiver of that abominable chill on him.

Abner was silent for a moment and then he went on, but from another quarter.

"Twice," said Abner, "the Angel of the Lord stood before me and I did not know it; but the third time I knew it. It is not in the cry of the wind, nor in the voice of many waters that His presence is made known to us. That man in Israel had only the sign that the beast under him would not go on. Twice I had as good a sign, and tonight, when Marks broke a stirrup-leather before my house and called me to the door and asked me for a knife to mend it, I saw and I came!"

The log that Abner had thrown on was burned down, and the fire was again a mass of embers; the room was filled with that dull red light. Dix had got on to his feet, and he stood now twisting before the fire, his hands reaching out to it, and that cold creeping in his bones, and the smell of the fire on him.

Abner rose. And when he spoke his voice was like a thing that has dimension and weight.

"Dix," he said, "you robbed the grazers; you shot Alkire out of his saddle; and a child you would have murdered!"

And I saw the sleeve of Abner's coat begin to move, then it stopped. He stood staring at something against the wall. I looked to see what the thing was, but I did not see it. Abner was looking beyond the wall, as though it had been moved away.

And all the time Dix had been shaking with that hellish cold, and twisting on the hearth and crowding into the fire. Then he fell back, and he was the Dix I knew—his face was slack; his eye was furtive; and he was full of terror.

It was his weak whine that awakened Abner. He put up his hand and brought the fingers hard down over his face, and then he looked at this new creature, cringing and beset with fears.

"Dix," he said, "Alkire was a just man; he sleeps as peacefully in that abandoned well under his horse as he would sleep in the churchyard. My hand has been held back; you may go. Vengeance is mine, I will repay, saith the Lord."

"But where shall I go, Abner?" the creature wailed; "I have no money and I am cold."

Abner took out his leather wallet and flung toward the door.

"There is money," he said, "a hundred dollars—and there is my coat. Go! But if I find you in the hills tomorrow, or if I ever find you, I warn you in the name of the living God that I will stamp you out of life!"

I saw the loathsome thing writhe into Abner's coat and seize the wallet and slip out through the door; and a moment later I heard a horse. And I crept back on to Roy's heifer skin.

When I came down at daylight my Uncle Abner was reading by the fire.

Special Surprise
Guest Appearance by . . .

CAROLE NELSON DOUGLAS

"Magic is a man's game," he told the reporter for the *Las Vegas Review-Journal* who sat beside him in the audience.

"In this town, for sure," she answered. "Except for Melinda at the Venetian, a female illusionist has never headlined in Vegas before. That's why I'm interested in your take on this one."

His "take" on this one was he could take her or leave her, and she had left him, long ago, not on her terms.

"Even you must admit," the reporter said, eyeing him slyly, "that her Mirror Image trick is a winner."

"It's all mirrors," he answered, snorting ever so slightly. No sense in demeaning his own act while dismissing that of a rival.

Rival?

Chardonnay LeSeuer was one of those tall black women with a whole lot of cream in her coffee. Looked like a freaking supermodel. Now she was "Majika" and making hay by playing both the sex and the race card: not just the second woman ever to headline on the Strip, but also the first black magician.

She was also an ex-assistant he had sent packing years ago for packing on a bit too much poundage. Sure, she looked pretty sleek now, but usually it was all downhill with women once the weight started piling up. How was he to know she'd get over putting on fifteen pounds because her kid had gotten that annoying disease? She'd missed a lot of rehearsals with that too.

Time had added assorted swags and sags to his six-foot frame as well, as if he were an outmoded set of draperies, but his magician's costume could be designed to hide it, as did the ignominy of a custom corset that also doubled as a handy storage device for assorted paraphernalia that shall remain nameless, at least to readers of the *Review-Journal.*

"Actually," he added, trying to sound affable, "I haven't seen this infamous Mirror Image trick yet."

"Why do you say infamous?"

"From what I've heard, it smacks more of a gimmick than legitimate magic."

"Aren't all magic tricks a gimmick?"

"Please. Not 'tricks.' It makes magicians sound like hookers. We use the term 'illusions.' We are frank about what we do but we don't debase it. There's a fine line."

"And how has Majika crossed over it?" the reporter asked, pencil poised. She was a twenty-something twerp with an overstudded left ear and an annoying manner, as if she knew something about him that he didn't.

By overstepping her bounds, he wanted to snap. Instead, he displayed that mysterious and vaguely sinister smile that was pasted on billboards high above the Strip and had been for fifteen years. It was pasted on his face now, too, thanks to Dr. Mengel. "We'll find out tonight, I'm sure."

Marlon Carlson sat back in the seat, startled when it tilted back with him. The damn Crystal Phoenix Hotel and Casino had gone first class in designing a house for this upstart woman. He'd had an exclusive gig at the Oasis down the Strip—as Merlin the Magnificent—for years, but the fact was the joint was getting a bit tacky. Every older stage show seemed shabby after Cirque du Soleil had hit town. That was the trouble with Vegas: it took millions to set up a theater specifically for a designated show meant to run for decades since the star got millions.

Refurbishing in mid-stream was the name of the game and he was getting tired of it, personally. He was getting tired, period, especially of the cosmetic surgery that had tilted his eyes to a Charlie Chan slant and drawn his neck skin back like a hangman's noose. At least he didn't look as artificial and aerodynamically taut as the eerily ageless Siegfried and Roy down the Strip. Yet. And at least he didn't have to work with cats, animals almost as annoying as the clichéd rabbit. He understood that Majika still resorted to producing the expected (another word for rabbit) in the illusion trade.

When he couldn't help shuddering at the indignity of resorting to the rabbit, which was literally old hat, the snippy young reporter had the gall to ask if he were cold, like he was somebody's Uncle Osbert instead of a first-rank stage magician at the top of his game.

He forced his attention to the stage, where the woman who now called herself Majika, slim and limber in spangled leopard leotard, was going through the motions of various sleight-of-hand illusions.

She was sleight of form again, he noted nostalgically. Always a looker, but not very cooperative. Usually his assistants considered it a signal honor to sleep with him. Well, maybe it was a less signal honor these days, but it was still a tradition at least.

She had no real assistants, except for various members of the audience she called onstage.

That's what was wrong with magic shows nowadays. They had all gone over to the proletariat. There was Lance Burton with his kiddie brigade at the Monaco, as if magic were still something meant to amaze and amuse the pre-teen set instead of a multimillion-dollar con game with almost forty million tourists a year to milk and bilk. There were the afore-considered Siegfried and Roy, in their off hours breeding rare albino lions and tigers and, perhaps someday, even some bloody bears. Oh, my. All for the good of the planet and mankind.

All Merlin the Magnificent did was mystify and collect his millions. At least Majika had no politically correct cause on display along with her lean form and her skimpy magical prowess.

His nose wrinkled despite itself, quite an achievement given his last surgery, as she coaxed a shy, fat middle-aged woman in a (sigh) floral-decorated sweat suit from one of the first rows of the audience onto the stage.

The usual cabinet had been wheeled center stage by the black-clad ninja stagehands Majika used for assistants. They came and went like ebony fog, no posing, no muscle-flexing. In fact, there was something weirdly boneless about their silent, supple forms, like electric eels gone upright. Frogmen in wet suits, that's what they evoked in their shiny Spandex jumpsuits covering head to toe to little finger. Disgusting.

This time the eternal magician's prop was presented with the mirror in plain view on the outside front, even framed in ornate gilt wood, as if it were made to hang on a wall. The simpering cow from the audience, obviously a plant, was finessed into the cabinet by the door swinging open on a dead matte-black interior.

Once the dupe was inside, the shadowy ninjas sprang from somewhere to spin the cabinet sideways. Majika stood proudly edgeways behind it, her figure as sleek as a diver's.

To the uneducated eye, the cabinet looked no more than two inches wide, like an ordinary mirror frame. Please! Marlon was getting a headache.

"How does she do that?" the reporter was whispering, nagging in his ear.

"Mirrors!" he snapped.

But he wasn't sure. How irritating.

The frogmen spun the cabinet . . . once, twice, three times.

Its side profile was always as black and narrow as a dagger's and Majika made sure to stand behind it fully visible, as if it were really that thin an edge.

He rapidly calculated angles, checked the wings and floor for hidden mirrors.

The audience gasped. . . .

. . . for out of the narrow edge of the dark mirror the woman in the gaudy sweat suit stepped, blinking as if emerging from the dark.

"My goodness," she murmured like the tourist born she was.

What a stooge! So annoying as to appear absolutely natural. He wondered what casting director Majika used.

The lithe magician gestured the woman to stand at her right side, then nodded to the dark men to spin the mirror again.

And this time the very same image of the sweat-suited woman

stepped out from the other edge of the mirror. Majika moved between them, her own figure reflected to infinity in the bland mirrored face of the cabinet front.

The split images of the woman from the audience eyed each other, and then began addressing each another.

"You can't be me."

"You must be me."

Twins. Simplest trick in the book. One backstage waiting to go on, the other planted in the audience. What a sucker ploy!

"How'd she do that?" the reporter prodded, her pencil waving in his face.

Watch the fresh peel, baby!

He leaned away from the unwanted contact. Twins, he was about to say, when Majika waved the two women together and they slowly converged until they melted into each other and only one stood there, looking like she needed to be pinched to wake up.

"How'd she do that?" the reporter persisted, insisted, as that ilk will.

"Mirrors," he said shortly, rising so he could beat the rest of the audience to the exit doors. It was hard work. They were all standing, blocking the rows and the aisles, giving Majika a standing ovation for the final illusion of her act. He didn't even glance stageward to catch the vaunted final fillip of the show: a white rabbit pulled from a black top hat that moments before had been flatter than a Frisbee. Even flatter than the edge of a spinning mirror.

⁓

"Chardonnay," he greeted Majika when she finally returned from the multiple bows to her dressing room, which he had managed to enter as if he had appeared there by design. It stunk of opening night floral arrangements, but the show had been running for eight months.

"Merlin," she answered. "I mean, Marlon. Dare I ask how you got in here?"

"Started early, honey. Shut the door. We have things to discuss."

She obeyed, just as she had used to when she'd needed the paycheck.

His confidence perked up. He was the maestro, she the upstart. "That mirror thing is a fairly effective trick," he said, smiling. God, it hurt.

"Works for me." She sat at her dressing table to swipe the glitter highlights from her face.

He wished she would wipe off that new expression of elegant self-satisfaction. Or had she always looked that way?

"Seriously," he added, "I think you might have something there."

"Really?" She spun toward him, bare-faced, looking as taut as a teenager.

He blinked like a tourist in the limelight. Something was wrong here. Unfair. Why should she be slim and unwrinkled, when she'd passed off his Babe-scale years ago?

"So how's your kid?" He had searched for the given name and given up.

"He died."

Silence always made him uncomfortable. He supposed firing her in the middle of that medical melodrama could have made it hard on . . . someone. He didn't like to hear about people dying. He never knew what to say, so he said nothing.

She seemed to expect no less from him. "So, did you like the show?" she asked.

"What's not to like?" Everything. "Glad you made such a great ... comeback. You look terrific." Spoken softly, like an invitation.

"Thanks. It's good to see you again too." She seemed pleased that he was here.

Oddly, that cheered him. He hadn't realized he'd needed cheer until now. "Really?"

"Well, you are the maestro. I'm flattered that you bothered to see my show."

"It's that Mirror Image trick that's the draw."

"Illusion," she corrected as swiftly as he had corrected the reporter.

She leaned an elbow on the dressing table, then her chin on her fist. Her image reflected to infinity behind her, thanks to the room's traditional parallel aisle of dressing table mirrors. It was all done with mirrors, and he was never done with mirrors, for he saw himself, small and wee, in a tiny corner of the reflected room behind her. His trademark mane of hair, now a dramatic white, was mostly extensions now. He was the sum of all the parts of his former illusions.

His heart fluttered. This moment was important. He knew it. For her, for him. He couldn't tell for which one it was more vital, just as one couldn't tell the twins from the Mirror Image illusion apart, even when they merged at the end.

"It's twins, isn't it?" He spoke without wanting to, hungry, urgent, worried.

"No, not twins."

"Not twins?"

She smiled, gently, as at a slow-witted child. "This is something totally new, my illusion."

"Nothing's new in magic. Nothing! It's the same dodge and burn the photographers used do to enhance photographs, only it's performed on the audience's eyes instead of a negative."

"Dodge and burn," she repeated. "I like the way you put that."

"Listen. I'm curious as hell, and I admit you've got me wondering. I really want to know how you do that."

She was silent. Signature illusions were a magician's bread-and-butter, big-time.

"A million dollars," he said, unable to stop himself. "I'll give you a million dollars if you show me the secret of that trick."

His words had surprised her as much as they had him.

"A million dollars." She savored them like bittersweet chocolate. "A million dollars would have saved Cody's life."

"Cody?"

"My son."

"Oh. Sure. Sorry. Sorry about that. So the disease, whatever, was terminal."

"Then it was. Not now."

He didn't know what to say, so he left his offer hanging there.

Apparently she saw it still twisting in the wind. "You have to promise not to tell anybody."

"Sure. I mean, no. Not ever."

"And you can't use it yourself without paying me a . . . royalty."

"I wouldn't want to use it. I mean, I'm not a copier. Haven't ever been. I just want to know." He realized this new, unexpected need was the deepest he'd felt in some time. "I don't understand it. It's not magic like I know it. I need to—"

"I understand need," she said, cutting him off as if uninterested in the sudden flood of genuine feeling that engulfed him. "I'll show you how the trick works."

"A million dollars," he repeated, awash in a foreign wave of gratitude.

He really had to know, more than anything in his life. What life? It was all magic show. She'd probably give the million to some foundation for the disease that had killed her son. So he'd have helped her after all. Life was strange, but magic was even stranger.

~ ∽ ~

It would be quite an event. She would only reveal her illusion by using him in it. He was to be the prearranged stooge hauled from the front rows of the audience. His hotel and her hotel had agreed to co-promote the one-time union of two major Strip magicians as if they were world-class boxers having a ballyhooed rematch.

Maybe they were.

She also stipulated that he wear his stage costume: glittering black sequined vest and satin cummerbund, the vaguely frock-coat-style jacket with the capelet built into the back. Even his corset. He had felt like blushing when she mentioned it. How did she know?

It was obvious, though, that she had to know the stooge's apparel before the illusion began. He knew he had no twin, but maybe she could make one. No one came to take an impression of his face beforehand, but makeup people could do incredible masks even from photos these days. It was more and more special effects instead of old-fashioned magic, like everywhere else in the entertainment industry.

He was even announced on the program, a parchment flyer tucked into the glossy photo-book about Majika and her show that cost the marks nine bucks a throw: Special Guest Appearance of Merlin the Magnificent by arrangement with the Goliath Hotel and Casino.

He sat down front, cricking his neck to look up at a stage he was used to looking down on people from. He felt like a kid dragged to a cultural outing, the local symphony maybe. There was a lot of show to sit through, and for a pro, it was all routine stuff, although the audience around him gasped and applauded.

He patted his palms together; no stinging claps from him. The racket, music to his ears when he was onstage, only hurt them now, especially the enthusiastically shrill whistles. His act never got whistles, but that was because it offered an old-fashioned dignity. He shrank a little in the disconcertingly mobile seat. Old-fashioned dignity did not sound like where it was at these days. He wouldn't outright copy Majika's mirror illusion, but borrow the best of it. And being part of it, going through it, was the easiest way to master another magician's illusion. You saw how it was done in an instant. Amazing that none of her audience stooges had been tempted to give away the trick, since it was the talk of Vegas and exposing it would cause a media frenzy. He was surprised that the Cloaked Conjuror at the New Millennium, who specialized in laying bare the mechanisms behind the magic, hadn't touched Majika's Mirror Image illusion.

When the mirrored cabinet was finally whisked onstage by the black-Spandexed minions, Marlon stared hard at the space above the wheels. No mirror halfway back to reflect the front wheels as the back and disguise an escape or entrance through the stage floor. In fact, Majika writhed underneath the cabinet like a sex kitten . . . or Eartha Kitt in heat, just to show the space was open and empty.

But not to worry. He'd soon know the way his "twin" would enter the box, although how she got that "two-melt-into-one-before-your-eyes" effect would be interesting to know. Probably mirrors again. So embarrassingly often, it was mirrors.

When she singled him out in the audience, he stood, nervous as a schoolboy at his first magic show. He was used to being in control, the king of the board, not a pawn.

As he headed for the six stairs to the stage he heard an audience member hissing, "Look at that kooky old guy, that big white hair! Televangelist Showman. Las Vegas!"

He held his cherished snowy pompadour high. It gave him an ecclesiastical air, he thought. He liked to consider himself as the high priest of magic in a town riddled with cheesy acolytes.

Chardonnay went through the usual chitchat with him: name, where he was from, what his hobbies were. The audience quickly caught on that he was more than the nightly guinea pig, that he was a noted magician himself, and laughed at his coyly truthful answers.

"Are you ready to face my mirror of truth and consequences?" she asked last.

He glanced over his sober, caped, black shoulder at the gaudy thing. "Of course. I am even more ready to meet myself coming from it than going into it."

That earned a few titters from the audience and then the gilt-frame door was swinging toward him like a horizontal guillotine aiming at his sutured neck. He ducked when he stepped up to enter the dark space behind the silvered door, thinking the opening might be too small for his height.

But nothing impeded him and in a moment the door had swung its matte-black painted interior shut on him with a finalizing snap.

He turned at once, feeling up . . . down . . . around for any panel that might give.

Nothing did. In fact, he felt no edges of anything, no limits.

Surprised, he took a step or two forward. Or four or five. Six, seven, eight! Backwards. Sideways. Nothing. And he could hear nothing, no muffled covering lines from Majika while the transfers were accomplished inside the mirrored cabinet. No transfers were accomplished. He couldn't even feel the cabinet jolted and manipulated by her accomplices as they spun the unit on the stage.

Nothing spun but his own baffled speculations. No way could such a paltry cabinet be so vast inside. No way, no illusion . . .

He was in a void. A soundless, motionless void. Not a hair's-width of light entered or escaped that void. It was as pitch black as a childhood confessional booth.

Used to mentally tracking time, Marlon tried to tote up the seconds, minutes he had been thus isolated. He couldn't compute it. Had no idea. His every expertise failed him here.

He would have pounded on the cabinet walls, broken the illusion, if he could have. But there was nothing to pound upon except the solid floor upon which he stood. Upon which he stood. He stamped an angry foot, a child having a tantrum. No sound, not even the pressure of an impact.

He searched his throat for a cry of protest or fear, but found it too tight and dry to respond to his panic.

And then, just like in that long-ago confessional, a small square of gray appeared in the darkness.

"At last! Where have you been?" he demanded. "There can't be much time to make our reappearance together."

"Time?" asked an odd, wheezing voice. "What's that? Be still. I need to absorb you."

Absorb him? "It's a little late for Method acting," he fussed. "If you can't do a reasonable impression of me right now this entire illusion is ruined."

Hmmm. A botched illusion wouldn't do much for Majika's hot new career. Perhaps this mess-up was for the best. One less rival was one less rival. "Where do we exit this crazy thing? I'm first."

"And the first shall be last," the wheezing voice noted, laughing soundlessly, or rather, with something like a death rattle.

"I don't understand," he said.

"This is where she fulfills her bargain. I have provided the faces and bodies of hundreds of mortal souls for her nightly exhibitions. It was always understood that I, the eternally shifting one, should eventually acquire a mortal body and soul of my own and escape this endless lonely dark."

Perhaps his eyes had finally adjusted to the sliver of gray light that shared the darkness with him. He imagined a wizened, warty figure not at all human, as perhaps the cat-suited and masked ninja-men might look if stripped of their shiny black skins.

The glimpse was enough to convince him that this was no derelict hired double, but something far less ordinary.

"You're a genie," he guessed, "like in a lamp, only in a mirror. And she found you somehow and you gave her a wish, her resurrection as a youthful woman and a magician, only she had to promise you . . . something."

"Not very much." The tone implied the creature had been studying him and found him wanting. "I did require a soul that had squeezed itself bare of attachments to this world, that had shriveled enough that there would be room for me to expand."

"You can't just . . . take me over!"

"Ah, but I can. That is my sole talent. I can replicate any being, any body. I got into trouble about that millennia ago, and some wicked magician—a real one—sentenced me to my lonely mirror."

"What kind of demon are you?"

"Explaining that would take too long. Although time is endless for me, I see by the spinning of my senses that we are expected to make our appearances upon the stage. I will warn you about one thing: my gift of replication responds only to the genuine. I can't control that. So it is and so shall you be and so shall I be when I become you. But freedom is worth the price."

"Freedom! And you would imprison me in your place? For eternity? No mortal soul deserves that."

"You are right." The creature's gray aura faded as it appeared to think.

Marlon knew a moment's relief and a sudden surge of hope for a new life, a better life, a kinder, gentler life. It was not too late . . . .

"I will not abandon you to the dark," the croaking voice whispered, very near now, but no more visible. "I will not deprive you of your beloved limelight. I am a master of transformations, and I can manage that. Watch and believe."

Marlon . . . Merlin the Magnificent . . . found himself blinking like a tourist under a bank of gel-covered spotlights. Red, blue, green they blazed, Technicolor stars in an artificial sky.

He was . . . himself. Standing on a stage as he did almost every night, and Majika was lifting one graceful arm to indicate his presence. His reappearance from the box. His deliverance. His rebirth. I will be good, I will, I will. Well, better.

He took the stage, spread his arms and cape, rejoiced in the magic of his vanishing and recovery.

Applause.

And then more applause, accompanied by fevered whispers and then shouts of wonder.

Majika had thrust her left arm out to introduce the second half of the illusion, the other Merlin the Magnificent standing on her other side.

Marlon turned his eyes uneasily, expecting to see the gray, shriveled, scrofulous thing from the dark.

Instead he saw a tall, white-haired man in fanciful evening dress . . . a man whose snowy mane had dwindled to a few threadbare strands . . . whose lumpy frame slumped like an overstuffed sack of extra-large baking potatoes . . . whose neck had become a jowly wattle, whose eyes were sunk in ridges of suet flesh.

For the first time he truly felt the horror in the story of Dorian Gray. Gray!

And before he could do or say anything, or even make a few more frantic mental promises to what or whom he couldn't say . . . before he could even take in the enormity of it all and the loss that loomed before him, the foul thing moved toward him—the man he was before he had changed his own mirror image—and sank into him like fog, or like an exiled part of himself.

Marlon drowned in the engulfing presence of Merlin, a Merlin cursed to live and die looking exactly as Marlon had not allowed himself to look, and happy for that.

Where Marlon went he couldn't say. It was dark. And narrow. And he heard and felt nothing and knew he'd go mad if he was kept here.

And then . . . slap! Snap! A sharp small sound and the world exploded again with light and applause. He gulped a deep, anxious breath of light-heated stage air, lifted his head and almost sniffed the sound of the applause. It was thunderous. Better than ever. He'd survived whatever nightmare the mirrored box had put him through.

Then, it became too much. The continuing racket crashed on his sensitive ears. He shrunk again, cowered, even as Majika lifted her arm the better to display him to the admiring audience.

His heart pounded against the palm of her hand.

His long white hair was full and thick again, luxurious, and she stroked it with her other hand.

Majika's giant face stared down with piercing eyes. His sensitive ears flattened at the horrid screeching of her voice in the microphone as she displayed her triumph of illusion: him.

Her face came close, smiling.

"You've been such a good boy tonight, Marlon," she whispered giddily as if to a confrere, "you'll have extra veggies in your after-show supper, and maybe even a big carrot from Mr. MacGregor's garden."

While his ears and tail drooped with self-recognition, he spied his former form, now bent and shuffling, hastening out of the theater before the crowd began its rush for the exits.

Occupational Hazard:
A Harry the Book Story

MIKE RESNICK

I have just given 75-to-1 against Lowborn Prince, who has not finished in the money since G. Washington chopped down the cherry tree, and I am wondering what kind of idiot puts five bills on this refugee from the glue factory when Benny Fifth Street walks up to me and whispers as follows:

"I saw you take that bet. Lay it off."

"What are you talking about?" I say. "Booking five hundred dollars on Lowborn Prince is as close as a bookie can come to stealing."

"Lay it off," he repeats.

"Why?" I ask.

He looks around to make sure no one is listening. "I just got word: the hex is in."

"Not to worry," I assure him. "I paid my hex protection to Big-Hearted Milton not two hours ago."

"You don't understand," says Benny Fifth Street. "Don't you know who made that bet?"

"Some little wimp I never saw before."

"He's a runner for Sam the Goniff!" he says. "And you know the Goniff. He's never bet on a fair race in his life."

The horses are approaching the starting gate. It's too late to lay the bet off, so I just make the Sign of the Pentagon and cross my fingers and hope Benny is wrong.

The bell rings, the gate opens, and Lowborn Prince fires out of there like he's Seattle Slew, or maybe Man o' War. Before they've gone a quarter of a mile he's twenty lengths in front, and I can see that Flyboy Billy Tuesday has still got him under wraps. He keeps that lead to the head of the stretch. Then Billy taps him twice with the whip and he takes off, coming home forty-five lengths in front. By the time Billy has slowed him down and brought him back to the Winner's Circle the race is official and the prices have been posted, and Lowborn Prince pays $153.40 for a two-dollar bet. But I didn't book a two-dollar bet. I pull out my pocket abacus and dope out what I owe the Goniff, and it comes to $38,870, and I know that I have to pay it or the Goniff will send some of his muscle, like Two Ton Boris or, worse still, Seldom Seen Seymour, to extract it one pint of blood at a time.

I hunt up Big-Hearted Milton, who is sitting at his usual seat in the clubhouse bar. As he sees me coming he pulls a dozen hundred-dollar bills out of his pocket and thrusts them at me.

"Here's your money back," he says. "I didn't deliver, so I won't keep it."

"That's fine, Milton. Now give me another thirty-seven grand and we'll call it square."

"That was never part of the deal," he says with dignity.

"Neither was letting a hex get by you."

"I *tried* to find you and give it back when I heard what was coming down," says Milton. "It's not my fault you were ducking out of sight because the cops were making the rounds."

"You *knew* Lowborn Prince was going to win?" I demand.

"I knew the hex was in. I didn't know who was going to win, because I didn't know who the Goniff was putting his money on. There were three other longshots in the race. It could have been any of them."

"What went wrong?" I ask. "You've broken lots of hexes for me."

"Yeah, but they were from normal, run-of-the-mill mages. Not this time."

"Who the hell does the Goniff have hexing for him?" I ask.

"You ever hear of Dead End Dugan?" says Milton.

"Dugan?" I repeat, frowning. "When did he get out?"

"Not *out*," Milton corrects me. "*Up*. They buried him in Yonkers, and that was supposed to be the end of it."

"So?"

"So he's a zombie now, and my magic isn't strong enough to counteract his."

"Look, Milton," I say, "this is serious. If I take one more beating like this, I'm out of business, and probably out of fingers and other even more vital parts as well. What am I going to do?"

"You need a real expert to go up against him."

"A voodoo priest, maybe?" I ask.

"Yeah, that might do it," says Milton.

I gather Benny Fifth Street and Gently Gently Dawkins and tell them we're leaving the track early, that we've got to find a voodoo priest before I can go back to work. Benny immediately suggests we buy plane tickets to Voodooland, but I explain that there isn't any such place, and Gently Gently says that he's got a friend up in Harlem who belongs to some weird cult and for all he knows it's a voodoo cult, and I tell him to offer his friend anything but make sure he brings his voodoo priest to my place, and I'll be waiting there until I hear from him.

So I go home, and I send Benny out to bring back some healthy food like blintzes and chopped liver and maybe a couple of knishes, and then there is nothing to do but sit around and watch the sports results on my new twenty-inch crystal ball. The big news of the day is Lowborn Prince, and it is so painful to watch that I almost can't eat my blintzes, even though I have loaded them up with sour cream and cinnamon sugar, but at the last minute I decide I have to practice a little self-denial so I only pour one container of strawberries on them, and I spread the chopped liver over little poker-chip-sized pieces of low-cal rye bread.

Finally, at about eleven o'clock, there's a knock on the door, and it's Gently Gently Dawkins. He walks in and tosses his hat onto a table.

"So where is he?" I demand.

"He's on his way up the stairs," said Gently Gently. "He's an old guy. He don't climb as fast as I do."

"And you left him alone?" I yell.

"Believe me, no one's going to bother him," says Gently Gently, and just as the words leave his mouth in hobbles this stooped-over, bald, wrinkled, old black guy, and I would say he was dressed in rags but Ezekial the Rag Merchant would take offense.

"*This?*" I say. "*This* is what you spent all day looking for?"

"I'm pleased to meet you too," says the old guy.

I turn to him. "You're really a voodoo priest?"

He shakes his head. "Do I *look* like an amateur?"

"Don't ask me what you look like and maybe we won't come to blows," I say. "If you aren't a voodoo priest, just what the hell are you and why are you here?"

"I'm here because this nice man—" he gestures toward Nicely Nicely Dawkins "—put the word out that he was looking for someone who could neutralize a zombie's hex." He smiles and taps his chest with an emaciated thumb. "You're looking at him."

"Okay, you're not a voodoo priest," I say. "What *are* you?"

"The answer to your prayers," he replies. "Also, I happen to be the only *mundumugu* in New York."

"What's a *mundumugu*?"

"You might call me a witch doctor."

"I might also call you a crazy old man who's wasting my time," I say.

He makes a tiny gesture in the air with his left hand, and suddenly I can't move a muscle.

"Oh, ye of little faith," he says with a sigh. "I ought to leave right now, but Dead End Dugan is giving a bad name to both hexes and corpses. My name is Mtepwa." He extends his hand, and somehow I extend mine, even though I am not trying to. "And you are Harry the Book. I am almost pleased to meet you."

He snaps his fingers, and suddenly I can move again.

"I hope you didn't take offense, Mr. Mtepwa, sir," I say. "It's been a bad day."

"I understand," says Mtepwa. "But tomorrow will be better."

"It will?"

"It will, or my name isn't Cool Jumbo Cool."

"But your name *isn't* Cool Jumbo Cool," I point out.

"Details, details," he says with a shrug.

"Uh, I hate to seem forward," I say, "but what is this gonna cost me?"

"I haven't decided yet," he says. "But whatever it is, I promise you'll be pleased with the price."

The fourth race at Belmont is coming up, and I'm getting really nervous. Bilgewater, who couldn't beat my mother around the track, even if she was carrying 130 pounds on her back and running with blinkers, is 120-to-1, and this time the Goniff doesn't even use a runner, he comes up and makes the bet himself: $1,800 on Bilgewater.

"That's a big bet," I note. "I'll probably have to lay some of it off."

"You can if you can," he says, and I realize that the word is out that Dead End Dugan has hexed the race and there is no way that any other bookie will take part of the bet. "I hear you've got a new boy working for you," continues the Goniff.

"Boy isn't exactly the word I'd use," I reply unhappily.

"I just want to do you a favor, Harry," he says. "Don't waste your money on another mage. I guarantee you that nothing in the field can beat Bilgewater. There's simply no way."

He utters a nasty laugh and walks off to his private box, and Mtepwa approaches me.

"That was Sam the Goniff?" he asks.

"That was him."

He looks after the Goniff, and nods his head. "I knew someone who looked just like him—a long time ago."

"Maybe it was just the Goniff when he was younger," I say.

"I doubt it," says Mtepwa. "This was before Columbus discovered America."

I wonder just how gullible he thinks I am, but we have more important things to discuss, and I tell him that the Goniff has admitted that Dead End Dugan has hexed the race and that nothing in the field can beat Bilgewater.

"Well," he says with a shrug, "if they can't, they can't."

"*What?*" I scream, and then lower my voice when everyone starts staring. "I thought you were here to put Dugan in his place!"

"You have undertakers to do that," answers Mtepwa. "I'm here to make sure that his hex doesn't work."

"But if no one in the field can beat Bilgewater . . . " I begin, but then there's a cheer from the crowd and I realize that the race has started and I turn to watch it, and I immediately wish I hadn't turned, because Bilgewater is already leading by ten lengths and as far as I can tell he hasn't drawn a deep breath.

I look at the rest of the field. Most of them are lathered with sweat, half of them are lame, and the rest spend more time watching the birds in the infield than the horses ahead of them.

"I should never have listened to Milton!" I mutter. "Voodoo priest my ass! I need a .550 Nitro Express and a telescopic site."

"Be quiet," says Mtepwa. "I must concentrate."

I don't know why, but I do what he says. Bilgewater enters the far turn fifteen in front, and Flyboy Billy Tuesday hasn't touched him with the whip yet, and then Mtepwa mumbles a little something that sounds like it's right out of *King Solomon's Mines*, and suddenly there is a big black-maned lion on the track, and he launches himself at Bilgewater, and the horse goes down and Billy Tuesday goes flying through the air and winds up in an infield pond, and the whole field circles around the lion, who is busy munching on the tastier parts of Bilgewater, and then the race is over and Benny Fifth Street and Gently Gently Dawkins are thumping Mtepwa on the back so hard I'm afraid they're going to damage him, and I shove them away.

The stewards post an Inquiry sign, and a moment later they announce that the lion has been disqualified and placed last, and the result is now official. And two minutes after that, the Goniff comes storming up to me, blood in his eye.

"I don't know how you did it," he says, and he's so hot I am surprised steam isn't shooting out of his nose and ears, "but it had better never happen again!"

"Don't bet on bad horses and it won't," I say cockily, because as far as I know this is the first bet the Goniff has lost since he was five years old (and no one ever saw the winner again).

"You listen to me, Harry the Book!" he says, shoving twenty large into my hand. "Kid Testosterone is fighting Terrible Tommy Tulsa at the Garden tomorrow night. I'm putting this on him to win by a knockout. If you pull anything funny, if you mess with my boy Dead End Dugan again, you won't be alive to gloat about it. Do I make myself clear?"

He turns on his heel and stalks off before I can answer, which is just as well because I have no idea what to say.

"Who is Kid Testosterone?" asks Mtepwa.

"It is possible that he is the worst fighter who ever lived," I say. "At the very least, he is the worst fighter still licensed to get his brains beat out. He has fought forty-seven times, and has been knocked out forty-six times. His greatest triumph was when he lost a unanimous decision to Glass Jaw Malone eleven years ago."

"I see," said Mtepwa.

"So what are we going to do?" I say. "The Goniff never backs down on a threat. If the Kid doesn't win, I won't be alive the next morning."

"No problem," says Mtepwa.

"No problem for *you*, Mtepwa," I say. "But what about *me*?"

"I've got twenty-eight hours to figure it out," he says. "And I wish you'd start calling me Cool Jumbo Cool. Mtepwa just doesn't seem right in this venue."

"Just get the Goniff and his zombie off my case once and for all, and I'll call you anything you want," I promise.

"Every occupation has its hazards," he says. "You shouldn't let this upset you."

"I don't mind being upset," I tell him. "It's being dismembered that bothers me."

⌒⌒⌒

I am just as upset when we show up at the Garden the next night. Mtepwa has gone into some kind of African swami trance, and only comes out of it an hour before the fight. I ask him what he was doing, and he says he was napping, that he's a 683-year-old man and he's had a lot of excitement and he needs his sleep.

"Did you solve our problem?" I ask.

"Well, actually, it's *your* problem," he explains. "Nobody's going to bother me no matter how the fight comes out."

"All right, did you solve *my* problem?" I say.

"I'm working on it."

"Well, work faster!" I snap. "If the Kid wins, I'm broke, and if he loses, I'm dead!"

"Fascinating problem," he said. "Rather like Fermat's Unfinished Theorem. Of course, if he'd simply paid me the five cattle and the virgin, I'd have shown him how to solve it."

"Will you please concentrate on Harry the Book's Unfinished Theorem?" I say pleadingly.

Before he can answer, I sense a presence hovering over me, and I turn and there is Sam the Goniff, smoking one of his five-dollar cigars, and with him is a guy who smells kind of funny and whose eyes seem to be staring sightlessly off into the distance and who has a lot of dirt under his fingernails, and I know that this is Dead End Dugan.

"Hi, Harry," says the Goniff. "I'm glad to see you're a fight fan. I'd hate to think that I'd have to go looking for you after the Kid knocks out Terrible Tommy."

"I'll be right here," I say pugnaciously, but that is only because I know that hiding from the Goniff is like hiding from the IRS, only harder.

"I'll count on it," he says, and heads off to his ringside seat with Dugan, and I notice that Seldom Seen Seymour is already there waiting for him, just in case he needs a little help collecting after the fight.

"Have you come up with anything yet?" I ask Mtepwa.

"Yes," he says.

"What is it?" I ask eagerly.

"I've come up with a sinus problem, I think," he answers. "Too much cigar smoke in here."

"What about Kid Testosterone?" I demand. "If he loses I die!"

"Then he can't lose, can he?" says Mtepwa.

"But if he wins, I'm not only broke, but I haven't got enough cash to cover the Goniff's bet, and Seldom Seen Seymour will take me apart piece by piece."

"Then he can't win, can he?" says Mtepwa.

"I've got it!" I say. "You're going to shoot him before the fight starts!"

Mtepwa just gives me a pitying look, and turns to concentrate on the ring, where they are carrying out what's left of the Missouri Masher, and then Kid Testosterone and Terrible Tommy Tulsa enter the ring, and the ref is giving them their instructions, such as no biting or kicking or low blows, and because this is New York he also tells them no kissing, and then they go to their corners, and the bell rings and they come out and Tommy swings a haymaker that will knock the Kid's head into the fourth row, but somehow his timing is off and he misses, and the Kid delivers a pair of punches that couldn't smash an empty wine glass but sudden Tommy's nose is bleeding, and he blinks his eyes like he can't believe that the fight is thirty seconds old and the Kid is still standing.

But the Kid is still on his feet at the end of the round, and it later turns out that one of the three judges actually gives him the round, and another calls it even, and that is the way the fight goes for three rounds, but I am not watching the fight, I am watching Sam the Goniff, and between the third and fourth round he somehow gets the Kid's attention and holds his fist out with his thumb down and I know he has just signaled the Kid to end it in the fourth round.

I am not the only one who has seen it. Mtepwa is staring right at the Goniff, and he just smiles, and I know he's got something up his sleeve besides his arm, but I don't know what.

The bell rings and the fighters come out for the fourth round. Terrible Tommy connects first, a blow to the solar plexus that should double the Kid over in pain, but instead Tommy screams and pulls his hand back like he's just broken it punching a concrete wall, and then they circle around until the Kid's back is to me, and suddenly Mtewpa starts mumbling again, and the Kid throws his money punch, and I look, figuring this is the end and Terrible Tommy is going down for the count, but it's *not* Terrible Tommy, it's the Goniff, and he takes the punch on the point of his chin and goes reeling around the ring, and the Kid starts pummeling him, and it occurs to me that the Kid looks a lot more like Rocky Marciano and a lot less like Kid Testosterone.

Every time he delivers what looks like a knockout blow, Mtepwa starts mumbling again, and no matter how much punishment the Goniff takes he stays on his feet. Finally the Kid winds up and knocks him through the ropes and he falls to the floor right in front of me.

"Is there something you'd like to say to me before you climb back into the ring?" I ask pleasantly.

"I ain't climbing back in there!" he mutters through bleeding lips.

"Yes you are," says Mtepwa, and against his will the Goniff gets to his feet and turns to face the ring.

"All right, all right!" he says. "I cancel the bet!"

"You don't even have to cancel," says Mtepwa before I can stop him. "Just promise you'll never bet with Harry again, or use Dead End Dugan to hex a sporting event."

"I promise," says the Goniff.

The instant the words are out of his mouth he collapses, the referee declares Kid Testosterone the winner, and the Goniff is carted off to the hospital.

"Thanks for nothing!" I say to Mtepwa. "We didn't cancel, so I still have to pay off! The bet was that the Kid would knock Terrible Tommy out, and he did!"

"The evening's not over yet," he replies, and indeed it isn't, because the Kid fails a urine test, which doesn't surprise anyone given that he made it all the way to the fourth round, and the fight is declared a draw—not a non-contest where I would have to return the Goniff's money, but a draw, where everyone who bet on either fighter loses and only those who bet there'd be a draw win.

———— ◦ ◦ ————

And that's the story.

Well, not quite all of it. I'm not a bookie anymore. I took on a full partner—Cool Jumbo Cool, who eventually decided that *this* was the payment he wanted—and these days we head a pretty successful betting syndicate.

Jumbo's really gotten into the swing of things; he *likes* this millieu. Tonight he's hexed the big game between the Montana Buttes and the Georgia Geldings. I gave Benny Fifth Street a promotion, and we've even got a couple of new runners. In fact, I have to close now. It's time to pass my money to Dead End Dugan and the Goniff and tell them where to lay our bets.

She's Not There

STEVE PERRY

Nobody is immune to Glamour.

In the ten years she'd had the talent, Darla had never come across anybody who had seen through it, far as she could tell. Old, young, men, women,—it fooled everybody, every time.

Not that she'd need it here: Fifteen feet away, the widow Bellingham snored fully-dressed upon her bed. The old lady had put down a bottle of very expensive champagne earlier at the party, and Darla could probably could bang a Chinese gong and not rouse her, but still . . .

She opened the last drawer of the jewel box, her movements slow and careful. The smell of cedar drifted up from the intricately-carved wooden box, which was probably worth more than Darla's car.

Ah. Here we go . . .

It was an oval pin about the size of a silver dollar. Inset into the platinum were thirty-some diamonds, fancy yellows, the majority of them a carat or so each. Not worth as much as clears and nowhere near the value of the intense pinks or fancy blues encrusting the pieces in the top drawer, of course, but that was the point. These were good stones—good—but not outstanding, and with what she could get from her fence, plenty to keep her going for six months.

One-carat gems of this grade were easy to move.

She limited herself to a job every three or four months, enough to keep her below heavy police radar—or at least it had done so for eight years.

Truth was, it had been almost too easy. Never a really close call. At first, it it had seemed a grand adventure, but it wasn't long before it turned into just a part-time job, no more exciting than shopping for fruit at New Seasons Market. Go in, pick out the organic apples you like, leave—without paying—and take a few months off, ta dah!

Disappointing in a way how easy it was, though certainly better than working for a living . . .

Six or seven million in fine jewelry here, and that just the daily-wear stuff. The really good pieces would be in a bank vault some-where . . .

Darla wrapped the pin in a square of black velvet and slipped it into her jeans pocket. She slid the jewelry box's drawer closed.

As always, she was tempted to clean the box out, but she knew better. Unique pieces were hard to move, worth only what the loose stones would bring, unless you wanted to mess around trying to find a crooked collector, and that was risky. This particular pin? It might not be missed for weeks or months. The top-drawer stuff sure; the bottom drawer? Maybe the widow would never even notice. When you could go in and plunk down a million bucks for a brooch or a necklace without having to look at your checkbook balance? A pin worth a couple hundred grand? Shoot, that was practically costume jewelry . . .

So, she'd take just the one piece.

The perfect crime, after all, was not one where the cops couldn't figure out who did it; it was one the cops never even heard about . . .

⌒⊃⊂⌒

Darla uttered the cantrip just before she pushed open the stair door into the apartment building's lobby. When she stepped through, she looked the same to herself, save for a slight bluish glow to her skin that told her the Glamour was lit.

The guard at the desk looked up. "Morning, Mr. Millar. Early start today, hey?"

Darla grinned and sketched a two-finger salute at the guard.

The armed man touched a button on his console and the building's door slid open. As she left, Darla waggled one hand over her shoulder, in what she thought was a friendly gesture. Silently, of course. Her Glamour fooled the eyes, but not the ears—if she spoke, she would sound like a twenty-something woman and not the sixty-something man she picked as a disguise.

She had been careful coming down the stairs to avoid the surveillance cams, too, since her trick wouldn't fool them, either.

When the real Mr. Millar exited for his morning walk, the guard wouldn't say anything—he wouldn't want anybody to think he was crazy . . .

It was a fantastic thing, her trick, even if it had a couple drawbacks: She had to touch somebody before it would work on them, and do that within a day, since the effects of the touch faded away after that. Still, it was impressive.

She had no idea why or how she had come by it. She had been

found in a dumpster as a baby, raised in an orphanage. The words to the cantrip were from a dream she'd had on the night she turned sixteen. Eventually, she had come to realize that, somehow, the dream had come true.

Magic? No such thing, everybody knew that. But here she was. She'd wondered about it over the years. She'd cautiously nosed around in a few places, but never found any other real magic, only people faking it. Why did it work? How? She didn't know. Still, you didn't have to be a chemist to strike a match, and apparently you didn't need to know jack about magic to use the stuff. Case in point.

Worrying over the reasons might drive her nuts if she let it, so she didn't try any more. She just thanked whatever gods there might be for bestowing it upon her and that was that.

She had a car, but she seldom used it on a job where public transportation was available. She walk to the bus stop. The TriMet driver would see her as a white-haired Japanese man, since she had touched his shoulder earlier in the day when she'd ridden the bus in this direction. She would exit six blocks from her apartment and walk home. Nobody could connect Darla Wright to the expensive Portland penthouse occupied by the widow Bellingham, even if the woman ever did notice she'd been robbed.

Smooth as oil on glass, no muss, no fuss, just like always, and she planned to sleep in until at least noon.

Life was good.

~~~

Darla strolled into her neighborhood Starbucks, next to Fred Meyer's, and inhaled the fragrances of brewed coffee and freshly baked pastries. She was scouting for a fattening cherry turnover she figured she'd earned, when she bumped into a good-looking guy about thirty who stopped suddenly ahead of her in the line.

"Oh, sorry," he said, turning to steady her. "My fault." He smiled. Nice teeth. Black hair, blue eyes, rugged features, pretty well-built under a dark green T-shirt and snug jeans. Three or four years older than she was, but that was nothing.

"No problem," she said. She returned the smile.

Ice cream, she thought, looking at him. To go with the pastry, hey . . . ?

No . . . She couldn't. Not today. She had to meet Harry at two, and she'd slept past noon, so Ice Cream here would have to wait. Business before pleasure.

There were plenty of other men in the pond, and she was going to have free time to do a little fishing, lots of time . . .

Nothing as obvious as running a pawn shop, Harry had a guitar store, a hole-in-the-wall place twenty minutes from Portland, in Beaverton. Beaverton was where Portlanders went to buy fast food and shop at the 7-Elevens, a bedroom community that had once been swamps and filbert orchards and beaver-dammed streams.

The guitars at Harry's ran from a few hundred bucks up to ten or fifteen thousand on the high end, mostly acoustic and classicals, and the place actually did a pretty good business. Today being Sunday, the shop was closed, but Harry answered the bell at the back door. She waited while the four big and heavy locks snicked and clicked, bolts sliding back, and the door, made of thick steel plate, swung quietly open on oiled hinges. Trust a crook to know how to protect his own stuff.

The shop smelled of wood, and some kind of finish that was not unpleasant, a sharp, turpentine-y scent.

"Layla. How nice to see you, as always."

Even Harry didn't get her real name. Darla was very careful.

"Harry. How business?"

"I can't complain. Come in. Some tea?" He was seventy-five, bald, thin, and wore thick glasses that kept slipping down his nose. He thought she was hot, though he'd never made a move on her.

"Thanks."

She sat at a table while Harry made tea. "Oolong today," he said.

Eventually, he sat the steaming cup in front of her.

"So, kiddo, whaddya got for me?"

She produced the pin, opened the velvet wrapping.

"Ah." He picked it up, pulled a loupe from his shirt pocket, held the pin up to the light. "Quality stones. Nice cuts, nothing outstanding. Say . . . fifty?"

"What, did I get stupid since you saw me last? Eighty," she said.

He smiled. "Might could go sixty, because I like you."

"It's a steal at eighty, Harry. Two and a quarter for the bigger stones, and maybe another ten or fifteen for the little ones. Plus seven, eight hundred for the platinum. Pushing a quarter million, and you can pocket half that."

"Honey, we both know it's a steal at any price, but since I'll have to fly down to Miami to move the rocks, sixty is a gift. You know how I hate air travel."

"Miami? What's wrong with Seattle?"

He pulled the loupe off and put the piece onto the table. "Too warm for Seattle. Even broken up, thirty stones this close will have to be moved a few at a time. Could take me months. Who has that kind of time at my age?"

"Warm? The, uh, previous owner doesn't even know it's gone."

"Alas, dear girl, I'm afraid she does. Mrs. Bellingham, widow of the late Leo Bellingham, owner of steel mills and shipyards, right? Probably pays her boy toys more than this bauble is worth, but she has definitely missed it."

Darla shook her head. "How could that happen? And how do you know it?"

He shrugged. "Maybe today was inventory day. Or it was a gift from a special friend with sentimental value. Who can say? All I know is, I talked to Benny the Nod this morning and he said the Portland cops had come to call upon him early, waving a picture of this very item." He tapped the pin.

"Sweet Jesus," she said.

"I doubt He would have any part of this, hon, though you can tithe if you want. So, sixty?"

"Yeah, well, I guess. Sure."

They drank more tea and he prattled on about some new classical guitar he'd just bought, Osage Orange this, cedar that, Sloane tuners, a genuine Carrith, look at the little owl inlay here—it all flowed into one ear and out the other. How unlucky was this? That the old woman had discovered the theft within hours of it happening? That cost her at least twenty thousand dollars!

There was just no justice . . .

~⌒~

As Darla drove her British racing-green Cooper Mini convertible along TV Highway back toward Portland, she relaxed a little. Yeah, okay, her latest theft had been discovered too quickly, but she was still sixty thousand dollars richer, Harry's cash, in used hundreds, was tucked away in her purse right there on the passenger seat. Life was still good. The sun was shining, the top was down, it was a lovely June afternoon, and she was free to spend the next few months lazing about, doing whatever she damned well pleased. Better than a poke in the eye with a sharp stick, hey?

She stopped at the light next to the Chrysler dealership on Canyon Road, tapping her fingers on the steering wheel as the Beatles sang "Hey, Jude" on the oldies station.

A heavyset teenage boy in baggy shorts and a sweatshirt with cutoff sleeves, a brim-backward baseball cap pulled low, his feet shod in big, clonky, ugly basketball shoes, strutted across the road in front of her. She couldn't see his eyes behind the dark shades he wore. Oh, please, kid! Who do you think you're fooling?

When he was almost past, on the passenger side, he pointed behind her and said, "Holy shit! Look at that!"

Darla turned to see what had impressed this wanna-be gansta kid.

She caught a blur in her peripheral vision, and turned back just in time to see the kid snag her purse —

"Fuck—!"

Darla put the car into neutral, set the brake, and jumped out of the car. She chased the kid, but he had a head start and he was a lot faster than he looked. He put on a burst of speed and she lost him behind the car dealership.

And what what she have done if she'd caught him? Kick his ass? She didn't know anything about martial arts. She had a nice folding knife, but unfortunately, that had been in her purse, too.

Son-of-a-bitch!

By the time she got back to her car, there was a line of traffic piled up behind it. She stalked back to the car, gave the finger to the fool behind her laying on his horn.

Fuck, fuck, fuck, fuck!

Sixty thousand dollars!

The hell of it was, she couldn't do anything about it! She could hear the conversation with the cop in her head:

Ah, you say you had sixty thousand dollars in cash in your purse? What is it you do for a living again, Miss?

Shit!

So much for the idea of six or eight months of goofing off. She was going to have to find another score. And soon. She was pretty much tapped out. She'd been counting on last night's job.

No fucking justice . . .

⁓◦◦⁓

Darla remembered a line she'd heard somewhere, when some reporter was interviewing a famous robber. "So, Willie, why do you rob banks?" And his answer had been: "Because that's where the money is . . ."

Probably never said that, but it made the point—you want to see who has the bling, you have to go where they flash it.

Which was why she was at a posh reception for some famous author at the Benton Hotel in Portland. Once she was past the gate keeper, having him see her as somebody who showed up at these things that he knew by sight, she became herself again, but she had to look the part, so she had dressed up for it. Heels, a black slinky dress, a simple strand of good black pearls, her short, dark hair nicely styled. Nobody inside would bother her, though the crowd was thick enough that somebody patted her on the ass as she squeezed through on her way to the bar. Apparently that cherry pastry hadn't added enough weight to matter . . .

She got a club soda with lime, then started shopping . . .

She winnowed her choices to two possibles.

One was a forty-something woman with gorgeous red hair and a great figure she worked hard to keep looking that way. She'd had a little plastic work done on her face, very subtle, but offset by a botoxed forehead that might as well have been carved from marble. She wore emeralds—earrings, a necklace, a ring that had to run four carats, all matching settings in yellow gold. The dress was a creamy yellow that went with the jewelry. Quarter million in shades of green fire. Nice.

The other prospect was a guy, maybe thirty-five, in an Armani tux. He was tanned and fit, with a little gray in his hair, and an easy smile, and though he wasn't sporting any monster rocks, he did wear a Patek Philippe watch—she guessed it was a Jumbo Nautilus in rose gold, worth about thirty grand wholesale. He had one ring on his right hand, a gold nugget inset with a black opal the size of a dime, that flashed Chinese writing in multiple colors as the opal caught the light when he raised his champagne glass to sip. That good an Australian opal might go ten grand. She wouldn't want either the watch or the ring, they'd be too hard to move, but he'd probably have other pieces laying around . . .

Men were both harder and easier for her. Looking like she did, she could get close to them and touch them enough to get feelings for somebody she could become. And more than a few rich men had offered to take her home—for their own purposes, of course, but still, it got her a lot of intelligence for a later visit.

So, the emerald lady or the opal guy?

Even as she thought this, the opal guy looked up and noticed her. He smiled at the man he was talking to, said something, and ambled in her direction.

Well, look at this. If he was going to do the work? Maybe that was a good sign . . . .

"What's a nice girl like you doing at a stuffy event like this?"

"Waiting for you, it seems," she said. She gave him her high-wattage smile.

He held his champagne glass up in a silent toast, as if to acknowledge her response to his pick-up line. "I'm Arlo St. Johns," he said.

"Layla Harrison," she said, giving him a name she'd made up for herself in the orphanage years ago. One of housemothers who wasn't too awful had been a big fan of the English rock invasion of the early sixties, and had lent Darla her books about the subject. She had discovered that Eric Clapton had written the song "Layla" after having fallen for George Harrison's wife, Patti. That woman must have been something, Darla had decided, since she had been the inspiration for at least three famous rock songs—"Something," by Harrison when he'd been with the Beatles; "Layla;" and "Wonderful Tonight," by Clapton.

Ran in the family, too—Pattie's little sister had been Donovan's muse for "Jennifer, Juniper," and had gone on to marry Mick Fleetwood of Fleetwood Mac . . .

"Penny for your thoughts?" he said.

"Worth more than that, I think."

"No doubt. Want to go get a drink or something somewhere a little less crowded?"

"What did you have in mind?"

"My place is much quieter."

She smiled. "Why not? Seen one writer, seen them all . . ."

⁓

St. Johns had a high-rise apartment downtown, and he drove them to it in a black Cadillac Escalade, still had the new car smell. Sixty, seventy thousand bucks worth of car. This was shaping up to be a fun evening. Guy was good-looking, well-mannered, was obviously doing well enough to drive a high-end SUV and to sport expensive, tasteful jewelery. Bound to have something laying around his place worth lifting.

She didn't have a lot of rules in her biz, but one of them was that she didn't get intimate—well, not too intimate—with her marks. Not that this was ironclad—she had slipped a couple of times—but it made her feel guilty stealing from somebody she'd slept with, and she didn't need that. Darla had built a pretty good rationalization about stealing from the rich and their insurers who wouldn't miss it; if she went to bed with somebody and had a really good time? It would feel wrong to take his stuff.

Pretending not to look, she easily managed to see the numbers he punched into the alarm keypad just inside the door. She committed them to memory, converting them to letters. The first letter of each word corresponded to the number of its position in the alphabet: Thus 78587 became GHEHG, which in turn became a nonsensical but memorable sentence: Great Hairy Elephants Hate Giraffes . . .

The apartment was gorgeous, decorated by somebody with money and taste. Oil paintings, fancy handmade paper lamps, Oriental carpets some family in Afghanistan must have spent years making. Upscale furniture, more comfortable than showy.

While St. Johns built them drinks at his wet bar, she went into the bathroom, took her cell phone from her purse, and programmed it to ring in thirty minutes. That would give them enough time to have a drink and talk a little, but not get to the rolling-around-and-breaking-expensive-furniture stage.

She went back into the living room.

St. Johns was funny, smart, and twenty minutes into their conversation over perfect martinis, she was thinking maybe she would sleep with him instead of burgling him. That would be okay.

But, she reminded herself, she was broke. She had a couple thousand in the bank, but her apartment rent was due, her car note, and her fridge was mostly empty. She needed the money more than she needed to get laid.

A shame. He really was fun. He was some kind of importer, specializing in Pacific Rim antiquities, he said, and there were a few pieces of Polynesian or Hawaiian or other island art carefully set out here and there that she suspected were probably worth a small fortune. Jewelry she knew, painting and sculpture, she didn't have a clue.

He smiled at her. "So, what do you do when you aren't attending boring social gatherings?"

"Not much, I'm afraid. When my parents died, they left me a fair-sized insurance policy. I had the money invested, so it brings in enough to keep the wolf from the door. I take classes in this and that, work out, travel a bit. Nothing very exciting."

He smiled bigger.

She smiled back. Oh, this wasn't just ice cream, this was Häagen Dazs Special Limited Edition Black Walnut, you could get fat just opening the carton. The temptation surged in her, a warm wave. She had enough to pay the rent and car note, barely, she could buy some red beans and rice and veggies, make it another week before she had to have some more money ...

In her purse, her cell phone began playing Pachelbel's Canon in D.

Crap! What to do? Shut the phone off and stay?

Because she wanted to do just that so much, she decided it wasn't a good idea. A matter of discipline. If she slipped, that could lead her down a dangerous slope. Just because it had always been good didn't mean it couldn't go bad.

Oh, well. She smiled, fetched her phone, touched a control.

"Hey, what's up?" A beat. Then, "Oh, no! That's terrible! Are you all right?"

St. Johns raised an eyebrow at her.

"No, no, I'll come over. I'll see you in a little while."

She snapped the phone shut. "I'm sorry. That was my girlfriend Maria," she said. "Her fiancé just dumped her and she's in a terrible state. I need to go see her."

"I knew it was too good to be true. I'll give you a ride."

"No, I'll catch a cab. She lives way out in Hillsboro, I wouldn't ask you to do that."

"It's no trouble. I don't have anything else planned."

"Really, I appreciate it, but no. Could you, uh, give me your number? I'd like to see you again."

"Oh, yes." He produced a business card that had nothing on it but his name and a phone number. "Take care of your friend," he said, smiling. "And do call me. I'd love to see you again."

"I will look forward to seeing you," she said. Unfortunately, you won't know who I am when I do ...

"Let me call a cab."

"Thanks, Arlo."

"My pleasure."

After he called, he walked her to the door, and rested his hand on her shoulder. There was a moment when she thought he would kiss her—and she wouldn't have objected—but it passed.

Another road not taken.

Too bad, but that's how life was. Sometimes, business had to come before pleasure.

⁓

Her taxi arrived. The night was warm, and she slid into the cab and gave the driver an address near a stop where she could catch a MAX train to a station near her place.

"Yes, madam," the driver said. He looked to be about fifty, and from his accent, she guessed he was Indian, or Pakistani.

It really was too bad about St. Johns.

The cabbie was chatty, going on about the warm weather and how the Bull Run Resevoir was low for this time of year. She responded politely, already thinking of how she was going to burgle St. Johns's apartment. If the Glamour had worked on voices, it would be a snap—she'd become St. Johns, tell the security guy she'd lost her key, and have him let her into the place. Take something the mark wouldn't miss, and adios.

Too bad St. Johns wasn't a mute—

Ah! Wait a second, hold on, she had something here . . .

"Beg pardon, Miss?" the cabbie said.

"Huh?" She looked at him.

"You made an exclamation? Are you in distress?"

She smiled. "Oh, oh, no, sorry. I was just thinking of something. I'm fine."

The cabbie smiled and nodded.

Actually, she was better than fine. She had come up with a terrific idea. Why hadn't it occurred to her years ago? It was so simple.

She paid the cabbie, gave him a nice tip—what the hell, she'd be flush again in a couple days, right? She walked to the MAX station. A light rail train arrived, and she got on, along with several others. She exited at the stop near her house. An old lady dressed in khaki slacks and a tie-dye T-shirt and running shoes got off the train and set off at a fast walk ahead of her. The woman had long, steely gray hair and a lot of smile wrinkles and was obviously in pretty good shape from the pace she set. You could do worse than to be somebody like that when you got old, Darla decided. But not for a real long time . . .

∽ ☙ ⌇

St. Johns needed to be out of the building, so she had to risk using her car. She parked near the exit to the garage early, and waited to see St. Johns' caddy leave.

At about nine in the morning, the Escalade pulled out.

Okay, kid, here we go . . .

Darla approached the building's street entrance. She put a hand on the doorman's sleeve as she asked to see the security man on duty.

Inside, she was conducted to the security desk. The man behind it looked up.

"Help you, Miss?" He stood and moved to the counter.

"Yes, I saw a car parked out front and there were two men in it who seemed to be watching the entrance," she said. "Probably it's nothing, but I thought I should say something about it."

"Two men? What kind of car? They still there?"

She shrugged. "I'm not good with cars. Like a van, maybe an SUV? Dark, kind of old, muddy? But they left."

"Uh huh. You get get the license number, ma'am?"

She shook her head. "Sorry."

"Ah. Well. Listen, we appreciate it. We'll, uh, keep an eye out for it." Probably thinking was a twit she was. Two men in a car, right . . .

She reached out and touched his arm. "Probably it's nothing," she said. "But these days, you can't be too careful."

"Yes, ma'am. That's true."

Darla stepped into a doorway in the next building and lit the Glamour. Show time . . .

"Morning, Mr. St. Johns," the doorman said. He opened the heavy glass door.

Darla smiled and nodded, knowing that her disguise was perfect.

She walked to the security desk.

"Mr. St. Johns. How may I help you sir?"

She shook his head and touched her throat. In a raspy voice as low as she could manage, Darla said, "Laryngitis." She coughed.

"Oh, sorry to hear that."

"Forgot my key," she said. Her voice was a passable imitation of a sick frog.

"No problem, sir." The guard opened a wide drawer, scanned the contents, and produced a door key. "Here you go. Drop it off when-ever."

Darla smiled, nodded, and coughed as she took the key.

Perfect. She didn't have to sound like St. Johns, she had set it up that her—his—voice was gone. Very clever, if she said so herself.

People were coming and going, and the guard's attention veered away from her.

There weren't any cameras on the elevators, at least none she'd seen the night before, but she lingered until a couple other people arrived to ride up. They would see her as Darla, and if there was a hidden camera on the elevator, the guard would see three people in it. How much track would he be keeping?

So far, it ran like a Swiss watch.

She opened the door, stepped inside—it wouldn't do for some-body to see her instead of St. Johns, though they might assume she was his special friend, since she had a key.

Inside, she shut the door and reached for the alarm pad, but real-ized that it was green. He hadn't even bothered to set it.

She shook her head. Man didn't turn on his alarm? He deserved to have his stuff stolen. Lordy.

In the bedroom, it took all of ten seconds to find the jewelry box—it was leather, trimmed in brass, and it sat atop a dresser made of what looked like ebony.

Darla opened the box.

My. There were gold coins, loose gems, mostly diamonds, but a couple of emeralds, a diamond-studded money clip that held three thousand dollars in hundreds. There was a banded 5K stack of hundreds next to that, but the band was broken and two were missing. There were a dozen platinum coins and ten platinum one-ounce ingots, and several sets of cuff links and tie pins, done in assorted gems—rubies, emeralds, sapphires . . .

Quickly, Darla decided what she could remove without it being immediately noticed. There were thirty-two gold coins, Eagles, and she took two of those. Nineteen loose stones, fourteen of which were one or two-carat, round-cut blue-white diamonds. She took one of the two-carat stones, and one of the single carats. She took two hundreds from the money clip, three from the banded stack. One of the platinum coins, one of the ingots. She considered the tie-tacks and cuff links and decided they were too easily missed.

Okay, a quick total: Couple gold Eagles, probably worth eight hundred each. The platinum Eagle was worth fourteen, fifteen hundred, probably, the ingot a little less, say twelve hundred, and that was money in her pocket, since they didn't have to be fenced. The diamonds were clean and clear, figure six, eight thousand on the smaller one, and at least twenty-five or thirty on the bigger one. Less Harry's cut on those, so say they were worth twenty thousand to her total, if she was lucky. With the cash, she'd net about twenty five grand total. Unless St. Johns did an inventory, he likely wouldn't notice anything was gone, and she'd buy herself three or four months of lie-about time. Not nearly as good as what she had gotten from the widow's place, but she had that laryngitis trick, and that would come in handy.

Once again, it was tempting to scoop it all into her pocket— there was enough here to keep her from having to score again for a couple, three years, maybe longer. But, no . . . Better to stick with what had kept her out of jail for all this time, greed was a killer. She sighed, and closed the jewelry box.

As she turned to leave, she noticed the corner of a box jutting out from under the bed. A bed with black silk sheets on it, she also noticed, and neatly made.

She stopped, bent, and pulled the box from under the bed. It was long, wide, and fairly flat, as big as a large suitcase, if shallower. She opened the box . . .

It was full of thousand dollar bills, stacked into rows, fifteen across and eight down, and the bills were loose and mostly used.

Holy shit!

She picked up one stack, her breath coming faster, and counted it. Then another stack. A third. The first had thirty, the second twenty-eight, the third, thirty-three. Non-sequentially numbered.

She did some fast math. A hundred and twenty stacks, say thirty bills in each stack on average.

Three million six hundred thousand dollars.

Oh, man!

What was St. Johns doing with this much cash under his bed?

Darla stared at the cash. If she took one or two bills from each stack, he might not even notice! She could take a hundred thousand, two hundred thousand, and unless he did a count, he wouldn't be able to tell. And even if he did that, she was pretty sure this wasn't money he wanted anybody to know about—it had the smell of something not quite legal . . .

Of course, she couldn't just walk into a bank and plunk down a couple hundred-thousand-dollar bills and expect that to fly without raising questions; but Harry knew people who could move big notes without batting an eye and he'd take ten or fifteen percent, no more than that . . .

Two bills from each stack. Two hunded and forty thousand dollars, she could give Harry the two-carat blue-white for his cut and—no, she decided, she'd put all that back. No point in risking this much for petty cash. With two hundred grand in her pocket, she could take a long damn time before she had to make another score.

Yes. That's how she would do it. Put the coins and gems back, pack a quarter of a million into her pockets—no more carrying it in purses, thank you very much—and walk away with a big smile under her Glamour . . .

Darla drove toward her place, using a long and winding route, to make sure she wasn't followed. She was almost home when she heard the sound of a police siren. She looked into the rearview mirror and saw a plain, tan Crown-Victoria with a blue light flashing on the dashboard behind her.

"Oh, shit!" she said. An icy wave washed over her, as if she'd been drenched in liquid nitrogen, turning her stiff with fear.

She pulled to the curb. This wasn't a traffic stop.

A tall, heavyset, balding man alighted from the car. He wore a cheap, badly wrinkled suit and brown shoes, and a tie that failed to reach his belt. Might as well have had a neon sign over his head flashing out the word "Cop!"

He walked to her driver's door.

"Would you step out of the car, please?"

"What's the trouble? Was I speeding?"

"No, lady, I'm a detective, I don't do traffic tickets. Out here, please, and keep your hands where I can see them."

Dead. She was dead. She had considered it over the years, what she would do if she was ever caught, but it had never seemed real to her, it had been so theoretical.

What was she going to do?

The Glamour.

Of course! In her panicked fear, she had forgotten she had a perfect weapon. She'd touch him, and when the moment was right, she'd distract him, change, and that would be that!

The woman? she'd say, when he turned around and saw an old man there, She went that way, she was running!

Okay, she'd be okay, she could do this. He'd have to pat her down, and that would be enough, his hands on her would be fine. A touch was a touch.

"Over on the sidewalk, please," he said.

She obeyed.

"What did I do?" she asked.

"You don't need me to tell you that. Step in there, please."

He pointed to a gate that lead to what looked like a small garden.

"Excuse me?"

"We don't want to do this out here."

"Do what out here?!"

The panic she'd felt came back. What was going on?

"Open the gate, please."

She did. He shut the wrought iron behind them. "Wow, look at that," he said.

She turned. "Wh-what?"

When she turned back to look at the cop he was gone.

In his place was an old woman.

Darla frowned. She knew this woman from somewere . . . ah, it was the old lady on the MAX train . . .

"Or this?" the old woman said, in a decidedly masculine voice.

The woman shimmered, and of a moment, Darla found herself looking at the cab driver who had taken her home from St. Johns—

And then, like a strobe light blinking on and off, the cab driver became the teenager who had stolen her purse, the good-looking guy she'd seen in Starbucks, and finally, St. Johns.

Blink, blink, blink.

Darla was too stunned to speak.

"Are we having fun yet?" he said.

She realized her mouth was open. She closed it.

He chuckled. "Sorry. I couldn't resist."

The meaning of it hit her. "You—you're like me," she said, her voice barely above a whisper.

"Yep. What you see isn't what you get, necessarily."

He laughed again. "I don't rob houses, my ambition is a little bigger than that, but I do okay. As you noticed when you spotted my cash box.

"How much did you take, by the way?"

"Two bills from each stack."

"Smart. I like bright women."

"Why are you—what—?"

"Well, I've been watching you for a while, Darla. Far as I can tell you and I are the only two of our kind. I'd propose a . . . partnership."

"Partnership?"

"Well. More than that, maybe. I mean, you are gorgeous and careful and clever, but there there are some advantages to what we can do together. Between the two of us, we could do bigger and better things than either of us can do alone. Imagine how much easier it would be be if we could be a couple that looked like anybody we wanted?"

She considered it. Yes. That would be something.

"Plus there are some other perks."

He shimmered and turned into a studly young movie star that Darla much admired.

"Or maybe . . . this?" He morphed into another young man, this one a match to a well-known rock star.

"We have a world of choice to offer each other, don't we?" He shimmered again, and reclaimed St. Johns. "Not that I think I would get bored with you as you stand. You are stunning, you know, but you also have a kind of variety to offer no other woman does."

She smiled back at him. "Even though I stole your money?"

"Because you stole my money. What do you think?"

She found herself nodding. Yes. There was an attraction, no question, and if she got tired of looking at him?

Well, he could fix that in an instant.

Because nobody was immune to Glamour . . .

Hostile Takeover

NINA KIRIKI HOFFMAN

I'm a thirty-year-old woman who lives at home with her mother. When guys do this, I suspect it's because they can't find a woman their age who will cook and do laundry and pick up after them the way their moms do. When a woman does it, the only legitimate excuse is that Mother is feeble and needs help.

My mother refuses to be feeble. I could cast a spell on her to make her feeble, but she has a rule: no witchcraft in the house. This is why I have to have an outside office to craft the spells I sell on my website. I have broken Mom's no-magic-in-the-house rule a couple times, but she really means it when she says she'll kick me out if I do it again without permission.

I tell people I still live with my mom because she needs my rent checks. I make twice as much money with my spell business as she does at her florist job. The checks meant something to Mom while Dad was defaulting on the alimony, but now that he wants to get back together with her, he's paying regularly, so my expressed reason for living with Mom is a lie.

What I really crave is living with someone who understands me. This is a big secret. Not my biggest one, but one of the top ten. My twin sister and I became witches the same day, and for a while we grew into our power together. We were close before we turned into witches, but afterward, we were so tight I had trouble loosening up enough to find a boyfriend. Tasha and I went to the same teacher and learned the same lessons. We practiced our arts on each other . . . until I took a turn toward the dark side, and she refused to follow. She got all mystical instead, dedicated herself to the powers of Air, and left me so she could pursue her new faith. Now she travels the world practicing weird rituals that don't get her anything but good will. I can see that being a bankable asset, but only if you spend it sometimes, which Tasha never does.

Mom's the only one in town who understands me. So she's stuck with me, whether she likes me or not.

～◌～

As part of my business practice, I hung out at the student union building at the local university. My regular spell customers knew to find me there, and I hooked up with new ones all the time. The right conversational opening gave people all the excuse they needed to complain. Once I knew their problems, I knew which spell to sell them.

The S.U.B. was a rambling building. There was a bowling alley/ video arcade in the basement, a food court on the second story, offices for university clubs and special interest groups scattered throughout, potted plants, meeting rooms, and snarls of conversational furniture everywhere. I could lurk there with impunity.

A boy witch bumped into me in the food court. I was waiting to buy a gyro, and he was heading toward a girl. In addition to sideswiping me and not apologizing, he totally dinged my witch radar.

I'd encountered other witches here and there on campus, but never somebody else with such powerful vibes.

"Hey," I said, giving New Witch Boy the up-down.

He brushed past me without answering. I wasn't the most beautiful woman in the world unless I worked at it, but I had style. Short dark hair in a clean cut, and single-color tailored clothes. I passed for college age all the time. Was this guy gay?

I wandered after him, not so much offended as intrigued. Maybe he didn't have witch radar and didn't recognize me for what I was. I'd met a number of powerful people, and power made its home in them in different places; I no longer expected anyone else's power to match mine.

"Shelley," he said, catching up to a girl who was hurrying away. I was disappointed. She had that blonde cheerleader look—long, washed-out hair, big blue eyes, lush lips, and big, pushy breasts—so beloved in teen-centric TV and too often in real life.

"Not *now*, Gareth," she said. Her voice incorporated acid. "My boyfriend's watching." She swung away, bobbing gently in front, and Gareth stood, his mouth half open in either idiocy or preparation for a remark that never made it past his teeth.

I stopped beside him. "If you're that interested in her, why don't you enchant her?"

His mouth closed and he stared at me with angry amber eyes.

"Hey, hey, I was just asking," I said.

"Get away from me," he said.

"Sheesh, you don't have to be nasty."

"Did my mother send you here to pester me?"

"No, but I'd like to meet her."

He blinked. "What?"

"If she's the type of mother who sends girls to torment her sons, she might be my kind of fun."

"Who *are* you?"

"My name's Terry Dane. Can I buy you a cup of coffee?"

"Terry Dane? Do you run that spell website?"

I smiled. "You're heard of me!"

He looked madder than ever. "What the hell do you think you're doing?"

I shrugged. "Making a living?"

"With those watered-down imitation spells? More like whole-sale fraud."

"Come on. Have you tried them?"

"I bought the spell for studying harder. It hardly helped at all."

"Did you dissolve it in hot water?"

"What?"

"You have to use hot water to make it truly active—the hotter the better."

"Oh—I thought—"

"I include instructions with the spells for a reason. It's not my fault if you ignore them. I'm feeling generous today, so I'll give you a replacement for the last one you messed up, but this is a one-time deal." I shrugged out of my backpack and rummaged through my sample case. The spells I carried with me were stronger than the mass-produced ones I made for mail order, on the principle of inter-mittent conditioning, and the desired-recapture-of-the-first-time syndrome. If your first hit was really effective, you kept thinking the next one would work just as well. Every once in a while I sent out the stronger versions through the mail to keep my regular customers coming back. "Here." I held out the little gray-paper-wrapped cube that was the "increased study skills" spell. "Hot water. Tea or coffee works."

He hesitated.

"Don't use it until you're cramming for something. The effect is temporary unless you reinforce it with actual studying on a regular basis. Wait until the night before the exam; it only helps you retain things for forty-eight hours, and that's an outside estimate. Why do you need something like this, anyway?"

"What do you mean?"

"Oh, come on. You're a witch. You could make your own."

He grabbed the spell and strode away without a backward look.

"So, no coffee?" I yelled.

About fifteen people turned to look at me. Usually I kept a low profile, but at the moment I was past caring. Had I just wasted a free spell on a guy who was going to ignore me?

"Hey, Terry? You got an attract spell on you?" asked Seth, a short guy with bad teeth and too many green pieces of clothing. One of my best customers. I'd slipped him a free "see yourself as others see you and figure out how to fix your obvious errors" spell once, the permanent version, because it increased the effectiveness of all the other spells I sold him. He had learned to smile with his lips closed, but he couldn't seem to overcome his penchant for green. "There's a girl I want to impress right over there."

"Sure," I said, instead of, "Another one? What happened to the last six girls you used an impress-her spell on?" The spells had to have worked, or why was he coming back for more? Maybe it was a case of wanting something until you actually had it, or maybe the short-term effect had kicked in. If you didn't actually interest the person you attracted after two or three exposures, the spell would wear off and the relationship was over. I fished out the red-wrapped spell Seth wanted—one of my best sellers—and he handed me fifty bucks.

"Thanks." He ran off. I wondered if I should use an attract spell myself and pursue Gareth, but he'd already vanished.

The next time I saw Gareth was in the supermarket by the produce section.

Ding! Ding! Witch in the vicinity! I turned from the mountain of Minneolas I was casing and saw Gareth squeezing an avocado. I decided to stalk him, since the straightforward approach hadn't worked.

He put three avocados in a plastic bag and turned to hand the bag to a woman. Ding! Okay, that was why two dings the first time, and maybe why he could ignore me so easily—he already had a companion witch.

"Gareth, I said *four*," she said.

A testy companion witch. Twice his age.

Two girls rushed up, stair-steps, wavy brown hair, with the same tawny eyes Gareth had. "Look, Mom! Stephanie found the brown sugar!" said the taller girl, and the other one said, "Lacey got the flour!"

"Good job, girls," said the woman, smiling down at them, an edge of enchantment in her expression. For sure the kids felt loved. Cheap trick. I had that one in my repertoire, but it was so easy I rarely used it. Maybe I should try it on Gareth. He was probably used to it, and would fall faster than someone never exposed.

A slender young woman, her brown-gold hair in short curls,

arrived and set a bag of raisins carefully in the cart, offering the mother witch a tight smile.

"Thank you, Rae," said the mother, her voice not so supple and graceful this time.

"What else do you need?" asked Rae.

Mom witch consulted her shopping list. "Chocolate chips."

"Why didn't you tell me before? Those were in the same aisle," said Rae. She frowned and marched away.

"Mommy, what else can we find?"

"Bread, girls," said the mother to the two girls, who jumped up and down. "Look by the back wall." She gestured toward the store bakery, and the two raced off, giggling. She held out the bag with three avocados to Gareth without a word, and he went back to the produce aisle.

I edged over to him, reached for an onion. "Okay, I get why you're allergic to witches," I muttered, "but I'm not your mother."

He jerked and dropped three avocados on the floor, starting an avocado avalanche. I snapped my fingers and stopped them all from tumbling, sorted them back into a stable pile. "You've got to work on your people-sensing skills," I said. "I didn't actually sneak up on you. You could have seen me in your peripheral vision."

"Are you following me?" He stood, picked up the three fugitive avocados, and placed them carefully with the others.

"Maybe."

"Get away from me."

"Am I totally unattractive to you?" That came out more plaintive than I liked. I didn't let Helpless Me out to play in public. This guy was demoralizing me, and I should probably move away from him. Instead, I said, "I can change."

"Why are you even interested in me? I'm not sending out signals, am I?" His eyes widened. "Did I put a spell on you?"

"Simmer down. I'm just short of witch company at the moment, and you're the first likely candidate I've sensed in a while."

"I'll be interested in you if you can teach me how to stop being a witch," he whispered, just as his mother swooped down on us.

"Didn't you find another avocado yet? What's taking so long?"

"Hey, Mom. This is Terry, my new girlfriend." Whoa! I was promoted! He went on, "Terry, my mother, Sally Mathis."

She stiffened immediately, worked hard, and came up with a smile. "Nice to meet you. You won't distract him from his homework too much, will you?"

"Is schoolwork a problem for Gareth?" I asked. Did she or didn't she realize I was a witch? Maybe she was one of those instinctive practitioners who had never explored the range of powers available to her. In which case, Gareth might be completely untrained. I could turn him into whatever I wanted.

I grabbed a perfectly ripe avocado and handed it to Gareth.

"He lacks concentration," said Gareth's mother. She was being pretty bitchy about her son to someone she didn't even know.

"I can help him concentrate," I said, in my best cat-purr voice.

"Wonderful," said Sally with a sour frown. "It's a thrill and a half to meet you."

"Likewise, I'm sure."

Gareth put the avocado I'd chosen in the bag with the others and handed it to his mother. "We're going for coffee."

"But—" said Sally.

I linked arms with Gareth, smiled at his mother, and led him away. I left my half-filled basket on top of a pyramid of cans of corned beef hash.

Outside, we headed for the nearest Starbucks. We both ordered the house blend, and I paid, since I'd offered to before. We settled at one of the tiny round tables, and I hunched toward him. "So what's your new agenda?" I asked. "It's quite a distance from 'get away from me' to girlfriend."

He hooked both hands behind his neck and pulled his head down like someone getting ready to be searched by cops. "I thought you could help me figure out how not to be a witch."

"Why would you want that? Are you totally not getting what a blast this is?"

He looked up. "She wanted the girls to get the power, but they didn't. She's scared of me having it."

"Are you still living at home?" I asked.

He nodded.

"Well, there's your first mistake. Get away from her." Like I could talk. My own mom was completely ready for me to move out. I was the one who wouldn't go.

"But I don't know how to—Dad's out of the picture. He hasn't paid child support in three years. There's four of us, and— She just barely managed my college tuition, even though I have scholarships. She can't afford to pay for a dorm room for me, and I—"

Couldn't he work his way through school? I guessed it depended on his skill set. "How old are you, anyway?"

"Seventeen."

"Oh." He couldn't even vote yet. But if he'd graduated high school early and gotten scholarships, why did he need spells to help him study? "How do you use your witchcraft on a day-to-day basis?"

"I don't."

"Not at all?"

"Not on purpose," he said, and flushed.

"How about your mom? What does she do with hers?"

"Woman things," he muttered, his gaze on the tabletop.

"What the hell does that mean?"

"She won't tell me. She does it at home in a room with the door closed. All I know is there's stinky incense involved, and words I can't hear through the door. The craft has passed from mother to daughter in our family for generations. She hates that I got it instead of the girls."

"Gareth," I said, exasperated. Then I thought, *No, he knows from rough women. I better be gentle or I'll lose him.*

I started over. "Okay, listen. I can't unwitch you—I don't know how—but I can teach you how to make it work for you."

"With those stupid spells you sell? I don't know much, but I can tell they don't work very well."

"They don't have to work well to sell well. I don't want to upset the social balance by giving anyone giant advantages in any of the areas I service. That might lead to scrutiny I don't want. I can teach you how to be a much better witch, but you have to agree to help me. If I train you in the business, you can make enough money to get your own place. What do you say?"

He stared at his coffee cup so long I thought he wasn't going to answer, but at last he said, "Okay."

⟋⟍

First I took Gareth home with me. I figured he should know what a mom was supposed to be like.

"It's mac and cheese again, Terry," Mom called from the kitchen at the back of the house as I ushered Gareth in through the front door, "unless you have other ideas."

"I have a guest, Mom." We passed through the living room and the hall into the kitchen, the heart of the house, where Mom and I spent all our together time after she got off work. The patina of a million cooked meals covered the kitchen ceiling in a yellow haze. The center of the room was a round table, often stacked with newspapers and mail, with just enough room for us to set our plates and silverware down. Sometimes we cleared the debris off, but it didn't take long to build up again. The kitchen colors weren't very inspiring, beige and brown, with a yellow fridge, all geared toward comfort and convenience. A cheese-and-boiling-pasta scent greeted us.

Mom stirred a pot on the stovetop, her silvering brown hair coming down from its neat coils around her head drift in long, limp tendrils around her face. She was flushed from the stove's heat and still wearing the white shirt and black suspenders she wore at the florist shop. It was a weird uniform that made her look more like a waiter than a flowership girl, but they liked that at Flowers While You Wait. "Gareth, this is my mom, Rebecca Dane. Mom, this is Gareth Mathis."

"Hi, Gareth! I hope you like mac and cheese. Terry, could you throw together a salad?"

"Sure." I checked the fridge and remembered why I'd gone to the supermarket in the first place. Produce! We were out. I sighed. "Well, I guess not, Mom. I forgot to shop."

"Frozen broccoli, then." She nodded toward the microwave. I got out the broccoli.

"Gareth, would you like something to drink?" Mom asked.

"That'd be great." He looked lost, standing in our kitchen, his hands clasped in front of his chest as though he were begging or praying, his brown-blond hair squiffed by the wind.

"Help yourself to whatever's in the fridge. Cups are in the cupboard over there."

Gareth poured himself some orange juice.

Mom asked, "Where'd you two meet?"

"At the supermarket," I said. "Gareth's a witch, but he hasn't had any training. I thought I'd get him started." I filled a glass with water and took a seat at the table.

"Really?" Mom put the lid on the mac and cheese and came to the table.

Gareth had gone red again. "Terry," he said, his voice squeaking in a surprising way.

"What?"

"Maybe he didn't want me to know he's a witch," Mom said. "It's okay, Gareth. I don't tell anybody these kinds of things. I appreciate Terry being up front about it, too. It's when she's keeping secrets that I get upset. Have a seat."

"Are you a witch, too?" he asked as he settled in a chair beside me.

"No, not at all," said Mom.

He turned to me. "So where'd you learn?"

"I had a teacher for about six years after I turned into a witch." I could take him to meet my mentor, but then I'd lose my chance to train him up to be my new twin and business partner. Besides, my mentor no longer let me cross her threshold. She was pretty strict about not dabbling in the dark arts.

"But you still live at home," he said. "And you think I should move out?"

"His mom makes him feel bad about what he is," I told my mom. "She's scared of him."

"Oh, honey," said my mom. She put her hands on Gareth's, squeezed. "So sorry you have to deal with that."

"Did Terry put a spell on you to make you say that?"

"Nope. No magic in the house," said Mom.

"He doesn't even know how to check for spells," I said. "I've got my work cut out for me."

"For once, I might actually approve of what you're doing," said my mother.

"So can I start his training here?"

Mom frowned, tapped her index finger on her mouth a couple times, and then nodded. "As long as it's just matter stuff, not spell-casting on people. For the dark stuff you have to take him somewhere else. Okay?"

"All right."

We had dinner, and afterward, Mom sat at the table with coffee and a crossword puzzle while I explained basic principles of magic to Gareth. Mom loves hearing this kind of stuff. It gives her insight not only into me but into my traveling twin, who blows home every once in a while. (I mean it about blowing, too. She brings the wind with her before she remembers to tell it to go outside and play.)

I said, "You have to perceive things to be able to affect them—or, at least, it helps. Do you ever sense things other people don't?"

"I don't know. How could I tell?"

"I knew you were a witch, and that your mom was, too. I learned it through my witch senses. Do you ever get strong feelings about people or things?"

His eyes narrowed, and he glanced past me, as though looking at something out a window, though he stared toward a wall. "I used to when I was little, but not for a long time. My mom's dresser set. Her brush. It's old. It felt like it might be able to—but she wouldn't let me touch it, after that time she found me waving it around."

"Hmm," I said. "Good news, probably. You have the senses. They're just asleep. Once we wake them up, you'll be able to do things. I'll try a spell to open your witch eyes. Wait here a sec. I have to get my kit." I ran upstairs, grabbed my traveling witch kit, and dashed back to the kitchen. I cleared newspapers off the table. "Mom, is this okay?"

"Does it hurt anybody?"

"Not physically. I don't know about the psychic consequences. It should show Gareth what he does and doesn't see."

"Gareth, are you ready for this?" Mom asked.

He laughed, with scorn in it. "Hey, I've seen her work before. I don't expect anything to happen."

Mom slanted a look at me. I smiled back at her. "Go ahead," she said.

I assembled dust of ages, scent of spring gone, sound of three high notes on a piano, and a trace of vanished sunrise. Power pooled in my palms as I bracketed my ingredients with my outstretched fingers. "Show us what he could see, and why he doesn't," I whispered, not a spell I'd ever said before. I wasn't sure if it would work. It didn't even rhyme.

The ingredients flared, mixed, and vanished, leaving a twist of smoke behind. The world shifted around us. Everything in the kitchen glowed with colored light, and streams or strings stretched between people and furniture, appliances, floor, ceiling, walls. Some pulsed, beads of light sliding along the strings between things intimately connected; some shimmered in time to the hum from the refrigerator.

In the midst of all this weaving, an overlay that didn't obscure the physical forms of things—translucent as it was pervasive—something hovered above Gareth's head. A miniature thicket of rose bushes, and trapped inside, a pair of eyes, their irises deep, shifting gray/golden/dark and shadow. The bushes had cleared from in front of them, so that they peered out, as if from a cage. They looked this way and that. Whatever they looked at deepened and intensified. They looked at me, and I felt warmth against my face as though I leaned toward a fire.

"What is this?" Gareth cried, and his extra eyes looked at Mom. She had been turning and gaping at the room, trying to take in everything at once, but now the power of the eyes' gaze focused her into concentrated Mom. She was taller, with a crescent moon in her hair—wrong symbol, I thought; Mom was hardly a virgin goddess—and a veil of golden haze surrounded her.

"What did you do?" Gareth asked, turning on me, and again I felt the warmth of his regard. I held out my hands, studied what the eyes made of me. I was cloaked in shadow so dark it made me look like a silhouette, but flashes of color rippled through my new outer skin.

"Why are you closed most of the time?" I asked.

"What are you talking about?" Gareth demanded. "What's with all these visions? Did you spike my orange juice?"

The eyes blinked, a shuttering of images—all the color left the world, then returned as the lids rose. The eyes rolled up until mostly white showed.

"Someone put a spell on you to blind you." I reached out, my hand a black spider against the green and red and dark glow of vines and flowers. "Do you want to be free?"

"Make it stop," Gareth said.

"I'm not talking to you," I muttered. With my shadowy hand, I touched the roses caging his vision, pressed this stem and that. A thorn bit my finger and I sucked in breath. Itching tingle spread from the puncture. The eyes stared at me. The shadow cloaking my outstretched hand faded as the itching tingle spread from my finger to my palm, and up my arm. My powers leached away as the shadow faded, revealing nothing but normal flesh, blood, and shirt.

Damned spell! Could it kill my witchness? I never thought anything could. In trying to save Gareth, was I dooming myself to being normal?

Before my darkness left me entirely, I murmured power words and picked more carefully through the roses, looking for help. The thorns sprouted and pricked my hands again. Weakness spread through me. Both my arms were bland.

Near the base of one of the vines, I found an aphid like a small hard bump, then another. I rested fingertips on their backs. "Small things, strengthen; change the balance. Shift the spell, let loose the sight. Sip the sap and wreck the roses; give me back my stolen might," I murmured, putting the remnants of my power into it. The aphids listened and grew strong, sucked the lifeblood out of the rose spell until it withered and fell away. They nestled in my palms, gleaming soft, fuzzy green, the size of kiwi fruits, full of the power they'd sucked from the spell.

Gareth groaned. "Stop it, Terry! Whatever you did, make it stop!"

I exchanged a glance with the eyes. They blinked again, then the lids closed, slowly, and all the extra color faded from the room.

"All right," Mom said, "what was that, Terry? Did you break a rule?"

"I just did what I said. We saw what Gareth would see if he used his witch senses."

"What, all that?" he said. "That was crazy."

"You have to get used to it." I sat in a chair at the table and rubbed one of the aphids against my cheek. So soft. It made a small, vibrating sound like a purr. I was exhausted, and a little worried: the rose had poisoned my power. My defenses were weak, now; if anything with power came at me, I could be badly hurt, though not destroyed, because of my secret protection. I needed to find a spell to restore me.

Chances were the rose spell had also poisoned Gareth's powers somehow, maybe paralyzed them. Now that it was gone, maybe he could get some joy out of his power. Maybe he'd be grateful. I hoped so. I wanted to use him in many different ways. "That's where you begin with your powers," I said. "See what you can see. Then decide how you want it to change, and work toward that."

"What does this have to do with those spells you sell?"

"I decide what the spells will do. I infuse them with power and direction. Once I craft the spells, other people can use them."

"You hypnotized me," Gareth said.

I sighed and rested my hands on the table, palms up, with the aphids in them. I wasn't sure what to do with my new friends. They solved the problem for me, sank into my palms. A flush of unfamiliar power flowed through my veins, mixed with the power the roses had sucked out of me, now come home.

I leaned back and closed my eyes, felt this foreign power move through me. It was a slivery power, like bamboo under fingernails, a power with hate in it, and strength, edged with elegance and beauty. "Tell me who you belonged to," I whispered, and learned about Gareth's mother, forced by her mother and grandmother to use her power when all she had wanted was to be normal. They had put a geas on her to pass her power to her daughters, but none of her daughters had been born gifted. A boy with gifts was an abomination. When she discovered Gareth's gifts, she locked them in a hedge of roses and put them to sleep. This was a power she had to renew constantly, as his witch eyes struggled to open.

And in the meantime, with that geas on her, continually unsatisfied, she twisted up in some truly unpleasant directions.

I accepted the foreign power as part of my arsenal. Strange to meet power darker than my own. Everyone I knew in the witch community thought I was the bad guy, the unnatural one who forced people into things against their will. I was as capable as Gareth's mother of mistreating other people.

I would take joy in foiling her.

Gareth shook my shoulder. "Terry?" he said. "Terry—it's happening again."

"What is?" I asked.

"The world looks screwy!"

I straightened and rubbed my palms together as a final thank-you to the aphids. I felt not only restored after the rose's poison but augmented.

I glanced around. The room seemed normal. I studied Gareth, and realized his aura had awareness in it now. He looked all around, panicked.

"Your witch eyes are open now, Gareth. You can close them if you don't like it, but you can also open them whenever you want. What you see, you can change."

"Can I change you? You look like the Grim Reaper."

"Really? Skull and all?"

He stared at my face. "Mostly it's the dark cloak. I guess I can see your face. Are you smiling at me?"

"I am, Gareth."

"How come your mom has a moon on her head?"

"I don't understand that myself. It's not there when I look at her. Have you figured out how to close your eyes yet?"

He glanced around, looking haunted again. Mom got to her feet, shaky, and went to the coffeemaker for a refill. She had some experience with weird witch effects—most of them from my sister, who was allowed to witch around the house, since she didn't hurt anyone. Mom hadn't had enough exposure to be relaxed about it, though.

"I can't—oh," said Gareth. "Oh, it's all gone again. Okay, good."

"Terry. Explanations?" asked Mom. She dumped extra sugar in her coffee and drank.

"Gareth's mom put a spell on him to close up his powers. Did you see the roses?"

"I did. Thanks, by the way, for making me part of the equation."

I couldn't tell if she was being sarcastic, but, even though I hadn't planned for her to see everything, I was glad she had. It meant she knew more about Gareth's problem. "She planted those to keep his powers asleep. She tends them constantly to make sure he's crippled. My spell messed hers up. Now his powers are awake, but he doesn't know how to use them. Can Gareth live with us, Mom? If he goes home, his mother might shut him down again."

Mom's frown was ferocious, but I knew she'd cave. She had the softest heart of anybody I knew.

"I have rules," Mom said, the start of her consent.

⸻

Gareth moved into the guest room. We went back to his house the next morning, when his mother was at work and his sisters had gone to school, to retrieve his belongings.

The house had no witch vibes. It looked like a TV sit-com house, not distinctive, not identical.

His room was a sad excuse for a boy's room. There were red roses winding in the wallpaper, and no pictures of cars, airplanes, metal bands, or things blowing up. His clothes were all neatly folded or hung on hangers—no dirty laundry on the floor or draped over the desk chair. I was more of a boy than Gareth was.

I'd brought a duffle bag for him. He put everything in it very neatly, then stuffed his backpack with a bunch of books.

On our way to the front door, I said, "So where's the room your mom uses for her rituals?"

Gareth looked over his shoulder toward a doorway I hadn't noticed before—and that disturbed me, because now that I know where to look, the witch vibes coming from it were incredibly strong. "We're not allowed to even open the door," he said, as I grabbed the doorknob. A stinging jolt shot through my hand, the same poison Gareth's roses had carried. I jerked back, shaking my hand. Weight in my other hand made me look: I saw one of the aphids, shrunk to the size of a marble, rising from my palm. As soon as it separated from my skin, I held it near the doorknob; it leaped the gap, fastened to the protect spell, and fed.

"What is that?" Gareth whispered.

"This is what freed you yesterday." I hadn't realized they could manifest again, but I was thrilled. Spellsuckers! A staggering number of household applications occurred to me. "I found them feeding on your mother's power-suppression spell, and helped them eat faster. They broke the spell for you. I wonder if they're yours?" The aphid on the doorknob was as big as a cantaloupe. My right hand, still tingling from the spell jolt, unhosted the second aphid, and I set it to join the first.

When they were both the size of fuzzy, pale-green watermelons, the tiny scritching sound of their feeding stopped and they dropped from the doorknob. I caught one, and Gareth caught the other. "Do you want the power?" I asked.

"What?"

I cradled my aphid in both hands, and it deflated, feeding me spell power again, exquisite hate and strength, a hot syrup both burning and sweet. "Put it down if you don't want the power." My voice was hoarse as my body adjusted to this influx. I was lucky to have had a taste the day before, otherwise I could see this killing me, as poisonous as it was—or it could have killed me if I hadn't had my special protection. What if someone random touched the doorknob?

I directed the power flow into a fireproof box in my mind. I could store this power and dilute it for personal use later.

The aphid vanished into my palm again.

"It's stuck! Ouch! It burns!" Gareth tried to shake the aphid off his hand, but it clung, a gelatinous mass, and shrank. He keened, a high, mindless wail.

He didn't have the defenses to handle this. I grabbed his hands as the aphid vanished under his skin and followed floods of power along dried riverbeds inside him, places where his witch power ought to flow. I couldn't stop the rush of hot new power, but I could soften it by adding power of my own, cold power I rarely tapped. He gasped over and over, and I saw that his mother's power didn't poison him either. He had been living with the restriction spell inside him long enough to acclimate to it.

The power rushed through all his channels and reached the river's source, burst through a wall, and uncapped the spring inside. I had to let go of him then, he burned so hot.

He screamed. I covered my ears with my hands and waited it out.

Finally he collapsed, twitching, on the floor.

I went to the kitchen to get a glass of water. I wasn't sure that was the right prescription, but I figured it couldn't hurt.

When I rejoined Gareth, he sat up and took the glass from me, and my shoulders, tight as corsets, loosened. I hadn't been sure there was anything left of his mind.

"I feel sick," he whispered.

"I know." He could talk! I relaxed even more. "Do you need anything I can get you?"

"An explanation?"

I laughed, relieved he could ask. I rose and grasped the door-knob. It didn't bite this time. I turned it and pushed on the door, but the door rattled: it was locked. Mechanical protection in addition to magical. I knew a lot of unlock spells, though, and the first one I tried worked. "Let's see what we earned." I hauled Gareth to his feet. He staggered, straightened, wiped sweat from his forehead with the back of his hand.

I let go of the doorknob and stepped back, giving him the choice. He studied me, then gripped the knob and turned it.

First thing out of the room was a smell, cold and rotten, like a cave where corpses were stored. The door opened inward. Gareth pushed it and let it swing. The floor inside was painted a light-sucking, tarry black.

"God," he said. "I'm glad I never saw this before. I couldn't sleep in the same house with this again."

His mother's altar took up the whole far wall, a black freize with niches in it where tentacled god-statues lurked, some veiled with dark lace, others staring, visible and revolting. On the flat stone bench below, a large brass bowl held ashy remains of burnt things and a scattering of small charred bones. A red glass goblet was half-full of dark liquid. A scorched dagger lay between the goblet and the bowl. A carved ebony box stood on the bench, too.

One of the god-statues waved three tentacles at me. I'd had dealings with him before. For a dark god, he had a great sense of humor. I wiggle-waved back.

"Let's go," Gareth said.

"Wait. Look in there with your witch eyes. See if there's anything you need to take."

"What?"

"Look."

Along the side walls of the room—any windows had been covered over—there were shelves full of magical aids and ingredients, and a small library of hide-bound books. Gareth stepped over the threshold into the room. A shudder went through him as he stood in the heart of his mother's power. "What am I looking for?" he asked.

"Something that belongs to you."

"I've never seen any of this stuff before."

I shrugged. He examined the shelves without touching anything. I wouldn't have touched, either. Everything looked dusty or dirty, even the ingredients I recognized.

After a tour of the room, Gareth stopped at the altar. He held his hand above the dagger, the bowl, the goblet, and finally the box. He lifted the box's latch and swung the lid up. Soft light glowed from inside. "Oh," he cried. His hand hovered, then dipped in. He lifted a fist and pressed whatever he held against his breastbone. When his hand lowered, there was nothing in it, and nothing on his shirt, either. He turned toward me. His face was alive with confused excitement.

The front door slammed open. "Who are you, and what are you doing in my house?" cried Gareth's mother. She saw the open door to her secret room, and shrieked.

"I'm the girlfriend," I said.

She stalked forward, her anger growing with every step, until her shadow towered above her, filled with lightning strikes in random directions.

"How dare you open that door?" she screamed, and then, when she saw that Gareth was in the room, she went silent, which was worse than the screams, though less ear-torturing.

At last she stepped forward, muttering words that hurt my ears. She slammed her left palm into my chest, sending a power-jolt through me that would have knocked me on my ass if I hadn't just processed a lot of her power. I was still humming with stolen strength, though, and her own power inside me shielded me from the new assault. She flicked her hand toward Gareth. A bolt of blue lightning shot out, sizzled through his shirt, scorched his chest. He staggered, straightened, planted his feet, and faced her.

"Okay," he said.

She gasped.

"I got your eviction notice, Mom. I'm moving in with Terry."

"What?" She stepped toward him. She laid her hand on his chest. "You—what?" Her voice was a whisper now.

"Good-bye." He pushed past her, and her hand slid off of him.

She ran to the bench and opened the ebony box, gasped again.

By that time we had grabbed Gareth's things and were headed for the front door.

❧

Mom made cocoa in the kitchen for us after Gareth had stowed his duffle and backpack in the guest room.

"He'll be able to pay rent and utilities," I said. "I'm hiring him as my assistant, so he should make plenty of money." Too bad his mother was so short-sighted. She hadn't known what a valuable asset she had. He was mine, now. Her mistake.

"Sure, sure," said Mom.

"I better protect you, Mom. His mother's really scary. She might come after us."

"Great," Mom grumbled.

"Are you okay with me spelling you a shield against her? She almost killed us."

"Terry!" Mom reached across the table and grabbed both my hands, clutched them tight. "Don't do dangerous things! How many times do I have to tell you?"

"I had to rescue him, Mom. You would have, if you saw what it was like at his house."

She softened. She reached for Gareth's hand. He ducked her,

then stilled and endured her touch.

"All right," my mother said. "Protect me, Terry."

Strange, almost scary happiness shot through me. Mom didn't trust me with magic; she knew my track record. She was giving me a new and precious chance.

I so didn't want to mess this up.

"Open your witch eyes," I told Gareth, "and watch what I'm going to do. This isn't a spell I sell anywhere."

I conjured magical armor for my mother, and she sat still for it.

After we washed dishes and cleaned the kitchen for the night, I followed Mom into her bedroom, leaving Gareth to settle himself in his new space.

"Lots of changes," Mom said.

"Yeah. Thanks so much, Mom." I sat on the bed. "Sorry I had to spring this on you without warning."

"Do you actually like the boy, Terry?"

"I don't know yet. He's got a lot of garbage to get through before he'll be useful."

She ruffled my hair. "There's my girl. I wondered where you went, honey. You've been way too nice all day."

I laughed.

Mom went to her closet. "I suppose you want to play with the pretties." She pulled her jewelry box from behind a stack of shoe-boxes on a shelf. Not a very secret hiding place. I had warded our house against burglars, though. She could have left the box in plain sight and it would have been safe.

I opened the box, touched the charm bracelet Mom's grand-mother had left her, the pearls my father gave her on their twelfth wedding anniversary, the malachite earrings she had given to her mother, taken back after her mother died. Buried under a tangle of chains, pendants, and bracelets, some of them gifts my twin Tasha and I had given her for various birthdays and Christmases, I found my heart.

I gave Mom my heart for her forty-fifth birthday. I made it into a really ugly brooch, red enameled and gaudy, with rhinestones. It was heavy and awkward to wear. If she ever pinned it to anything, it would drag down the material.

She treasured it the way she treasured everything my twin and I ever gave her, but she never wore it, which was just as well.

I knew Mom would never break my heart the way Gareth's mother had treated his. She wouldn't use my heart as a tool to supplement her own desires. As long as I kept my heart safe and separate from my body, I could not be mortally wounded, though I could be hurt—a lot. Now that Gareth had reclaimed his heart, he would be vulnerable to kinds of assaults he had been immune to before. I could make that work for me.

I held my heart in my hand just long enough to warm it, then hid it among the rocks and metal in Mom's jewelry box. I closed the box and handed it to my mother. She tucked it away.

She kissed my cheek good night.

Doppelgangster

LAURA RESNICK

It wasn't no surprise that Skinny Vinny Vitelli got rubbed out. I mean, hey, I'd nearly whacked him myself a couple of times. So had most guys I know. Not to speak ill of the dead and all that, but he was an *irritating* bastard. Vinny could pick an argument with a plate of pasta. He could piss off the Virgin Mother. He could annoy the dead—so it wasn't exactly a big shock when he *became* one of them.

A couple of nuns taking a cigarette break found his body in an alley early one morning. He'd been done with four slugs straight to the chest. Which was a little strange, actually, because Vinny always wore the bulletproof vest he got the time he whacked that Fed.

It's not what you're thinking. It was personal, not business. Vinny caught the guy in bed with his underage daughter. The vest was lying right there on the floor, and after Vinny impulsively emptied a whole clip into the guy's torso, he decided the vest was A Sign. (Did I mention he was a pretty religious guy?) See, Vinny had always been afraid of dying exactly the way he'd just killed the Fed who'd been stupid enough to take off his bulletproof vest while humping a wise-guy's seventeen-year-old daughter right there in her father's house. (Feds. They breed 'em dumb.)

So Vinny picked the vest up off the floor, put it on, and never took it off since. I mean *never*. Just ask his wife. Well, if you can find her. She hot-tailed it straight down to Florida before the corpse was cold and ain't been seen since. She was making plans for her new life right there at Vinny's funeral, yakking on her cell phone with her real estate agent while the casket was being lowered into the ground.

"It's a funny thing," I said to Joey (the Chin) Mannino while the grieving Mrs. Vitelli kicked some dirt into her late husband's open grave with the toe of her shoe while telling her real estate agent she expected to be in Florida by nightfall.

"Huh?" Joey didn't really hear me. He was stroking his scarred chin as he stared lovesick at the Widow Butera. She was glaring back at him. A very beautiful woman, even at forty-five, but bad news for any guy.

"Give it up, Joey," I advised.

"I can't." He shook his head. "I've asked her to marry me."

I slapped my forehead. "Are you nuts?" One of the mourners frowned at me, so I lowered my voice. "She's had three husbands, and they're all dead. Don't that tell you something?"

"She's been unlucky."

"Her *husbands* have been unlucky. All three of them. So I'll lay odds that number four is gonna be real unlucky, too."

"It's not her fault, Vito."

"No, but being married to her is so unlucky it crosses over into dumb."

Her first husband got hit just because he was having dinner with Big Bobby Gambone at Buon Appetito the night Little Jackie Bernini decided to kill Bobby and didn't feel too particular about who else he sprayed with his Uzi. That was the start of the first Gambone-Bernini war. Well, a beautiful woman like that couldn't stay widowed forever. So three years later, during the second Gambone-Bernini war, she married a hit man from Las Vegas who the Gambones brought into town to teach the Berninis a lesson. But then the Berninis brought in their own hit man from Boise to deal with him, and ain't *nobody* tougher than those Boise guys. So the Widow was widowed again. Then, maybe because she was tired of marrying Gambones who got whacked out, the Widow shocked everyone by marrying Bernini Butera, who was everybody's favorite pick to head the Bernini family next . . . until Joey clipped him last year. That hit pretty much ended the third Gambone-Bernini war. But from the way the Widow Butera was glaring at Joey across Skinny Vinny Vitelli's grave now, it didn't look like she had forgiven Joey for stuffing her third husband into a cement mixer in New Jersey.

"What'd she say when you asked her to marry you?" I asked Joey.

"She told me she'd rather fry in hell." He shrugged. "She'll come 'round."

I shook my head. "Joey, Joey, Joey . . ."

He gave a friendly little wave to the Widow Butera. She hissed at him. The priest, Father Michael, smiled vaguely at her and said, "Amen."

So, to take Joey's mind off the Widow, I said, "Anyhow, like I was saying before, it's a funny thing."

"What's a funny thing?"

"About Vinny."

"No, no," Connie Vitelli was saying into her cell phone as she shook Father Michael's hand, "the condo's got to have an ocean view, or no deal. Understand?"

"Funny?" Joey said. "Oh! You mean about the vest, right?"

"Yeah." I shook my head when Father Michael gestured to me to throw some dirt onto the coffin. Hey, I didn't kill Vinny, so no way was I doing the work of deep-sixing him. Not my problem, after all. "Why'd Vinny take off that vest for the first time in five years? It ain't like him. He was a religious bastard."

"I think you mean superstitious." Joey's an educated guy. Almost read a book once.

"Okay, superstitious. Vinny always thought he'd get killed if he ever took that thing off. And, sure enough, look what happened. So why'd he take it off? It don't make sense."

"You mean you didn't hear, Vito?"

"Hear what?"

Connie was shouting into her cell phone, "Speak up! Are you driving through a tunnel or something? I'm getting tons of static!"

Vinny's daughter, now twenty-two years old and reputedly still a virgin, stepped up to the grave, made a face at her father's coffin, and then spit on it.

"Poor Vinny," said Father Michael, who looked like he'd taken a fistful of Prozac before coming here. "He will be missed."

"Not by anybody I ever met," muttered Joey.

I said to Joey, "What is it that I didn't hear?"

"Oh! The strange thing is, Vito, Vinny was still wearing his vest when they found his body."

"Huh? So how'd four slugs wind up in his chest?"

Joey shrugged. "It's a mystery. No holes in the vest. No marks at all, like it was never even hit. But as for Vinny's chest . . ." Joey grimaced.

While I thought about this, Connie Vitelli said, "But how big is the master bathroom?"

"So, Joey, you're saying that someone clipped Vinny, then put that vest back on him? For what? A joke?"

Joey shook his head. "That vest never came off him, Vito."

"Of course it did. How else did four bull—"

"The cops said the fasteners on Vinny's vest were rusted and hadn't been disturbed for years."

"Jesus. So it's true what Connie said. Vinny even *showered* in that thing!"

"Uh-huh."

I frowned at Joey. "But what you're saying . . . I mean, how did the bullets get past the vest and into Vinny's chest?"

"That's what's got the cops stumped."

"And why'd the cops tell *you* this?" Cops don't usually say nothing to guys like us besides, "I'll get you into the Witness Protection Program if you cooperate."

"I don't think they meant to tell me," Joey said. "It just sort of slipped out somewhere during the seven straight hours they spent interrogating me yesterday."

"Oh, *that's* why you weren't at the wake."

Joey nodded wearily. "I'm thinking of suing them for the emotional trauma caused by missing a dear friend's wake, as well as the stain they have placed on my good reputation."

"How come they think you're the one who whacked him?"

"Well, you know, I had that argument with Vinny last week at Buon Appetito."

"So what?"

"So it turns out there were three undercover Feds in the place at the time, and they took it the wrong way when I held a steak knife to Vinny's throat and said I'd kill him if I ever saw him again."

"Man," I said, sick at how unfair it all was. "You just have to be so careful these days. Watch every damn little word."

"Tell me about it."

"Whatever happened to the First Arraignment?" I said.

"Amendment."

"Whatever."

"I admit," Joey said, "I thought about whacking Vinny."

"Sure."

"Who didn't?"

"You said it."

"But it's not like he didn't deserve it," Joey said.

"Absolutely," I said as Vinny's son opened his fly and pissed on his father's grave.

"So I don't see why the cops have to get so bent out of shape just because someone finally *did* whack Vinny."

"Me neither."

"And just because I'm the last guy anyone saw threatening to kill him, the cops ruin my whole day. Now is that fair? Is that the American way?"

"It really stinks." I patted Joey on the back. "Just out of curiosity, *did* you kill him?"

"No. I was proposing to the Widow Butera at the estimated time of death."

"Did she alibi you to the cops?"

"No."

Women.

"So I wonder who did it?" I said.

"Could've been any one of a hundred guys," Joey said.

"More," I said.

"Yeah."

The Widow Butera stepped up to Vinny's grave and looked down at it for a long moment. Then she crossed herself, glared once more at Joey, and started walking to her car.

When Connie Vitelli got off the phone for a split second, Joey and I paid our respects so we could get the hell out of there.

"Such a shame," Joey said politely to Vinny's widow. "Him being so young and all."

"Not that young." Connie shook her head. "And I think dementia was setting in already. He was seeing things."

"Seeing things?" Joey said. "Then 'dementia' probably isn't the right word, because that's when—"

"Oops! I gotta take this," Connie said as her cell phone rang.

"Wait a minute," I said. "What things was Vinny seeing? Feds stalking him? Hitters from the Bernini family coming after him?" If we knew, we might be able to figure out who'd whacked him.

Connie rolled her eyes. "Himself, if you can believe it."

"Huh?"

"The day before Vinny died, he came home in a cold sweat, babbling about how he had just bumped into the spitting image of himself on the street outside Buon Appetito. The guy was even dressed like Vinny. Right down to the bulletproof vest. Go figure." Connie shrugged off the idea that her husband's perfect double was out there somewhere and added, "Now I've really got to take this call. Thanks for coming, fellas." She turned away and said into her cell phone, "Hello? Oh, good! Thanks for getting back to me today. Yes, I'll be out of the house by tonight, so put it on the market right away."

"So Vinny was losing his mind," I said.

Joey nodded towards Connie and the kids. "And you're surprised by this?"

"No, I guess not."

Which is why I didn't think any more about it. Not then, anyhow. Not until three days later, which was when a dinner-and-dance cruise accidentally found Johnny Be Good Gambone's body floating in the Hudson River.

"But it can't be Johnny," I said to Joey Mannino when he told me about it.

"It is. Positive ID, no doubt about it."

"No, it can't be, because—"

"Vito, pull yourself together," Joey said. "Two of our guys dead in one week. We're going to the mattresses."

"It can't be Johnny, because I saw him alive at the same time they were fishing that corpse out of the river."

"It must be the Berninis doing these hits. Who else would have the nerve? Those bastards! Well, if they want another war, we'll give them another w—"

"Joey, are you listening to me? I'm telling you, whoever they found in the Hudson, it wasn't Johnny Gambone, because I had dinner with him last night!"

Joey stared at me. "Are you losing your mind, too?"

"No! They're just putting the wrong name on the corpse."

But when we showed up at the mortician's to inspect the body, I saw there'd been no mistake. That was Johnny Gambone lying on that slab, no doubt about it. Who else in the world had a purple tattoo of a naked broad on his shoulder with the word "Mom" written across it?

"So you're not still denying that's Johnny?" Joey prodded.

"Couldn't be anyone else, but . . ."

"But?"

"But, I'm telling you, I was having dinner with him that evening. We talked about Vinny's death. Johnny told me that, no matter how much we hated Vinny, it was our job to find out who'd clipped him, because we can't just let people go around killing made guys without even asking first. Especially not *our* made guys."

"Vito, that's impossible. According to the cops, Johnny had already been dead for thirty-six hours by the time you had dinner with . . . with . . ."

"Something's not right," I said.

And whatever was not right became even more wrong a couple of days later when Danny (the Doctor) Bardozzi, best known for chopping up four members of the Gambone family and passing them off as ground ostrich meat at an East Village restaurant which went out of business soon after Danny was indicted, was found dead.

I know what you're thinking, but we didn't do it. We didn't even *know* who did it, just like we didn't know who'd clipped Johnny and Vinny. We were knee deep in bodies by now, and we had no idea who was stacking them up.

"And the *way* the Doctor was killed," Joey told me as we walked along Mott Street, "is really strange."

"You mean compared to the normal way Vinny was killed, with four bullets pumped into his chest and not a scratch on the bulletproof vest he was wearing at the time? Or the normal way Johnny Gambone was found floating in the river while I was watching him eat linguine and bitch about his indigestion?" Okay, I was feeling irritable and got a little sarcastic.

Joey said, "Listen, Danny showed up at Bernini's Wine and Guns Shop in a panic, armed with two Glocks and a lifetime supply of ammo, and locked himself in the cellar. There's no way in or out of the cellar except through the one door he'd locked, and—because Danny was acting so crazy—there were a dozen Berninis standing right by that door trying to convince him to come out."

"And?"

"Next thing they know, they hear a few shots go off. So they break down the door and run downstairs. Danny's alone. And dead." Joey grimaced. "Shotgun. Made a real mess."

"But you said he had two Glocks."

"That's right. And, no, there wasn't a shotgun down there. Not before Danny locked himself in ... and not when the Berninis found him there."

"Then it wasn't a shotgun. He blew his own head off with a Glock."

"No. His guns hadn't even been fired, and there was buckshot everywhere. Just no shotgun."

"In a locked cellar with no windows and no other door? That's impossible."

"Like it was impossible for you to be eating dinner with a guy whose two-day-old corpse was floating in the Hudson River at the time?"

"We're in trouble," I said. "We've got something going on here that's bigger than another war with the Berninis."

"That's what they think, too."

"What? You mean they ain't blaming us for Danny's death?"

"How could they? I just told you what happened. They know we're not invisible, and neither are our guns. In fact, they knew something strange was happening even before we did, because they knew they didn't kill Johnny Gambone."

"We've got to have a sitdown with the Berninis."

"I've called one for tonight. At St. Ignazio's. I gotta have dinner at my mother's in Brooklyn first, but I'll be there."

~~~

St. Ignazio's was dark and shadowy, lit only by candles. The whole place smelled of incense and lingering perfume . . . The Widow Butera's perfume, I realized, as I saw her kneeling before a statue of Saint Paula, patron saint of widows.

Father Michael and two guys from the Bernini family were waiting for me in an alcove on the other side of the church.

"Is Joey here yet?" I asked the Widow Butera.

"What do I care? What do I care about any of you fiends?" She rose to her feet and came towards me. "I hate you all! Every single one of you! I spit on you! I spit on your mothers' graves!"

"So you haven't seen him?"

She shook her fist at me. "Stay away from me!"

"Hey, I'm not the one trying to make you a widow for the fourth time. So don't yell at *me*, sister. And . . ." I frowned as wispy white things started escaping from the fist she shook at me. "Are those feathers? Whatever happened to praying with rosary beads?"

She made a really nasty Sicilian gesture and stomped towards the main door in a huff just as Joey entered the church. The poor guy's face brightened like he'd just met a famous stripper.

He asked her, "Have you thought any more about my proposal? I mean, take all the time you need, I just won—"

"Get out of my way!" she shrieked. "Don't ever come near me again! Don't even look at me!"

"Maybe we'll talk later?" Joey said to her back.

She paused to look over her shoulder at him. "Amazing," she said in a different tone of voice. Then she left.

"You're late," I said to Joey.

"Sorry. Couldn't be helped."

"Gentlemen," said Father Michael, smelling strongly of sacramental wine as he came close to us, "the Berninis are eager to begin this summit, so if you—"

"Summit?" I repeated.

"Sitdown," said Joey.

"Oh."

"So if you'll just take your seats . . ."

"You're fucking late," said Carmine Bernini. He was Danny (the Doctor) Bardozzi's cousin by marriage, and also the world's biggest asshole.

"But we haven't been waiting too long," added Tony Randazzo. He was a good-looking kid who'd been a soldier in the Bernini family for a few years. A stand-up guy, actually, and I'd let him date my daughter if I didn't think I'd probably have to kill him one day.

"Would anyone care for some chips and dip?" Father Michael asked. "Maybe some cocktails?"

"We ain't here to fucking socialize," said Carmine.

"Don't curse in church," said Joey.

"Well, please fucking excuse *me*."

Like I said—the world's biggest asshole. "Never mind the refreshments, Father," I said. "This'll just take a few minutes." I looked at Carmine. "Let's lay our cards on the table."

So we did. And what these guys told me about Danny Bardozzi's death got my full attention.

"He said *what*?"

Tony said, "Danny came into the shop that day and said he'd just seen his perfect double, his spitting image."

"His doppelgänger?" said Father Michael.

"Yeah, his doppelgangster," said Carmine. "He was fucking freaking out. In a cold sweat, shaking like a virgin in a whorehouse, babbling like a snitch with the Feds. Scared out of his mind."

"Because he'd seen this doppelgangster?" I said.

"Yeah. He said it meant he was gonna die."

"He was right," I said. "But how did he know?"

"Perhaps he knew that, traditionally," said Father Michael, "seeing your doppelgänger portends your own death."

"No shit?" said Carmine.

"No sh . . . Um, yes, really," said Father Michael.

"But we got more than people *pretending* their deaths here, Father," I said.

"No, *portending*," the priest said. "Seeing your doppelgänger is, in popular folklore, a sure sign that you're going to die."

"Weird shit," said Carmine.

"Even weirder," I said, "Danny ain't the only one around here who's seen a doppelgangster." I told them about Skinny Vinny telling Connie he'd seen his own perfect double the day before he died.

"Johnny Gambone did, too!" said Father Michael, swaying a little. "My God! I didn't realize . . ." He wiped his brow. "Just a few days before his body was found, Johnny told me after Mass that he'd seen a man who looked very much like himself, dressed the same, even bearing the same tattoo—but nowhere near as handsome."

"He always was a vain sonofabitch," said Carmine.

"So he saw his double, too, then," I said. "All three of these guys died after seeing their doubles."

"And died in such strange ways," Tony added.

"Yes," said Father Michael. "Almost as if meeting the doppelgänger doesn't just presage death, it actually curses the victim, making him utterly defenseless against death when it comes for him."

"So once you see this fucking thing, that's it?" said Carmine. "You're as good as whacked?"

"That would explain how bullets somehow got past or around Vinny's vest," I said.

"And how someone walked past all of us without being seen," said Tony, "and got through a locked door to kill Danny."

"So we're dealing with . . . what?" I said. "Witchcraft? Some kind of curse? The Evil Eye?"

"It's some weird fucking shit," said Carmine.

Father Michael fumbled behind the skirts of the shrine of the Virgin and pulled out a bottle of wine. He uncorked it, gulped some down, and then said, "Black magic. What else could it be?"

"Fucking creepy."

"And whoever is doing it is damn good," I said. "I had dinner with Johnny Gambone's doppelgangster and didn't even know it wasn't the real guy."

"But no one has seen Vinny, Johnny, and Danny since they were found dead, right?" said Father Michael. "I mean . . . no one has seen their doubles since then?"

I hadn't even thought about that. "No," I said. "That's right. The last time I saw Johnny's double—the last time anyone saw it, as far as I know—was before his body was found."

"So . . ." Father Michael took another swig. "So whoever is doing this sends a doppelgangst . . . doppelgänger after the victim to curse him with inevitable death. And then, after the victim is dead, the perfect double continues carrying on the victim's normal life until the death is discovered."

"And then what?"

"Then it . . . " Father Michael shrugged. "It probably disintegrates into whatever elemental ingredients it was originally fashioned from."

"So if you hid the fucking body well enough, it would be years before anyone even knew you'd made the hit. Hey, this black magic is some fucking great stuff! If I could learn to do it—"

"Whoever *has* learned to do it," I said, "is out to kill all of us. Get it? We've got to stop him before we're all dead!"

"Vito's right," said Joey. "We're all in danger."

My cell phone suddenly rang, making us all jump a little. (Hey, if you thought someone was about to kill you that way, wouldn't you be a little jumpy, too?) I pulled the phone out of my pocket. "Hello?"

"Vito?" said Joey at the other end. "I'm coming from my mother's, and I'm still in Brooklyn. Stuck in traffic. You'd better start the sitdown without me. I'll get there as soon as I can."

My blood ran cold as I stared at the Joey sitting here with me, absently stroking his chin the way the real one often did. Choosing my words carefully, I said, "Seen anything strange lately?"

"Huh?"

"Anyone familiar?"

"Well . . . my mother, obviously."

"No one else?"

"What are you talking about?"

"Okay, good," I said with relief. I like Joey, I'd miss him if he was the next one to die. "Listen to me very carefully. *Stay right where you are.* Call me back in an hour."

"But Vito—"

"Just do it!" I hung up.

"Who was that?" asked Joey.

I jumped him, took him to the floor, and started banging his head against the stone. "Vito!" he screamed. "Vito! *Stop!* What are you doing? *Ow!*"

"Vito!" cried Father Michael "Stop!"

"Fucking maniac," said Carmine.

"Thought you'd get Joey Mannino, did you?" I shouted at the doppelgangster. "Well, think again, you bastard!"

"This is one of them?" the priest shrieked.

"Yes!" I kept banging its head against the floor. "And it's gonna tell me who's behind these hits!"

Its eyes rolled back into its head, it convulsed a few times, and then its head shattered like dry plaster.

"Whoa!" said Tony.

I looked down at the mess. Nothing but crumbled dust, lumps of dirt, and feathers where the thing's head had been. Then its body started disintegrating, too.

"I think you whacked it, Vito," said Tony.

Father Michael poured the whole rest of the bottle of wine down his throat before he spoke. "Well . . . I guess this means that Joey is safe now?"

"Not for long," I said. "Whoever did this will make another one the moment he knows this one has been . . . Wait a minute!"

"Vito? What is it?" said Tony.

"Maybe it's not a *he*," I said.

"Huh?"

"Think about it! Who would hit the Berninis *and* the Gambones? Who hates *both* families that much? Who wants all of us dead?"

"You saying the fucking Feds are behind this?"

"No, you asshole! I'm saying the one person who hates both families equally is behind this!" I grabbed a handful of the crap that had been Joey's doppelgangster a minute ago and waved it at these guys. "*Feathers!*"

"Vito, this is a very serious accusation," said Father Michael, slurring his words a little. "Are you absolutely sure?"

"Huh?" said Tony.

"Just fucking follow him," said Carmine as I ran for the same exit that the Widow Butera had taken.

<hr />

I kicked in the door of her apartment without knocking. I'd figured out her scam by now, so I expected the feathers, the blood sacrifices, the candles, the chanting, and the photos of Bernini and Gambone family members.

I just didn't expect to see my own perfect double rising out of her magic fire like a genie coming out of a lantern. I pulled out my piece and fired at it.

"*Noooo!*" screamed the Widow Butera. She leapt at me, knocked my gun aside, and started clawing at my face.

"Kill it! Kill it!" I shouted at the others.

Carmine said, "I always wanted to do this to you, Vito," and started pumping bullets into my doppelgangster while I fought the Widow. Father Michael ran around the room praying loudly and drenching things in holy water. Tony took a baseball bat—don't ask me where he got it—and started destroying everything in sight: the amulets and charms hanging everywhere, the jars of powders and potions stacked on shelves, the cages containing live chickens, and the bottles of blood. My perfect double shattered into a million pieces in the hail of Carmine's bullets, and the pieces fell smoldering into the fire. Then Tony kicked at the fire until it was scattered all over the living room and started dying.

"It's a fucking shame about the carpet," Carmine said as chickens escaped the shattered cages and started running all over the room.

" . . . blessed are thou, and blessed is the fruit of they womb . . ." Father Michael was chanting.

"What else can I break? What else can I break?" Tony shouted.

"I'll kill you all!" the Widow screamed. "You're all dead!"

"Too late, sister, we're onto you now. You've whacked your last wiseguy," I said as she struggled in my grip.

"Three husbands I lost in your damned wars!" she screamed. "I told them to get out of organized crime and into something secure, like accounting or the restaurant business, but would they listen? *Noooo!*"

"Secure? The fucking restaurant business? Are you kidding me?"

"The Berninis and Gambones ruined my life!" The Widow Butera shrieked. "I will have vengeance on you all!"

"Repent! Repent!" Father Michael cried. Then he doused her with a whole bottle of holy water.

"*Eeeeeeeeeee!*" She screamed something awful . . . and then started smoking like she was on fire.

I'm not dumb. I let go of her and backed away.

The room filled with smoke and the Widow's screams got louder, until they echoed so hard they made my teeth hurt ... then faded. There was a dark scorch mark on the floor where she'd been standing.

"Where'd she go?" I said.

"She'll never get her fucking security deposit back now," said Carmine, looking at the floor.

Tony added, "No amount of buffing will get that out."

"What the hell happened?" I said, looking around the room. The Widow had vanished.

Father Michael fell to his knees and crossed himself. "I don't think she was completely human. At least, not anymore. She had become Satan's minion."

"Huh. I wondered how she kept her good looks for so fucking long."

"That's it?" I asked Father Michael. "She's just ... gone?"

He nodded. "In hell, where she belongs." After a moment, he added, "Mind you, that's only a theory."

"Either way," I said, "I'm kinda relieved. I know we couldn't just let her go. Not after she'd hit three guys and tried to hit me and Joey, too. But I really didn't want to whack a broad."

"What a fucking pussy you are, Vito."

"Carmine, you asshole," I said, "the sitdown was successful. We found out who's behind these hits, we put a stop to it, and there ain't gonna be no new war. So now get outta my sight before I forget my manners and whack you just for the hell of it."

"Did I mention how much fun it was pumping a whole clip into your fucking doppelgangster?"

My cell phone rang, making Father Michael jump.

"Damn." I knew who it was even before I answered it. "Hello?"

"Vito," said Joey, "I've been sitting here in my car, not going anywhere, just like you said, for a whole hour. Now do you want to tell me what the hell is going on?"

I looked at the scorched spot the Widow had left in the floor and tried to think of the best way to break the news to him. "So, Joey . . . would you still want to marry the Widow Butera if you knew she'd been trying to whack you and everyone you know?"

The Necromancer's Apprentice

LILLIAN STEWART CARL

Robert Dudley, Master of the Queen's Horses, was a fine figure of a man, as long of limb and imperious of eye as one of his equine charges. And like one of his charges, his wrath was likely to leave an innocent passerby with a shattered skull.

Dudley reached the end of the gallery, turned, and stamped back again, the rich fabrics of his clothing rustling an accompaniment to the thump of his boots. Erasmus Pilbeam shrank into the window recess. But he was no longer an innocent passerby, not now that Lord Robert had summoned him.

"You beetle-headed varlet!" his lordship exclaimed. "What do you mean he cannot be recalled?"

Soft answers turn away wrath, Pilbeam reminded himself. "Dr. Dee is perhaps in Louvain, perhaps in Prague, researching the wisdom of the ancients. The difficulty lies not only in discovering his whereabouts, but also in convincing him to return to England."

"He is my old tutor. He would return at my request." Again Lord Robert marched away down the gallery, the floor creaking a protest at each step. "The greatness and suddenness of this misfortune so perplexes me that I shall take no rest until the truth is known."

"The inquest declared your lady wife's death an accident, my lord. At the exact hour she was found deceased in Oxfordshire, you were waiting upon the Queen at Windsor. You could have had no hand . . ."

"Fact has never deterred malicious gossip. Why, I have now been accused of bribing the jurors. God's teeth! I cannot let this evil slander rest upon my head. The Queen has sent me from the court on the strength of it!" Robert dashed his fist against the padded back of a chair, raising a small cloud of dust, tenuous as a ghost.

A young princess like Elizabeth could not be too careful what familiar demonstrations she made. And yet, this last year and a half, Lord Robert had come so much into her favor it was said that her Majesty visited him in his chamber day and night . . . No, Pilbeam assured himself, that rumor was noised about only by those who were in the employ of Spain. And he did not for one moment believe that the Queen herself had ordered the disposal of Amy Robsart, no matter how many wagging tongues said that she had done so. Still, Lord Robert could hardly be surprised that the malicious world now gossiped about Amy's death, when he had so neglected her life.

"I must find proof that my wife's death was either chance or evil design on the part of my enemies. The Queen's enemies."

Or, Pilbeam told himself, Amy's death might have been caused by someone who fancied himself the Queen's friend.

Lord Robert stalked back up the gallery and scrutinized Pilbeam's black robes and close-fitting cap. "You have studied with Dr. Dee. You are keeping his books safe whilst he pursues his researches in heretical lands."

"Yes, my lord."

"How well have you learned your lessons, I wonder?"

The look in Lord Robert's eye, compounded of shrewd calculation and ruthless pride, made Pilbeam's heart sink. "He has taught me how to heal illness. How to read the stars. The rudiments of the alchemical sciences."

"Did he also teach you how to call and converse with spirits?"

"He—ah—mentioned to me that such conversation is possible."

"Tell me more."

"Formerly it was held that apparitions must be spirits from purgatory, but now that we know purgatory to be only papist myth, it must be that apparitions are demonic, angelic, or illusory. The devil may deceive man into thinking he sees ghosts or . . ." Pilbeam gulped. The bile in his throat tasted of the burning flesh of witches.

"An illusion or deception will not serve me at all. Be she demon or angel, it is Amy herself who is my best witness."

"My—my—my lord . . ."

Robert's voice softened, velvet covering his iron fist. "I shall place my special trust in you, Dr. Pilbeam. You will employ all the devices and means you can possibly use for learning the truth. Do you understand me?"

Only too well. Pilbeam groped for an out. "My lord, whilst the laws regarding the practice of magic are a bit uncertain just now, still Dr. Dee himself, as pious a cleric as he may be, has been suspected of fraternizing with evil spirits . . . my lord Robert, if you intend such a, er, perilous course of action as, well, necromancy . . . ah, may I recommend either Edward Cosyn or John Prestall, who are well known in the city of London."

"Ill-nurtured cozeners, the both of them! Their loyalty is suspect, their motives impure. No. If I cannot have Dr. Dee I will have his apprentice."

For a moment Pilbeam considered a sudden change in profession. His beard was still brown, his step firm—he could apprentice himself to a cobbler or a baker and make an honest living without dabbling in the affairs of noblemen, who were more capricious than any spirit. He made one more attempt to save himself. "I am honored, my lord. But I doubt that it is within my powers to raise your . . . er, speak with your wife's shade."

"Then consult Dr. Dee's books, you malmsey-nosed knave, and follow their instructions."

"But, but . . . there is the possibility, my lord, that her death was neither chance nor villainy but caused by disease . . ."

"Nonsense. I was her husband. If she had been ill, I'd have known."

Not when you were not there to be informed, Pilbeam answered silently. Aloud he said, "Perhaps, then, she was ill in her senses, driven to, to . . ."

" . . . to self-murder? Think, varlet! A fall down the stairs could no more be relied upon by a suicide than by a murderer. She was found at the foot of the staircase, her neck broken but her headdress still secure upon her head. That is hardly a scene of violence."

Pilbeam found it furtively comforting that Lord Robert wanted to protect his wife's reputation from hints of suicide . . . . Well, her reputation was his as well. The sacrifice of a humble practitioner of the magical sciences, now—that would matter nothing to him. Pilbeam imagined his lordship's face amongst those watching the mounting flames, a face contemptuous of his failure.

"Have no fear, Dr. Pilbeam, I shall reward you well for services rendered." Lord Robert spun about and walked away. "Amy was buried at St. Mary's, Oxford. Give her my respects."

Pilbeam opened his mouth, shut it, swallowed, and managed a weak, "Yes, my lord," which bounced unheeded from Robert's departing back.

⁓◦⌣⁓

The spire of St. Mary's, Oxford, rose into the nighttime murk like a admonitory finger pointing to heaven. Pilbeam had no quarrel with that admonition. He hoped its author would find no quarrel with his present endeavor.

He withdrew into the dark, fetid alley and willed his stomach to stop grumbling. He'd followed Dr. Dee's instructions explicitly, preparing himself with abstinence, continence, and prayer made all the more fervid for the peril in which he found himself. And surely the journey on the muddy November roads had sufficiently mortified his flesh. He was ready to summon spirits, be they demons or angels.

The black lump beside him was no demon. Martin Molesworth, his apprentice, held the lantern and the bag of implements. Pilbeam heard no stomach rumblings from the lad, but he could enforce Dr. Dee's directions only so far as his own admonitory fist could reach. "Come along," he whispered. "Step lively."

Man and boy scurried across the street and gained the porch of the church. The door squealed open and thudded shut behind them. "Light," ordered Pilbeam.

Martin slid aside the shutter concealing the candle and lifted the lantern. Its hot-metal tang dispelled the usual odors of a sanctified site—incense, mildew, and decaying mortality. Pilbeam pushed Martin toward the chancel. Their steps echoed, drawing uneasy shiftings and mutterings from amongst the roof beams. Bats or swallows, Pilbeam hoped.

Amy Robsart had been buried with such pomp, circumstance, and controversy that only a few well-placed questions had established her exact resting place. Now Pilbeam contemplated the flagstones laid close together behind the altar of the church and extended his hand for his bag.

Martin was gazing upward, to where the columns met overhead in a thicket of stone tracery, his mouth hanging open. "You mewling knotty-pated scullion!" Pilbeam hissed, and snatched the bag from his limp hands. "Pay attention!

"Yes, Master." Martin held the lantern whilst Pilbeam arranged the charms, the herbs, and the candles he dare not light. With a bit of charcoal he drew a circle with four divisions and four crosses. Then, his tongue clamped securely between his teeth, he opened the book he'd dared bring from Dr. Dee's collection, and began to sketch the incantatory words and signs.

If he interpreted Dee's writings correctly—the man set no examples in penmanship—Pilbeam did not need to raise Amy's physical remains. A full necromantic apparition was summoned for consultation about the future, when what he wished was to consult about the past. Surely this would not be as difficult a task. "*Laudetur Deus Trinus et unus,*" he muttered, "*nunc et in sempiterna seculorum secula . . . .*"

Martin shifted and a drop of hot wax fell onto Pilbeam's wrist. "Beslubbering gudgeon!"

"Sorry, Master."

Squinting in the dim light, Pilbeam wiped away one of his drawings with the hem of his robe and tried again. *There.* For a moment he gazed appreciatively at his handiwork, then took a deep breath. His stomach gurgled.

Pilbeam dragged the lad into the center of the circle and jerked his arm upwards, so the lantern would illuminate the page of his book. He raised his magical rod and began to speak the words of the ritual. "I conjure thee by the authority of God Almighty, by the virtue of heaven and the stars, by the virtue of the angels, by that of the elements. *Domine, Deus meus, in te speravi. Damahil, Pancia, Mitraton . . .*"

He was surprised and gratified to see a sparkling mist began to stream upwards from between the flat stones just outside the circle. Encouraged, he spoke the words even faster.

" . . . to receive such virtue herein that we may obtain by thee the perfect issue of all our desires, without evil, without deception, by God, the creator of the sun and the angels. *Lamineck. Caldulech. Abracadabra.*"

The mist wavered. A woman's voice sighed, desolate.

"Amy Robsart, Lady Robert Dudley, I conjure thee."

Martin's eyes bulged and the lantern swung in his hand, making the shadows of column and choir stall surge sickeningly back and forth. "Master . . ."

"Shut your mouth, hedge-pig!" Pilbeam ordered. "Amy Robsart, I conjure thee. I beseech thee for God his sake, *et per viscera misericordiae Altissimi*, that thou wouldst declare unto us *misericordiae Dei sint super nos.*"

"Amen," said Martin helpfully. His voice leaped upward an octave.

The mist swirled and solidified into the figure of a woman. Even in the dim light of the lantern Pilbeam could see every detail of the revenant's dress, the puffed sleeves, the stiffened stomacher, the embroidered slippers. The angled wings of her headdress framed a thin, pale face, its dark eyes too big, its mouth too small, as though Amy Robsart had spent her short life observing many things but fearing to speak of them. A fragile voice issued from those ashen lips. "Ah, woe. Woe."

Pilbeam's heart was pounding. Every nerve strained toward the doors of the church and through the walls to the street outside. "Tell me what happened during your last hours on earth, Lady Robert."

"My last hours?" She dissolved and solidified again, wringing her frail hands. "I fell. I was walking down the stairs and I fell."

"Why did you fall, my lady?"

"I was weak. I must have stumbled."

"Did someone push you?" Martin asked, and received the end of Pilbeam's rod in his ribs.

Amy's voice wavered like a set of ill-tempered bagpipes. "I walked doubled over in pain. The stairs are narrow. I fell."

"Pain? You were ill?"

"A spear through my heart and my head so heavy I could barely hold it erect . . . ."

A light flashed in the window, accompanied by a clash of weaponry. The night watch. Had someone seen the glow from the solitary lantern? Perhaps the watchmen were simply making their rounds and contemplating the virtues of bread and ale. Perhaps they were searching for miscreants.

With one convulsive jerk of his scrawny limbs, Martin scooped the herbs, the charms, the candles, even the mite of charcoal back into the bag. He seized the book and cast it after the other items. Pilbeam had never seen him move with such speed and economy of action. "Stop," he whispered urgently, "Give me the book, I have to . . . ."

Martin was already wiping away the charcoaled marks. Pilbeam brought his rod down on the lad's arm, but it was too late. The circle was broken. A sickly-sweet breath of putrefaction made the candle gutter. The woman-shape, the ghost, the revenant, ripped itself into pennons of color and shadow. With an anguished moan those tatters of humanity streamed across the chancel and disappeared down the nave of the church.

Pulling on the convenient handle of Martin's ear, Pilbeam dragged the lad across the chancel. His hoarse whisper repeated a profane: "Earth-vexing dewberry, spongy rump-fed skainsmate, misbegotten tickle-brained whey-faced whoreson, you prevented me from laying the ghost back in its grave!"

"Sorry, Master, ow, ow . . . ."

The necromancer and his apprentice fled through the door of the sacristy and into the black alleys of Oxford.

Cumnor Place belonged not to Lord Robert Dudley but to one of his cronies. If Pilbeam ever wished to render his own wife out of sight and therefore out of mind, an isolated country house such as Cumnor, with its air of respectable disintegration, would serve very well. Save that his own wife's wrath ran a close second to Lord Robert's.

What a shame that Amy Robsart's meek spirit had proved to be of only middling assistance to Lord Robert's—and therefore Pilbeam's—quest. No, no hired bravo had broken Amy's neck and arranged her body at the foot of the stairs. Nor had she hurled herself down those same stairs in a paroxysm of despair. Her death might indeed have been an accident.

But how could he prove such a subtle accident? And worse, how could he report such ambiguous findings to Lord Robert? Of only one thing was Pilbeam certain: he was not going to inform his lordship that his wife's ghost had been freed from its corporeal wrappings and carelessly not put back again.

Shooting a malevolent glare at Martin, Pilbeam led the way into the courtyard of the house. Rain streaked the stones and timber of the facade. Windows turned a blind eye to the chill gray afternoon. The odors of smoke and offal hung in the air.

A door opened, revealing a plump, pigeon-like woman wearing the simple garb of a servant. She greeted the visitors with, "What do you want?"

"Good afternoon, Mistress. I am Dr. Erasmus Pilbeam, acting for Lord Robert Dudley." He offered her a bow that was polite but not deferential.

The woman's suspicion eased into resignation. "Then come through, and warm yourselves by the fire. I am Mrs. Odingsells, the housekeeper."

"Thank you."

Within moments Pilbeam found himself seated in the kitchen, slurping hot cabbage soup and strong ale. Martin crouched in the rushes at his feet, gnawing on a crust of bread. On the opposite side of the fireplace a young woman mended a lady's shift, her narrow face shadowed by her cap.

Mrs. Odingsells answered Pilbeam's question. "Yes, Lady Robert was in perfect health, if pale and worn, up until several days before she died. Then she turned sickly and peevish. Why, even Lettice there, her maid, could do nothing for her. Or with her, come to that."

Pilbeam looked over at the young woman and met a glance sharp as the needle she wielded.

The housekeeper went on, "The day she died her ladyship sent the servants away to Abingdon Fair. I refused to go. It was a Sunday, no day for a gentlewoman to be out and about, sunshine or no."

"She sent everyone away?" Pilbeam repeated. "If she were ill, surely she would have needed an attendant."

"Ill? Ill-used, I should say . . . ." Remembering discretion, Mrs. Odingsells contented herself with, "If she sent the servants away, it was because she tired of their constantly offering food she would not eat and employments she had no wish to pursue. Why, I myself heard her praying to God to deliver her from desperation, not long before I heard her fall."

"She was desperate from illness? Or because her husband's . . . duties were elsewhere?"

"Desperate from her childlessness, perhaps, which would follow naturally upon Lord Robert's absence."

So then, Amy's spear through the heart was a symbolic one, the pain of a woman spurned. "Her ladyship was of a strange mind the day she died, it seems. Do you think she died by chance? Or by villainy, her own or someone else's?"

Again Pilbeam caught the icy stab of Lettice's eyes.

"She was a virtuous God-fearing gentlewoman, and alone when she fell," Mrs. Odingsells returned indignantly, as though that were answer enough.

It was not enough, however. If not for the testimony of Amy herself, Pilbeam would be thinking once again of self-murder. But then, his lordship himself had said, *a fall down the stairs could no more be relied upon by a suicide than by a murderer.*

The housekeeper bent over the pot of fragrant soup. Pilbeam asked, "Could I see the exact staircase? Perhaps Lettice can show me, as your attention is upon your work."

"Lettice," Mrs. Odingsells said, with a jerk of her head. "See to it."

Silently the maid put down her mending and started toward the door. Pilbeam swallowed the last of his soup and followed her. He did not realize Martin was following him until he stopped beside the fatal staircase and the lad walked into his rump. Pilbeam brushed him aside. "She was found here?"

"Yes, master, so she was." Now Lettice's eyes were roaming up and down and sideways, avoiding his. "See how narrow the stair is, winding and worn at the turn. In the darkness . . ."

"Darkness? Did she not die on a fair September afternoon?"

"Yes, yes, but the house is in shadow. And her ladyship was of a strange mind that day, you said yourself, Master."

Behind Pilbeam, Martin muttered beneath his breath, "The lady was possessed, if you ask me."

"No one is asking you, clotpole," Pilbeam told him.

Lettice spun around. "Possessed? Why would you say such a thing? How . . . What is that?"

"What?" Pilbeam followed the direction of her eyes. The direction of her entire body, which strained upward stiff as a hound at point.

The ghost of Amy Robsart descended the steps, skirts rustling, dark eyes downcast, doubled in pain. Her frail hands were clasped to her breast. Her voice said, "Ah, woe. Woe." And suddenly she collapsed, sliding down the last two steps to lie crumpled on the floor at Pilbeam's feet, her headdress not at all disarranged.

With great presence of mind, Pilbeam reached right and left, seizing Martin's ear as he turned to flee and Lettice's arm as she swooned. "Blimey," said Martin, with feeling.

Lettice was trembling, her breath coming in gasps. "I did not know what they intended, as God is my witness, I did not know . . . ."

The revenant dissolved and was gone. Pilbeam released Martin and turned his attention to Lettice. Her eyes were now dull as lead. "What have you done, girl?"

"They gave me two angels. Two gold coins."

"Who?"

"Two men. I do not know their names. They stopped me in the village, they gave me a parcel and bade me bring it here."

"A parcel for her ladyship?"

"Not for anyone. They told me to hide it in the house was all."

Pilbeam's heart started to sink. Then, as the full import of Lettice's words blossomed in his mind, it reversed course and bounded upwards in a leap of relief. "Show me this parcel, you fool-born giglet. Make haste!"

Lettice walked, her steps heavy, several paces down the hallway. There she knelt and shoved at a bit of paneling so worm-gnawed it looked like lace. It opened like a cupboard door. From the dark hole behind it she withdrew a parcel wrapped in paper and tied with twine.

Pilbeam snatched it up and carried it to the nearest windowsill. "Watch her," he ordered Martin.

Martin said, "Do not move, you ruttish flax-wench."

Lettice remained on her knees, bowed beneath the magnitude of her defeat, and made no attempt to flee.

Pilbeam eased the twine from the parcel and unwrapped the

paper. It was fine parchment overwritten with spells and signs. Beneath the paper a length of silk enshrouded something long and hard . . . Martin leaned so close that he almost got Pilbeam's elbow in his eye. Pilbeam shoved him aside.

Inside the silk lay a wax doll, dressed in a fine gown with puffed sleeves and starched stomacher, a small headdress upon its tiny head. But this was no child's toy. A long needle passed through its breast and exited from its back—Pilbeam's fingertips darted away from the sharp point. The doll's neck was encircled by a crimson thread, wound so tightly that it had almost cut off the head. A scrap of paper tucked into the doll's bodice read: *Amy.*

Again Pilbeam could hear the revenant's voice: *A spear through my heart and my head so heavy I could barely hold it erect.* So the spear thrust through her chest had been both literal and symbolic. And Amy's neck had been so weakened it needed only the slightest jolt to break it, such as a misstep on a staircase. A misstep easily made by the most healthy of persons, let alone a woman rendered infirm by forces both physical and emotional.

It was much too late to say the incantations that would negate the death-spell. Swiftly Pilbeam re-wrapped the parcel. "Run to the kitchen and fetch Mrs. Odingsells," he ordered Martin, and Martin ran.

Lettice's bleak eyes spilled tears down her sunken cheeks. "How can I redeem myself?"

"By identifying the two men who gave you this cursed object."

"I do not know their names, master. I heard one call the other by the name of 'Ned' is all."

"Ned? If these men have knowledge of the magical sciences I should know . . . ." She did not need to know his own occupation. "Describe them to me."

"One was tall and strong, his black hair and beard wild as a bear's. The other was small, with a nose like an axeblade. He was the one named Ned."

Well then! Pilbeam did know them. They were not his colleagues but his competitors, Edward Cosyn, called Ned, and John Prestall. As Lord Robert had said, they were ill-nurtured cozeners, their loyalty suspect and their motives impure.

Perhaps his lordship had himself bought the services of Prestall and Cosyn. If so, would he have admitted that he knew who they were? No. If he had brought about his wife's death, he would have hidden his motives behind sorrow and grief rather than openly revealing his self-interest and self-regard . . . . *God be praised*, thought Pilbeam, he had an answer for Lord Robert. He had found someone for his lordship to blame.

At a step in the hall Pilbeam and Lettice looked around. But the step was not that of the apprentice or the housekeeper. Amy Robsart walked down the hallway, head drooping, shoulders bowed, wringing her hands.

Lettice squeaked in terror and shrank against Pilbeam's chest.

With a sigh of cold, dank air, the ghost passed through them and went on its way down the hallway, leaving behind the soft thump of footsteps and the fragile voice wailing, "Ah woe. Woe."

⁓

Pilbeam adjusted his robes and his cap. Beside him Martin tugged at his collar. Pilbeam jabbed the lad with his elbow and hissed, "Stand up straight, you lumpish ratsbane . . ."

"Quiet, you fly-bitten foot-licker," Lord Robert ordered.

Heralds threw open the doors. Her Majesty the Queen strode into the chamber, a vision in brocade, lace, and jewels. But her garments seemed like so many rags beside the glorious sunrise glow of her fair skin and her russet hair.

Lord Robert went gracefully down upon one knee, his upturned face filled with the adoration of a papist for a saint. Pilbeam dropped like a sack of grain, jerking Martin down as he went. The lad almost fumbled the pillow he carried, but his quick grab prevented the witching-doll from falling off the pillow and onto the floor.

The Queen's amber eyes crinkled at the corners, but her scarlet lips did not smile. "Robin, you roguish folly-fallen lewdster," she said to Lord Robert, her voice melodious but not lacking an edge. "Why have you pleaded to wait upon us this morning?"

"My agent, Dr. Pilbeam, who is apprenticed to your favorite, Dr. Dee, has discovered the truth behind my wife's unfortunate death."

Robert did not say "untimely death," Pilbeam noted. Then her Majesty turned her eyes upon him, and his thoughts melted like a wax candle in their heat.

"Dr. Pilbeam," she said. "Explain."

He spoke to the broad planks of the floor, repeating the lines he had rehearsed before his lordship: Cumnor Place, the maidservant overcome by her guilt, the death-spell quickened by the doll, and behind it all the clumsy but devious hands of Prestall and Cosyn. No revenant figured in the tale, and certainly no magic circle in St. Mary's, Oxford.

On cue, Martin extended the pillow. Lord Robert offered it to the Queen. With a crook of her forefinger, she summoned a lady-in-waiting, who carried both pillow and doll away. "Burn it," Elizabeth directed. And to her other attendants, "Leave us." With a double thud the doors shut.

Her Majesty flicked her pomander, bathing the men and the boy with the odor of violets and roses, as though she were a bishop dispensing the holy water of absolution. "You may stand."

Lord Robert rose as elegantly as he had knelt. With an undignified stagger, Pilbeam followed. Martin lurched into his side and Pilbeam batted him away.

"Where are these evildoers now?" asked the Queen.

"The maidservant is in Oxford gaol, your Majesty," Robert replied, "and the malicious cozeners in the Tower."

"And yet it seems as though this maid was merely foolish, not wicked, ill-used by men who tempted her with gold. You must surely have asked yourself, Robin, who in turn tempted these men."

"Someone who wished to destroy your trust in me, your Majesty. To drive me from your presence. My enemy, and yours as well."

"Do you think so? What do you think, Dr. Pilbeam?"

What he truly thought, Pilbeam dared not say. That perhaps Amy's death was caused by someone who intended to play the Queen's friend. Someone who wished Amy Robsart's death to deliver Lord Robert Dudley to Elizabeth's marriage bed, so that there she might engender heirs.

Whilst some found Robert's bloodline tainted, his father and grandfather both executed as traitors, still the Queen could do much worse in choosing her consort. One could say of Robert what was said of the Queen herself upon her accession, that he was of no mingled or Spanish blood but was born English here in England. Even if he was proud as a Spaniard . . . .

Pilbeam looked into the Queen's eyes, jewels faceted with a canny intelligence. *Spain*, he thought. The deadly enemy of Elizabeth and protestant England. The Spanish were infamous for their subtle plots.

"B-b-begging your pardon, your Majesty," he stammered, "but I think his lordship is correct in one regard. His wife was murdered by your enemies. But they did not intend to drive him from your presence, not at all."

Robert's glance at Pilbeam was not encouraging. Martin took a step back. But Pilbeam barely noticed, spellbound as he was by the Queen. "Ambassador Feria, who was lately recalled to Spain. Did he not frequently comment to his master, King Philip, on your, ah, attachment to Lord Robert?"

Elizabeth nodded, one corner of her mouth tightening. She did not insult Pilbeam by pretending there had been no gossip about her attachment, just as she would not pretend she had no spies in the ambassador's household. "He had the impudence to write six months ago that Lady Robert had a malady in one of her breasts and that I was only waiting for her to die to marry."

His lordship winced but had the wisdom to keep his own counsel.

"Yes, your Majesty," said Pilbeam. "But how did Feria not only know of Lady Robert's illness but of its exact nature, long before the disease began to manifest itself? Her own housekeeper says she began to suffer only a few days before she died. Did Feria himself set two cozeners known for their, er, mutable loyalties to inflict such a condition upon her?"

"Feria was recently withdrawn and replaced by Bishop de Quadra," murmured the Queen. "Perhaps he overstepped himself with his plot. Or perhaps he retired to Spain in triumph at its—no, not at its conclusion. For it has yet to be concluded."

Lord Robert could contain himself no longer. "But your Majesty, this hasty-witted pillock speaks nonsense, why should Philip of Spain . . ."

" . . . wish for me to marry you? He intended no compliment to you, I am sure of that." Elizabeth smiled, a smile more fierce than humorous, and for just a moment Pilbeam was reminded of her father, King Henry.

Robert's handsome face lit with the answer to the puzzle. "If your Majesty marries an Englishman, she could not ally herself with a foreign power such as France against Spain."

True enough, thought Pilbeam. But more importantly, if Elizabeth married Robert then she would give weight to the rumors of murder, and might even be considered his accomplice in that crime. She had reigned for only two years, her rule was far from secure. Marrying Lord Robert might give the discontented among her subjects more ammunition for their misbegotten cause, and further Philip's plots.

Whilst Robert chose to ignore those facts, Pilbeam would wager everything he owned that her Majesty did not. His lordship's ambition might have outpaced his love for his wife. His love for Elizabeth had certainly done so. No, Robert Dudley had not killed his wife. Not intentionally.

The Queen stroked his cheek, the coronation ring upon her finger glinting against his beard. "The problem, sweet Robin, is that I am already married to a husband, namely, the Kingdom of England."

Robert had no choice but to acknowledge that. He bowed.

"Have the maidservant released," Elizabeth commanded. "Allow the cozeners to go free. Let the matter rest, and in time it will die for lack of nourishment. And then Philip and his toadies will not only be deprived of their conclusion, they will always wonder how much we knew of their plotting, and how we knew it."

"Yes, your Majesty," said Lord Robert. "May I then return to court?"

"In the course of time." She dropped her hand from his cheek.

He would never have his conclusion, either, thought Pilbeam. Elizabeth would like everyone to be in love with her, but she would never be in love with anyone enough to marry him. For then she would have to bow her head to her husband's will, and that she would never do.

Pilbeam backed away. For once he did not collide with Martin, who, he saw with a glance from the corner of his eye, was several paces away and sidling crab-wise toward the door.

Again the Queen turned the full force of her eyes upon Pilbeam, stopping him in his steps. "Dr. Pilbeam, we hear that the ghost of Lady Robert Dudley has been seen walking in Cumnor Park."

"Ah, ah . . . ." Pilbeam felt rather than saw Martin's shudder of terror. But they would never have discovered the truth without the revenant. No, he would not condemn Martin, not when his carelessness had proved a blessing in disguise.

Lord Robert's gaze burned the side of his face, a warning that matters of necromancy were much better left hidden. "Her ghost?" he demanded. "Walking in Cumnor Park?"

Pilbeam said, "Er—ah—m any tales tell of ghosts rising from their graves, your Majesty, compelled by matters left unconcluded at death. Perhaps Lady Robert is seeking justice, perhaps bewailing her fate. In the course time, some compassionate clergyman will see her at last to rest." *Not I*, he added firmly to himself.

Elizabeth's smile glinted with wry humor. "Is that how it is?"

She would not insult Pilbeam by pretending that she had no spies in Oxfordshire as well, and that very little failed to reach her ears and eyes. And yet the matter of the revenant, too, she would let die for lack of nourishment. She was not only fair in appearance, but also in her expectations. He made her a bow that was more of a genuflection.

She made an airy wave of her hand. "You may go now, all of you. And Dr. Pilbeam, Lord Robert will be giving you the purse that dangles at his belt, in repayment of his debt to you."

"Yes, your Majesty." His lordship backed reluctantly away.

What an interesting study in alchemy, thought Pilbeam, *that with the Queen the base metal of his lordship's manner was transmuted to gold.* "Your Majesty. My Lord." Pilbeam reversed himself across the floor and out the door, which Martin contrived to open behind his back. Lord Robert followed close upon their heels, his boots stepping as lightly and briskly as the hooves of a thoroughbred.

A few moments later Pilbeam stood in the street, an inspiringly heavy purse in his hand, allowing himself a sigh of relief—ah, the free air was sweet, all was well that ended well . . . . Martin stepped into a puddle, splashing the rank brew of rainwater and sewage onto the hem of Pilbeam's robe.

Pilbeam availed himself yet again of Martin's convenient handle. "You rank pottle-deep measle! You rude-growing toad!" he exclaimed, and guided the lad down the street toward the warmth and peace of home.

The Night of Their Lives

MAX ALLAN COLLINS

I spent the first week in the shantytown near the Thirty-first Street Bridge, nestled in Slaughter's Run. The Run was a non-sequitur in the city, a sooty, barren gully just northeast of downtown. For local merchants it was a festering eyesore—particularly the ramshackle Hoovervilles clustered here and there, mostly near the several bridges that allowed civilization passage over this sunken stretch of wilderness.

For men—and women—down on their luck, as so many were in these hard times, the Run was a godsend. Smack dab in the middle of the city, here were wide open spaces where you could hunt wild game—pigeons, squirrels, wild dogs, and the delicacy of the day: Hoover hog, also known as jackrabbit.

In the Thirty-first Street Jungle, a world of corrugated metal and tar paper and tin cans, I met "former" every-things: college professor, stock broker, haberdasher, and lots of steel mill workers, laid off in this "goddamn Depression." I don't know that I ever heard the latter word without the former attached.

Saddest to me were the families—particularly the women who were alone, their husbands having hopped the rails leaving them to raise a passel of dirty-faced, tattered kids. A ragamuffin-laden woman, even an attractive one, was unlikely to find a mate in this packing-crate purgatory.

Since Thursday of last week I'd been wandering the streets near the Central Market, where hobos haunted the rubbish bins. The weather was pleasant enough: a cool late April with occasional showers and lots of sunshine. I hadn't shaved the whole time; I wore a denim work shirt, brown raggedy cotton trousers, and shoes with holes in the soles covered by cardboard insteps. My "home" was a discarded packing crate in an alley off Freemont Avenue, behind a warehouse, in the heart of the city's skid row district.

When I talked the chief into letting me take this undercover assignment, he'd suggested I take my .38 Police Special along. I said no. All I'd need was a few personal items, in my canvas kit bag. I never went anywhere without my kit bag.

"It's a good idea," the chief had said. He was a heavyset, bald, grizzled man who spoke around an ever-present stogie, frozen permanently in the left corner of his mouth. "As just another hobo, you can gain some trust … we can't get this riff-raff to cooperate, when we haul 'em in on rousts. But they might talk to another bum."

"That's the theory," I said, nodding.

Of course, if I told the chief my *real* theory, he'd have fitted me for a suit that buttoned up the back—you know the kind: where you can't scratch yourself because your arms are strapped in?

It had been three weeks since the last body had been found. The total was at eleven—always men, dismembered "with surgical precision," whose limbs turned up here and there, washed up on a riverbank, floating in a sewage drainage pool, wrapped in newspaper in an alley, scattered in the weeds of the Run itself. Several heads were missing. So was damn near every drop of blood from each victim's jigsaw-puzzle corpse.

Because the butcher's prey was the faceless, homeless rabble washed up on the shores of this Depression, it took a long time for the city to give a damn. But the Slaughter Run Butcher was approaching an even dozen now, and that was enough to interest not just the police, but the press and the public.

The mission at Fourth and Freemont was always crowded—unlike a lot of soup kitchens, they didn't require you to pay for your supper by sitting through a hell-and-damnation sermon. In fact, I never saw anybody seated in the pews of the little chapel room off the dining hall, although occasionally you saw somebody sleeping it off in there; the minister was a mousy guy with white hair and a thin black mustache. He didn't seem to do much beside mill around, touching bums on the shoulder, saying, "Bless you my son."

The person who really seemed to be in charge was this dark-haired society dame—Rebecca Radclau. If the gossip columns were correct, Miss Radclau was funding the Fourth Street Mission. Though schooled in America, she was said to be of European blood—her late father was royalty, a count it was rumored—and the family fortune was made in munitions.

Or so the society sob sisters said. They also followed the movie-star lovely Miss Radclau to various social functions—balls, ballet, theater, opera, particularly fund-raisers for the local Relief Association. She was the queen of local night life, on the weekends.

But on weeknights, this socially conscious socialite spent her time dressed in a gray nurse's-type uniform with a white apron, her long black hair up in a bun, standing behind the table ladling bowls of soup for the unfortunate faceless men who paraded before her.

Even in the dowdy, matronly attire, she was a knockout. The soup was good—tomato and rice, delicately spiced—but her slender, top-heavy shape, and her delicate, catlike features, were the draw. Men would hold out their soup bowls and stare at her pale face, hypnotized by its beauty, and grin like schoolboys when she bestowed her thin red smile like a blessing.

"I'd like a piece of *that*," the guy in front of me in line said. He was rail thin with a white stubbly beard and rheumy eyes.

"She seems friendly enough," I said. "Why not give it a try?"

"She don't fraternize," the guy behind me said. He was short, skinny, and bright-eyed, with a full beard.

"Bull," the first guy said, "shit." He lowered his voice to a whisper. "I seen her and Harry Toomis get in her fancy limo out back … it comes and picks her up, you know, midnight on the dot, every night, uniformed driver and the works."

"Yeah?" I said.

"Yeah," he said. "Anyway, I seen the night Harry Toomis got in the limo with her, and she was hanging on 'em like a cheap suit of clothes."

The other guy's expression turned puzzled in the maze of his beard. "Say—whatever *happened* to Harry? I ain't seen him in weeks!"

Somebody behind him said, "I heard he hopped the rails, over to Philly. Steel mills out there are hiring again, word is."

We were close to the food table, where I picked up a generous hunk of bread and took an empty wooden bowl; soon I was handing it toward the dark-haired vision in white apron and gray dress, and she smiled like a madonna as she filled it.

"You're the most beautiful woman I've ever seen," I said.

"Thank you," she said. Her voice was low, warm; no accent.

"I feel I've known you forever."

She looked at me hard; her almond-shaped eyes were a deep brown that approached black—it was as if she had only pupils, no irises.

"You seem familiar to me as well," she said melodically.

"Hey, come on!" the guy behind me said. "Other people want to eat, too, ya know!"

Others joined in. "Yeah! This goddamn Depression'll be over before we get fed!" I smiled at her and shrugged, and she smiled warmly and shrugged, too, and I moved on.

I sat at a bench at one of the long tables and sipped my soup. When I was finished, I waited until the food line had been shut down for the evening, then found my way back to her.

"Need some help in the kitchen?" I asked, helping her with one handle of the big metal soup basin.

"We have some volunteers already," she said. "Maybe tomorrow night?"

"Any night you like," I said, and tried to layer it with as much meaning as possible.

Then I touched her hand as it gripped the basin; hers was cool, mine was hot.

"I wasn't always a tramp," I said. "I was somebody you might have danced with, at a cotillion. Maybe we did dance. Under the stars one night? Maybe that's where I know you from."

"Please ..." she began. Her brow was knit. Confusion? Embarrassment?

Interest?

"I'm sorry to be so forward," I said. "It's just ... I haven't seen a woman so beautiful, so cultured, in a very long time. Forgive me."

And I silently helped her into the kitchen with the basin, turned, and went out of the mission.

The night sky was brilliant with stars; a full moon cast an ivory glow upon skid row, giving it an unreal beauty. An arty photograph, or perhaps a watercolor or an oil in a gallery, might have captured this landscape of abstract beauty and abject poverty. Rebecca Radclau might have admired such a work of art, on her social travels.

From around a corner, I watched as her dark-windowed limousine arrived at midnight, pulling into the alleyway where an impossibly tall, improbably burly chauffeur stepped out and opened the door for her. She was still wearing the dowdy gray uniform of her missionary duties. A sister of mercy.

She was alone.

She slipped into the back of the limo, her uniformed gorilla of a driver shut her inside, and they backed out into the street and glided away into the ivory-washed night.

Perhaps I'd misjudged her.

Or perhaps tonight she just wasn't thirsty . . .

———— ⌣⌣ ————

For the next two nights I worked in the kitchen, washing the wooden soup bowls the first night, drying them the next—and there were a lot of goddamn bowls to wash and dry. She would move through the small, steamy kitchen as if floating, attending to the next night's menu with the portly little man who was the cook for the mission, and in her employ.

Rumor had it he'd been the chef at a top local hotel that had gone under in '29. Certainly the delicately seasoned soups we'd been eating indicated a finer hand than you might expect at a skid-row soup kitchen.

I would catch her eye, if possible. She would hesitate, our gazes would lock, and I would smile, just a little. She remained impassive. I didn't want to push it: I didn't repeat my soliloquy of the first night, nor did I add to it, or present a variation, either. I tried to talk to her with my eyes. That was a language I felt sure she was easily fluent in.

The next night, as I went through the soup line, she said, "We won't need you in the kitchen tonight," rather coldly I thought, and I went to one of the long tables, sat, sipped my soup, thinking. *Damn! I screwed up. Came on too strong. She needed to think she was selecting me.*

And just as this thought had passed, I felt a hand on my shoulder: hers.

I looked up and she was barely smiling; her catlike eyes sparkled.

"How was your soup?"

I turned sideways and she loomed over me. "Dandy," I said. "I never see *you* trying any. Don't you like the company?"

"I never eat ... soup."

"It's pretty good, you know. Rich enough even for your blood, I'd think. Want to sit down?"

"No. No. I never fraternize."

"I've heard that."

"I just wanted to thank you for your help." And she smiled in a tight, businesslike way. Others were watching us, and when she extended her slender fingers toward me, and I took them, we seemed to be shaking hands in an equally businesslike way.

Nobody but me noticed the tiny slip of paper she'd passed me.

And I didn't look at it until I was outside, ducked into my alley home.

Midnight, it said.

Written in a flowing, lush hand. No further instructions. No signature.

But I knew where to be.

She stepped out of the back door of the alley, looking glamorous despite the dowdy uniform being damp with sweat and steam, black tendrils drifting down into her face from the pile of pinned-up hair. The whites of her eyes were large as she took in the alley, looking for me, I supposed. She seemed perplexed.

When the limousine glided into the alley next to the mission, and the tall burly chauffeur got out to let her in, I stepped from the recess of a doorway, kit bag in hand, and said "You did mean midnight, tonight?"

She jumped as if I'd said "boo."

She touched her generous chest. "You startled me! When I didn't see you, I thought you'd misunderstood . . . or just stood me up."

I went to her; took her hand and bent from the waist and kissed her hand, saying archly, "Stand up a lovely lady like yourself? Pshaw."

I'd always wanted to say "Pshaw," but it never came up before.

She smiled slyly, a thin smile that settled in one pretty dimple of her high-cheekboned face. "Did you think this was a date?"

"I had hoped."

"Mister . . . what is your name?"

"Jones, or Smith, or something. Is it important?"

"Let's make it Smith-Jones, then."

"Sure! That's high-tone enough. And may I call you Rebecca?"

"I prefer Becky."

"All right."

The chauffeur was standing with the limo's rear door open. His face was shadowed by his visor, but I could make out a firm jaw and a bucketlike skull.

"Let's not stand out here talking," she said, suddenly glancing about, almost furtively.

"Why not? You're not mistaking a member of the Smith-Jones clan for the sort of riff-raff you don't care to be seen with?"

"Please get in. What is that you have there?"

"Just my old kit bag. I don't go anywhere without my old kit bag—it contains what few possessions I still have."

"Fine. But do please get in."

The chauffeur moved forward, and I had the feeling that if I didn't get in, he'd toss me there.

"Ladies first," I said, bowing, gesturing, and she quickly ducked in.

I followed. The leather seats smelled new; they were deep and comfortable—like living-room furniture, not the backseat of a car.

"Mr. Smith-Jones, I wanted to express my gratitude to you, this evening."

She was unpinning the black hair; it fell in cascades to her shoulders. She shook her head and it shimmered and brushed her shoulders, flipping up at the bottom.

"Gratitude?" I asked. "For what?"

"For your help, these last several days."

"In the kitchen? Jeez, lady . . . Rebecca . . . Becky . . . it's only fair. You've been always good to guys like me, down on their luck, making sure we get a square meal once in a while."

"I've known adversity myself," she said solemnly. It sounded silly, but I managed not to laugh.

"So . . . uh . . . how exactly do you intend to express your gratitude?"

She touched my hand; she looked at me with those iris-less dark eyes. She seemed about to say something provocative, something sensual, something seductive. What she said was: "Food."

"Food?"

"Food. Real food. A real meal. Prepared by a five-star chef."

"No kidding. I had something else in mind . . ." I grinned at her lecherously, and she just smiled. " . . . but I'll settle."

She didn't let it go. *"What* else did you have in mind, Mr. Smith-Jones?"

I sighed. Looked down at my tattered clothes. Shook my head. "I shouldn't even kid about it. How can you look at somebody like me . . . unshaven . . . dirty clothes . . . breath that would knock a buzzard off a dung wagon . . . and think of me in any other way but one of pity?"

She patted my hand. "That's not necessarily true, Mr. Smith-Jones. I can look at you and see . . . possibilities. I can see the man you were—the man you still are, underneath the bad luck and the hard times."

"That's kind of you to say."

Her cool hand grasped mine. "And I don't think your breath is bad at all . . . I think it smells sweet . . . like night-blooming jasmine . . ."

She leaned forward; her thin but beautiful lips parted—they were scarlet, but I wasn't sure she was wearing lip rouge—and she touched her lips to mine, delicately. Then she touched my unshaven cheek with the slender, long-nailed fingers of one hand and stared soulfully at me.

"You're a fine man, Mr. Smith-Jones. We're going to clean you up . . . a bath . . . a shave . . . an incredible meal. You're going to have the night of your life . . ."

The Radclau mansion was a modern brick castle beyond a black wrought-iron gate; three massive stories, its turreted shape rose against the clear night sky in sharp silhouette, the moon poised above and to the right as if placed there for the sole purpose of lighting this imposing structure.

"This is really something," I said. "When was this built?"

"Just a few years ago," she said.

We were around the side of the building now, gliding into a garage which opened automatically for us—whether the chauffeur triggered it somehow, or someone inside saw us coming and lifted the drawbridge, I couldn't say.

"I recruited one of the top local architects to build something modern that would evoke my family home," she said.

"Where *was* the family home?"

"Europe."

"That doesn't narrow it down much."

"Just a little corner of eastern Europe. You probably wouldn't even have heard of it."

Maybe I would have.

We stepped from the cement cavern of the four-car garage into a wine cellar passageway that led to an elevator.

"I was never in a private home that had an elevator," I told her; the leather strap of my canvas kit bag was tight in my hand. The chauffeur—whose bucketlike skull turned out to have two dead eyes, a misshapen nose, and grim line of a mouth stuck on it—was playing elevator operator for us.

"Why, Mr. Smith-Jones," she said, looping her arm in mine, smiling her wry one-sided dimpled smile again, "I find that difficult to believe."

The elevator, a silver-gray chamber, rose to the fourth floor and opened onto a red-painted door in a cream-colored plaster alcove.

"We're in one of the guest towers," she said. She stepped out into the alcove with me, still arm-in-arm. "These are your quarters . . . you'll find everything you need, I think. I just guessed on your size. If I've got it wrong, just pick up the phone and ask for me. We can accommodate you. Then, let us know when you're ready to dine . . ."

She smiled—both dimples this time—and ducked back into the elevator, whose doors slid shut, and she was gone.

"I'll be damned," I said, and in the little alcove, it echoed.

The red door was unlocked, and opened onto a vast modern living room—plush white carpet, round white leather sofa, deep white armchairs, sleek decorative figurines, black-and-white decorative framed prints, a fireplace, a complete bar, a radio console, you name it. Everything but the kitchen sink. Everything but mirrors.

Beyond the living room was a bedroom; it was another white room, with one exception: the round bed was covered with red silk sheets. On the wall, over the bed, was a huge, bamboo-framed, sleekly decorative watercolor of a black panther, about to strike.

In the closet hung a full-dress tux—white tie and tails, pip pip. And the size *was* right, down to the black size nine and a half shoes, so shiny I could see my face in 'em, but probably not hers . . .

I tossed my kit bag on the bed, and checked out the bathroom; it was bigger than most apartments. On the white marble counter (and there *was* a mirror in here, at least) I found a straight razor, a brush and cup and shaving soap, and fancy French imported after-shave cologne. Also deodorant powder, and toothbrush and Pepsodent.

She apparently wanted me clean and smelling good, for dinner.

I made sure the guest-room door was locked, and stuck a chair under the knob to make double-sure, before stripping down to take a long, elaborate, very hot bubble bath. After two weeks of the hobo life, I was ready to take advantage of Miss Radclau's hospitality and soak off the slime.

Dressed to the nines, looking like neither a hobo nor an under-cover cop in my white tie and tails, I picked up the phone and said, "Mr. Smith-Jones is ready to dine."

Within minutes, a knock at the door announced the chauffeur, who was serving as a room-service man this time; he wheeled in a cart with several covered dishes.

"Please wait for the lady, sir," the chauffeur said, in a voice as dead as his eyes. "Madam is still dressing."

"Sure," I said.

It was another ten minutes before another knock came, and I hadn't even peeked under the dull, nonreflective lids of the hot dishes. I didn't want to be an ungracious guest.

I answered the door, bowing, with an arch, "*Enchante.*"

But it almost caught in my throat, because as I was bowing I found myself staring into her round, ripe decolletage.

I backed up awkwardly. "You're sure a sight."

She floated inside. Madam still looked undressed: her astonish-ingly low-cut gown was a vivid dark red and clung to her as if wet. Her waist was tiny, her hips flaring, but she was too tall, too long-legged, to have an hour-glass shape; she was wearing open-toed heels that brought her to my eye level. Her toenails were the same bright red as the dress and her lips.

She gestured theatrically to herself, with both hands. "I trust this is better than the apron?"

"Than the apron and the gray uniform," I said. "Maybe not just the apron . . ."

Her laugh was long and sultry. She was draped in an exotic, incenselike perfume, which was making me feel woozy.

She gestured with a slender red-nailed hand toward the tray with the covered food.

"Please dine," she said.

I pulled up a comfy chair that was a little short for the tray; it made me feel like a child. Before I sat, I asked, "Aren't you joining me?"

"I've eaten."

I doubted that.

"Please," she said, "I take great pleasure from watching you enjoy yourself. The carnal pleasures are so . . ."

"Pleasurable?" I offered, lifting a round lid; the fragrance of prime rib rose to my nostrils like a cobra from a snake charmer's basket, only I was the one doing the biting, sinking my teeth into the tender, very rare, succulent meat.

"I know I promised you the work of a five-star chef," she said, perched nearby on the arm of the couch, legs crossed, giving me a generous view, hands clasped in her lap, "and that is the work of a master, but . . . I could tell that you had . . . *basic* appetites."

She rose and switched on the radio and drifted back to her perch on the couch arm. A dance band was playing "Where or When." She swayed gently to it, her black hair shimmying.

"This is swell," I said. The prime rib, Yorkshire pudding, and browned potatoes were, in fact, delicious. No salad, no vegetable. But what the hell—it was free. So far.

She watched me with what seemed to be genuine pleasure, eyebrows raising as she savored me savoring every bite, her thin, pretty mouth tied up in a cupid's bow of shared bliss. Why she was getting such a vicarious glow out of watching me dig into the rare roast beef, I couldn't say. But I had a pretty good hunch . . .

I touched my napkin to my lips, sipped the red wine she had risen to pour for me, in a goblet-sized glass, and aid, "This is a hell of a public service program you got here, lady."

"I don't single just *anyone* out, you know." She looked almost hurt by my remark. "Once in a while, working in that line, serving up soup . . . I see someone . . . special. Someone who shouldn't be there. Someone who . . . deserves better. Deserves more."

She leaned in and the incenselike smell of her was overwhelming; her mouth locked onto mine and her kiss as sweet, much sweeter than mere wine . . .

The lights were off, suddenly, as if she'd willed it, and she led me into the bedroom, where the red gown slipped off and confirmed my suspicion that there was nothing, not even the slightest, wispiest step-in, underneath. A window allowed some moonlight to filter and her slender, yet full-breasted, wide-hipped, long-limbed frame was like some artist's dream of female perfection. And a horny artist, at that.

She drew me onto her bed, and laid me down on it cool silk sheets, and climbed on top of me, to grant my yet another gift. The erect blood-red tips of her breasts were as hypnotic as the intoxicated and intoxicating almond eyes, as she rode me, and I kept waiting, lost in her as I was, with my left hand dropped down along the side of the bed, waiting for her head to dip toward my throat, but it didn't, and when her face lowered, it was merely to kiss me again, deeply, passionately, as we flew together to some high, fevered place . . .

⁓

Maybe she was just some rich-bitch society girl who felt sorry for (and had a yen for) poor down-and-out schmucks like me, or like the poor down-and-out schmuck I was supposed to be. Maybe the suspicions that had brought me here were unfounded. Maybe I was the only dishonest one in this bed.

It had seemed a reasonable theory—what better place for an ancient monster to hide than behind the mask of a modern monster? The mass murderer that the city took the Butcher of Slaughter Run for would be the perfect disguise for a demon of the night.

And how better for the beast to gather its victims than behind the mask of an angel of mercy?

She seemed to be sleeping; the perfect globes of her bosom rose and fell, heavily, gloriously, in what seemed to be slumber. But as I stared at her, leaning on one elbow, her eyes popped open, startling me.

"What's wrong?" she asked.

"Nothing," I said. "I was just . . . admiring you."

She smiled a little, a pursed-lipped, kiss of a smile. "In what way?"

"Physically. You're a handsome woman. The handsomest I've ever seen. But it's more than that."

"Oh?"

"I admire what you're trying to do. Helping guys like me out."

She laughed. "I told you—I don't make love to all of them."

I shook my head. "I didn't mean that. Not everyone who's . . . advantaged takes the time to give a little back."

"I know. Please don't take this in a condescending manner, Mr. Smith-Jones, but the 'little people' of society, they're the life's blood of the 'advantaged.' It seems to me the least an advantaged person can do is, now and then, make life a little better for someone less fortunate."

"Well, you've certainly made my life better, tonight "

She smiled, and it seemed, suddenly, a sad, bittersweet kind of smile; the thin red lips looked black in the near dark. "Good. That was my desire."

She leaned forward and kissed me, gently, tenderly, then buried her face in my shoulder, and I had a sudden flash of what was about to happen, and pulled away. Her fangs were distended; her eyes were wide and here was no longer any difficulty in telling the pupils from the irises, because the latter were a ghastly yellow.

Naked, I jumped out of the bed; she was poised there, on all fours, as if mimicking the panther on the wall looming over her.

"You are from a privileged, moneyed family, aren't you, Miss Radclau?"

Her response was a deep, throaty snarling sound; I wasn't sure she was capable of speech, at this point.

"You think just 'cause I'm a bum, I can't do a damn anagram?" I asked, and I swung viciously at her, and it landed.

A punch on the jaw, even with all my weight behind it, wouldn't be enough to knock her out—she had metamorphosed into something beyond human, stronger than a mere man—but it had surprised her, and threw her on her back, which was where I wanted her.

The kit bag was out from under the bed in a flash and the pointed stake and the mallet were in my hands in another flash, and I drove my knee into her stomach, and the stake into her heart. She yowled with pain; it was a wolflike sound. Blood bubbled from around the stake, and I hammered it again, and it sunk deeper, and she yowled again, but her eyes weren't yellow anymore.

And they weren't savage, anymore, either.

Her expression was sad, and maybe even grateful.

She was still alive when I raised the machete—heaving under the pain, her hands clutching the stake but unable to remove it, slender fingers streaked with her own blood, a perfect match to her nail polish.

"I know you acted out of compassion," I said. "I know you gave me, and the other men, the best night of their lives, before taking those lives, when you wouldn't have had to. You could have just been a beast. Instead, you were a beauty."

She seemed to be smiling, a little, when the machete swung down and severed her head from pale, pale shoulders.

⁓

I had no trouble getting out of the place. I took the elevator down to the wine cellar passage to the garage with the bloody machete in hand in case I had to ward off the gorillalike chauffeur or any other minions of the night who might appear.

But none did.

I found a button in the garage and pushed it and the door swung up and open and I ran out into a cool, clear night. At the first farmhouse, I called in to the station, and told them to wake the chief.

"He's not going to like it," the desk sergeant said.

"Just *do it.*" I couldn't tell him I'd stopped the Slaughter Run Butcher or I'd be up to my eyeballs in reporters out here. "Understand, sergeant?"

I could hear the shrug in his voice: "If you say so, Lieutenant Van Helsing."

Road Dogs

NORMAN PARTRIDGE

PART ONE

Kim Barlow was two months in the ground when her brother first learned she was dead.

Glen got an e-mail from a deputy sheriff up in Arizona. Of course, the message had been gathering virtual dust for a couple of months in Glen's inbox, because Glen hardly ever checked his mail. Not because he couldn't. Sure, the rig was forty miles off the Texas coast, but there were computers around. What there wasn't was anyone Glen Barlow heard from that way. Except for Kim, and Kim had been pretty quiet since Glen tossed her boyfriend through her living room window last Christmas Eve.

Glen had only clocked a couple months with the company, but the Installation Manager liked him well enough to okay emergency leave. Some young suit from Houston was headed back to the mainland after touring the rig, and Glen caught a ride into Galveston on the company chopper. Seventeen hours later he parked his truck in front of the El Pasito sheriff's office. He'd already talked to that emailing deputy on a cell phone he'd forgotten in the Ford's glove compartment when he ditched the mainland for his time offshore. Glen used that cell phone about as much as he used his e-mail account.

The deputy—whose name was J. J. Bryce—had spent most of the day waiting for Glen to show up. One look at the guy and Bryce shook his head. He shook his head when he saw Glen's pickup, too. Try to describe that old hunk of Ford in a report, he'd note the color as rust or primer, take your pick. And the guy who drove it was pretty much the same way. Headed towards forty with the years starting to show. Bryce was real familiar with the type. A drifter—one of those guys who was wiry as a half-starved animal. And that might mean you were talking jackrabbit, or it might mean you were talking coyote. Sometimes it was hard to tell going in.

But Bryce already had an opinion about this guy. He'd heard all about Barlow tossing Kale Howard through that living room window last Christmas Eve. In fact, he'd heard more about it than the talk that went around the cop shop. Not that any of that mattered right now. The way the deputy saw it, right now things were all business.

The two of them sat down in the deputy's cramped office and ran the drill. There wasn't much to look at. Not in the office. Not in the file Bryce had on Kim Barlow's death. But Glen looked, and he took his time about it, and that wasn't something the deputy much liked.

After a while, Glen closed the folder and slid it across the desk.

"Having a hard time buying this," he said.

"No buying it, really. It's what happened."

"You don't have a suspect?"

"You read the report, Mr. Barlow. You don't have a suspect in a case like this."

"You talk to that asshole Howard?"

"Yeah. I talked to Kale. Read his file, too."

"Then you know he used to beat up my sister."

"I know that. But I also know that Howard didn't do this. No man could have."

Glen just looked at the guy—kind of grinned, didn't say one word—and Bryce all of a sudden felt his pulse hammering, because it most definitely wasn't the kind of look you got from a jackrabbit.

Glen Barlow said: "You'd be surprised what some men can do."

There it was. Cards on the table, and all in the space of ten minutes. But the gents named Bryce and Barlow hadn't quite played out the deck, so they went a few more hands. Bryce reminding Glen about the restraining order, warning him how hard he'd go if Glen went after Kale Howard. Glen asking questions, the deputy batting them off or not answering them at all. The words exchanged weren't getting either man anywhere he wanted to go, or anywhere he wanted to take the other. The two of them were running neck and neck, and neither seemed to like that very much.

Finally, Glen said: "I want to see the pictures."

"Look, Barlow. I understand that your sister was your only living relative. You know the land out there. As far as we can figure it, she was alone, rock-climbing at Tres Manos. She must have taken a fall. After that . . . well, she was hurt pretty bad. She had a broken leg. It was a couple days before anyone found her. Something got hold of her before then . . . a pack of coyotes, or maybe a big cat. We had some experts in and they said—"

"I don't care what they said. Kale's mixed up in this some way. Wouldn't surprise me if he wanted a little protection after

I tossed him through that window. Maybe he got himself a pit bull."

"We checked that out, Mr. Barlow. Kale doesn't have a dog."

"That doesn't change anything. I still want to see the pictures."

"Trust me on this. You don't."

"How many times you want to hear me say it?"

The deputy drew a deep breath and tried to hold his temper.

"You want me to, I'll say it again."

Bryce was so pissed off, he could barely unclench his jaw, but he got the job done. "Okay, Barlow. You want pictures, pictures is what you'll get."

The deputy yanked open a file cabinet harder than he should have and tossed another manila folder across the desk. Barlow looked at those photos for a long time—the way Bryce figured time, anyway.

"All right," Glen said finally. He closed the folder, slid it across the desk, and got up so quickly that he took Bryce by surprise. There was more that the deputy needed to say, but Barlow didn't give him the chance. He slammed Bryce's office door before the deputy could say another word, and a handful of seconds later he slammed the door to his busted-ass pickup hard enough to leave a shower of rust on the ground. Then he drove straight out of El Pasito, foot hard on the gas. Past the town's lone bar . . . past the funeral home . . . past the gun shop . . .

Two miles into the desert, Glen Barlow laid rubber and pulled over.

The goddamn deputy was right about those pictures.

At the base of a dying yucca tree, Glen puked his guts dry.

⁓⊃⊂⁓

J. J. Bryce filed the folders on the Kim Barlow case and shared the story of his run-in with her older brother with the sheriff. He sat around the office killing time, but he just couldn't take it sitting there with the sunset slicing through the Venetian blinds and the edge of the desk marred by cigarette burns from the lazy-ass deputy who'd had it before him.

So he clocked out and got in his own pickup, a brand-new Ford which was a hell of a lot shinier than the one Glen Barlow drove. That didn't make Bryce feel any better, though. He was still boiling, and there wasn't much he could do about it at the moment—El Pasito only had one bar and Sheriff Randall didn't like anyone who wore a badge drinking there.

So Bryce drove out of town, south, towards Guadalupe. He figured he'd swing by a Mexican grocery store he knew in Dos Gatos. The place was about thirty miles out of his way, but that'd give him some time to cool off before heading home. Besides, you could get pork carnitas at the grocery, already marinated and ready to go. Bryce figured he'd grab a sixer and some tortillas while he was at it. Later on, he'd drop those carnitas in the banged-up cast-iron skillet he used on the barbeque, watch the stars wink on in the sky while he downed a couple of brews, and the night would go down easy.

Or easier, anyway.

❧

By the time the deputy edged his speedometer past seventy and got the A/C cranking just right, Glen Barlow had chugged half a warm Dr Pepper that had been playing tag with a bunch of burger wrappers on the floor of his truck. The good Dr didn't do much for him besides wash the taste of puke out of his mouth. Still, that was a plus.

Glen drove south. Same road as Bryce, but in the opposite direction. He didn't plan to be on the road long. There was a crossroad just ahead, a narrow unpaved lane jagging west through creosote, coyote brush, and amaranth.

Down that road was where Glen Barlow was headed, because there was other stuff he needed to know. Stuff a guy like Bryce wouldn't tell him. But that was okay—Glen knew where he could find some answers. It was the same place he'd left a whole mess of questions when he cut out of town last December.

That thought chewed on him. He hung a left, pulled over at the side of the dirt road and took another swallow of warm Dr P. For the first time that day, he felt nervous. And that was strange, considering the cards he'd been dealt in the last few hours.

A yank on the handle and the truck door creaked open. Glen climbed out of the cab and stood there in the dry heat. He was dog-tired after a full day behind the wheel, but he couldn't relax. Still, he tried. He needed to catch his breath before going any further.

He closed his eyes for a minute. There were crickets out there somewhere . . . sawing a high, even whine that wouldn't go away. Glen was so used to being on the rig, listening to the sea and the gulls and the equipment. It was weird listening to something different. But he wasn't really listening, no matter how hard he tried. He was thinking. Remembering last Christmas Eve . . . remembering pulling to a stop right here, as a cold December moon shone above.

Right here in the same place that he was standing now. Glen churned the last gulp of soda in his mouth. He thought about that night and the nights that had come since then, and he thought about where those nights had taken him. Full circle. Right back to the place he'd begun.

He shook his head, glancing at his reflection in the banged-up driver's door mirror.

Guess you only have one gear, you stupid bastard.

Glen almost laughed at that. But he didn't. Instead, he spit warm Dr P on the dirt road. Then he climbed in the truck, keyed the engine, and kicked up some roadbed, leaving that wet patch on the ground for the thirsty red earth to drink up.

⁓⁓⁓

Lisa Allen was still beautiful, of course. That hadn't changed in the handful of months since Glen left town. But a whole lot had. Glen knew that coming through the door of the house they'd once shared.

No kiss for him tonight. Not even a hug. They sat in the kitchen, a couple of beers on the table. The back door was open behind Glen's shoulder, and he could smell the herbs in the little patch of garden scrabbling along the side of the house. Sage, rosemary, thyme . . . probably a whole lot of other stuff out there that Lisa's hippie parents had sung about back in the sixties when they built the adobe on a scrubby patch of Arizona notmuch. Of course, Glen didn't say that, even though it was the kind of thing that would have made Lisa laugh back in the days when his coat hung in a closet down the hall.

Back then, things were different.

Those crickets were still out there somewhere, sawing that high, even whine. But Glen ignored them. Instead he listened to the words coming out of his own mouth, surer and steadier than he could have imagined. And he listened to Lisa's answers, which were just as sure and just as steady.

"You saw those photos, Glen. Kale couldn't have done that."

"Maybe. Maybe not."

"The cops told you what they pieced together, didn't they? Kim was out at Tres Manos . . . you know how she loved it out there. They found her rock-climbing gear. She was on that wall south of the third fist, and she must have had an accident. God knows how long she was out there alone—"

"Or maybe she wasn't alone. And maybe it didn't happen that way. Maybe someone just wanted it to look like it did."

"Jesus, Glen. Did you listen to the cops at all?"

"Yeah. I listened to them tell me what made sense to them so they could slot a file into a cabinet pretty damn quick."

"So what do you plan to do about it?"

"A lot of that depends on you. I only know what my gut tells me . . . and that's that I need to get Kale Howard in a place where he's going to do some straight talking. I want to hear what he has to say about this, and I want to look into his eyes when he says it."

"You tried that before, Glen. If you remember, it didn't work out so hot."

"Yeah." Glen stared at Lisa. "I remember."

And Glen did remember. All of it. Images came at him like hard popping jabs. He and Kale had exchanged a couple of simple, unvarnished words. And then Kale Howard had thrown a punch that rocked Glen solid, and Glen's hands were on the rangy bastard, handling him the way you handle a chicken leg when you're real hungry and you just want to tear it apart at the joint. Which meant that Kale had exited the room through a plate-glass window before Glen even realized what he was doing.

"Look, Lisa. I only came here for one thing. You need to tell me where Kale is."

Surprised, she raised an eyebrow. "Who'd you talk to over at the cop shop, anyway?"

"Some joker with a roll of nickels up his ass. Guy named Bryce."

"And he didn't tell you?"

"Tell me what?"

"Things changed after you cut out of town last December. Kale moved in with Kim."

"You're kidding."

"Not a chance."

"And he's still there? That's what you're telling me? He's living in her house?"

"It's his house, Glen."

Lisa stared at him.

"Kale and Kim drove up to Vegas on Valentine's Day and got married. Kim left him everything."

<hr />

A bitter laugh caught in Glen's throat. "Okay," he said. "Things are beginning to make sense now."

"Don't you think the cops thought that, too?"

"If they did, they sure as hell didn't show it. They found my sister torn to shreds out at Tres Manos. Her climbing gear was scattered around, and she had a broken leg, and they figured . . . *Gee, there are coyotes around here, aren't there?* So they did the math the easy way and wrote the whole thing off as an accident *times two.*"

"Uh-uh. Not the way it happened. This may be a small town, but you've got to give the cops some credit. They grilled Kale. They were all over Kim's house. They didn't find a thing."

"Hard to find what's locked up in a bastard's head . . . unless you're willing to use the right tools, that is."

"You'd better think about that. You know the law around here. You try something like that . . . twice? And with a guy who's got a restraining order against you? It'd be crazy."

"Yeah. Maybe that's exactly what it would be. And maybe that's the way it should have been all along. The truth is that I stopped short when I tossed Kale through that window. You know that better than anyone, Lisa. I should have whipped that dog until I was sure he'd turn tail and run. If I'd done that, maybe Kim would still be alive. Hell, if I'd done that, maybe I wouldn't have had to leave."

"You never had to leave. That was your choice."

"No. It was your choice, Lisa . . . you made it when you called the cops and stopped me cold last December."

⁓

The words were out of Glen's mouth before he even knew they were in his brain. Lisa stared at him like he'd just crawled out from under a rock. Seeing that expression, Glen knew it might as well have been that night last December, with the kitchen door closed to the cold and the herbs cut back against the frost and an icy wind rattling the window at his back. His left eye throbbing from the sucker shot Kale Howard had landed just before getting his miserable excuse for an ass tossed through the living room window, Glen trying to explain to Lisa how he knew in his gut that kind of punishment wasn't enough for a guy like Howard, how a guy like that needed more if he was going to get the message.

He'd never forget that moment, just as he'd never forget the anger that flared inside him when Kim admitted for the first time how things really were with Howard, or what he was certain needed to be done with that anger, or what he'd done with it in the moments after his sister's confession. And he'd sat there that December night in Lisa's kitchen with all those things roiling inside him, and no way to get an explanation past his lips that could make sense to the woman he loved.

It didn't make sense to her now. "You're saying that if it weren't for me, everything would be okay today?"

Glen took a breath, but he didn't say a word.

"Jesus, Glen. You're not really sitting here saying I'm responsible for Lisa's death, are you?"

"No. But you're the one called the cops when I told you I was going back over there."

"And I told you I'd do that. You walked out of here with a *gun*, Glen."

"I was just going to scare him. That coward would have been across the state line by midnight."

"C'mon. You don't know how Kale would have reacted when he saw a gun. And when it comes to the cops, I would have called them anyway. Remember, I'm the one who reported Kale as an abuser. Hell, I would have let Kim move in here until things straightened out if she would have done it. I made the offer while Kale was locked up. She wouldn't even admit that they had a real problem."

"Sometimes people can't handle what happens to them."

"They have to."

"And what if they aren't strong enough?"

"You help them get strong." Lisa sighed. "But you can't live their lives for them. You can't walk through the fire they've got to walk through. And you can't burn down your own life because they're not strong enough to do the job. But that's what you did. To yourself, when you walked out of here with that gun. To me, too . . . and to us. And you paid the price for it. But it could have been worse."

"I don't see how."

"I do. If I hadn't stopped you that night, you'd probably be sitting in a jailhouse, serving time for murder. We both know that's true."

Glen shook his head.

"Maybe that's where I'll end up still," he said.

Now it was Lisa's turn to look at him without saying a word.

"Guess we're done here," Glen said.

"Yeah. I guess we are."

Glen stepped to the door. There was a phone on the counter. "Hate to do this," he said, and then he unplugged the phone, cradling it under his arm.

"One other thing before I go," he said.

"What's that?"

"Your cell phone, Lisa. Hand it over."

~ ❦ ~

Glen hit the gas, bulleting down that red road. Suddenly, it was just like it had been six months before. Lisa and his life in the rearview, God knew what ahead.

At least the cops wouldn't be waiting for him at the end of that road tonight. That wouldn't happen, now that he'd taken Lisa's phones. From Lisa's place, it was a long walk to anywhere.

But he hadn't had a choice in the matter. No way he could afford a rerun of last December's action. That night, Sheriff Randall himself had responded to Lisa's 911 call. The old man had been quick about it, too, heading Glen off at the point where the dirt road that led to Kim's place met highway blacktop.

After Kale Howard got into the act, Glen ended up in lockup for a week on an assault charge. Of course, Howard had gotten the restraining order, dropped the charges—all like that.

Kale took some heat, too, but in the end he got off with probation and counseling . . . and soon he was back with Kim, who wasn't talking to either Lisa or Glen.

That wasn't the worst of it, though. Glen had issued his own sentence, and in retrospect he was one hard-ass judge. Because somehow, he had turned out to be the bad guy. In the eyes of the law, and his little sister, and in Lisa's eyes, too.

And maybe even in his own eyes. Because he was the one who hit the road, not Kale Howard. He was the one who didn't hang around when things went bad with Lisa, and with Kim. He was the one who didn't talk to either of them for months. He couldn't dodge that fact any more than he could make up for it now.

More than anything, that was what drove him forward. He cut the wheel harder than he should have and hit the blacktop, heading north. He tried to bury the regrets he'd felt while sitting at Lisa's table, and the familiar longings that went along with them. But he couldn't manage the trick. Though his gaze traveled the road ahead—tracking the painted line that gutted its center—his thoughts lingered behind.

He could still see Lisa there, sitting at that table. It had been six months since he'd seen her, but the way things had been six months ago was not exactly far-removed in his memory. He imagined what it would be like, burying his head in her hair again, touching her, going to bed with her, getting up in the morning together. That's the way it still was, in one small place inside him. And if he were another kind of guy, maybe he could have made it happen all over again . . . and just that way.

———— ∽◡ ————

But that was the pure hell of it. Because Glen Barlow wasn't another kind of guy . . . and the worst thing about it was he knew that better than anyone. Even better than the other kind of guy who at that moment was stepping through Lisa Allen's front door.

That guy's name was J. J. Bryce.

The deputy put a sixer on the counter, and set the bag with the tortillas and carnitas he'd bought at that Mexican grocery store next to it. He undid his gunbelt and put it on a chair. Then he bent low, gave Lisa a kiss, and passed her a beer.

"Has Barlow been here yet?"

Lisa shook her head. But that was just a comment about Glen, not an answer to J. J.'s question.

The real answer took a minute . . . a popped bottle cap . . . a deep swallow.

"Oh, yeah," she said finally. "He's been, and he's gone."

———— ∽◡ ————

J. J. sighed loud and long, staring down at the place the phone should have been.

"Jesus," he said. "This guy."

"I told you how he is. And you said you could handle him."

"For that little job, I would have needed some of those gloves the bomb-disposal boys use. Man, what a handful of dynamite. Your boy Barlow was ready to go to war as soon as he stepped into my office.

One quick chew of my ass and he was out of there. I didn't get to say a word about Kale and Kim getting married—"

"Yeah. I noticed. I got to drop that bomb myself."

"Did you tell him about us?"

"Are you kidding?"

"Hell, someone's got to tell him."

"Oh, sure. That would have been a sweet followup to the news about his sister marrying the guy who used to beat the crap out of her. Hey, maybe we should invite him over to dinner and break the news. We could hold hands, and he could carve out his own heart with a steak knife."

"Don't play that, Lisa. Barlow walked out on you . . . *and* his sister. If he wants someone to blame for that, he can go find himself a mirror."

Lisa laughed sharply. "Funny thing is, I think he'd agree with you."

"Well, that doesn't mean squat to me. He walked out six months ago, and you didn't hear from him until today. I'll bet he didn't keep in touch with his sister, either. Now, I'm not exactly sure what happened to Kim out there at Tres Manos. Hell, I'm not even sure Kale Howard didn't have something to do with it. But one thing I'm sure of is that Glen Barlow did dirt to both of you when he left town, and now he's here trying to make things right when it's way too late to tote that load."

"Wow. You sound just like him. If he would have stuck around, I bet you would have rubber-stamped his plan for the rest of the night."

"What plan?"

J. J. sipped his beer and listened while Lisa laid it out for him.

When she was done, he took a deeper swallow.

Then he drained the bottle.

"That goddamn coyote," he said, and he stepped outside.

<hr>

J. J. flipped open his cell phone and called dispatch. It was dark now, and a light breeze was blowing from the west. Lisa watched as J. J. moved over to the barbeque. He took off the lid and scraped down the grill while he talked. She couldn't hear his words, just clipped short sentences. But his tone told the story, and that tone was all business.

Across the table, an empty chair waited. Lisa saw Glen sitting there an hour before. She saw J. J.'s empty beer bottle on the table, right now. She heard the words of both men, sizing up things in ways that really weren't that different.

The breeze carried the smell of sage, rosemary, and thyme through the open door. Glen had always trimmed back the rosemary way too tight. He said it made the plant grow stronger. J. J. was the kind of guy who thought anything you put in your mouth should come from the grocery store. She wondered if he ever noticed the herb garden at all.

Lisa had been with J. J. two months. The relationship had started slow and easy, then come on fast. Bryce was a *what you see is what you get* kind of guy. You wanted to know how he felt about something, all you had to do was ask. He'd tell you. And things worked best if they operated that way from his side of the equation, too. He wanted to know something, he'd ask you straight out. It was never that way with Glen. Glen could be as silent as a shadow. Sure, the two men weren't exactly yin and yang or night and day, but Lisa definitely didn't have a problem figuring out which one was left brain and which was right—

Mr. Left Brain stepped through the door.

"Change of plans," J. J. said. "Dinner's on the backburner."

"What do you mean?"

"Jeff Keats is out sick tonight, and Einar Cerda's transporting a couple of prisoners over to county lockup. That Garcia kid from California's pretty much running the show, and he's out on a domestic dispute call. Since all I've got is a suspicion your boy Barlow is going to jump a restraining order, there's no way Glen gets priority. Besides, I wouldn't want to put the kid up against Barlow and Kale Howard, even if he was available. Not by his lonesome, anyway. You ask me, both those guys belong in strait-jackets."

"Can't they call in someone from the day shift?"

"Sure. They could start with Randall, like they did last Christmas Eve. He'd love that."

"Who then?"

"Well, if someone's stupid enough to be proactive when nothing's happened yet, he might head out there. Someone with a solid knowledge of the parties involved. Of course, an idiot like that would have to put his off-duty self in the middle of things and worry about lawsuits later—"

"If you're saying that you're doing this off the clock, I'm going with you."

"Don't be crazy, Lisa. Let's leave that job to your buddy the road dog. I think he's made for it."

Bryce grabbed his gunbelt from the chair and buckled it on.

"Well," he said, "I guess I'll go catch some bad guys and get our phone back."

Lisa laughed, then kissed him.

"Thanks," she said.

"No need, darlin'. But let's not let this get too complicated. You just remember who's going to walk through the door when this is over."

"I'll remember," she said.

"Okay." Bryce stepped outside. "Be back soon. Don't worry."

"I won't."

"Liar."

Lisa laughed again. Another kiss that was too quick, and then J. J.'s truck was raising a cloud of dust as he headed for the highway. Lisa watched him go, and she kept on watching after the dust settled and the truck had disappeared from view.

The night air was cool.

The crickets had gone quiet.

Lisa sat on the back step and tried to think of nothing at all.

⌒⌒⌒

Behind the house he'd shared with Kim Barlow—the same house he'd once exited through a window thanks to her brother Glen—Kale Howard eyed Tres Manos.

The place the *Anglo* locals called The Hands was a sight to see, even from this distance. It was something different every time you looked at it. Red as a thickening puddle of blood in the hard light of afternoon. Black as the devil's silhouette in the hours past midnight . . . and right now, with silver moonlight creeping up its backside, it was as smoky and ethereal as a dream any fool could climb.

Kale smiled. Though he stood in darkness, that same moonlight crept up his spine like a dozen furious scorpions in a hurry to plant stings at the base of his brain. In his world, that wasn't unfamiliar feeling, and it dug down to his core like a grave robber's shovel, churning up secrets buried in the deepest, darkest corners of the shriveled black hunk he called his soul.

There were visions in that place that would have made a sane man slash his wrists. Visions of women like Kim Barlow as they screamed their last screams, and visions of Kim Barlow herself, on the final night of her life, out there in the desert beneath a towering hunk of rock that might as well have been a gigantic tombstone.

They weren't exactly Kale's visions. Not completely. They were owned in part by the thing that lived inside him, the disease that sent those scorpions scurrying across his spine. But the visions were nothing to be feared, any more than he feared the silhouette of Tres Manos in the distance. And, hell, if he raised a hand right now, he could cover up that mother-of-all tombstones where Kim had died, and he could do the job with one little finger. This he did. And just that fast, every memory of Kim Barlow vanished from his mind except that very last one . . . and, for Kale, that was the one worth keeping.

The moonlight brought it home. As its clean halo broke over the rim of The Hands, the memory shimmered in the clear white light surrounding Kale's raised finger. Quite suddenly, his raised finger itched as if those ghostly scorpions had launched their own dark visionquest, scrambling across the enormous sandstone tombstone that rose from the desert of Kale's hand, jabbing barbed tales into that tower, reducing it to fine grains, burrowing through Kale's flesh and blood and bone until they unearthed that bedrock of hidden memory.

Kim's final fright . . . and just as final understanding.

For Kale, that single moment defined his entire relationship with

Kim Barlow. He understood that . . . just as he understood that it paid to take his time when those moments rose from the shadows. They were the ones that truly counted.

He'd taken his time with Kim, all right. Together, they'd gone to Tres Manos, sharing a picnic dinner as dusk turned to night. Kale had made sure Kim understood the lies he'd told, stripping them away from the truth with the same relish he stripped meat away from a bone. And when he was finished doing that little job he did another, taking what he wanted from Kim in the shadow of a great tombstone he could eclipse with a single finger.

He took it in a fury born of cursed moonlight and patience and spite. Under other circumstances Kale would have lingered with the memory, but it was time for it to go. His mind cremated every image, and his pointing finger curled into a fist along with its neighbors, and his fist tightened. Chrome skull rings gnashed on his fingers like five monsters grinding bones to make their bread. The moon crested about the towers. Kale extended his fingers. He had to. Each one was lengthening now, growing black claws that sliced the shadow he cast.

Those ghostly scorpions raised tails and drove spikes home, and the venom of the moon delivered fresh visions to Kale's mind . . . visions of Kim's brother. The bastard had been in Kale's head all day. Even when the moon was shining on another part of the world, he'd known Glen Barlow was coming. The scorpions had told him so, and he had trusted each sting of warning, and each scent raised by his daylight visions.

And he'd scented the bastard, all right . . . even in his visions. The oil burning in Barlow's old pickup had scalded his nostrils, and he'd smelled the bastard's sweat as he stood out there in the desert, and he'd retched at the stink of Barlow's puke as the hardcase gave up his misery in the dull heat of dusk. And now the visions were stronger. Barlow was coming closer. Barlow was almost here. That burning motor oil was a hot rag in the mouth of the night, and the stink of gun oil etched in the whorls of Barlow's fingerprints bore the raw perfume of vengeance.

The fact that Barlow had a gun didn't worry Kale, for the bullets in Barlow's pistol did not bear the acrid stench of a single grain of silver. That meant Kale had nothing to fear from the weapon. And if Kale did not fear Barlow's gun, he would not fear Glen Barlow. Not when his own fingers were tipped with razor claws that could slice flesh to ribbons. Not when growing teeth twisted and scraped in his mouth, carving a brutal path against thickening gums.

And that wasn't the end of it. Soon Kale's jaws were heavy with fangs. Black bristles of fur spiked from a dozen monsters tattooed on his arms. Moonlight poured over the desert, and Kale's shadow stretched across the sand as he grew larger—tendons cording over lengthening bone, muscles getting heavier.

But the moon was carving him down, too. It whittled away everything but the basics, the way those jabbing scorpions had chiseled at the sandstone tower in his vision . . . cutting away everything that had once protected Glen Barlow, skinning hesitation and fear from Kale's heart, tearing off every mask he had ever been forced to wear.

Moonlight carved the werewolf as brutally and efficiently as the Reaper's own predatory scythe. And what the moon left behind was the same . . . and nothing but.

PART TWO

As he neared Kim's house, Glen killed the headlights. He pulled the pickup to the side of the road, parking beneath an old mesquite tree a hundred yards from the entrance to her property. Night had dropped its veil, but there were still shadows here. The gnarled branches overhead netted the stark silver light of the full moon, casting twisted shadows on the hood of Glen's old truck.

Glen reached under the seat and grabbed his pistol. He stepped from the truck and cut a path through the night, following the road at a slow trot until he came to the rock-lined drive leading to Kim's house. He stood there for a moment, in full moonlight now. If anyone inside the house was looking through a window, they'd surely see him . . . but every window was dark, and so were the rusted railroad lanterns hanging from the heavy-beamed overhang that covered the front patio.

There weren't any other houses nearby. Just that silver moonlight, and desert that didn't so much as ripple until it ran into Tres Manos, many miles away. Quietly, Glen moved down the final twenty feet of the drive. He put a hand on the hood of Kale's Mustang as he passed by, but the car was as cold as the house was dark.

Sand crunched lightly beneath Glen's boot heels. Out on the road, a driver shifted gears. Glen ducked low, but the car didn't enter Kim's driveway. Headlights cast cold beams over the front of the house as the car passed by. Glen caught a quick glimpse of his reflection in the bedroom window, the light trapping his image on the pane for what seemed a long moment. Then the light moved on, smearing across the rest of the house, sweeping the shadows beneath the patio overhang as it passed, revealing the heavy slab of a front door and the old string of chili peppers hanging there . . . and, past that, a weathered sheet of plywood, still nailed over the front window.

Glen shook his head. Maybe Kale was too lazy to fix the window, or maybe the bastard didn't want anyone looking inside. It didn't matter to Glen. One way or another, he planned to take a good long look in the house. As the sound of the passing car's engine faded in the distance, he stepped onto the flagstone patio and crossed through the shadows beneath the overhang. Here the air was heavy with the fragrance of climbing roses; the plants wound around stout support posts like gnarled muscles, vines heavy with blooms cradled by the overhang above.

It was darker here, but Glen's night vision was good. He spotted a stack of cut piñon near the boarded-up window. Grabbing a length of it, he pressed his back to the brick wall near the heavy slab of a front door.

Glen tossed the piñon across the patio. The log clattered loudly against flagstone as it landed fifteen feet away. If anyone was inside the house, they wouldn't be able to ignore the noise.

Glen waited. No sound from within, and no lights came on. His breaths came faster now, and the butt of the pistol jammed into his jeans nudged at his belly.

Needles of silver light pierced the roses overhead as the moon rose higher.

The sweet fragrance of the flowers was heavy on the night air.

Glen filled his lungs with it.

He tested the doorknob.

It was locked.

Damn. Glen drew another breath . . . but this time he choked on it. Because suddenly there was another smell—a sour animal stink, as if something dead was trapped up there in the rose vines.

And then there was a sound. Glen jolted as a hunk of piñon clattered over the flagstones at his feet and bounced off the door—the same hunk of wood he'd tossed just a few moments before. He spun quickly, drawing his pistol as he turned toward the thing that had thrown the log . . . the thing that had been stalking him since he'd first stepped from his truck.

Because this was no man. Something down deep in Glen's gut recognized that before his mind could accept it. The shadow that faced him was enormous . . . and grinning . . . and red-eyed . . . and it moved much faster than Glen could possibly move.

It came straight at him. Before he could raise his pistol, the thing caught him with one hairy shoulder and hammered him against the door. The hanging chili peppers went to powder behind his back. The shadow snatched his wrist and yanked him forward, and Glen was suddenly spinning like a child launched from a Tilt-A-Whirl, heels scrapping over flagstone and then rising above it, the thing's clawed hands tight on his wrist . . . tighter still when the monster cracked the whip.

Glen's body was jerked so hard he was sure his left shoulder had popped from its socket. But it wasn't his left shoulder he needed to worry about. It was the right one, which slammed into the plywood covering the broken window with such force that the panel cracked and planted splinters in his flesh.

Glen dropped to the ground. The thing's hands were off him for just a couple seconds as it drew back. Then it charged again, fanged teeth gleaming in the patchwork light beneath the overhang.

It was almost on top of him when Glen realized he was still holding the pistol. Pain dug a trench from his wrist to his shoulder as he jacked his aching elbow into position and pulled the trigger. The gun bucked in his hand. The thing screamed and fell back. Blood splattered across the flagstone, and a wet hunk of meat smacked against the ground. Glen fired again—straight at the thing's chest this time—and fired once more as the monster stumbled back.

The 230-grain hollow-points did their work. Another slug drove the shadow-thing backward. It crashed against one of the patio posts—the overhang shuddering as the creature bucked in pain, its blood showering flagstones in wet droplets.

Glen fired again, and the monster howled.

Dead rose petals rained down.

And the shadow charged through them with renewed ferocity. Glen raised the pistol one more time, but it was too late. Before he could pull the trigger, the creature's bristling forehead cracked hard against Glen's chin. Simultaneously, a knotted shoulder drove into his gut, jamming him against the cracked plywood covering the broken window.

This time, the plywood didn't hold.

This time, Glen went straight through it.

And the werewolf followed.

⁓⁓⁓

Kale sprang through the gaping plywood maw. There was the bastard. Right there—a hunk of human piledriver stretched out on the hardwood floor.

Somehow Barlow had managed to hang on to his pistol. Kale slapped it away with a fistful of claws. Not that the gun did Barlow any good without silver bullets. Kale's wounds were already scarring over. Lead slugs couldn't do more than slow him down.

He grabbed Barlow's collar, snarling at him. And the look on Glen's face? Man . . . it was priceless, as if someone had just lit up his flat-earthed little world with a full bucket of hellfire.

If a wolf could have laughed, Kale would have done it. The scorpion fury trapped inside him demanded that Barlow die hard. It'd been too damn tough keeping the leash on during the year he'd lived with the bastard's sister. Caging his anger when Barlow gave him static about never holding a job for long . . . or the way he'd dip into Kim's wallet when he needed some cash . . . or a million other things. Sometimes he'd lose it, and Kim would pay the price. Sure. Had to be Kimmy who paid, because he'd kept Kim on a leash of her own.

And it was a short one. Kimmy'd had things he wanted. A damn fine little house in the middle of nowhere, and money in the bank, and not too many relatives around to muddy the water. So waiting had been the ticket. First for the marriage license . . . next for the will. And that meant that most of the time Kale bit back his anger, but sometimes he couldn't help himself. He'd let loose . . . especially when it was getting close to the full moon and the scorpions started crawling up his spine.

And that wasn't bad, really. Not all bad, anyway. The scorpions, the fights and the violence . . . they gave Kale an excuse to get the hell out of Dodge. Usually he'd head to Vegas. Enjoy a couple days on the Strip, then do a little cruising in the desert. Grab someone traveling alone, out where it didn't matter. He had his way about it, he favored himself some dark-haired little piece of sweetmeat. Maybe one with a little something extra to go with the gristle. He'd catch one alone at a rest stop or a backwater motel—some place like that. Have some fun with her, then chow down. Clean the bones and bury them. Strip her car and sell it to a chop shop while the best parts of the little skank were still warm in his belly, then head home with a fat bankroll in the pocket.

No sweat, Kimmy. I picked it up gambling. Now let me drive you

over to Tucson and we'll have dinner. Hey, we can even stay the night
at that place you like. I want to make things up to you . . . and I'm really
sorry about that fight we had, okay?

Uh-huh. That was the way it worked.

Sweet when he needed to be.

Not so sweet when he didn't.

And right now, with Kim six feet under and most of her worldly
possessions banked, Kale didn't have a shot glass worth of *sweet* in
him. Barlow started scrambling, one hand reaching for that pistol
on the floor. Kale grabbed him before he could reach the useless
weapon, slamming Glen into the wall hard enough so that the boy
damn near punched an outline in the sheetrock.

The werewolf didn't stop there. He piled into Glen before he
could hit the ground, ramming him against the wall again . . . and
again. Next he jammed a clawed hand under Barlow's chin, and this
time he did the job right—hammering Glen's thick skull straight
through the sheetrock.

A wrench of his wrist and he pulled Barlow out of the divot,
twisting his neck into a patch of moonlight shining from the back
window. Ruby beads rolled down Glen's sweaty face. *Yeah*, Kale
thought, twisting harder. *Bring on the blood!*

He picked up Barlow and heaved him against the far wall. Glen
crashed into a clean square of moonlight, grunted, tried to move. But
Kale was on him before the hardcase could even twitch an inch. This
was it—the final bit of business before the deed got done. Because
right now, all Barlow really knew was that some kind of monster was
putting him through the spin cycle. For Kale, killing Kim's brother
would be useless unless the bastard realized the identity of the nightmare doing the deed.

Without that little moment of recognition, Kale's satisfaction-meter would register *zip*.

With it, that sucker would notch off the scale. The werewolf's claws snaked through Barlow's hair and gave his head an attentive yank. At the same time, Kale raised his other hand, and moonlight caught the chrome skull rings circling his black fingers.

Those fingers danced before Glen Barlow's eyes.

Fanged teeth sparkled with rictus smiles.

Hollow-eyed skulls filled with moonlight.

Barlow stared as if hypnotized, pupils dilating into deepening pools of realization. Kale howled in triumph, but Barlow wasn't even looking at him. He just kept staring at those rings.

And why wouldn't he stare?

It was a hell of a thing to figure out a few seconds before you died.

It was a hell of a thing to realize that the monster crouching over you was the man you'd come to kill.

<hr>

So Glen did the only thing he could do.

He looked the monster dead in the eye.

The switchblade he'd hidden in his boot *snicked* open in the moonlight.

The werewolf caught the gleam a second too late. Glen jammed the knife between Kale Howard's ribs, burying the blade to the hilt before ripping it to the side. Black blood spilled over Glen's right hand. He pulled back and stabbed the creature again, lower this time. Kale roared as if his guts were about to spill out of his belly.

But they didn't. The werewolf's wounds were already healing.

His left hand plunged downward, razor claws splayed in a driving arc that split the skin of Glen's right forearm. Muscle shredded as Kale dug those nails deep, burying four long fingers between Glen's bones.

Glen dropped the knife, and the well-honed blade dug into the floorboards as Kale closed his fist around Glen's ulna. Glen would have screamed if he could have sucked a breath. The werewolf's other hand snaked through Glen's hair, then deeper—claws digging tunnels between scalp and skull until they found purchase in the tendons at the back of Glen's neck.

The monster jerked Glen's head back, stretching his neck into the kill zone, trapping him between hands buried in neck and wrist. Wounds spilled blood across the corded length of Glen's neck. Kale's black lips drew back. A mouthful of spit slapped Glen in the face, and then Kale's jaws closed around his neck.

Savage teeth tore into muscle. Arterial blood geysered against the werewolf's pelt. Halogen headlights cored the jagged plywood hole across the room. It seemed the light would swallow Glen faster than Kale could. He closed his eyes against it, but he couldn't escape its stark power.

Outside, a car door slammed.

There were voices. The werewolf's ears perked, and he turned toward the light.

For Glen, the reprieve didn't seem to matter.

If the Marines had arrived, they were too goddamned late.

⁓

Of course, it wasn't the Marines.

And it wasn't J. J. Bryce, either.

There were three of them, and every one looked just a little bit like Kale Howard—even the one who didn't have a set of *cojones* hanging between her legs.

Glen had never met any of Kale's siblings.

But all it took was one glance, and he knew this bunch fit the bill.

⁓ ◡ ⁓

The Howards were all over brother Kale in a matter of seconds. Dwayne—the largest of the boys—waded in first, backhanding the wolf with a handful of silver rings. Kale howled as if doused with acid, but he didn't turn tail. No. He spit blood and bared his teeth, but he never got the chance to test his game on his eldest brother. Joe—shorter, faster, and meaner—had already closed in from one side, skinning his belt from his jeans. Before Kale could make a move, Joe had looped that thirty-two-inch length of snakeskin around his brother's neck in one well-practiced motion.

The belt whispered through hammered silver as Joe yanked it tight. The buckle closed over Kale's windpipe like a pair of channel locks, the horrible metal burning its brand into his flesh. Unable to breathe, Kale blacked out for an instant and started to drop.

In the second it took for him to make the trip to the floor, Kris—the oldest and roughest of Kale's siblings—stepped forward. Tanned, cougar-lean, and dressed in black jeans and a tank top, she looked like the kind of woman who should be demo-ing combat knives at a survivalist convention in Vegas. She jammed the barrel of a nickel-plated .45 against her baby brother's temple and tore a strip off him with a voice seasoned by whiskey and cigarettes.

"Make another move, dog, and I'll splatter your brains all over this room."

"Better save those silver bullets, Kris." Dwayne hovered over Glen. "Looks like this other boy's been bit."

Kale's sister swore under her breath as she turned to examine Glen's wounds. From jawbone to wrist, Barlow's right side was a shredded mess of meat and gristle. Any bastard suffering similar wounds under another circumstance would have slipped into shock by now, but Kris knew that wasn't going to happen to Barlow . . . not if the werewolf virus were pulsing through his blood.

She ignored his mangled arm, and the pistol that lay next to it, examining the flesh torn by the werewolf's attack. Yep. This was more than a claw job. Kale had put his fangs straight into the cowboy's arteries, but he hadn't finished him off. The wounded man's heart was still beating, and from the look of things the virus was already doing its work. Barlow's wounds were beginning to heal, a cuff of scar tissue slowly knitting over the flesh of his wrist. The only upside was that Barlow was freshly infected. His metabolism was operating at a slower rate than Kale's, so he wasn't an immediate threat.

"Better put a bullet in him, sis," Joe said. "That full moon ain't goin' anywhere for hours yet. I don't want to have to deal with two dogs if he turns."

"Brush up on your homework, idiot," Kris said. "It takes longer than that for the virus to set. This cowboy won't do any turning until the next full moon. The most he'll do right now is some serious healing up."

She smiled down at Glen.

"If we let him live long enough, that is."

But there was no way in hell Kris Howard was going to let this desert rat live. She'd made that decision as soon as she'd learned that the cowboy had been bit.

Yep. That was the way it had to be. Kris was the one who made the decisions around here. She'd been doing that since her parents decided to crawl inside a bottle when she was just a kid. Even then, her deadweight brothers were just along for the ride.

And Kale, hell . . . time hadn't done him any favors. He was still her scrabble-brained little brother, half nuts even on nights when the moon was just a fingernail clipping up there in the sky. That's why she'd cleaned up after him so many times in the years since he'd gotten his ass chewed by a werewolf down in Mexico.

Of course, having a werewolf in a family of thieves was mostly a real plus, but Kris could see that this wasn't going to be one of those times. Damn . . . it'd been awhile since Kale tore up that little showgirl in Reno, but this clusterfuck tonight made that mess look like a picnic. Kale had opened Kim's brother like a can of Alpo. Anyone who watched forensic TV shows could collect enough evidence in this slaughterhouse to convict every Howard in the room . . . plus their dead-ass parents, who were back in Texas taking dirt naps.

So the whole deal sure enough screwed the pooch, but what could she do about it? Jagged wedges of Glen Barlow's skin stuck to the wall like some serial killer's warped painting; his blood was soaking into the cracked floorboards; the headbutt-pitted sheet-rock was clotted with hanks of his hair. Kris was sure she'd have to burn down the house before they made a permanent exit tonight.

And that really bit, because the plan had been to sell the damn thing for a good chunk of cash after Kale knocked off his latest bride. But there was more chance of their parents growing fresh livers and crawling out of their plywood caskets down there in Texas than there was of her selling this house. Kris figured the best she could hope for when she finished up this business tonight would be an empty box of matches. And the way she saw it, the bloody mess of a man at her feet had to have figured out the score about the whole deal—including the growling moron who at that moment was straining against a snakeskin leash.

Kris stared down at Glen Barlow, cocking her head in Kale's direction.

"Guess you know the family secret," she said.

"Yeah . . . and I think I figured out the family business, too."

Kris smiled. The bloody cowboy sucked a breath. Surprisingly, only part of it whistled through his windpipe. Had to be the virus was burning a trail through Barlow's torn-up excuse for a circulatory system faster than Kris had expected. But she wasn't particularly worried about that. After all, she was the one holding the gun with the silver bullets.

"So, you're the guy who tossed my baby brother through a window, huh?"

"Yeah."

"Looks like tonight you're reapin' what you sowed."

"Well, it was a dirty job . . . " he started, coughing up a thick rope of blood.

"Yeah . . . but somebody had to do it," she finished.

"You know how it goes."

"You bet I do. But there's a problem with that, Tex. Kale sure ain't the most obedient pup in the kennel, but he's my brother. And in our family, we take care of our own. I figure you can understand that."

Another cough, and maybe another *yeah* mixed in there, too.

"Sure. Add it up, we're not that different, you and me. I'm here to help Kale. You're here to do right by your sister. Hell, I understand that. Some guy chews your baby sis down to the bone and leaves her in the middle of nowhere for the buzzards to peck. Plus, he ends up with everything she owned in the world. You've got a right to go all *Charlie Bronson* on him, but you're a little late for that. To tell the truth, you're late for anything that doesn't include taking a silver bullet."

That did it. Barlow tried to rise. Just doing that, it looked like his head was going to topple off his torn-up neck and end up in his lap. Kris nearly laughed, and the only thing that stopped her were the scars closing over Barlow's wound.

He was healing faster now, but Kris knew there wasn't enough *fast* in the world to get the job done for him before she finished saying her piece. "You wanted to fix things, Barlow, you should have done it last Christmas. It's too late now. Your sister's in a hole. And if there's still a squeaky little cage turnin' in your guts, let me tell you something: that hamster's dead, amigo. Whatever you wanted to do, it's way past time to do it now."

"You said that."

"Yeah. I did. But you cost me a fat bankroll tonight, so forgive me if I take a minute to show you the error of your ways before I put a hunk of silver in your brain. See, I don't want you feeling the least little bit like a hero when you get your ass kicked into eternity. You're not any kind of hero, *amigo*. Let's get that straight."

Barlow was quiet now. Had to be it was sinking in. He didn't say a word.

Kris checked the pistol, chambered a round.

"Let me wrap it up for you, now that you're catching on. I've got a real simple way of looking at life. The way I see it, what you do is who you are . . . and what you don't do, too. And, buddy, when it comes to your sister, and when it comes to the guy who killed her, you didn't do much."

Barlow held his silence. All he gave her was a stare.

And that was enough. Hell, that stare was plenty.

Kris raised the pistol.

"I see you get the message," she said. "End of sermon. It's time for the piper to get paid."

⁓

The werewolf virus had jacked Glen's metabolism into a molten overdrive. His mind raced with quick-cut impressions, hundreds of them—Kris' .45 . . . and her smile . . . and the other two Howard boys watching him from across the room . . . and their snarling werewolf brother straining against the snakeskin leash, eager for another taste of Barlow's flesh—the slightest movement of each member of the Howard clan cataloged in a fraction of a second, and every image filed for action and reaction if Glen could only move.

He had to do that. If the virus set quickly enough . . . if the full moon shone at the correct angle . . . his lupine brain understood that he could move faster than he'd ever moved before. And it was happening already. His wounds were closing as if some heathen god had decided to dam him up. Scar tissue crackled over his carotid artery. New skin covered exposed muscle and tendon, cells multiplying with an insane rapidity.

Glen's dropped pistol lay just a foot away. Synapses fired as his brain ordered his hand to grab the pistol . . . but, damn . . . he couldn't even wriggle his fingers yet, let alone lift his arm.

"Don't even think about it," Kris said, kicking the gun across the room.

She bent low, pressing the .45 barrel against his temple.

"Here we go," she said. "Enjoy the ride."

Glen sucked a breath. Kris began to squeeze the trigger.

Across the room, another pistol cocked sharply.

A man's voice came from the other side of the ragged plywood hole.

"Drop the gun," J. J. Bryce said. "And do it now."

⁓ ∽ ⌣

The hard-eyed woman did as she was told. One look at the bloody man on the floor and Bryce had a serious crime scene flashback— Kim Barlow dead in the shadow of Tres Manos—but this time he was looking at her brother, soaked in his own gore on a dusty hardwood floor.

"Get away from him," Bryce said.

The woman raised her hands and stepped backward, retreating from the dull illumination of the room's single standing floor lamp. Bryce leaned through the splintery plywood gap, tracking her movement with his pistol.

That was when he noticed that the woman wasn't alone. Two men stood in the shadows on the other side of the room. One of them reached for a wall switch while the other slipped a loop from around the neck of a . . .

Jesus. Some kind of hairy *thing* . . . a thing with claws, and teeth, and—

It settled on its haunches.

In another instant it would spring—

Bryce's brain didn't need any more input. He fired his pistol. The slug punched the freak backward. The lights went out. The two men scrambled in the dark, but J. J. couldn't see them. He couldn't see anything—

Except a pair of red eyes, low to the floor then rising, closing on him like coals shoveled by the devil himself.

⁓

The nickel-plated .45 gleamed in a patch of moonlight. Glen was with it, his body trapped in the dead-white fire. And it seemed as if the pistol Kris Howard had used to control her werewolf brother were melting there on that same moonlight forge . . . its gleaming ivory grips scorching the silver slugs that lurked within.

The stink of silver nearly made Glen retch. His stomach roiled at the thought of touching the weapon, but he knew that the .45 was his only chance.

So did Kris Howard.

She grabbed for the pistol.

Glen did, too.

⁓

Several shots rang out inside the house, but J. J. Bryce was barely aware of them. Gripping his own pistol tightly in his fist, he scrambled to his feet as he came out of a tumble with the red-eyed creature.

It had rolled over the top of him, continuing across the flagstone patio before righting itself. Quickly, it launched a second attack, charging him like a freight train. Bryce wasn't set, but he fired his pistol three times in quick succession. Every slug found its target, dead center in the thing's chest. It didn't matter. The monster bit off an anguished scream and kept coming, and it slammed into the deputy so hard that he was airborne in an instant.

A glance to the side. White teeth gnashing inches from Bryce's face. His pistol clattered against the patio. Then he started to drop. He realized he'd be coming down hard on a flagstone slab a second before his skull slammed against it, realized too that the monster would be on top of him before another second could tick off the clock.

The cop landed hard.

Kale knew he had to finish him off quickly and get back inside the house. He'd heard the gunshots. Chances were they'd come from Kris' .45 instead of Glen Barlow's pistol. But who had the gun? That was the question—

"Hey, boy."

Kale spun toward the open doorway.

He had his answer.

He didn't like it.

The werewolf sprang. Eyes gleaming, teeth bared, claws ready to tear through Glen Barlow in a ferocious explosion of rage.

For Glen, it was just like staring into his own heart.

He didn't stare long.

He pulled the trigger.

In a bright blast of muzzle flash, everything went away.

PART THREE

J. J. Bryce lay on the flagstones, out cold, but Glen ignored the fallen cop.

The .45 still filled his hand. The silver bullets inside the weapon were encased in a steel clip buried beneath ivory grips. Glen knew that. Still, holding the pistol was like holding a live rattler, ready to sink fangs into his skin if he so much as twitched.

But he couldn't put the pistol down.

The truth was, he didn't know if he'd ever put it down.

Behind Glen, three people lay dead in the house. He'd killed Kris first, then the other two. He didn't even know their names. He'd killed all three of them in a matter of seconds, the animal fury of the werewolf virus surging through him as if it were in control of the gun. Kale was dead, too—his sternum shattered by a silver bullet that had torn through muscle and heart, finally burying itself in his spinal column. He lay on the flagstone patio, and looking at him there was no clue that he'd ever been anything different than the human monsters who lay within the walls of Kim Barlow's house.

But Kale had been something different. Glen knew that as he stared down at the corpse of the man he'd wanted to kill so badly, just as he knew that his rage was as dead as the cursed bastard who'd murdered his sister. Now it had been replaced by another fire, a hunk of brimstone buried inside him that was torched by the light of the full moon.

Glen wasn't the kind of man who prayed, but he hoped he wouldn't feel that fire when he watched the sun rise in just a few hours.

If he watched the sun rise.

If he stuck around long enough to do that.

Glen's grip tightened around the .45. He knew what the silver bullets in the gun could do to him, the same way he knew what the moon above would do to him the next time it rose in the night sky, full and bright.

Just one bullet. That's all it would take.

Just one, and he'd never end up like Kale Howard.

Glen raised the pistol. He placed the barrel beneath his chin.

And he waited. He waited for a sign . . . a sign from somewhere . . . or someone . . . perhaps a sign from Kim. Right or wrong, the things he'd done tonight he'd done for her. So he waited for an acknowledgment, a rush of images his brain could catalog the way it had cataloged every movement and expression of the people he'd just killed.

The ivory pistol grips were slick with his sweat. The gun barrel dug into the taut flesh beneath his chin. That brimstone fire inside him was cooking his heart now. Suddenly Glen heard words, down there in the sizzle.

But they weren't Kim's words.

They belonged to another, and he'd heard them earlier this night.

What you do is who you are . . .

The words were lost for a moment, sizzling in the brimstone roar. It was as if something inside Glen wanted to incinerate them, the same way he'd burned down the woman who'd spoken those words. But they came around again, surer this time . . . as if they were his own.

What you do is who you are . . .

Glen lowered the pistol.

. . . and what you don't do, too.

❧

The sound of his cell phone brought Bryce around. It was still dark—a glance at his watch told him it was just past midnight.

Damn. His skull was pounding in time with the phone's insistent ringtone. J. J. reached for his cell, but it wasn't there. It was over on the patio, murky LCD light glowing as it chirped like a confused little bird. And there was his pistol, right next to it, and—

That thing he'd wrestled lay on the patio, too. Only it didn't look like a wolf anymore. Now the damn thing looked like Kale Howard. And now J. J. remembered. He'd cracked his head on the patio when he'd taken that fall. In the moment before he'd passed out, Glen Barlow had appeared in the doorway with a nickel-plated .45 in his hand. He'd looked like a refugee from a zombie movie, but he'd gunned down the monster beneath the patio overhang.

And now Kale Howard lay dead in its place.

Bryce stared at Howard's corpse for a long moment.

Goddamn, he thought. *Well . . . goddamn.*

Because there wasn't much else you could think. Not if you could add two and two. And even with a knock on the head, J. J. could do that. He moved on to the next order of business and tried to rise, but his legs wouldn't quite make the trip. And the rest of his body . . . Jesus. It felt like his right arm wasn't even there.

What the hell was going on? He was ass-down in the dirt, leaning against something hard. He couldn't move his right arm at all. Damn thing was asleep, bent above his head, stuck there as if tied.

Bryce leaned to the side and looked up. He was handcuffed to the driver's door of a truck. Not his own truck—Barlow's piece-of-shit rustbucket . . . which hadn't even been there when J. J. pulled in a couple hours ago.

Oh shit. With his free hand, Bryce patted his pocket. His keys were gone.

His brand-new Ford was gone, too.

That son of a bitch, Bryce thought. He settled back against Barlow's truck, and he stewed about it. Might be he'd have to sit here a while before someone came along. But that was okay. He was in no rush to discuss his stolen vehicle . . . or tonight's business.

Still, the wheels started turning in his head. Maybe that wasn't a bad thing. Sooner or later, he'd have to decide what the hell he was going to say.

To Sheriff Randall.

And to Lisa, too.

PART FOUR

In the months since he'd left El Pasito, Glen had a lot of time on his hands. That was good. There was a lot he needed to think about in the wake of the bloodbath out there in the desert. Things had changed for him . . . a lot of things. Everything.

But as the days closed into night, what he thought about most was Kim. He'd always felt responsible for her. After all, he was her big brother. That reaction was as natural as breathing. But he was starting to understand that Kim had made her own decisions in life, and he wasn't responsible for them any more than he was responsible for the trouble they'd brought her way. They were Kim's choices, not his. And she'd shut him out when making them, and she'd shut him out when they went bad . . . especially when it came to Kale.

And maybe that was part of the reason for his anger. She'd shut him out, and then she was dead before either of them could change the way things were. Maybe that was the reason he hadn't heard his sister's voice in the desert on the night he'd nearly taken his own life.

Maybe he hadn't know her well enough to ask for that kind of help.

Maybe she was still shutting him out.

They were brother and sister, sure. They'd shared memory, time, and blood. But Glen had never known the secrets Kim kept locked up in her heart. And he wondered if you ever could know that about someone else, no matter what ties you shared.

Just lately, he'd been thinking about that a lot. He hadn't reached any particular conclusions, but there was one thing he was sure of. In the time since he'd left El Pasito, he was beginning to understand his own secrets, and he was beginning to understand his own heart.

He wondered if someone else was beginning to understand those things, too.

〜◯◯〜

It wasn't easy to find a pay phone anymore, but Glen turned one up.

He had to buy a phone card from a little Cajun girl working the till in the convenience store before he could make his call. The phone was on a pole across from the gas pumps. There weren't a lot of people around, just a lot of kudzu. And that was okay with Glen. This wasn't a conversation he wanted to share with anyone.

He dialed Lisa's number.

A man picked up on the third ring. "Hello?"

Glen didn't say a word.

"Hello?" the man said again. "Hey . . . is anyone there?"

A click on the line, and the familiar voice was gone. Glen hung up the receiver.

Well I'll be damned, he thought, that voice still there in his head. *J. J. Bryce and Lisa Allen.*

He stood there a minute, thinking about it. A truck roared by on the two-lane highway, heading toward Baton Rouge. Glen shook his head, grinning. A lot had surprised him just lately, and he couldn't see a single reason why this should be any different.

But, right now, that was okay with him.

Really, it was.

⸎

Man, if there was one thing J. J. hated, it was hang ups.

He turned away from the phone. At least it hadn't been another lawyer calling. Since the gunfight at the Barlow Corral, he'd had enough of lawyers. And administrative leave. And state and county investigators.

And the questions some of those guys asked. Especially that forensic specialist who'd discovered that the Howard clan had been gunned down with silver bullets. He'd asked if J. J. had any ideas about those. "Hell," J. J. had said. "Maybe Barlow thought he was the Lone Ranger. The guy was definitely crazy enough."

As it stood, investigators had connected the Howards to six murders in four states. Three of the victims had been married to Kale. Seemed he'd do the killing, and then his sister would come in a few months later and cash in the chips. She'd been smart enough to keep a low profile, mostly, and that had definitely been her MO in El Pasito. No one in town had even know that Kale had a sister—or a couple of brothers—out there at the house. Hell, that was probably why they kept the front window boarded up.

Anyway, J. J. was glad the deal was wrapping up. Next week he was going back to work. A couple months after that . . . well, the whole thing would probably be forgotten.

One could hope, anyway.

Lisa was sweeping the patio when J. J. stepped through the door. He was carrying a couple bottles of Pacifico, and he handed her one. She took a sip, and that was an improvement. The beer was good and cold.

"Who was on the phone?" she asked.

"Hang up. Don't you hate those?"

She nodded. They sat on the back step for awhile. J. J. drank his beer and talked about going back to the cop shop. She listened. After awhile, he said, "I think I'll drive over to Dos Gatos. Get some of those pork carnitas. We can have a barbeque tonight."

"Sounds good."

A few minutes later, he was gone.

Lisa sat there on the step, staring at Tres Manos in the distance. Afternoon clouds drifted in from the east, casting shadows over The Hands. Lisa sipped her beer and watched the clouds hang there. They hung a good long while, until the wind chased them off.

Lisa finished her beer, then got her clippers from the tool shed.

She worked in the herb garden.

She trimmed back the rosemary.

She trimmed it tight.

Ninja Rats on Harleys

ELIZABETH A. VAUGHAN

It was a dark and stormy night.

Well it was, damn it. The cold air slapped me in the face as the glass doors of the ER waiting area slid open. Any warmth my tattered bathrobe held was gone in an instant as the wind wrapped around me. The rain had stopped for now, but the entire parking lot gleamed under the lights, as did the ambulances, their flashing lights reflecting off the puddles and my van.

My bloodstained slippers were soaked as I slapped across the parking lot. I cradled my purse and those damned discharge instructions as I fumbled for my keys. I opened the passenger side door, set the purse carefully on the seat, and then slammed that sucker shut with all my strength.

I was pissed, and who could blame me?

Nothing like being attacked in your own home by a hideous, stinky white possum and his ninja hench-rats at an ungodly hour of the morning. We'd fought them off, Wan and I, with naught but our bare hands and a bottle of toilet cleaner.

Well, okay, Wan had a sword. And he killed most of them. But I'd done my fair share, although it was my own blood on my slippers.

Wan is a mouse. An ancient Chinese mouse, as far as I can figure. He hasn't been very forthcoming. He's been good company since he moved in about a month ago. He was teaching me tai chi and I was teaching him football. I had to admit, it was nice to have someone around . . . to have company. And yes, my social life does suck that bad.

He talks. Did I mention that?

At any rate, a few hours ago, we'd been attacked by people . . . animals . . . who also talked and who clearly knew more about Wan than I did. One of the rats had bitten through my finger, hence the visit to the ER.

Slamming the door had not been the best idea, since Itty and Bitty, my poor little white dogs, had been cowering under the seats in the back. They scrabbled up, put their feet on the window and howled for attention.

My cowardly fat white Westies, who tend to fart when under stress. I opened the rear passenger door and petted and cooed over them for a minute, paying attention to the slash on Itty's nose. The possum had gotten her at one point in the fight, but it was only a slight scratch. I got them calmed back down, shut the door, and headed around to mine.

Wan was standing on my purse when I heaved my weary body into the driver's seat. He stood at the summit, his sword over his back, his arms crossed over his chest. "We should stay and talk with the learned doctor, Kate."

The doctor also seemed to know more about what was going on than I did. I sighed, looking at the ambulances. "Wan, he's going to be busy for quite some time. I want to go home and take a shower."

"He possesses knowledge that we do not have," Wan argued.

"Why do we leave a potential ally behind us?"

"Because my hand hurts," I snapped. "Because I'm filthy, and tired, and the dogs are scared." I struggled with my seat belt using my bandaged hand. "Because that nurse said that the Doctor would be working on those accident victims for hours. Because I'm not drinking that hideous coffee, and because . . . " I snapped the belt in place and turned to glare at Mr.-Holier-Than-Thou-Talking-Mouse. "Because I don't know who is friend or foe until you tell me what the hell is going on!"

Wan glared right back and I promised myself that if he told me to be one with my pain I was going to pitch him right out the window and drive off.

The damn mouse looked away. "You hold the keys, Honorable Lady."

I jammed them in the ignition and started the van.

⁓

What a surprise. There isn't a lot of traffic on the expressway at four in the morning on a Saturday.

Who'da thunk it?

I pulled out of the hospital grounds, and headed up Monroe Street toward Douglas. I'd take the expressway home. Wan sat silent, which was fine with me. I needed to think.

It had taken me aback when the ER Doctor told me he knew my injury was from a ninja rat bite. Believe me when I say that I hadn't put that down on any forms. He'd taken pains to make sure the nurse didn't hear him, too, come to think of it. I narrowed my eyes as I pulled onto Douglas. His steel gray eyes had been sharp, sharp enough that he had probably known about Wan hiding in my purse.

But did that mean that I could trust him?

I turned onto the entrance ramp to the expressway, chewing my lower lip. Well hell, I was trusting a talking mouse, now wasn't I? And I hadn't exactly asked him for ID, now had I?

My front window was fogging up, so I reached for the blower dial. Cold air flowed over my feet before I could get it set on defrost. We'd almost be home before it warmed up. I shivered and set the cruise control at sixty-two. The last thing I needed was a ticket.

My hand throbbed as I tilted the rearview mirror to look at the dogs. They were sound asleep on the backseat, exhausted, poor babies. I adjusted the mirror back with a wince. There were lights in the distance behind us. Far enough back not to worry about just yet.

I pulled my injured hand back and rested it on my chest, steering with my left hand.

"We should not return to the house," Wan stated firmly. "They will be waiting for us."

I sighed. He had a point, but I didn't really want to hear it. "All right. I'm too tired to argue. A hotel then, but we will have to smuggle in the dogs." I sighed, and checked the rearview mirror. If a hotel would let us in. I looked like hell. The lights behind us were getting closer. They were coming fast. Looked like motorcycles out for an evening cruise.

"Perhaps we could shelter in the home of a friend?" Wan asked carefully.

I stiffened. This was a sore point, and he damn well knew it. When I'd given up on my dreams, my fantasy writing, I'd walked away from friends who shared those dreams. Gamers, writers, dreamers and geeks, I'd cut them out of my life. "Oh sure," I snapped.

"I'll just show up with bloody slippers, dogs, a talking mouse and they'll be glad to—"

The rumble of a gunned Harley cut me off. I glanced at the rearview mirror. The motorcycles had caught up with us, about twelve from the looks of things. They'd surround us, then pass as they—

Movement caused me to glance out my side window. A big Harley, a Fat Boy, had pulled up even with the van. I glanced at the tank first, seeing the logo then noticed the rider's leg looked . . . odd. I looked up and gasped.

"KATE!" Wan shouted beside me.

The rider was a rat, a giant rat, riding a Harley, and glaring at me through its ninja mask. With a big white ugly possum perched on its shoulder. The possum caught my gaze and gave me an open-mouth hiss, waving its walking stick.

I swerved wildly.

The bikes all swerved with me, moving as if we'd rehearsed it. The rumble strip complained as my tires hit and I jerked the wheel back, frantic to stay on the road.

The dogs started barking, not sure what was happening, but sure they could scare it away. The bike in front of me put on its brake light, and I hit the brake as well, instinctively.

"No, Kate." Wan urged. "Do not stop."

"But . . ." I said.

"It will put us at their mercy, of which there is little." Wan's voice cut like a knife. "Go!"

Wan may be small, but that command made me jam my foot on the gas. The van leaped forward, and the biker swerved to the side, then gunned it to stay in front of me. The ninja rat driver turned his head to look at me, his eyes dark, beady, and vicious.

I swallowed hard. "How did they get so big?" I asked in a whisper.

"Magic," Wan said.

Duh. I risked a quick glare in his direction but the little snit was back down on the seat, digging in my purse, pulling out my cell phone and the Doctor's card. "Call 911," I said.

"And what do I say?" Wan asked as he opened the phone.

He had a point. I gripped the steering wheel with two hands, and focused on the road. The bikes kept weaving around me, trying to drive me off the road but I hung on grimly.

Then that one in front apparently decided to clip me and I saw my chance. Big mistake on his part. No amount of magic was going to stop me. He swerved in front, and I gunned the van.

She did me proud, surging forward just enough to clip his rear fender. The rat wiped out, barely avoiding my front tire as he and his bike hit the pavement and slid off. Metal screamed and sparks flew as the bike and the rat slid away.

Bet that ninja outfit was a whole lot of protection.

But even as I gloated the one by my window moved closer. I had a brief glimpse of the possum hefting up its walking staff and—

THWACK!

Tiny cracks blossomed in my side window.

That started the dogs to howling, dancing in the back seat and farting for all they were worth. I swore and swerved again, pressing on the accelerator, but the rats stayed right next to the van.

I glanced down at the speedometer. Sweetmother of— Where were the police? Normally I'd have a small army of Toledo PD on my ass waiting to write me six tickets for going this fast. But noooo— never one when ya—

The possum jumped on the hood.

One little claw grabbed the windshield wiper, and his other held that damn staff. He was grinning that toothy grin again, chanting something muffled by the glass. The staff started to glow. Not good, not good. I panicked. I wanted him off the glass, off the—

I hit the washer.

Blue fluid squirted up under his chin. *WHAMP* went the wipers, and the possum went flying off to the side, with any luck possum pie by the road.

One of the ninja rats lunged and caught him by the tail just before he hit the ground.

My heart was pounding in my throat. For an instant, the possum was swinging from his tail, spitting out washer fluid and pointing at me. Then with a flip, he landed on the back of the rat, and they fell away from the van, moving over a lane. They all did.

"Wan," I said nervously. "Wan, I think . . ."

Wan was talking into my phone excitedly in what sounded like Chinese.

"English, Wan!" I shouted. The possum was gesturing at the front of the van, and pointing at the—

BHAM.

The front tire blew.

The dogs were howling, Wan was howling, hell I was probably howling but I didn't care, My only focus was to control the van, and my teeth rattled with the effort.

The noise was terrific, the rubber from the tire flying in every direction. Sparks fountained up from the rim and my poor old minivan was steering like a dead cow. With metal screaming, the hot smell of rubber and dog farts, the van went off the side, over the brim and down to rest at an angle off the road.

The air bag exploded, punching me in the face. The silence was eerie as it deflated and I unwrapped my hands from the wheel. "Is everyone—"

CRACK!

The possum shattered my window.

I covered my head instinctively as bits of safely glass exploded into the Van. I could barely hear Wan over the howling of the dogs, because I was completely focused on the rat snarls as they reached for me. Their claws sank into the arm of my bathrobe and my flesh as they tried to pull me out through the window.

Sorry boys, my fat middle-aged butt wasn't budging. They could tug and pull all they wanted—

One of them reached in and opened the van door. A sharp blade appeared and sliced through my seat belt.

I fell out, onto the ground. The rats grabbed my robe and dragged me away from the van through the wet grass. The dogs howled and I had just enough time to pray they stayed in the van when I was dropped to the ground.

I looked up to find myself surrounded by man-sized ninja rats. The possum perched on one's shoulder, glaring down at me. I took a deep breath, then wished I hadn't. That possum wasn't man-sized but he still stunk to high heaven. Ugh.

"You have offended, fat one. Now you die."

The rats all pulled daggers.

Er. I blinked up at him, confused. What about threats, rantings, that kind of thing? I mean, really . . .

"She dies, you die."

We all looked to see Wan standing on the seat of the car, backlit by the dome light of the minivan. Wisps of fog were gathered around his feet. He had his sword out and pointed at the ninjas. "Move away from her if you value your lives."

It would have been very impressive had he been more than a few inches tall.

The rats chuckled, and even I smiled. Wan looked so earnest, standing there with his sword in his hand.

"She dies," the possum laughed. "And then we beat the information out of you, traitor."

Okay, not so funny now.

I leaped up, dodged one of the rats and hit the possum right on the snoot. Impressed?

The only problem is it didn't happen that way. My middle-aged fat body wouldn't leap up for nothing. So I did the best I could. I kicked one of the rats right on the shins. Smartly.

He dropped his knife and clutched his leg. Some ninja.

All eyes were focused back on me. "Kill her," the possum snarled.

Wan squeaked his battle cry and darted forward, but that whole man-sized-rat thing was working against him. I tried desperately to crawl away, my robe catching under my knees. The rats laughed, my cowardly dogs howled from the van, and I was sure I was dead.

One rat grabbed my shoulder and flipped me over, his teeth and knife gleaming. He was bringing the knife up to plunge into my stomach. I watched in horror as the gleaming blade arched over me.

There was a crackling flash, a stench of sulfur, and one dead rat falling down on top of me. The lightning caught him right in the chest.

I scrabbled back, trying to get out from under the smoldering, twitching corpse without throwing up. As my legs slipped clear, more bolts shivered over my head, seeming to almost hang in the air before striking the rats. I pressed myself flat to the grass and risked a glimpse.

It was the doctor from the ER.

He looked taller somehow, his white lab coat glowing and his stethoscope swinging wildly around his neck. The street lights reflected off his high forehead, and his long grey ponytail swung behind him.

He looked damn fine, to my way of thinking.

The fact that he was standing with both feet firmly braced as he flung lightning at the rats with ease also worked for me.

The rats were diving for cover, throwing themselves to the ground to hide behind the motorcycles they'd left scattered around.

The possum went for my van.

I felt the pressure of tiny paws on my shoulder and a whisper in my ear. "Stay down, Kate. I will protect you."

"The dogs," I screamed, trying to climb to my feet. My slippers slipped on the grass.

The doctor heard me. With a flip of his wrist, he sent a bright blue ball our way, floating, zeroing in on us like a missile. It zipped past my shoulder, and for a brief moment light flared around me. When it faded, I was pinned under the weight of a man-sized mouse, standing on my back.

Needless to say, the rats were focused on the doctor. Their tails lashing, hissing, regrouping to attack him. I'd be okay. "Wan, please," with what little breath I had, I begged. "Save my babies."

Wan hesitated, then to my utter relief charged the van, sword in hand, his battle cry more impressive now. The possum had climbed in the driver's seat, but his head turned to look at the angry man-sized mouse charging his way.

I took a few deep breaths, certain that there'd be more help coming. But the expressway was empty, and there were no flashing cop cars. No, just a lovely bright colored macaw flying at the rats, slashing with its beak and claws. And the lightning bolts, being slung from the doctor's fingers at the rats.

Lightning. I felt oddly calm about the whole thing. Of course lightning. What else . . .

The possum was charging toward me.

Uh-oh. It occurred to me that just laying there was not a good idea. I needed to be running, or at least trotting, away from this madness.

Wan was chasing the possum, as were Itty and Bitty, barking madly. I struggled to my feet, just as the possum threw something at me. A globe of light again, sparkly white and lovely.

I threw up my hands to ward it off, even as Wan chopped at the possum.

The globe of light splattered over me, soft and warm, like a blanket. Just like a blanket, in fact, it was expanding, clinging, covering me quickly, my chest, mouth, and nose.

I couldn't breathe.

The stuff wrapped tight, and started to constrict, forcing what air I had out of my chest. I struggled, pushed at it, but while I could move it, I couldn't break it. I had a brief moment to be thankful that there was no one around. I probably looked like a bag lady fighting a garbage bag.

Arms surrounded me. The Doctor. I could see those gray eyes, feel his arms around me. Was that a macaw on his shoulder?

There was no air left. Interestingly enough, I actually felt my eyes roll back into my head as I lost consciousness.

～◦◦～

I woke up and smelled the coffee.

Floating just on the edge of sleep, I took a deep breath, trying to get the caffeine in my system through my lungs. Deep and rich and dark, I could almost taste it on the back of my tongue. Clearly I was dead, and heaven smelled like frenchroast.

Warm. I was warm as well, laying wrapped in a blanket on what felt like a sofa. There was weight on my feet, which could only be Itty and Bitty. Poor things, they were probably exhausted from their . . .

From something. I couldn't remember exactly. I was wrapped in a soft blanket, on a couch. Did I fall asleep watching a game?

As much as I wanted coffee, I also wanted to float off again, just drift off for a while. But now sounds started to invade my private, perfect world. Voices, soft and persistent, with the clink of a spoon against a cup and the sound of coffee being poured.

"You shouldn't have approached her at all. You've put her in danger."

"Such was not my intent." Wan was speaking, but he sounded louder than normal. Sleep would have to wait, it seemed.

"But after so long," Wan continued. "I'd been alone for so long . . . she is a friend. A good person."

"And a mundane. With no knowledge, no skills. She's not going to be—"

Hell, that was the Doctor. It came back then. The attack, the rats . . . the doctor throwing lightning bolts. I opened my eyes, blinking at the sun pouring into a strange living room. My dogs were asleep on my feet.

Crap. I was naked under the blanket.

"How long have you been with her?"

"A little more than a month." Wan answered. He sounded apologetic. "Can you make her forget this? Forget me?"

What? I started to struggle with the blanket at that point, clutching it close while trying to sit up. Itty and Bitty snorted and shifted, but they didn't even raise their heads.

"Kate?" Wan's voice came from behind the sofa.

I freed my arms and tried to push myself up, which jarred my wounded hand. I muffled my curse as I managed to sit up. "No one's mucking about in my head." I growled, trying to clear my throat and talk at the same time.

Wan came around the end of the sofa, still man-sized, a pleased look on his face. "You are well?"

"I am naked." I snarled, lifting a hand to smooth my hair back. I pulled it back to find my hand smeared with dirt, and white sticky stuff. "Oh, ick."

"No one is going to muck around in your head. After this long, I couldn't make you forget, even if I wanted to." The Doctor came around the other corner of the sofa, a white mug in each hand. Steam rose from the cups, taunting me.

"Coffee." I wiped my hand on the blanket, and reached out like a babe for a bottle.

The Doctor wisely surrendered one of the mugs. He sat on the coffee table, opposite me.

I ignored him, taking my first sip, eyes closed with pleasure. It tasted as good as it smelled. I sighed, and sank deeper into the cushions.

The Doctor . . . hell if I could remember his name . . . studied me with those sharp steel-gray eyes. "Your clothes were ruined, filthy and soaking wet. *We*," he emphasized the word, "stripped them off you and wrapped you in the blanket."

Wan still hovered, his sword slung over his shoulder. It felt funny to have to look up at him. When I did, his tail flicked up and he clutched it with both paws. "Are you well, Kate?"

"I am not," I scowled at both of them. "What happened?"

"What do you remember?" The Doctor leaned forward as he asked the question, and laid two fingers on the inside of my wrist. His skin tingled against mine.

I pulled my hand back, and rubbed my eyes. "Not being able to breathe."

"You collapsed, Kate." Wan drew a deep breath, his ears twitching. "You fell, lifeless—"

"She's fine, Wan." The Doctor said. "You lost consciousness, but we got the stuff off you quickly."

I frowned, looking at the sunlight pouring through the windows. "How long was I out?"

Wan darted a glance at the Doctor. "Doctor McDougall saw fit to cast—"

"I bespelled you. We needed to move fast, and I didn't have time for arguments. More coffee?" Doctor McDougall rose, supreme in his overblown confidence, and disappeared behind the couch.

Wan stood there, clutching his tail.

I relented, and patted the cushion next to me.

Wan removed his sword, and set it on the coffee table. He sat next to me, his tail reaching out to wrap around my wrist. I was never going to get used to that. But he'd spent a thousand years practicing.

"I feared for you, honorable lady." Wan's warm fur rubbed against my arm. "This man removed the spell on you, then scooped you up in his arms, demanding I follow."

"What about the possum?" I asked. "Did you get him?"

Wan shook his head. "He escaped, along with the remaining rats." He leaned closer, his ear twitching. "Can we trust this man?"

"Do you have a choice?" Doctor McDougall stood over us, coffeepot in hand. I opened my mouth, but he shook his head as he poured. "Eat first. Argue later."

I glared at him over the rim of my mug. "Shower first. I can eat and argue at the same time."

"I'm not surprised." The Doctor replied mildly.

"I will assist you, Kate." Wan sprang up, taking his sword and pulling the strap over his head.

I let him help me up, still clutching my precious caffeine, and the blanket. The Doctor preceded us, turning on lights and getting towels. What a surprise, the bathroom was huge, with a walk-in shower and spa tub. I leaned against the sink for a minute, just taking in the glory of the room, trying not to drool.

"I'll leave you to it," MacDougall said as he left.

"Kate," Wan said softly.

I turned, setting the mug down by the sink, the blanket twisting around my legs. I smiled at him. "It seems so odd, to look you in the eye."

"The spell will not last much longer, or so he said." Wan hesitated, then gave me a deep bow. "I wish to offer my humble apologies. I have brought danger upon you, honorable lady, and I am deeply shamed."

"Wan," I reached out and touched his shoulder. "I don't know what MacDougall said to you, but this is not your fault."

He straightened, shaking his head to negate my words. I could see the pain in his eyes, beady though they might be. On impulse, I reached out and hugged him, sliding my hands under the sheath of his sword.

Wan hesitated for a moment, then wrapped his paws . . . arms . . . around me and buried his face in my hair. His fur was warm and soft, and I could feel the strength in his arms. Paws. Whatever.

"I will defend you with my life," he whispered.

I tightened my arms around him, then released, making sure my blanket stayed up. "Go eat. I'll be quick, and maybe then we will get answers."

"Take your time, Kate." Wan said. "We are safe within this home."

I closed the door behind him, and turned to look at myself in the mirror. Lord, I looked like hell. I started the shower, and sank down on the toilet to let it warm.

Could we trust McDougall? Hell if I knew. I mean, points for saving my life and all, but . . .

On the other hand, we didn't have a lot of alternatives. Seems the public library was a tad short on information about "possums, the use of magic by." We had to get some information from somewhere. McDougall was a place to start.

But as I shed my blanket and stepped into the shower I reminded myself of one thing: Wan had some explaining to do of his own. He hadn't come clean, and apologies aside, he damn well better.

To hell with it. For the next few minutes all I was going to think about was soap and hot water. I poured half a bottle of shampoo in my hand, and started scrubbing.

I was enjoying the second rinse when the door of the bathroom opened.

I froze, as the cold air swirled around the hot steam and made me shiver. "Wan?"

"The spell wore off," McDougall said quietly. His voice echoed in the tiled room. "I found some clothes for you."

I couldn't see him through the shower wall, but I knew he was there. I covered myself, feeling very naked and vulnerable, suddenly convinced that he had X-ray vision. It occurred to me that I was naked, in a stranger's house, a stranger that threw lightning and had talked about mucking with my head. With only a mouse-sized mouse as a protector.

"How do you like your eggs?"

Er . . . it took a moment to wrap my head around that question. "Scrambled."

"Cheese?"

Okay, it was hard to be suspicious of a man offering to cook for me. "Sure." I paused for a minute, but he didn't move. "Thank you, Dr. McDougall."

There was a longer pause. "My name is Sean. But I go by 'Mac.'"

That seemed to require a response. "Thank you, Mac."

The door closed, and the steam started to build back up again. I turned off the water, and stood there dripping for a moment, feeling like I'd somehow missed an important part of that conversation.

⁓⌇⁓

"Magic exists." Mac said.

My forkful of eggs poised in midair as I glared at him. "That's it? That's all you're going to tell us?"

"Yes. More toast?"

I stuffed the eggs in my mouth and glared at him. They were

perfect, light and fluffy with just the right amount of cheese. I can't cook an egg to save my life.

"That seems unfair." Wan was sitting on a small chair in the center of the table, sipping tea from a tiny cup. His sword hung on the back of the chair. "We need to know—"

"You don't need to know," Mac said. "Kate is mundane. Normally I'd be telling her that she'd had a fever dream or was hallucinating—"

"Lovely," I muttered through my eggs.

"I need to know more," Mac replied. "And consult with my colleagues. I will take you home, and ward the house. That will keep you safe for now."

I rolled my eyes, and slipped Itty and Bitty each a piece of toast. They were at my feet, taking anything they could get and begging for more.

"But first," Mac said. "I need to know what you protect."

"I don't know what you are talking—"

"Not you," Mac said, staring down at Wan.

Wan tilted his head to the side, and set his cup down. "How is it that I must speak when you remain silent?"

"I came when you called." Mac said.

Wan studied him for a moment, then gave him a nod. "So be it." He stood, and pulled a white paper napkin from the holder. He spread it out on the table, and then turned to retrieve his sword.

Mac and I reached out to clear away the butter, jam and other items, leaving the table clear. Wan walked to the middle of the napkin, and knelt down. He set the sword down in front of him, and then bowed, knocking his head three times three, moving with great dignity.

He lifted the sword then, and removed the red tassel at the base of the hilt. He set that to one side, and rapped the sword down three times on the table.

The hilt sprung open.

Mac and I leaned forward to watch, almost bumping heads.

Wan removed a small bundle wrapped in white silk from the hilt, and set the sword aside. He placed the bundle before him, and again, prostrated himself before it. Normally I would have been impatient, but I was caught up in his approach to that bundle. To Wan, it was worth his life.

Wan raised his head, reached out and pulled the cloth back. There, on the white silk, lay a necklace. Putting his hands under the silk, he arranged it in an oval.

It was lovely, with heavy jade pieces, bright green against the white. The pendant that hung from the necklace was almost circular, and an odd color. It looked rough, like the inside of an oyster, yet it seemed to sparkle with all colors in its depths.

For just a moment, I seemed to feel the necklace around my head, resting cool against my collarbones, then warming against my skin. The pendant would lay upon my breast, heavy yet light, with . . .

"It's lovely, Wan." I whispered.

"You look upon—"

I could barely hear him. The necklace seemed to call to me, and on impulse I reached out and brushed the pendant with my finger, just wanting to feel—

"Kate, NO." Wan shouted.

My finger touched the scale and the world went white.

I was floating, suspended between earth and the heavens, hanging freely as if underwater, clouds all around me.

I gasped at the change, then gasped again when cool air rushed into my lungs, with a taste of rain and spring on the air. I breathed again, filling my body with energy and light, lost in the sensation.

The clouds eddied around me, heavy with mist, white and intangible. I started to try to tread the air, to see if I could turn, but my hands passed through the clouds, collecting the heavy drops within. I couldn't move.

Something else could, though. I caught the movement out of the corner of my eye. There was a rumble, as if of far distant thunder on a sunny day. I saw a huge form moving in and out of the clouds, flowing like a snake. I had a quick glimpse of scales that glittered all colors of the spectrum, then a huge head reared up before me.

I'd seen enough to know a dragon. No wings, just a fierce, lovely face and huge teeth and claws. A museum print come to life, the only source of color in the white billowing clouds.

It saw me. Not just me, it saw through me somehow, right down to my soul and I shook as I hung there, pierced by its gaze. Then it threw its head back, and shook it's mane, and laughed.

The heavens resounded, and the earth trembled with the sound, as if all of creation shared the joy of this being. For it did not mock, nor was it threatening. It was a joyful sound, and my heart shared in its delight.

It coiled around me, massive and powerful. It's . . . no . . . his eyes were warm and bright, considering me as if part of a series of endless possibilities. The laugh came again, and I felt it in my chest, as if it delighted in this strange happening.

"Let it be so," a voice thundered, and I was thrown back, pitched into a body of flesh and muscle.

"Kate, Kate, speak to me." Wan's voice sounded odd in my ear. He was on my shoulder, tugging at my earlobe.

Mac kneeled by my chair, one hand at my wrist, the other on my chest. I blinked at him, and took a breath, feeling so very odd.

"What happened?" Mac demanded.

"I don't—" I licked my lips, and swallowed. How the hell did you explain . . . ?

"Oh, Kate." Wan's voice was sorrowful. "You should not have done that."

What had I done?

~ ⌒ ~

Itty and Bitty raced ahead of us into the house as we walked in. Mac went first. Wan was on my shoulder, alert and ready for trouble.

Nothing had been touched. Even the computer room and Wan's library were intact.

"I'll go out and cast the wards. You'll be safe within the house." Mac said.

"The dogs," I started.

Mac nodded. "I'll do the backyard as well." He slipped out the sliding door.

I turned to the kitchen, determined to make a pot of coffee. Wan stayed silent as I worked. He'd been babbling in the car, about sacred guardians and destiny, until I had a headache and Mac's eyebrows had climbed into his hairline. I'd told Wan to shut up in no uncertain terms.

Yes, I knew he had things to tell me, but it could damn well wait until I'd had more coffee. About a gallon should do it.

Wan seemed to think that I'd offended the gods by my actions, but I remembered the joy in the dragon's laugh. I might have upset the balance of things, but I don't think he minded that much. In fact, I rather thought he'd delighted in it, truth be told.

I offered Mac some coffee when he came back inside, but he just shook his head. "I need to contact people. Don't leave this house until you hear from me. The possum is still out there."

Swell.

Mac turned to Wan. "Guard her with your life. Whatever has happened, Kate is extraordinary now. See to her safety."

Wan bowed. Mac gave me a nod, and left.

I sighed, taking a long sip of my coffee. Hell of a few days. I dreaded checking email and messages, but that could wait. Poor Wan was about to bust with talk, and I needed to hear it. "All right, Wan. Tell me what this all means."

I figure he'd bust right out, but he just jumped down to the counter and stood looking at me, his sword over his shoulder. "Kate, I thought you were extraordinary before you touched the sacred necklace."

I hid a smile in the rim of my mug. "So what did I do, exactly?"

Wan drew himself up, and took a deep breath—

Someone knocked on the front door. Itty and Bitty raced for the entryway, farting like crazy and barking their fool heads off.

I sighed. Wan leaped for my arm, and climbed up. "Careful, Kate. The Doctor's wards are strong but we should have a care."

"It's probably the mailman." I put the cup down, and headed for the door, only to find a small army of guys with tattoos and leathers on the other side, staring at me grimly.

"Uh ..."

"Lady, your van was found with our stolen hogs alongside I-75. WHAT THE HELL HAPPENED?"

Uh-oh.

THE END—or is it?

Stalked

KELLEY ARMSTRONG

I had to get rid of the mutt.

Killing him would be easiest but, unfortunately, out of the question. If Elena found out, she'd be pissed. Ten years from now, I'd still be hearing about it: "Clay couldn't even get through our honeymoon without killing someone."

She'd laugh when she said it . . . in ten years. Right now, she'd be furious.

She'd argue there were better ways to handle the situation. I disagreed. The mutt knew we were in town and that by sticking around, he was taking his life into his hands. If he'd skittered into the shadows and stayed out of our way, I'd have said, "Fuck it," and pretended not to notice. After all, it was my honeymoon.

Even if he'd just stood his ground and refused to hide, I wouldn't have made a big deal of it. Beaten the crap out of him, yes. Had to. The Law was the Law, and it stated that a non-Pack werewolf had to cede territory to a Pack one. Unfair, maybe, but if you let one mutt break the rules, the next thing you knew, they'd be camping out back at Stonehaven, knocking on the door, asking if they could use the facilities.

But this mutt wasn't hiding or defending his territory. He was stalking Elena. He'd been following us all morning and was now sitting across the restaurant, gaze glued to her ass as she bent over the buffet table.

When your mate is the only female werewolf, you get used to other wolves sniffing around. I'd spent the last eighteen years dealing with it or, more often, watching her deal with it. With Elena, interference is not appreciated. She can fight her own fights, and gets snippy if I rob her of the chance. But this was our honeymoon, and damned if I was going to let this mutt spoil it. He had to be dealt with before Elena realized he was stalking her. The question was how.

When Elena walked back to the table, the mutt had the sense to busy himself gnawing on a sparerib.

"You okay?" she asked as she slid into her seat. "You've been quiet since the Arch."

The mutt had started following us there.

"Just hungry. I'm fine for now."

"I should hope so. After three plates." She buttered her bread, then studied me. "Are you sure you're okay?"

"I don't know. . . ." I shrugged and pretended to ease back in my chair, then lunged and snagged bacon from her plate. I folded it into my mouth. "Nope, still hungry."

She brandished her fork. "Then get your own or—"

I snatched another slice, too slow this time, and she stabbed the back of my hand. I yelped.

"I warned you," she laughed.

The women at the next table stared in horror. Elena glanced their way. Five years ago, she would have blushed. Ten years ago, she would have found an excuse to leave. Today, she just murmured a rueful "Whoops," and dug into her potatoes.

I got another plate of food, avoiding the temptation to pass the mutt's table. He'd made a point of staying downwind outside and now sat partially obscured by a pillar, too far away for his scent to carry. For now, I'd let him think he was safe, undetected.

When I came back, Elena said, "I think I have an outing idea for us. Someone behind me in line was talking about a state park. Could be fun." Her blue eyes glittered. Of course, we shouldn't go during the day when there are people around."

"Nope, we shouldn't." I speared a ham slab. "This afternoon, then?"

She grinned. "Perfect."

❧

When you resort to everyday activities on your honeymoon, you know, it's not going well. Planning our second run in as many days meant Elena was bored and trying very hard not to let me know it.

The first couple of days had been great. With two-year-old twins at home, the only time we normally got away was when our Alpha, Jeremy, sent us to track down a misbehaving mutt. Being on a mission doesn't mean we can't enjoy ourselves. There's nothing like celebrating a successful hunt with sex. Or working out the frustration of a failed hunt with sex. Or dulling that edge of pre-hunt excitement with sex.

But there was also something to be said for skipping the whole "track, capture, and maim" part and being able to go straight to a hotel room, and lock the door. Still, we could stay in there for only so long before we got restless, and when we came out, we'd discovered a problem with our honeymoon destination: there wasn't a helluva lot to do.

~⌒~

Back at the hotel, we called home and talked to the kids. Or they listened as we talked, and had their answers interpreted by Jeremy. As much as we loved our daily call, we spent most of it braced for the inevitable "Momma? Daddy? Home?" or in Kate's case: "Momma! Daddy! Home!" Jeremy managed to spare us this time stopping as soon as Logan asked "Momma where?" and bustling them off with his visiting girlfriend, Jaime.

Next. Jeremy and Elena would talk about the kids and discuss any new Pack or council business. Normally, I'd listen in and offer my opinion—whether they wanted it or not—but today I told Elena I was going downstairs to grab a map and a bottle of water, and took off.

~⌒~

I was reasonably sure the mutt hadn't followed us from the restaurant, but wanted to scout to be absolutely certain. We'd walked to the Arch and then to the restaurant, meaning we'd had to walk back, which gave him the opportunity to follow. A cab would have solved that, but if I'd voluntarily offered to spend time trapped in a vehicle with a stranger, Elena would have been on the phone to Jeremy, panicked that my arm was reinfected and I was sliding into delirium.

So I'd suggested we take the long route back. The mutt hadn't followed. Maybe he'd had second thoughts. If he'd heard the rumors about me, he'd know he could be setting himself up for a long and painful death. But if he'd believed that, he should have hightailed it the moment he crossed our path. So while I hoped, I didn't trust.

I grabbed a brochure on state parks, stuffed it into my back pocket, then headed out the front door to circle the hotel. I got five steps before his scent hit me. I stopped to retie my sneaker and snuck a look around.

The bastard was right across the street. He sat on a bench facing the hotel, reading a newspaper. Cocky? Or just too young and inexperienced to know I could smell him from here?

I straightened and shielded my eyes, as if scanning the storefronts. When I turned his way, he lifted the paper to hide his face, but slowly. Cocky. Shit.

Normally, I'm happy to show a cocky young mutt how I earned my reputation. At that age, one good thrashing is all it takes. But damn it, this was my honeymoon.

I crossed the road and headed into the first alley.

~~~~~

There were two ways the mutt could play this, depending on why he was stalking Elena. It could be his misguided way of challenging me. Stupid—any wolf knew his mate wouldn't lift her tail for the first younger male who sauntered her way. Only a human would fly into a jealous rage and call a man out for it. But if challenging me was his goal, he'd follow me into the alley.

Or he might really be after Elena. He wouldn't be the first mutt to think she might not object to a new mate.

I walked far enough into the alley to disappear, then crept back along the wall, lost in its shadow, stopping when I could see the hotel door. After a few minutes, a car horn blasted and a figure darted through the heavy traffic. It was the mutt, heading straight for the hotel.

I circled around the block, then came in the hotel side entrance, beside the check-in desk. I stopped there, partially hidden by a huge fake plant. The stink of the plastic fern overpowered everything else.

I peered through the fronds. There he was, hovering at the other end of the desk, sizing up the staff. Hoping to get our room number? I stepped out. Just as he turned, a pale blond ponytail bounced past on the other side of the lobby. Elena.

I turned away from the mutt before he realized I'd made him. I opened my mouth to hail Elena, then stopped. If she saw me, she'd head over here. Better for her to keep walking and I'd catch up outside the front doors—

Shit. He'd walked in the front doors. His scent would still linger there, and Elena had a better sense of smell than any werewolf I knew. I started walking fast to cut her off. She caught sight of the brochure rack and veered that way.

"Elena!"

I yanked the park guide from my back pocket and waved it. I moved to the left, blocking her view of the mutt. She couldn't smell him from here, but she was in charge of the Pack's mutt dossiers and might recognize him.

"Got the maps," I said. "I was looking for water. I can't find a damn machine—"

She directed my attention to the gift shop.

"Shit. Okay, let's grab one and go."

Out of the corner of my eye, I saw the mutt watching us. Elena's gaze traveled across the lobby, as if sensing something. I took her elbow and wheeled her toward the gift shop.

She peeled my fingers from her arm. "I'm looking—"

"The gift shop's behind you."

"Where I just pointed. No kidding. I'm looking for the parking garage exit. I was going to say we can get a drink on the way. It's too expensive here."

"Good. I mean, right. The stairs are back there, by the elevators."

She nodded and let me lead the way.

The park wasn't busy, so avoiding humans was easy. That took some of the challenge out of it, but a new place to run is always good.

We spent most of the afternoon as wolves, exploring and playing, working up a sharp hunger for the hunt. We'd found a few deer trails, but all our tearing around scared the small herd into hiding. Probably just as well—in places like this, people pay attention to ripped-apart deer carcasses, and we'd have felt guilty later, knowing we'd nudged the line between acceptable and unacceptable risk. We settled for rabbits, the fat dull-witted sort you find in preserves with few natural predators.

The snack was enough to still the hunger pangs without making us sleepy, so we followed it up with more games, these ones taking on an edge, the snarls sharper, the nips harder, fangs drawing blood, working up the inevitable conclusion—a fast Change back and hard, raw sex that left us scratched and bruised, happy and drowsy, stretched on the forest floor, bodies apart, feet entwined.

I was on my back, shielding my eyes from the sun shifting through the trees, too lazy to move out of its way. Elena lay on her stomach, watching an ant crawl across her open palm.

"What about a second stop for our honeymoon?" I asked.

Her nose scrunched in an unspoken "What?"

"Well, I know this isn't shaping up to be everything you'd hoped . . . ."

"This afternoon was." She grinned and rubbed her foot against mine. "I'm having a good time, but if you're not . . ."

How the hell was I supposed to answer that? *No, darling, our honeymoon sucks. I'm bored and I want to go somewhere else.*

If it was true, I wouldn't have minded saying so, though I supposed, being a romantic getaway, I'd have to phrase it more carefully. Walking away from a threat set my teeth on edge, but it was better than having this mutt ruin our honeymoon. Still, given the choice between staying and making Elena think I was having a shitty time, something told me option one—even if it meant fighting a bigger, younger werewolf—was a whole lot safer.

"I'm fine," I said. "You just seemed a little . . . bored earlier."

Alarm brightened her eyes and she hurried to assure me she was, most certainly, not bored. I should have known. Any other time, Elena would have no problem admitting it. But a honeymoon was different. It was a ritual and, as such, came with rules, and saying she was bored broke them all.

Shortly after I met Elena, I'd realized that, while she squirmed and chafed under the weight of human rules and expectations, there was one aspect of them she embraced almost to the point of worship. Rituals. Like Christmas. Ask Elena to bring cookies for the parent-and-tot picnic and she'll buy them at the bakery, then dump them into a plastic container so they'd look homemade. But come mid-December, she'll whip herself into a frenzy of baking, loving every minute because that's part of Christmas.

When the subject of "making it official for the kids' sake" came up,

I knew she'd want the ritual—a real wedding, the kind she'd dreamed of eighteen years ago when we'd bought the rings, her face lit up with dreams of a white dress and a new life and happily ever after.

Instead of the happily ever after, she got a bite on the hand and the kind of new life that had once existed only in her nightmares.

I won't make excuses for what I did. The truth is that your whole life can change with one split-second decision and it doesn't matter if you told yourself you'd never do it, or if you stepped into that moment with no thought of doing it. All it takes is that one second of absolute panic when the solution shines in front of you, and you grab it . . . only to have it turn to ash in your hand. There is no excuse for what I did.

After I bit Elena, it took eleven years for her to forgive me. Forgetting what I'd done to her, though, was impossible. It was always there, lurking in the background.

When Elena vetoed a wedding, I thought it was just the weight of human mores again—that it didn't feel right when we already had kids. So I'd decided I'd give her one as a surprise. Jeremy talked me out of it and it was then, as he waffled and circled the subject of "why not" that I finally understood. There could be no wedding because every step—from sending invitations to walking down the aisle— would only remind her of the one she'd planned all those years ago, and the hell she'd gone through when it fell apart.

But the honeymoon was one part of the ritual we hadn't discussed. So, if a wedding was out, the least I could do was give her that.

I'd made all the arrangements, trying to create the perfect honey-moon. My way of saying that I'd screwed up eighteen years ago and I was damned lucky we'd ever reached the stage where a honeymoon was even a possibility.

The mutt resurfaced at dinner, spoiling my second meal in a day. Not just any meal this time, but a special one at a place so exclusive that I—well, Jeremy—had to reserve our table weeks ago. It was one of those restaurants where the lighting is so dim, I don't know how humans can see what they're eating or find what they're eating—the tiny portions lost on a plate filled with inedible decorations. But it was romantic. At least, that's what the guidebook said.

It matched Elena's expectations, and that was all that mattered. She'd enjoy the fussy little portions, the fancy wines, the fawning waitstaff, then fill up on pizza in our room later. Which was fine by me . . . until the mutt showed up.

As I was returning from the bathroom, he stepped into the lobby to ask the maître d' for directions. Our eyes met. He smiled, turned, and sauntered out.

I knew I should walk away. Take care of him later. But there was no way I could enjoy my dinner knowing he was prowling outside. And if I didn't enjoy it, Elena wouldn't enjoy it, and we'd get into a fight about why I'd take her someplace I'd hate only to sulk through the meal. I was determined to make it through this trip without any knock-down, drag-out fights . . . or, at least, not to cause any myself.

I waited until the maître d' escorted a couple into the dining room, then took off after the mutt.

I found him waiting for me in the lane behind the restaurant. He was leaning against the wall, ankles crossed, eyes closed.

Who raises their kids like this? That was the problem with mutts. Not all mutts—I'll give them that. Some teach their sons basic survival and a few do as good a job as any Pack wolf, but there are far too many who just don't give a damn. At least in a Pack, if your father doesn't teach you properly, someone else will.

Here stood a perfect example of poor mutt-parenting skills—a kid stupid enough not only to challenge me, but to feign confidence to the point of boredom, lowering his guard in the hopes of looking "cool." Now I had to teach him a lesson, all because his father couldn't be bothered telling him I wasn't someone to fuck with.

Werewolves earn their reputations through endless challenges. Twenty-seven years ago, when I'd wanted to protect Jeremy on his rise to Alphahood, I didn't have time for that. So I'd sealed my reputation with a single decisive act, one guaranteed to convince every mutt on the continent that the infamous child werewolf had grown into a raging lunatic. To get to Jeremy, they had to go through me, and after what I did, few dared try.

I could only hope this mutt just didn't realize whom he'd challenged and, once he did, a few abject apologies and a brief trouncing would set the matter straight and I could get back to my honeymoon.

I walked over and planted myself in front of him.

He opened his eyes, stretched, and faked a yawn. "Clayton Danvers, I presume?"

So much for that idea . . .

I studied him. After a moment, he straightened, shifting his weight and squirming like a freshman caught napping during my lectures.

"What?" he said.

I examined him head to foot, eyes narrowing.

"What?" he said again.

"I'm trying to figure out what you've got."

His broad face screwed up, lips pulling back, giving me a shot of breath that smelled like it'd never been introduced to mouthwash.

"So what is it?" I asked. "Cancer, hemorrhagic fever, rabies . . ."

"What the hell are you talking about?"

"You do have a fatal disease, right? In horrible agony? 'Cause that's the only reason any mutt barely past his first Change would call me out. Looking for a quick end to an unbearable existence."

He let out a wheezing laugh. "Oh, that's a good one. Does that line usually work? Scare us off before you have to fight? Because *that's* the only reason a runt like you would have the reputation of a psycho killer."

He stepped closer, pulling himself up straight, just to prove, in case I hadn't noticed, that he had a good five inches and fifty pounds on me. Which did *not* make me a runt. I'd spent my childhood being small for my age, but I'd caught up to an average size. Still, mutts like to point out that I'm not as big as my reputation, as if I've disappointed them.

"You do have a daddy, right?" I asked.

His face screwed up again. "What?"

"You have a father, don't you?"

"Is that some kind of Pack insult? Of course, I have a father. Theo Cain. Maybe you've heard of him."

I knew the Cains. Killed one of them a few years ago in an uprising against the Pack. "And your daddy warned you about me? Told you about the pictures?"

"Pfft." He rolled his eyes. "Yeah, I've heard about those. Photos of some dude you carved up with a hatchet."

"Chain saw."

"Whatever. It's bullshit."

I eased to the side, getting my nose away from his mouth. "And the witness? He's still alive, last I heard."

"Some guy you paid off."

"The pictures?"

"Photoshopped."

"It was almost thirty years ago."

"So?"

I shook my head. The problem with stupid people is you can't reason with them. Waste of my time while my meal was getting cold and Elena was spending our romantic dinner alone.

Screw this.

I surveyed the dark service lane. There was never a convenient Dumpster when you needed one I eyed the garbage cans, eyed Cain, sizing him up. . . .

"So when do we fight?" he asked.

"What?"

"You know. Go *mano a mano*. Fight to the death. Your death, of course. I'm looking forward to enjoying the spoils." His tongue slid between his teeth. "Mmm. I gotta thing for blondes with tight little asses, and your girl is fine. Bet she'll fix up real nice."

"Fix up?"

"You know. Get some makeup on. Get rid of that ponytail. Trade the jeans for a nice miniskirt to show off those long legs. You gotta keep after chicks about things like that or they get comfortable, let it slide. Not that she isn't damned sweet right now, but with a little extra effort, she'd be hot."

I shook my head.

"What?" he said "You've never tried?"

"Why would I?"

"Why *wouldn't* you?"

I opened my mouth, then shut it. Another waste of time. He wouldn't understand my point of view, no more than I understood his. "So you think if you kill me, you get Elena?"

"Sure, why not?"

"If it didn't require my death, I'd be tempted to go along with it, just to watch you tell her that."

"Whatever." He rolled on his heels. "Let's get this over with. I'm hoping you brought your chain saw, 'cause otherwise, this fight isn't going to be nearly as much fun as I was hoping, with your fucked-up arm and all."

I stopped, then slowly looked up, meeting his gaze. "My arm?"

"Yeah, Brian McKay said you busted his balls last year for having some sport with a whore. He said something was wrong with your arm. You kept using your other one. Tyler Lake says he did it, as payback for what you did to his brother."

"Yeah? Did he mention which arm it was? This one?"

I grabbed him by the throat and pinned him to the wall, hand tightening until his face purpled and his eyes bulged.

"Or was it this one?"

I slammed my fist into his jaw. Teeth and bone crackled. He tried to scream, but my hand against his windpipe stifled it to a whimper.

I dragged him down the wall until his face was level with mine, and leaned in, nose to nose. "I'd say that will teach you not to listen to rumors, but you're a bit thick, aren't you? I'm going to have to—"

A thump to my left stopped me short. I glanced over as the

restaurant rear door swung open. We were behind it, a dozen feet away, out of sight. I held Cain still as I watched and listened, ready to drag him into the alley if a foot appeared under that door.

Garbage can lids clattered. They were right next to the door. No need to step outside. Just dump the trash—

Cain let out a high-pitched squeal—the loudest noise he could manage. Then he started banging at the boarded-up window beside him. I tightened my grip, my glower warning him to stop. A foot appeared under that door, someone stepping out. I dropped the mutt and dove around the corner.

"Hey! Hey, you there!"

I pressed up against the wall. Footsteps sounded. A man yelled at Cain, mistaking him for a drunk. The mutt mumbled something about being jumped, struggling to talk with a broken jaw.

I gritted my teeth. Ending a fight by alerting humans was bad enough. Trying to set them on my trail? That toppled into full-blown cowardice.

I shook it off and retreated before someone came looking for the "mugger."

⁓

Back in the restaurant I longed to visit the washroom and scrub Cain's stink off me. But I'd been gone too long already. So I grabbed a linen napkin from a wait station, wiped the blood from my hands as I strode through the dining room, and tossed the cloth onto an uncleared table.

Elena looked up from the last bites of her meal.

"Hey, there," she said, smiling. "Thought you'd made a fast-food run on me."

"Nah." I took my suit coat from the chair and slipped it on, blocking the mutt's smell and covering the blood splatter. "Something didn't agree with me."

"Lunch, I bet. That's the thing about buffets—lots of food, none of it very good. So, is dessert out of the question?"

I shook my head. "Just give me a second to finish dinner."

⌒⌒⌒

Our hotel was a few blocks from the restaurant, so we'd walked. Heading back, I had to switch sides every time we turned a corner, staying downwind from Elena, and keeping a foot's gap between us. She didn't notice the extra distance. Neither of us was much for public displays of affection, so walking hand-in-hand wasn't expected.

That worked only until we got to our room. She leaned against me as she pulled off her heels, then ran her hand up the back of my leg, grinning upside down, hair fanning the floor. She swept it back as she stood, her hand sliding up my leg and into my back pocket.

"Pizza now?" she asked. "Or after we work up an appetite?" I tugged her hand out, lacing my fingers with hers, elbow locked to keep her from getting close enough to smell Cain.

"Hold that thought," I said. "I'm going to grab a shower."

Her brows shot up. "Now?"

"That problem in the restaurant? I'm thinking it might be something I rolled in this afternoon. My leg's itching like mad. Let me scrub it off before I pass it along."

Her head tilted, the freckles across her nose bunching as she studied me, her bullshit meter wavering. Normal-Elena would have called me on it, but honeymoon-Elena was struggling to avoid confrontations just as much as I was, so after a moment, she shrugged.

"Take your time. I'll catch the news."

———⌒◡⌒———

I ran my hands through my hair and lifted my face into the spray. My forearm throbbed as the hot water hit it. Tomorrow I'd pay for overworking the damaged muscle, but it was worth it if Cain took home proof that Clayton Danvers's arm was definitely not "fucked up."

For two years, I'd been so careful in every fight, convinced no one would notice. I was favoring my left. I should have known better. Like scavengers, mutts could sense weakness.

Damn Brian McKay. If Elena had listened to me, we wouldn't have had to worry about him talking to anyone. When he'd killed a prostitute in El Paso, Jeremy sent us after him, but left his punishment up to Elena, as he often did these days. To me, the answer was simple. McKay was a vicious thug and we should eliminate the threat while we had the excuse. Elena had disagreed and we'd let him off with a beating. Let him return home to spread his story about my arm.

I squeezed the water from my hair as I moved out of the spray and looked down at the pitted rut of scar tissue. All these years of fighting without a permanent injury and what finally does it? One little scratch from a rotting zombie. At the worst of the infection, I'd been in danger of losing my arm, so I couldn't complain about some muscle damage.

But if rumors were already circulating, I had to squelch them. And maybe even that wouldn't be enough. Was Theo Cain's son only the first in a new generation of mutts who'd heard the stories about me and fluffed them off as urban legends or, at least, ancient history?

I'd first cemented my reputation to protect Jeremy. Now I had fresh concerns—a mate, kids . . . and a fucked-up arm that was never going to get any better. So how was I going to convince this generation of mutts that Clayton Danvers really was the raging psychopath their fathers warned them about?

I rubbed the face cloth over my chest, hard and brisk enough to burn. I didn't want to go through that shit again. What the hell would I do for an encore? What *could* I do that wouldn't have Elena bustling the twins off to a motel while she reconsidered whether I was the guy she wanted raising her kids?

Elena understood why I'd taken a chain saw to that mutt. If pressed, she might even grudgingly admit it had been a good idea. Anesthetic ensured the guy hadn't suffered much—the point was only to make others think he had. Still, only in the last few years had she stopped twitching every time someone mentioned the photos. Admitting I might have been right didn't mean she wanted to think about what I'd done. And she sure as hell wouldn't want me doing it again.

I shut the taps and toweled off, scrubbing away any remaining trace of Cain.

As I got out, I could hear the television from the next room. So the news wasn't over. Good. I had no interest in local or world events—human concerns—but Elena would be engrossed in them. Distracting her was always a challenge . . . and a sure way to clear my head of thoughts that didn't belong on a honeymoon.

I draped the towel around my shoulders, then eased open the

door to get a peek at the playing field. Through the mirror, I could see the bed. An empty bed, the spread gathered and wrinkled where Elena had sprawled to watch the news.

A sportscaster was running through scores. Shit.

I tried to see the sitting area through the mirror, but the angle was wrong. It didn't matter. If she was finished with the news, I'd lost my chance to play. I gave my dripping hair one last swipe, tossed the towel on the bathroom floor, walked into the suite, and thumped onto the bed, springs squealing.

"All done. Still ready to work up that—?"

The room was empty.

I strode to the door, heart thudding as I sniffed for Cain. I knew my fears were unfounded. No way could he get Elena out of this room . . . not without blood spattered on the walls and carpet.

But what if he'd been lurking outside the door? If she'd heard him? Peeked out and he bolted? She'd give chase.

I opened the door and was crouching at the entrance when a yelp made me jump. Down the hall, a middle-aged woman stumbled back into her room, chirping to her husband. For a moment, I thought "Hell, I wasn't even sniffing the carpet yet." Then I remembered I was naked.

I slammed the door and stalked into the bathroom for a towel. Humans and their screwed-up sensibilities. If that woman saw Elena dragged down the hall kicking and clawing, she'd tell herself it was none of her business. But God forbid she should catch a glimpse of a naked man. Probably on the phone to security right now.

Towel in place, I cracked open the door. When I was certain it was clear, I crouched, smelling the carpet. No trace of Cain. A quick glance around, then, holding the door open with my foot, I leaned into the hall for another sniff. Nothing.

I paused for a few deep breaths, sloughing off the fear, then strode into the room to search for clues. The answer was right there, on the desk. A page ripped off the notepad, Elena's looping handwriting: *salty crab+no water=beverage run.*

Shit.

As I pulled on a T-shirt, I told myself Cain was long gone. I'd had him in a death-hold before he could lay a finger on me. A sensible mutt would take it as a lesson in arrogance, swallow the humiliation, get out of town, and find a doctor to set his jaw before he was permanently disfigured. But a sensible mutt wouldn't have gotten himself into that scrape in the first place.

Cain would back off only long enough to pop painkillers. Then the humiliation would crystallize into rage. Too cowardly to come after me, he'd aim a sucker punch where he thought I was most vulnerable: Elena, who'd just strolled out alone into the night, having no idea that a mutt had been stalking her all day because I hadn't bothered to tell her.

Shit.

As I tugged on my jeans with one hand, I dialed Elena's cell phone with the other. Elena's dress, discarded on the chair, began to vibrate. Beneath lay it the purse shed taken to dinner, open, where she'd grabbed her wallet, leaving the purse—and her cell phone—behind.

I grabbed my sneakers and raced out the door.

⌒⌒⌒

I didn't bother checking the gift shop. Elena had already decreed the water there too expensive. Jeremy and I might have had some lean times during my childhood, but Elena knew what it was like to wear three sweaters all winter because you couldn't afford a coat. Even if she could now buy the whole damned gift shop, she wouldn't give them three bucks for water that cost a dollar down the block.

Normally, I respect that, but this was one time when I wished to hell she'd just spend the damned money.

I strode out the front doors, stopped and inhaled. A couple glowered when they had to drop hands to walk around me. I scanned the road, sampling the air. Finally it came. Elena's faint scent on the wind. I hurried down the steps.

———⌒⌒———

There was a convenience store on the corner, but Elena's trail crossed the road and headed down the very alley where I'd lain in wait for Cain that afternoon. What the hell was wrong with the shop on the corner? Was the water ten cents cheaper three blocks away? Goddamn it, Elena!

Even as I cursed her, I knew I was really angry with myself. I should have warned her about the mutt. If I'd honestly believed I could keep her in my sights twenty-four hours a day, then I was deluded. Elena would see no reason why she shouldn't run out at night for water. She was a werewolf; she didn't need to worry about muggers and rapists. But a pissed-off mutt twice her size?

I broke into a jog.

———⌒⌒———

The moment I stepped into the alley, I smelled him. He must have been lying in wait outside the hotel, formulating a plan. Then his quarry had sailed out the front doors . . . and waltzed straight into the nearest dark alley.

By the time he got over the shock at his good fortune, he'd lost his chance to catch her in the alley. She'd exited, walked a block then . . . cut through another alley.

Goddamn it!

I raced to that alley, then pulled up short. Cain stood at the far end, his back to me, gaze fixed on something across the road. Elena.

I could drive him toward her . . . if she'd known he was coming. I circled to the next side road, hoping to cut him off. As I approached the end, I moved into the shadows.

Elena was still there. I could sense her, that gut level calm that says she's near.

The streets and sidewalks were empty. Our hotel was in a business section of town. That had looked good when I'd picked it online—surrounded by restaurants and other conveniences. But we arrived to discover those conveniences weren't nearly so convenient when they closed at five, as the offices emptied.

Around the corner, I saw yet another quiet street, vacant except for a lone shopper gazing at the display of a closed clothing store. I had to do a double-take to make sure it was Elena. It certainly looked like her—a tall, slender woman in jeans and sneakers, her pale blond hair hanging loose down the back of her denim jacket. But window-shopping? At a display of women's business suits? This honeymoon was boring her even more than I thought.

As she studied the display, her gaze kept sliding to the right. I squinted to see what was drawing her attention, but the streetlights turned the glass into a mirror, reflecting . . . Reflecting Cain across the road behind her.

She knew he was there. I exhaled in relief. The sound couldn't have been loud enough for Elena to hear, but she went still, then pivoted just enough to see me.

She grinned. Then her smile vanished as she jerked her attention back to the window and motioned, palm out, for me to stay put.

A quick sequence of charade moves as she kept her gaze on the display. Nose lifting to inhale, fingers gesturing to the alley to her right, the stop signal again—warning me there was a mutt in that alley.

Another flurry of gestures to say she'd handle it and I could settle into backup mode. Then, midmotion, she stopped. A slow smile, teeth glinting in the darkness. Seeing that smile, I knew what she was thinking before she glanced over, lips forming the word.

"Play?"

My grin answered.

～⌒～

No game is fair—or much fun—when one of the parties doesn't realize he's playing. So Elena took care of that first. She started by drumming her fingers against her leg, her head twisting his way, a subtle hint that she knew Cain was there and was growing impatient waiting for his next move.

While I couldn't see the mutt, I could picture him, poised at the end of the alley, rocking on the balls for his feet, seeing Elena's signals but afraid to misinterpret.

She glanced over her right shoulder, hair sweeping back as her face tilted his way, and I didn't need to see her expression to imagine that too. I'd seen it often enough. Lips parted, eyes glittering beneath arched brows, a look that translated, in human or wolf, into "Well, are you going to come get me or not?"

Cain shot from the alley so fast, he stumbled. Elena laughed, a husky growl that made me lock my knees to keep from answering it myself. As Cain recovered, she turned my way with a grin. Then she took off, in a sprint, hair flashing behind her.

Cain teetered on the curb and stared after her in confusion and disappointment, the human telling him that a woman running in the other direction wasn't a good sign. She stopped at the next corner and turned to face him.

He stepped off the curb. She took a slow stride back. Another forward, another back, and it wasn't until the dance had gone on for five paces that the wolf instinct finally clicked on and he realized that to her, running away meant not "I'm trying to escape" but "catch me if you can."

His broad face split into a grin. He winced, slapping a hand to his broken jaw. When he looked up, Elena was gone. One panicked glance around, then he started to run.

⌒⌒⌒

Had Elena been a wolf playing this mating ritual for real, she'd have ditched Cain after five minutes, deciding he either wasn't interested enough or competent enough to track her and, either way, wasn't worthy of her attention.

He kept losing her trail and backtracking. Or he'd glimpse a pedestrian down another road and take off that way before his nose finally told him it wasn't her. Without a Pack, a werewolf grows up immersed in human society, feeling the instincts of a wolf, but not trusting them, not knowing what to do with them.

Cain seemed to be running on pure lust and enthusiasm which, while amusing, wasn't much of a challenge . . . or much fun.

After he backtracked over my trail twice—thankfully not noticing—Elena decided it was time to end this segment of the game before Cain realized there was a third player. She'd intended to take it to the next level anyway. Hunting in human form was like playing "catch me" with this mutt—not very challenging .. and not much fun.

She led him to a park down by the river, then darted into a cluster of shrubs to Change. Cain caught up quickly—Elena had made sure he'd been right behind her. This time, once he realized what she was doing, there'd been no indecision. After a few seconds of trying unsuccessfully to see her naked through the bushes, he tore off to find a Changing spot of his own.

I guarded Elena until I heard Cain's first grunt, assuring me he wasn't about to change his mind. Then I ducked into a hiding place and undressed.

When I came out, Elena was already lying in the shadows, tail flicking against the ground, eager to be off. Seeing me a dozen feet away, she let out a soft chuff, her blue eyes rolling, saying, "Settle in—this could take a while."

I was looking around when Cain's bushes erupted in a flurry of rustling, punctuated by very human grunts. He'd barely begun.

Elena's head slumped forward, muzzle resting on her forelegs as a sigh rippled through her flanks. I growled a laugh and loped off to set up the playing field.

I lay on a flat rock overlooking the path, nose twitching as the river scents wafted past, making me salivate at the smell of fish. I hooked my forepaws over the rock and stretched, back arching, nails extending, foot pads scraping against the rough broken edge. I'd been waiting a while, and I could feel the ache in my muscles, urging me to get up, get moving, get running.

I stretched again and peered over the edge. The perfect launch-pad. Elena would lead Cain along the path, and with one leap, I'd have my workout. The chase, the hunt, the takedown—all more satisfying than the actual fight.

A low whine cut through the night. I lifted my head, ears swiveling as they tracked the sound to a brown wolf a hundred feet away. Cain, whining for Elena, probably worried she'd given up and taken off.

After a moment, she appeared, a pale wraith sliding silently from the shadows. Cain let out a sharper whine and danced in place like a domestic dog seeing his master come home.

Elena continued toward him, taking her time, tail down, head high. She stopped about six feet away, making him come to her, gaze straight ahead, a queen granting her subject permission to approach.

Cain paced, keeping his distance. Her body language was perfectly clear—she was establishing hierarchy—but he didn't know what to make of it, and kept pacing.

When he didn't accept the invitation to approach and sniff her, Elena started turning away. Again, clear wolf behavior, not snubbing him, just coquettishly saying "Well, if you aren't interested. . . ."

Cain went still. As she presented him with her flank, his head lowered, hackles rising. I leapt to my feet, nails scrabbling against the rock, a warning bark in my throat, but before it could escape, he sprang.

Cain grabbed Elena's shoulder, teeth sinking in, whipping her off her feet. I raced down the slope as he threw her in the air. She hit the ground, spun, and dove at him, snarls slicing through the night. Cain let out a yelp of surprise and pain as she ripped into him.

I skidded to a stop fifty feet away, still unseen. Ears forward, eyes straining, sight now the most critical sense as I watched and evaluated.

After a moment, I retreated to my perch, my gaze fixed on them, ready to fly back down if the battle turned against Elena.

They continued to fight, a rolling ball of growls and fur and blood. I could smell that blood, his and hers, the latter making a whimper shudder up from my gut. I shook it off and locked my legs, standing my ground.

Finally, Elena backed away, snarling, head down, hackles up. Cain got to his feet, shaking his head, blood spraying. As he recovered, Elena glanced in my direction, wondering whether she should finish this herself or follow through on the plan.

My muscles coiled and uncoiled, as my gaze fixed on him, twice her size, too much for her to handle if she didn't have to, praying she made the right choice, the safe choice. Of course she did. With Elena, common sense always wins over ego. With one final, lip-curling snarl, she ran for the path.

She'd covered half the distance when her muzzle jerked up and she swerved, circling an oak tree and going back the other way. I was scrambling up when I caught the scents: dog and human. I followed the smell and saw a man walking a terrier, heading this way.

Elena looped back, darting a weaving path around every obstacle she could find, trying to buy time. I glanced at the dog walker. An elderly man and an old dog, creeping along, oblivious and unhurried.

As Elena circled a small outbuilding, she dipped, paw probably catching a rodent hole, not enough to make her stumble, but slowing her down. Cain lunged. He caught only a mouthful of tail hair. As his snarl of frustration reverberated through the park, the old dog lifted his muzzle in a lazy sniff, then went back to dawdling along beside his master.

Elena disappeared behind the building. A yelp, loud enough even to make the man look up. Elena's yelp. I sprang to my feet. She shot from behind the building, a pale streak, low to the ground, running full out now, Cain on her heels.

A third shape raced from behind the building, larger than the first two. *That* was Cain—I could make out the odd drop of his jaw. My gaze swung to Elena and the new mutt behind her. Cain had brought backup.

I crouched, ready to leap from the rock. The man and dog rounded the corner, bringing them right into my path below. I looked over my shoulder, at the long route, then at Elena, now tearing across the park, heading for the river, getting farther from me with each stride.

A split second of hesitation and then I leapt, sailing over the man and dog and hitting the ground hard on the other side. The little dog started yelping, a high-pitched *aii-aii-aii*. The old man wheezed and sputtered, his gasps echoing the pound of my paws as I raced away.

With my first sprint, I started closing in on Cain. But he wasn't the one I was worried about. I recognized the other mutt's scent now. Brian McKay. The mutt who'd spread the rumor of my injured arm.

McKay wasn't an arrogant kid like Cain. He was an experienced mutt with a deadly reputation. And he was right on Elena's tail, the gap between us only getting larger.

Come on, circle around! Bring him back to me!

I knew she couldn't. She finally began to veer, but east, toward the river, heading up an embankment to a set of train tracks. At the top, she started to run back down, then sheered again, staying the course. McKay bought the fake-out, turning to race down the hill, probably hoping to cut her off in descent. When she swerved back, he tried to stop himself, but spun too sharp, losing his footing and tumbling down the embankment.

I adjusted my course, heading straight for McKay. He saw me bearing down on him and found an extra spurt of energy, flying to his feet, bruises forgotten as he bolted after Elena.

The clatter of nails on wood told me she was on the train tracks. As we crested the embankment, I saw her tearing along the railway bridge, Cain a half-dozen strides behind.

I caught up with McKay at the bridge's edge. I launched myself and landed on him. We went down fighting, rolling and biting, ripping out fur and flesh.

Last year, fighting in human form, McKay had pushed me closer to my limits than I'd been in years. He was a first-rate fighter and a decade my junior. I'd reached the age where those extra years were starting to make a difference and my arm hadn't made it any easier. In wolf form, though, it was all about teeth and claws. There I had the advantage, understood how to use the wolf, how to be the wolf better than anyone else, mutt or Pack.

That didn't make it an easy fight. McKay had a score to settle. I'd sent him packing from El Paso with broken bones and a bloodied face. The worst, though, were the bruises . . . the ones on his ego. When he took home the story of my "fucked-up" arm, the obvious question would be, "If his arm's in such bad shape, why couldn't you take him?" I'm sure McKay came up with a reasonable story—in his version, I'd probably had every Pack brother at my side—but that wouldn't stop the cut from stinging. He'd had a chance to beat me and he'd blown it.

We rolled, struggling for a hold, fangs slashing, aiming for that critical throat bite. I managed to get close, but ended up with a mouthful of fur. When I drew back, he butted his head against the bottom of my muzzle. Pain blinded me. I staggered, head shaking.

McKay let out a snort of a laugh and charged. I kept shaking my head, acting disoriented, until the last moment. Then I sidestepped. He swung around. In midturn, when he was off-balance, I dove, hitting his side. I knocked him off his feet and we skidded over the grass, plowing through a small bush, twigs crackling.

He yanked his head down, instinctively covering his throat. I slashed at his belly instead. A yelp of surprise and pain as my fangs ripped through flesh. He tried to scramble up, legs kicking, claws scratching any surface they could reach, tearing through my coat, scraping the skin beneath. His teeth clamped down on my hind leg, chomping through to bone. A gasp burbled up, but I pushed it back before it reached my throat. If I let go, he'd run. Here was my chance to prove I wasn't growing old or soft, wasn't crippled with a fucked-up arm. My chance to squelch the rumors by taking out the very mutt who'd started them.

I bit down on his belly, ignoring the pain as he chewed on my leg. When I had the best grip I could manage, I ripped back with everything I had, eyes shut against the flood of hot blood as his stomach tore open, intestines spilling out.

He let go of my leg then. He twisted around, as if he could still escape. I grabbed him by the throat and whipped him into a bridge girder. A huge chunk of flesh came free, filling my mouth with blood. I dropped him. He fell, shuddering, dying. I bit the back of his neck, swung him up, and pitched him into the river below.

A quick kill, but during those few minutes, the blood pounding in my ears blocked everything else and it was only as McKay's body splashed into the water that I finally heard Elena's snarls. I started running. My hind leg throbbed from the bite, but it wasn't broken or gushing blood. Good enough.

Halfway down the bridge, she'd stopped and was facing off with Cain, head down, ears back, fur on end. At first, the mutt seemed uncertain, prancing forward, then back, like a boxer bouncing on his heels waiting for the signal. As I rocketed down the tracks, paws pounding the railway ties, he dropped into fighting position, as if hearing the sound he'd been waiting for: the arrival of his backup.

I slowed, rolling my paws, footfalls going silent. Then, right behind him, I hunkered down and let out a low growl. He turned, and had he been in human form, he would have fallen over backward. On four legs, he did an odd little stumble, paws scrabbling against the gravel as he veered toward me.

I snarled, teeth flashing, blood flecks spraying as I shook my head. He glanced over my shoulder, probably praying the blood came from some bird or rabbit. Seeing no sign of McKay, he knew, and swerved back, in flight before he'd finished his turn. He made it two strides before Elena landed in his path, snapping and snarling.

I backed up two steps and sat. He looked from Elena to me, the challenger and the road block. Confused, he kept glancing back as if to say, "You're going to jump me, aren't you?"

Elena gave up and rushed him. She caught him in the chest, knocking him backward. They went down fighting.

It didn't last long. Cain was spooked and distracted, knowing his buddy was dead and the killer sat five feet away, waiting to do the same to him. He managed to do little more than rip out tufts of fur while Elena sank her teeth into his flank, his shoulder, his belly.

Finally, when one bite got too close to his throat, the coward kicked in. He threw himself from her and tried to make a run for it. Elena flew onto his back. She grabbed his ear between her teeth, chomped down hard enough to make him yelp, then yanked, leaving tatters. He howled and bucked. She leapt off the other side, putting him between us again.

He flipped around and took a few running strides my way. I growled. He looked from Elena to me, hesitated only a moment, then flung himself between the girders and plummeted into the river.

As Elena leaned through the metal bars to watch him, I circled her, inventorying her injuries. A nasty gash on her side was the worst of it. A lick to wipe away the dirt. When I tried to do a more thorough job, she nudged me aside, then checked me out, nosing and licking my back leg, before deciding the bite wasn't fatal and moving up beside me.

We watched Cain flail in the water below.

She glanced at me. "Good enough?" her eyes asked.

I studied him for a moment, then grunted, not quite willing to commit yet. An answering chuff and she loped off across the bridge. I went the other way.

───⌖───

We toyed with Cain for a while, running along the banks, lunging at him every time he tried to make it to shore. When he finally showed signs of exhaustion, Elena gave the signal and we left him there.

A lesson learned? Probably not. Give him a year or two and he'd be back, but in the meantime, he'd have to return to his buddies with a shredded ear and without McKay, and no matter what slant he put on the story, the meaning would be clear: situation normal. I wasn't suffering from a debilitating injury or settling into comfortable retirement with my family. I'd bought myself a little more time.

❧

Elena lifted her head peering into the bushes that surrounded us.

"Don't worry," I said "No one can see."

"Something I really should have checked about ten minutes ago."

She pushed up from my chest, skin shimmering in the dark. She sampled the air for any sign of Cain.

"All clear." A slow stretch as she snarled a yawn. "One of these days, we're actually going to *complete* an escape before we have sex."

"Why?"

She, laughed. "Why, indeed."

She started to slide off me, but I held her still, hands around her waist.

"Not yet."

"Hmm." Another stretch, her toes tickling my legs. "So when are you going to blast me?"

"For taking off and running down alleys at midnight?"

"Unless you slipped something past me in the wedding vows, I think I'm still entitled to go where I want, when I want. But do you really think I'd go traipsing down dark alleys in a strange city for a bottle of water? Why not just stick a flashing 'mug me' sign on my back?"

"Well, you did seem a bit bored. . ."

"Please. That mutt's been following us since this morning. I was trying to get rid of him."

"What?"

"Yes, I know, I should have warned you. I realized that later, but you worked so hard to plan our honeymoon and I didn't want this mutt ruining it. I thought I'd give him a good scare and send him packing before you noticed him sniffing around."

"Huh."

I tried to sound surprised. Tried to look surprised. But her gaze swung to mine, eyes narrowing.

"You knew he was following us."

I shrugged, hoping for noncommittal.

She smacked my arm. "You were just going to let me take the blame and keep your mouth shut, weren't you?"

"Hell, yeah."

Another smack. "That's what you were doing at dinner, wasn't it? Breaking his jaw. I thought it looked off, and I could swear I smelled blood when we were walking back from the restaurant." She shook her head. "Communication. We should try it sometime."

I shifted, putting my arm under my head. "How about now? About this trip. You're bored." When she opened her mouth to protest, I put my hand over it. "There's not a damned thing to do except hole up in our hotel room, run in the forest, and hunt mutts—which, while fun, we could do anywhere. So I'm thinking, maybe it's time to consider a second honeymoon."

She sputtered a laugh. "Already?"

"I think we're due for one. So how's this? We pack, head home, see the kids for a couple of days, then take off again. Someplace where we can hole up, run in the forest and *not* have to worry about tripping over mutts. A cabin in Algonquin . . ."

She leaned over me, hair fanning a curtain around us. "Wasn't that where I suggested we go when you first asked?"

"I thought you were just trying to make it easy on me, We can rent a cabin anytime. I wanted this to be different, special."

"It was special. I was stalked, chased, attacked . . . and I got to beat the crap out of a mutt twice my size." She bent further, lips brushing mine. "A truly unique honeymoon from a truly unique husband."

She put her arms around my neck, rolled over, and pulled me on top of her.

Corpse Vision

KRISTINE KATHRYN RUSCH

Joe Decker couldn't remember who poured him into the taxi that brought him to Le Café du Dôme. Either way, it had to be one of the Midwestern boys—gangly Jim Thurber or the new guy —whatsisname? William?—Shirer. Neither of them knew Decker had a room at the Hôtel de Lisbonne—him and everybody else at the *Trib* except that old stick Waverly Root. Of course, without that old stick, the paper wouldn't get out every day for the ex-pats and tourists to read in their little Left Bank cafes. Some were saying—mostly the folks over at the *Paris Herald*—that an alcoholic wave was sweeping through the offices of the *Paris Tribune*, making it damned impossible to get anything out, let alone a daily paper.

Like the deadbeats at the *Herald* could talk. What they said about the *Trib* applied to the *Herald* as well: Each and every day, a goodly proportion of the staff was insensate due to drink—half because it was there and half because it wasn't.

Joe Decker didn't drink when he worked. He drank after he worked, and then only because he didn't want to face his typewriter in that little room off Boulevard St. Michel. If anyone had told him he'd be writing hack in Paris while he was supposed to be writing his brilliant first novel, he would've laughed.

He'd come to Paris with $300, his typewriter, and one tiny suit-case of clothes, figuring that, with the franc worth damn near nothing against the dollar, he could afford one year, one year of typing, one year of thinking, thinking, thinking. Six months later, he had 5,000 words of unadulterated horseshit and fifty dollars, barely enough to pay for the room which he was heartily sick of.

Besides, no one in Paris had heard of Prohibition or if they had, they thought it one of those crazy American ideas that would never work.

Oh yeah sure, it would never work. It had never worked him into a huge thirst, which he tried to slake on nights like this when he'd turned in his copy on some stupid tourist gala no one here gave a good goddamn about but which actually got sent home because the folks back at their parent paper, the *Chicago Tribune*, thought such things were the important goings-on in Paris.

He remembered heading down the twisty back stairs of the *Trib* building, the presses thudding, the air hot with fresh ink. Funny man Thurber had come along and Whatsisname Shirer, still all googly eyed because he hadn't seen anything like this back in Ioway or Illanoise or wherever the hell he was from, and they'd planned one drink, just one—and the next thing Decker knew he woke up in this taxi with a throbbing headache and a mouth that tasted of three-day old gin.

In his exceedingly bad French, he'd asked the cabby where they were going. The cabby just waved his hand imperiously and said, "Le Dôme, Le Dôme," and Decker wasn't sure they were heading to the Dôme because Thurber or Whatsisname had told the cabby to go there, or because the cabby, like every other French taxi driver, knew the Dôme was the place to take drunk Americans so that they could get home.

Decker's head was too fuzzy to conjure the words to get the taxi to the Hôtel de Lisbonne. Besides, he wasn't sure he had the scratch. The ride to the Dôme was gratis—or would be if he couldn't find a franc or two—because someone there would cover the fare, if not one of the patrons then one of the uniformed police officers who paced the beat near the taxi stand.

He would have to promise to pay them back. And he would pay them back. He had paid everyone back, which was about the only good thing he could say about himself at the moment.

Nothing he did was any damn good, not even the daily copy he wrote for the *Trib*. The words were fine, the prose was solid, the assignments stank. His friends were just as miserable as he was (although, as Wave Root said, miserable in Paris is like happy everywhere else), and there wasn't even a woman in the picture. Well, not a relationship woman. There'd been more than Decker's fare share of one-night women. He might have even had one tonight.

The thought made him search his pockets as the taxi pulled up on the Rue Delambre side of the Dôme. The café had been on this corner for nearly thirty years, but only since the War had it become a haven for Americans. Know-it-all Hemingway, the only one of Decker's acquaintances who had finished his novel after he arrived in Paris, called it one of the three principal cafes in the Quarter, and the only one filled with people who worked.

No one who worked was there now. The tables on the terrace were empty, the chairs pushed out expectantly. A glow fell across them from the café's open doors.

Decker staggered out of the taxi, handed the driver the lone franc he'd found in his front pocket, and had to grip the pole marking the taxi stand to keep from falling.

Not only did he have a throbbing headache, but wobbly legs as well. He had to stop drinking, that was all there was to it.

"Coffee?"

Decker still had one arm wrapped around the pole. He thought maybe the ubiquitous uniformed policeman had spoken to him, but he didn't see an ubiquitous uniformed policeman. Instead, he saw an elderly man sitting against the wall, beneath the awning that someone should have rolled up by now.

"Or are you one of those British gentlemen who prefer tea?"

The old man spoke the oddly clipped English that Parisians learned—not quite British upper-class, but not quite British lower-class either. Continental English, Root called it. Incontinent English, Thurber always amended when Root had left the room.

"Water would probably help," Decker said, not sure he should let go of the pole.

"Water *will* help. Alcohol dehydrates the system. That is half of what causes the so-called hang over."

The old man put a deliberate space between "hang" and "over." It was those kinds of errors that Decker usually found funny. The French often mangled English idioms, like the time the editor at *Le Petit Journal* had introduced Decker to his assistant, calling the man "my left hand" — and not meaning it as any kind of joke.

"*Monsieur,*" the old man said with a wave of a hand. "*Une bouteille d'eau.*"

Decker was going to tell him that the waiters here never showed up when you wanted them, and certainly wouldn't show when there were only a few customers, but the waiter who appeared, happily prying the top off a bottle of water, contradicted his very thought.

Of course, the old man wasn't just French. He had to be a regular. French regulars were prized at places like this, places which the Americans had taken over, like they had taken over most of Montparnesse just south of the Luxembourg Gardens. It was essentially an extension of the Latin Quarter without being in the Latin Quarter at all. It had been that way since the 16th century when Catherine de Medici had expelled students from the university. They had set up shop here and called it Montparnesse.

Decker knew such things about Paris, indeed, he had become a font of Paris trivia in his two years at the *Tribune*, all learned with bad schoolboy French and only a modicum of charm.

"It would be nice if you joined me," the old man said to Decker as the waiter put down the empty bottle and a single, rather grimy glass.

"Easier said than done," Decker said, not certain he could let go of the pole and remain standing.

The old man had a croissant in front of him and, despite the hour, a cup of coffee. He wore a proper black suit but no hat, which looked odd in the thin light. His hair was a yellowish white, speaking of too many hours in cafes around cigarette smoke.

As Decker lurched closer, using tables and the occasional chair to maintain his balance, he realized that the old man's beard was yellowish brown around his mouth. His fingers were tobacco stained as well. But he held no pipe and no cigar or cigarette had burned to ash in the tray in the center of the table.

Decker made it to the table and sank into the chair the old man had pushed back for him. It groaned beneath his weight. He tugged his suit coat over his stained white shirt. He had to look as filthy as he felt.

The old man poured water into the glass. The water looked clear and fresh despite the fingerprints on the side of the glass.

"You are an American newspaper man, yes?" the old man asked.

"Yes," Decker said, not that it was a hard guess, given their location.

"Joseph Decker, the American newspaper man, yes?" the old man said.

It gave Decker a start that the old man knew his name. "Is there another Joe Decker in Paris?"

The old man ignored the question. "I have a story for you, should you take it."

Everyone had a story for him. Usually it was the kind of thing tourist rumors were made of, like why there were no fish in the Seine. But the old man didn't look like someone who would give Decker a song and dance.

Of course, Decker wasn't yet sober, so he had to assume his judgment about all things—like the kind of man the old man was based on how he appeared—was probably flawed.

"It's two a.m.," Decker said, "and—"

"Three a.m.," the old man said.

"Three a.m.," Decker said with a flash of irritation, "and I'm drunk. If you're serious about this story thing, we'll meet here tomorrow when I've had a chance to sleep this off, and we can talk then."

"I do not go out in the daylight," the old man said.

Two years ago, Decker would have rolled his eyes. But by now, he'd seen and heard everything. There were guys on the copy desk who didn't go out in the daylight either, saying it hurt their precious eyes.

Decker went out too much in the daylight, seeing things that sometimes he wished he hadn't.

He flashed on her then, body crumpled beneath Pont Neuf, feet dangling over the edge of the walkway along the banks of the Seine, pointing toward the river.

He closed his eyes and willed the image away.

"And that is why I do not," the old man said. "You see them too."

Decker opened his eyes. The old man was staring at him. The old man's eyes were blue and clear, not rheumy like Decker had expected. Maybe the old man was younger than Decker thought. He'd met a number of those guys in Paris—men in their forties who could pass for someone in their eighties by their clothing, their white hair, and their gait.

"I don't see anything, old man," Decker said.

"Nonsense," the old man said. "It is why you drink."

"I drink because I'm lonely," Decker said. *Because he kept writing the beginning to that damn novel over and over while Know-it-all Hemingway sat in this very café with his stupid notebook and scribbled story after story, book after book. Decker drank because he hated writing puff pieces for the folks back home, puff pieces about touristy restaurants and American musicians and writers like Know-it-all Hemingway. Decker drank because the stories he wanted to cover "would discourage the tourist trade from coming here." He drank because Paris wasn't the answer after all.*

"You drink," the old man said, "because it closes your mind's eye. I have watched you. You see too much."

"You've *watched* me?" Decker was getting more and more sober by the minute. "You're following me?"

"If you recall," the old man said with the patience people reserve for drunks, fools, and children, "I arrived before you did. But I must confess that I have been waiting for you."

"Me and all the other American hacks," Decker said.

The old man smiled, revealing tobacco-stained teeth. The smile was friendlier than Decker expected. "Admittedly, you American hacks, as you say, are dozens of dimes—"

Decker winced.

"—but I, in truth, have been waiting for you."

Decker drank his water. It did clear his head, although he wasn't entirely sure he wanted his head cleared. "What's so special about me?"

"You see," the old man said again.

This time, Decker did roll his eyes. He drank the last of his water, and stood up. "Old man, I'm so damned drunk that this conversation isn't making sense. How about I meet you here tomorrow at midnight, and I promise to be sober. Then you can tell me your story."

"It is your story," the old man said.

"Whatever you say," Decker said, taking the bottle of water and heading north.

He had a hell of a walk—at least for an exhausted drunk. Normally he wouldn't have minded the jaunt up to the twisty little streets near the Sorbonne. The Hôtel de Lisbonne was on the corner of Rue Monsieur-le-Prince and Rue de Vaugirad. All he had to was walk the Boulevard St. Michel toward the Seine and he'd be in his bed in no time.

But he usually avoided the Boulevard St. Michel. He avoided a lot streets in Paris, at least on foot. The old man was right; Decker saw things. But he usually attributed those things to drink or to too much imagination.

The soldiers he always saw marching through the Arc de Triomphe wore no uniforms he recognized. They marched in lock-step, their heads turned side to side as if they were little tin soldiers with moving parts.

But he didn't always see the soldiers there. Sometimes he saw a flag that he didn't recognize with a Fylfot in the middle. The Fylfot, an ancient elaborate cross, was supposed to ward off evil. But he somehow got the sense that the Fylfot itself—at least as used here—was the evil.

On the Boulevard St. Michel, he saw students rioting in the streets. The students were grubby creatures, with long hair and carrying signs that he did not understand. Sunshine shone on them, although he only saw them when it was dark.

Because of these visions, he studied Paris history, and found nothing that resembled any of it. The soldiers were unfamiliar, just like the flag, and the students too filthy to belong to any modern generation. He could dismiss such things as figments of his imagination.

But the woman—she had been real.

He had touched her, her skin cold and clammy and gray from the elements. Her eyes had been open and cloudy, her lips parted ever so slightly.

He had found her six months into his trip to Paris. Shortly after, he had wandered into the offices of the *Trib*, such as they were, and offered up his services.

Novelist, eh, kid? The man at the copy desk had asked.

Yessir.

You know how many novelists we get here, hoping for a few bucks? At least two a day. Sorry.

I have experience …

Those fateful words. *I have experience.* And he did. From his college newspaper to the *Milwaukee Journal*—yes, he had been a good Midwestern boy, once too, a boy who didn't like near beer. A boy who actually had dreams for himself.

Five thousand words of horseshit later, stories about the tourists (*Mr. and Mrs. Gladwell arrived this afternoon on a trip that has taken them from their home in Lincoln, Nebraska, to New York City through London, and now here, in Paris, where they are staying at the Ritz …*), stories about everything except the woman, crumpled beneath Pont Neuf.

Somehow he made it to the Hôtel de Lisbonne without seeing anyone, real or imaginary. The front desk was empty, so he reached over it and grabbed his key.

As he climbed the dark narrow stairs to his room, he heard a typewriter rat-a-tat-tatting. Someone was working on something, maybe a short story, maybe a novel, maybe a freelance piece for *Town and Country*.

He unlocked his room and stepped inside, then stared at his own typewriter, gathering dust beneath the room's only window. A piece of paper had been rolled in the platen since sometime last month, with only a page number on the upper right hand corner (27), and a single lowercase word in the upper left.

… the …

As if it meant something. As if he knew what he was going to do with it.

The paper was probably ruined, forever curlicued, although it didn't matter. If he finished typing on that page, he could pile the other twenty-six pages on top of it, flattening it out.

If he sat down now, nearly sober, the old man's words still echoing in his head (*You see them too*), he would write:

The woman discarded at the foot of the bridge looked uncomfortably young. Her brown hair was falling out of Gibson Girl do, now horribly out of fashion, her lips painted a vivid red. Part of the lip rouge stained her front teeth. If she were alive, she would turn away from him, and surreptiously rub at that stain with her index finger.

He looked away from the typewriter, from that little accusatory "the." The description of the woman did not fit with the bucolic piece he had been writing, a memoir of Germantown Wisconsin in the days before the war, when he had been a young boy, and his father was still alive, tinkering with his new Model T, his mother tutting the dangers in the new-fangled machinery, the bicycle he himself had built from a kit, with the help of the man who lived next door.

Those were the kind of books people read now, memories of times past, not bloody, dark stories about dead women on Paris streets.

Decker took off his suit and hung it up, although he didn't brush it out, like he should have. He lacked the energy. As he pulled off his shirt, he realized the stains were worse than he had thought. Long, brown stains up front, looking like blood.

He was thinking of blood, though. He wasn't going to let his imagination win.

Besides, he still had one clean shirt. He needed to take the bundle to the laundry, along with his suit, so that he could look pressed and sharp again, instead of rumpled and disreputable.

He left his undershirt, boxers, and socks on, and tumbled onto the bed, the saggy mattress groaning beneath his weight. The bed hadn't even stopped bouncing by the time he had fallen asleep.

—⁓—

She was there in his dreams, her rich brown hair piled on top of her head, with a few curls cascading around her face. She sat on the edge of the bridge, feet dangling over the Seine, leaning back toward the road. Her eyes smiled, her lips—a perfect cupid's bow, just like the drawings she mimicked—rouged darker than her cheeks. The makeup softened her living face, making her seem as unreal as the women in the advertisements.

While her hair was old-fashioned, her clothing was not. No buttoned down shirtwaist for her with a long skirt that fell to her ankles. She wore a black skirt that grazed her knees, silk stockings with a perfect line up the back, and a blouse so soft that it seemed almost indecent. Around her neck, a simple St. Christopher's medal, and a delicate gold cross with a tiny diamond in the center. A gold band on her right hand, a band she twisted when she saw him approach, a frown creasing her lovely forehead.

He stopped beside her. She was American—he knew that without asking—and he held his reporter's notebook in his left hand, a pen in his right.

Her face shut down when he asked her name. And then her eyes clouded over, and her mouth opened ever so slightly.

The St. Christopher's medal disappeared and the gold ring too. But the expensive necklace, the gold cross with a diamond in the center, remained, as if it were her calling card.

He woke up thinking about it, twisted to one side, the bottom of the cross bent slightly as if she had fallen on it against the stone walkway.

She had worn no stockings when he found her body, and the sensible shoes, made for walking in a strange city (he knew that as clearly as if she had told him) had been replaced by thin heels, the kind flappers wore with their knee-length dresses and opera-length pearls.

He woke up thinking of the difference between the smiling girl in his dreams and the dead woman on the walkway, her skin cold against his fingertips.

He stared at his typewriter, his fingers itching to finish that sentence.

. . . *the* . . .

The.

The woman discarded . . .

Discarded.

He got dressed, and stumbled out of his room, ostensibly searching for breakfast, but really on his way to get another drink.

⁘

Still, that day, he made it to midnight without taking a nip from the bottle he kept at the bottom of his desk drawer. He didn't take the glass of wine offered with dinner, nor did he drink the shot of vodka offered to him by the White Russian he'd met while waiting for the American tourists he was supposed to interview in Le Procope.

He arrived at the Dôme exactly at midnight, sober as a judge. Decker had pressed his suit and worn his last clean shirt, mostly as an apology for the way he had looked the night before.

He hadn't examined himself in the mirror until this morning, but even then he had looked a fright—his hair standing on end, his nose bulbous, the capillaries in his cheeks bursting from too much drink. His eyes were red rimmed and he knew his breath was bad enough to kill any small rodent unfortunate enough to cross his path.

So he cleaned up, although no one at the *Trib* noticed, except Whatsisname Shirer, the kid from Ioway or Illanoise. Whatsisname Shirer had raised his eyebrows, but hadn't made a single remark, smart ass or otherwise, and so no one else seemed to notice.

Thurber was busy making up the news. Root was working, trying to get someone at the copy desk to expand the notes his so-called reporters had turned in. Most everyone else was so bleary-eyed that they would think they were imagining Decker in his spiffed up clothes and slicked-back hair.

Alcoholic wave indeed. It had become an alcoholic ocean, and he was seeing it for the very first time.

The Dôme had customers this night, at least a dozen sitting on the terrace, with more inside. The interior was grayish blue from all the cigarette smoke—it looked like a fog had blown through Paris and gotten stuck only inside the Dôme.

Outside, a group of men crowded around one of the tables. Decker recognized some of them from the *Transatlantic Review*. They spoke earnestly to each other, one of them shaking the stem of his pipe at a bespectacled man in an American felt hat.

Decker avoided them, just like he'd taken to avoiding Know-it-all Hemingway. Instead he circled to the other side of the terrace, near the taxi stand. This evening, one of the ubiquitous uniformed policemen paced, hands clasped behind his back.

The Dôme seemed normal, not like something out of a painting, the way it had the night before.

Because Decker was concentrating on its normality, he almost missed the old man, sitting at the same table, his back against the café's glass windows. Another man sat with him, younger, sharply French with his narrow face, black hair, and up-to-the-minute gabardine suit.

Decker wandered over toward them, as if they weren't his destination at all. When he reached the table, he pulled out the only other chair and sat.

"You're lucky I remembered," he said.

"I knew you would." The old man wore the same suit. His eyes were as clear as Decker had thought. "You have not had a drink."

Damn that incontinent English. Decker couldn't tell if the old man had asked a question or made a statement. "I told you I'd be sober. You told me you had a story."

The younger man stared at Decker as if he thought he was rude. Maybe he was.

"I said, I had a story *for you*." The old man emphasized the last two words.

Decker looked at the younger man. "Maybe some introductions would be a good place to start."

"Maybe not," the old man said. "We shall perform the—how do you say?—niceties after we have determined what disturbs you the most."

"What disturbs me the most," Decker said, "are people who waste my time."

He shoved the chair back, about to stand, when the old man touched his arm. The old man's skin was cold. In spite of himself, Decker shivered.

"Americans are impulsive," the old man said to his companion. "And somehow they have come to embrace a lack of politeness as if it is a virtue."

"Look," Decker said, almost adding "old man" like he had done last night when he was drunk. That had been rude, but not intentionally rude. "I deal in hard, cold facts. The first hard cold fact you learn about damn near anybody is his name, which you're not willing to tell me. So I'm not willing to stick around. See ya, pal."

This time he did stand. He was going to repeat the same walk he'd made the night before, up the Boulevard St. Michel. Maybe he should walk around the Luxembourg Gardens instead, meander instead of go directly.

He was nearly to the group of *Transatlantic Review* writers when the old man said, "The students, they will be in the street tonight. And tomorrow, the flag will fly over the Arc de Triomphe."

Decker stopped in spite of himself. A shiver ran down his spine. He hadn't told anyone about those waking dreams. Not even when he was drunk. Probably not even when he was black-out drunk, since he got quieter and quieter—a man who knew how to keep secrets, Root used to say, when he was the one who poured Decker into a taxi.

Decker pivoted. He walked back to the table, as the old man had known he would. But the old man did not smile like a man who had won an argument. Instead, he remained grimly serious. The younger man continued to stare.

"The soldiers leaning out of the Hôtel de Ville, do you not notice how blond they are?" The old man's voice was soft.

The other man watched Decker avidly, as if everything depended on his response.

The Hôtel de Ville was Paris's city hall. And he'd only seen soldiers there once, in the middle of a summer afternoon, as heat shimmered on the boulevards and he sat outside, trying to find a bit of air in a city not used to extreme warmth.

"They wore helmets," Decker said, knowing that was an admission.

"But they were fair-skinned, no?"

"Stocky," he said, wishing he hadn't responded. But that was what he had noticed, how stocky and square they were, as if the uniforms they wore with their unrecognizable helmets made them as solid as a boxer in the beer halls near Milwaukee.

"And they wore this symbol on their arms." The old man pushed a piece of paper forward with a Fylfot drawn on it.

In spite of himself, Decker sat back down. "Who are they?"

"A nightmare," the old man said. "One we pray we will not have. But our prayers will be for nothing. Because only strong nightmares leach backwards."

"Backwards?" Decker asked, thinking of the woman. Was that a backwards nightmare? He had seen her six months after he arrived—years ago now—and he dreamt of her every night, awakening from those dreams unsettled.

"The soldiers," the old man said. "They are little boys now, playing with battered tin soldiers from before the War. If, indeed, they are healthy enough to play. Most are hungry. Some are starving."

Decker frowned. Even when he was sober, Decker didn't understand the old man. The old man spoke nonsense. But a nonsense that Decker found enticing, in spite of himself.

"Starving?" Decker said. "Then why don't you do something?"

"Why don't you?" the old man asked. "Your country pushed for reparations. Your President Wilson. Somehow he knew how to cure the world. He made it sicker."

"Congress never ratified that treaty," Decker said, wondering why they were talking about the Treaty of Versailles conference from six years ago, from before he even arrived in the City of Light.

"And that makes it all better, no?" the old man said. "Leadership provided by your president here in Paris failed at home, so the fact that the other countries—"

"*Grand-pére,*" the young man said, touching the old man's arm. "That is enough. He is not responsible for his country's follies."

"They are all responsible," the old man said.

Decker was frowning now.

"You were telling me about soldiers and little boys," Decker said, trying to get past this confusion. "Soldiers, little boys, and backwards nightmares."

"They are not nightmares," the younger man said. "They are visions. The future, haunting us here and now."

Decker frowned. "The future?"

The young man nodded. "Events so powerful they reach backwards to us. We have seen the soldiers for generations now. We have not understood them until—what is it you call it?—the Peace of Paris."

"You understand it now?" Decker asked.

"We understand that they are Germans."

"Marching into Paris." Decker snorted. "Are you hoping for this?"

Three men from nearby tables stared. Most everyone here served in the War or had lost someone who had.

"No," the younger man said, holding up his hands. "It is the worst kind of tragedy. But we do know, from the students who are also a vision leaching backwards, that Paris herself will stand."

"The students." Decker wasn't going to ask any more and he wasn't going to reveal what he had seen. He was assuming the younger man meant the grubby students he had seen some nights as he walked up the Boulevard St. Michel.

"St. Sulpice stands. Notre Dame stands. Le Tour Eiffel stands. In the distance, away from the shouting, you can see Sacré Coeur. The bridges remain. If the Germans were to destroy Paris, they would bomb the bridges so that no army could follow. Then they would destroy the monuments to destroy our souls."

Decker couldn't resist any longer. "How do you know the students appear later?"

"They are less solid."

"You can't touch them?" Decker asked.

"No," the younger man said. "You have not tried?"

He had avoided everything. He had avoided the students and the soldiers and the flags. He heard the whispery voices, and figured they had come from his own drunkenness.

"Can you touch current nightmares?" Decker asked.

"Only reality," the old man said.

Her skin, cold against Decker's fingers. So she *had* been real. Had he spoken to her once? Holding his notebook? Wanting to know who she was?

Why would he have spoken to her? He wasn't yet working for the *Trib*. He was playing at being a famous writer, the American James Joyce, yet to publish his *Portrait of the Artist as a Young Man*.

"Ah," the old man said, peering into Decker's face. "Something precipitated your visions. You did not see them when you first came to Paris."

Decker looked at him. The old man's skin was papery thin, his eyebrows so bushy they seemed to grow toward his scalp.

Paris had been clean. Paris had been pure. Truly the City of Light, all beauty and glistening stone, history calling to him.

Not like Milwaukee. Milwaukee had turned dark, especially near the lakefront. He had seen corpses of sailors, washed against the rocks, their uniforms still sodden with the waters of Lake Michigan. He had screamed the first time, and people had run to him, not to them, not even when he pointed . . . .

He shook his head. He did not want to think of this. He did not want to remember it, how each street had something, someone, who sprawled along a road or had been shot on apartment steps or had been squashed flat by a new-fangled motorcar.

Sometimes two, sometimes three per block. He had walked with his eyes closed, and his mother—his beautiful tiny mother—whispering that he had to do something else, something that took him away from death.

Write your novel, she had said. *I will tell people of my son, the famous writer.*

And she had given him all of her pin money, money he knew she relied upon to get away from his father.

His father, who drank.

"What was it that precipitated these visions?" the old man asked. "A drink, perhaps. You like your drink."

Decker stared at him, feeling his gaze go flat with anger.

"No, it could not be drink," the younger man said. "Or he wouldn't continue drinking. It's got to be hereditary. Let me see your hands."

Decker closed his hands into fists. He didn't want these people to touch him. He looked at the old man.

"You said you had a story for me."

"I have a city of stories, if you're willing to listen," the old man said. "But first, we must see the root of your vision."

Decker stared at him, then slowly, reluctantly, extended his right hand.

He had first seen her on the Champs Elysées, a vision in white. She looked like the old world blending with the new, her Gibson Girl hairdo, the wide-brimmed hat (with ribbons trailing it) that she carried in her left hand. Her dress was narrow, with a flip just near the knees, her stockings perfect, her shoes solid, old-fashioned, buttoned-up leather.

He had seen no Parisian woman dressed like that—mixing styles. Parisian women had their own style, a lot more fluid, a lot more suggestive, and all of them wore cloche hats (if they wore hats at all). She smiled when she saw him, a broad, wide American smile, the kind that held nothing back.

He tipped his hat to her. She laughed and continued onward as if she had known they would see each other again.

Of course they had. She had been looking at the sights, such a tourist, and he had been moving from park bench to park bench, staring at the monuments.

He had talked with her on Pont Neuf, more than once. She had laughed and flirted and never once told him her name. No one seemed to want to tell him names.

The thought disconcerted him for a moment, and the image of her laughing face wavered. He heard voices all around him, male voices mostly, and the air filled with tobacco smoke. An old man was peering at the palm of his hand as if it held the secrets of the universe.

And then she was back, looking at him sideways. She was holding his hand, palm up, as if she could see his future in it. She was young, enjoying Paris. He hadn't enjoyed Paris until her. Not like this—climbing the Eiffel Tower and going to Versailles to see the gardens, wandering through the Louvre, and eating bread and cheese for lunch in the Tuileries.

And he wrote. How he wrote. The novel, abandoned, he didn't care about Lincoln. He wrote instead about—

. . . the woman, discarded, like abandoned laundry at the base of the bridge. Her killer, dark, darker than anything Edgar Allan Poe could imagine in his darkest Rue Morgue dreams. The man carried her from the bridge itself, down the side, preparing to dump her in the Seine when someone called out . . .

He looked up, saw the younger man staring at him with something like horror, the old man with eyes full of compassion.

"Corpse Vision," the young man said. "You have Corpse Vision."

Decker wasn't sure he wanted them to tell him what Corpse Vision was, although he had a hunch he knew.

The memories scrolled backwards—like the nightmares the old man had mentioned—the first homicide call on the police beat, near one of the speakeasies by the lakefront. The dead man wore spats and a snazzy hat that blew toward Decker in the wind. He caught the hat, knew enough to carry it back to the detective, and as he did, his foot brushed the corpse, his ankle actually hitting the dead man's elbow.

A little bit of nothing—a bit of a shiver, a bit of a chill—but not much more until he returned to the *Journal's* city room. He found a typewriter and banged out his recollections, handing the paper to the copy desk for expansion. He went back to the desk to type a few impressions, like he used to do, for the novels he would someday write. But first, he rested his cheek on his fist and closed his eyes.

Spats rose from the sand, backwards, like a Charlie Chaplin film being rewound, shaking his fist at someone near on the docks. A flash of a knife, a dropped bottle of gin, some money clanging against the wood, and Decker opened his eyes, terrified of his waking dream.

The next morning, he went to the lakefront as follow-up, at least that was what he told himself, and instead, he saw the sailors, washed up on the rocks, the air cold off Lake Michigan, and two little boys, standing in the middle of the corpses, fishing.

That was when Decker screamed. The last time he screamed when he saw a corpse.

But not the first time.

The first time—Lord, he'd been ten. On his grandfather's farm. His father had come back from the stream, looking grim, the female barn cat following him, crying plaintively. Decker should have followed his father, but he was already afraid of the man. So he went to the stream, saw the tiny kitten corpse on one of the rocks, touched it—the cold damp fur—and turned.

The man behind him had no eyes. He was tied to a tree, his skin filled with holes, birds sitting on his shoulders and pecking at his face.

Decker had screamed and screamed. His father had come first, pulled him away, told him he was a baby—he knew it was spring and every spring, his grandfather took the pick of the litter for barn cats and drowned the rest so the farm didn't get overrun with cats.

Someday, his dad had said grimly, *this'll be your job.*

But Decker only dimly heard the words. Instead, he stared at the dead man tied to the tree, the birds taking chunks out of his face as if he were a particularly delectable roast. Decker wanted to bury his own face in his dad's chest, but he knew better.

He also knew he needed to gather himself, to stop being so upset, but he couldn't. He couldn't. He sobbed and sobbed and finally his dad picked him up like a sack of potatoes and slung him over his shoulder, carrying him back, Decker hiccoughing, his father whacking his butt with every single hitched breath.

His mother came into his room that night when he screamed again, the dead man alive in his room as a vision, running from men Decker dimly recognized. They would catch the dead man, carve him up, tie him to the tree, and laugh when they told him the birds would get him. They laughed. And Decker recognized the laughs.

But that wasn't why he screamed. He screamed at the sunlight afternoon invading his dark room, the trees no longer there leading down to the stream, the bank where he'd happily played just a few years before.

His mother had come and shushed him. She had cradled him as if he were still a baby, and rocked him, but she said nothing.

Except when she thought he was asleep, she went back to the room she shared with his father—*You promised*, she said.

I did not send him down there, his father said. *He went on his own.*

You should have watched him.

You coddle him.

He doesn't need to see.

At his age, I was drowning kittens. I had killed chickens and butchered pigs. I fished. You deny him childhood.

That isn't childhood, she said. *See what it has done to you.*

You used to love me, his father said.

Before the darkness ate you, she said. *Before it ate you alive.*

"You could spend your whole life in escape," the old man said, again misusing idioms. It was the odd choice of words that brought Decker back to the Dôme, not the fact that he wanted to be back.

The men from the *Transatlantic Review* had left. In their place, a group from the *Herald*. One of the reporters tipped his hat to Decker, who nodded. He couldn't for the life of him think of the man's name.

"Each place will be new and fresh until death," the old man said. "Then you will see—and in Europe, there is much death to see."

"I'm not seeing corpses," Decker said before he could stop himself. Not that he admitted anyway. He drank too much to remember what he saw. And what he did remember the old man called backwards nightmares.

"You are not looking," the old man said. "You have deliberately blinded your most important eye."

Decker was getting a headache, and he was starting to wish for a drink. This had been a mistake. He didn't like being sober, not any more.

"You lied," Decker said. "You said you had a story for me. This whole meeting has been nothing but gibberish."

He stood, conscious of how odd he felt. He didn't want to be near these men. He didn't want to be at the Dôme. He wanted to talk to his mother, and she was thousands of miles away, probably worrying about him, like she did. She worried.

She thought he could outrun the family curse. The old man just said he couldn't.

Decker didn't want to think about any of it.

"We will be here tomorrow night," the old man said.

"I won't," Decker said.

"Unless you finish the story," said the younger man.

"We would love to read it," the old man said.

"Sure," Decker said. And he would love to start over, that fresh bright attitude he had brought to Paris so far gone that he couldn't even remember how it felt.

Maybe he could recapture it somewhere else. He had heard nice things about Vienna. There was another sister paper in Geneva—or maybe that was a sister to the *Herald*. United Press operated out of most countries.

He could leave in the morning. He didn't need the language skills. He hadn't had all that many in France. Besides, French was the language of diplomacy. He spoke it just badly enough for people to take pity on him.

He was going to go speak it badly now at the nearest bar he could find. He would speak it until he couldn't talk any more, until he didn't think about all the things the old man had brought back into his mind. He would be so bleary-eyed drunk that maybe he wouldn't even dream.

❧

But he made the mistake of stopping in his room first. He wanted more cash, which he found rolled up in his socks in the bottom drawer of the shabby bureau. Anyone would know to look in the sock drawer for money. It was a testament to how honest the staff was at the Hôtel de Lisbonne that no one had stolen his stash.

How honest or how lax. He couldn't remember the last time they cleaned his room.

He wiped a finger over the typewriter, removing dust. His eye caught the edge of that paper.

... the ...

He sat down, xxed out the "the," and typed:

Sophie Nance Brown, daughter of Mr. and Mrs. Harcourt Brown lately of Newport, Rhode Island, in what the police initially reported as a bungled suicide attempt.

(Although, he thought, how could it have been bungled if she did indeed die?)

The body, discovered by an American tourist, fell on the walkway beneath the Pont Neuf. A witness claimed she had jumped off the bridge's wide stone railing, laughing as she fell.

But the American tourist contradicted these things, saying no one could have seen her fall. He found her at 7 a.m. Any witnesses would have had to be on the bridge in the middle of the night.

The American also pointed to her missing stockings and mismatched shoes. Her traveling companion, one Eleanor Rose Stockdale of Battle Creek, Michigan, said Miss Brown had never traveled anywhere without her St. Christopher's medal and her grandmother's solid gold wedding ring, both missing.

Police now believe Sophie Nance Brown is the third victim of a killer who play tricks on investigating officers. The witness who claimed she had fallen matched the description of a man seen carrying an unconscious woman to the base of the bridge around midnight.

Anyone with information about this most interesting case should contact the Prefect of Police.

Decker stared at the words. The paper did indeed come out of the platen curled, but he didn't care. The story was good enough for the *Trib*, if it published crime news like that (which it did not, afraid it would scare the tourists). But the story wasn't really good, just good enough.

He had written the facts as he had been trained. But that wasn't what he *knew*.

What he knew was this:

The woman discarded at the foot of the bridge looked uncomfortably young. Her brown hair was falling out of Gibson Girl do, now horribly out of fashion, her lips painted a vivid red. Part of the lip rouge stained her front teeth. If she were alive, she would turn away from him, and surreptiously rub at that stain with her index finger.

She *had* turned away from him and wiped at the stain, the very first time she had seen him. Sophie Nance Brown, of Newport and Westchester and points south. Sophie Nance Brown with the laughing eyes, who said she had come to Paris for the *adventure.*

But her index finger was broken, bent backwards at an angle painful to look at, even now, when he knew she could feel nothing.

She had felt something. She had felt too much something when she went to the bridge after a long dinner on the Right Bank with friends. She wanted to feel the breeze in her hair, look at the moonlight over the Seine. She asked her traveling companion, Eleanor Rose Stockdale of Battle Creek, Michigan, to accompany her, but Eleanor Rose, a sensible girl, had heard that nice people did not stand on the bridges at night and had declined.

Later, Miss Stockdale would say she thought saying such things would discourage Miss Brown, but other friends said nothing discouraged Miss Brown when she set her mind to something.

Miss Brown had met a young man who had captured her fancy. Her interest in him was what she wanted to discuss with her friends at dinner. Knowing him had caused an ethical dilemma for her, especially since she was so far from home. He lived alone in a solitary room in one of the more disreputable hotels near the Sorbonne.

Miss Brown worried that she was too old-fashioned for the new morality, but too young to press the young man into something less exciting, something more permanent.

Instead of listening to her, Miss Brown's friends teased her "mercilessly." They laughed their way through dinner, interrupting her, until she grew angry, threw down her napkin along with a few francs and left the restaurant, heading for the Pont Neuf.

The Pont Neuf was suggestive, Miss Stockdale said, because Miss Brown found it romantic.
Miss Brown stood in the center of the bridge, peering out over the Seine at the famed lights of Paris, thinking that no woman should stand in such a spot alone. The light played with her old-fashioned hairstyle and her modern clothing, her ankles nicely turned out, the skirt accenting her shapely legs.

He had noticed that. He had noticed the contradiction from the start.

Decker paused, his wrists aching. He had them bent at an odd angle. His headache had cleared for the first time since he started drinking in Paris.

He wasn't writing news any longer—or at least, he wasn't writing news that he recognized. He was writing something else, *seeing* something else, something he didn't want to think about.

The pages had piled up on the small desk beside his typewriter. The voice was odd. It wasn't his, and it wasn't exactly the voice of impartial journalist. He was edging into something else, something his editors would disapprove of—"worried" and "thinking" and "noticing"—actual viewpoints, which were not allowed in the dispassionate prose of journalism.

Decker rolled another sheet of paper in the platen, ready to type that damning "the" again, ready to leave it, and count all of this as an aberration.

Instead, he continued:

He had watched her since she got off the boat. She wore a wide brimmed hat with a red ribbon, fanciful and old-fashioned. Her clothing hinted at a girl who wanted to break out of the old ways, but her hair spoke of a girl who cherished what had come before.

Almost Parisian. Modern, yet grounded in the past. He loved his city, and he wished others would as well. But he did not love the tourists, particularly the American ones, with their loud braying laughter and their lack of manners.

Although they grew their women tall and beautiful in America. Solid women, with high cheekbones and flashing eyes.

He followed her to her hotel, then watched her, meeting her first on the Champs Elysées, then finding her in the Tuileries, regaling her with stories of his novel—every young man in Paris these days had a novel—his notebook clutched in his hand . . . .

Decker stopped. Those memories, the things he saw, they weren't his? He frowned, trying to see something else, trying to remember when he had first met her. The date—

He dreamed of her. He dreamed of her, *after* he had found her. Six months into his stay in Paris.

Six months.

But he had never seen her, touched her, laughed with her. He hadn't really encountered her until he saw her half-naked foot hanging off the walkway, her shoe dangling over the sparkling waters of the Seine.

Only it wasn't her shoe. The killer changed the shoes. That was his little joke. He tossed her sensible shoes in the water and gave her little Parisian heels, delicate shoes that he had bought just for this purpose . . . .

Not Decker. *Him,*

Etienne Netter, whose apartment in the Seventh Arrondissement had been in his family for six decades. His parents long dead, his mother distressed when he came home from the War with "haunted eyes."

"But at least I am home, Mother," he said plaintively, when so many young men had not come home. She had not seen what he had seen, how the blood turned French fields into mud, all for the sake of a few meters of advancement that would probably be lost the following day.

They said the Americans changed it all, with their energy and their numbers and their willingness to get killed. The Americans, big and hearty, like their women, who were stupid but lucky and somehow managed to end the war.

They liked him, these American women. They thought him their pet Frenchman. They thought his accent "quaint," his smile "romantic," his desire to write novels "almost American," even though the French had been writing novels before America was a country.

He charmed them, relaxed them, promised them he would show them the sights—and he did. He did. He showed them their own venal faces in the Seine before he raised their skirts, ripped off their stockings, and proved to them that French men hadn't lost all of their dignity in the trenches.

His mother, before she died, said he had lost his soul on the battle-field, that he had come home a shell, not a man at all, filled with dark compulsions not French. She tried to take him to church, but he would not go, not even to her funeral, after she had died, stepping in front of one of the automobiles that she so despised for ruining the lovely streets of Paris.

Stepping—that is what he told the police. She had lost track of where she was in the conversation, and she had stepped—

But she had not stepped. She had stumbled, after a shove, after she called him a monster, and said she wished he had died on the battlefield along with his soul.

Sometimes he thought she was right. He had seen the darkness coming for him those early days in the woods, lurking beyond the tanks and the flying machines, past the machine guns with their rat-a-tat-tats and their spray of bullets, the bodies falling, falling, falling in the mud. Beyond that, the darkness rose over the fields and extended across Europe, and he saw it coming toward him, then filling him, until there was no room for anything else.

He could pass on the darkness—he had done so with that beautiful American—but as he watched the hope die in her eyes, he remembered how that felt, and he could not, he would not, let her live with that. So he took the life from her, knowing (although she did not know) that it was no longer worth living.

He had taken her St. Christopher's medal because it should not touch darkness. He had left the medal and the ring she wore in the poor box at Notre Dame. He did such things, venturing into churches only for that, then escaping before the darkness polluted them as well.

Sometimes he thought he should have stumbled in front of that automobile instead of sending his mother there. Sometimes he thought he should have died, just as she said, in the mud-and-blood soaked fields, along with his friends. Sometimes he thought.

And sometimes, he did not.

Decker could not look at what he had written. He stacked the paper inside one of his folders and tied it shut with a ribbon, just like he used to tie the pages of his novel inside the folder, proud of his day's work.

This day—this night—he was not proud. He was spent.

He had seen things he had hoped to never see again.

Corpse Vision, the old man's grandson had called it.

Whatever it was, Decker despised it, much as the man he had written about, this Etienne, had despised the darkness in himself.

～◦～

As Decker walked to the Dôme the following night, the folder under his arm, he saw the darkness lurking. It hid in the shadows, wearing uniforms he did not recognize—that symbol the grandson had drawn—marching in lock-step.

Nightmares seeping backwards.

But Etienne had been a nightmare seeping forward.

Decker winced. He did not want to think about it.

He hadn't had a drink in three days. His alcoholic wave was over.

He also hadn't been to the *Tribune* in three days. He wondered what Root would think, what Thurber would say. Maybe they were already searching for him, although no one had come to his room at the Hôtel de Lisbonne—or if they had, he had been too absorbed to hear their knock.

This time, Decker arrived before the old man. Decker sat at the old man's table, sipping coffee and eating ham, cheese, and bread, much to the disapproval of his waiter, who wanted to serve the coffee long after the meal was done.

Know-it-all Hemingway sat in a corner, scribbling in his journal. He did not look up as Decker came onto the terrace, and Decker did not call attention to himself.

But as he looked at Hemingway now, he saw something that startled him—an insecurity, a fear, so deep that Hemingway might not have known it existed. Superimposed over Hemingway—like a ghost in a Dadaist painting—was an old man with a white beard and haunted eyes. He hefted a shotgun and rubbed its barrel against his mouth.

Decker looked away.

The old man—his old man, not the spirit surrounding Hemingway—sat at the table, his grandson beside him.

Decker didn't ask where they came from. He didn't remark on their silent entrance. Instead, he handed the folder to the old man.

The old man untied the folder, opened it, and scanned the pages, handing them one by one to his grandson.

Decker read upside down, embarrassed by the words, their lack of cohesion, their meandering viewpoint. When the grandson saw the name Etienne Netter, he stood.

"My thanks," he said and bowed to Decker. Then he walked away, leaving the pages beside Decker's plate.

Decker did not touch them. The old man picked them up and put them back in the folder, which he tied shut, making a careful bow.

"It is more than I could have hoped for," he said. "You have saved lives."

Decker shook his head. "I didn't do anything."

"This man, this Netter, he is a new breed. You have heard of Jack the Red, no? Saucy Jack?"

"The Ripper," Decker said. "Decades ago. In London."

"The first of his kind, we think," the old man said. "If there had been one such as you, perhaps he would have been stopped."

"He was stopped," Decker said. "He only killed five."

"That we know of," the old man said.

He set the papers under his own plate, then extended his hand. "I am Pierre LeBeau. I run *Noir*, the central newspaper in the City of Dark."

Decker couldn't take the misstatements any more. "City of Light," he said. "We call Paris the City of Light."

LeBeau nodded. "Light has its opposite. You have seen the dark. You write of it. You know what is coming."

"Only because you tell me that it is," Decker said. He sipped his coffee, pleased that his hand remained steady. "How come I've never seen your paper?"

"As I have said, you kept your most important eye deliberately closed." LeBeau put his hand on top of the folder. "The paper has grown since the War. Before, we were a single sheet. During, we ran four. After, we grew to five, then ten, now eighteen. We need an English language edition. We will start with four pages on the expatriate community."

"More meeting the boat," Decker said. "More puff pieces."

"No puff, as you say," LeBeau said. "Warnings, perhaps. Stories that do not run in your *Tribune* or the *Herald*, things only hinted at in the fictions your friends write for the *Transatlantic Review*."

"Who would read it?" Decker asked, surprising himself. Normally he would ask about pay before readership.

"People like my grandson," LeBeau said.

"Where did he go?"

"He will take Etienne Netter and extinguish his darkness. Then he would help the police find justice."

"He'll kill him?"

"No," LeBeau said. "But this Netter might wish he were dead when my grandson has finished with this. For Netter will realize what he has done and why, and with the revival of his soul, he will feel remorse so painful that death will be the only way out. Yet death will be impossible for decades. It is our smallest but best measure of revenge."

Decker felt a chill run down his back. The conversations with LeBeau, as circular as they were, were beginning to make sense.

"We will pay triple what you earn at the *Tribune* for the first six months," LeBeau said. "Raises every quarter thereafter if you continue to perform."

"Perform?" Decker asked.

"You must follow the darkness," LeBeau said. "See where it will lead."

"And if I don't?"

LeBeau smiled. "I shall buy you your next drink. You will become one of the—what do they call it?—casualties of the licentiousness of Paris. There will be no novel, no more hack work as you call it, no more typing. Only drinks, until one day not even the drinks will work. You will go to a sanatorium, and they will try to help you, but you will be one of the hopeless ones, the ones who has rotted his mind and his body, but has not managed to destroy the vision that has haunted you since you touched that kitten decades ago."

It no longer surprised Decker that LeBeau knew so much about him. Nor did LeBeau's description of his future surprise him. Decker had seen it already, as his father drank more and more, until finally his grandfather drove his father away to "a hospital" where they would "help" him. No one had ever seen him again.

His mother would not speak of him. She had lived too close to his darkness. She feared it for her son.

But running from it hadn't worked. He had simply become a drunk in Paris instead of in Milwaukee. Even if he had no magic vision, he had a future like the one LeBeau had described.

And the writing had taken away the urge to drink.

Even if the things he wrote had chilled him deeper than anything else.

"I never met her, did I?" Decker asked the old man. "Sophie. I never did meet her."

LeBeau looked at him. "You met her. Her spirit, after she had died. She wished she had been with you instead of this Etienne. She used your similarities to pull you in. She wanted him stopped. She did not want him to harm anyone else."

It sounded good. Decker wasn't sure he believed it, but he wanted to. Just like he wanted to believe that *Noir* existed, that he would be paid three times his *Tribune* salary, that his Corpse Vision actually had a purpose.

"I suppose I can't tell anyone what I'm doing," he said.

LeBeau shrugged. "You can tell," he said. "They will not believe. Or worse, they will not care, any more than you care for them."

LeBeau glanced at Hemingway, still scribbling in his notebook. Decker looked too. Hemingway raised his head. For one moment, their eyes met. But Hemingway's were glazed, and Decker realized that Hemingway had not seen him, so lost was he in the world he was creating.

They were all creating their worlds. The expatriate reporters with their chummy newspapers in English, hiding in a French city that did not care about their small world. The novelists, sitting in Parisian cafes, writing about their families back home.

And the old man, with his darkness and nightmares looming backwards.

Decker already existed in darkness. He could no longer push it away. He might as well shine a light on it and see what he found underneath.

"I'll take four times the salary," he said, "and a raise every two months."

The old man smiled. "It is, as you say, a deal."

He extended his hand. Decker took it. It was dry and warm. They shook, and Decker felt remarkably calm.

Calmer than he had felt in months.

Maybe than he had felt in years.

He did not know how long *Noir* would be in his future. But he did know that his tenure there would be better than anything he had done in the past.

Anything he had seen in the past.

He opened his most important eye, and finally, went to work.

The Unicorn Hunt

MICHELLE WEST

Hunting the Unicorn in the big city isn't exactly a simple proposition. Unicorns being what they are, sleek bastards, they're steeped in old lore, as if lore were magic.

Some of the lore is true, mind you; there's always a bit of truth in any old legend, if you know how to sift through the words. Words often get in the way. Maggie's my sometime partner, when it comes to things that exist outside of whatever passes for normal. She's got half a family—which is to say, herself and the kids—and a full-time job, besides. But she's got a bit of a temper, and a memory that just won't quit. She takes the whole business personally.

Me? I never did.

I was raised by my grandmother, a tough old woman with a mouth like a soldier's, and a pretty strong right hand to boot. She had some standards, expected good grades, and carried a weary disdain about life that pretty much seeped into everything I ever tried to do. It wasn't so much that she laughed at me—although I might have mentioned she was a touch harsh—as that she saw through me.

It was hard to dream much, in my grandmother's house. And make no mistake, it was her damn house. Small, squat building, red brick painted in a drab grey, porch up the backside of the house and round the side to the front. Garden for days, and in a city house, that says something. She didn't much believe in grass; it was a waste of water and sun, in her opinion. No, she grew useful things. Herbs, spices, fruits, vegetables. No flowers for her either, although I sort of liked them when I was younger. Flowers in her garden always withered and died, and I learned not to plant 'em.

You get odd communities in the city. My grandmother was at the centre of ours. When she wasn't drinking, she was often on that porch, and she had words of wisdom for any poor sucker who happened to stop within earshot of her chair. She had a cane that she used like a gavel—she sure as hell didn't need it for walking—and a voice that could make thunder seem sort of pleasant.

But I learned to love her. It was an uphill battle, for the early years of my childhood, and much of the affection I feel for her is hindsight and odd memory. She told me things I hated, when I was young, and watching them prove true was both a liberation and a bitter reminder that that old woman *knew* things.

She didn't believe in magic.

Which isn't to say that she didn't believe in Unicorns or Elvis sightings. She thought astrology was idiotic, thought crystals were stupid, and could spend whole days deriding the healing powers of just about any newfangled fad. She had God's ear, in a way—she believed in God—but whatever he had to say to her, she didn't share.

But I was talking about Unicorns.

Because Maggie got it into her head that she had to have one. Time of year. Time of month—I don't know. Maggie's like her own mystery, as different from my Gran as night from day; part of the same continuum, if you look close enough, but really, how many people do?

"Mags," I told her, "this is stupid."

Maggie, hefting her six-month-old onto the perch of her left hip, gave me The Look. Shanna, her oldest, is four, and because Shanna is both capable of listening and repeating what she hears, Maggie's gotten a little less verbose when she's in a mood. Doesn't matter. The Look pretty much says it all.

So when she turned it on me, I shut up for a bit. Not for long; living with Gran, I learned how to talk. If I hadn't, I'd've probably been a mute—that woman could *talk*. "Look, you've got Connell and Shanna to think about now."

"I'm thinking about them," she said, in that cast-iron voice of hers. "It's not for me."

Now, Maggie's no idiot. "Look, you *know* the stuff about healing powers and unicorn horns is just shit. Besides, they look healthy enough to me."

Connell obliged by spitting up on her left shoulder. It's not one of his most charming activities, but we're both used to it by now. Maggie, determined, didn't even bother to reach for something to clean herself off. And Connell, being the age he is, can swallow or spit with equal comfort. I glared at him, but he just thought it was funny. He usually does.

Baby laughter is a type of disease; it rots the brain. I spent a few minutes descending into that language that isn't really language at all, and after liberating my finger and my glasses—both of which he'd grabbed—I turned back to Maggie.

"You're not getting enough sleep."

She looked like she was fit to spit herself. "It's not sleep I need," she snapped.

⌘

Creation is an act of defiance. Whose, it's hard to say. Unwanted pregnancies happen all the time, and if you've the mind, you can end 'em. But Maggie's a special case. I've known it for a while. My grandmother told me, before she passed away.

Maggie moved in two houses down the street, and let her grass go to seed the first summer, which is high on the list of mortal sins as far as my Gran was concerned. But there are worse sins—barely— and she sent me along to check things out.

Turns out Maggie, being single, was in that constant state of exhaustion that also comes with being newly parental, and, as she put it, either the grass went or she did. Given that Maggie has eyes to die for (and a temper to die by), I thought it was a fair trade, and after introducing myself, I trudged on back to Gran's place. And then trudged back to Maggie's with a lawn-mower. I'm not that fond of gardening, in case I hadn't made that clear, but there are forces of nature you just don't ignore, and Gran had decided that this partic- ular woman needed some help.

After I added a new layer of burn to the upper side of my arms and face, I asked my Gran why she was so interested in Maggie. And the old woman gave me The Look—oddly enough, it's pretty much the same as Maggie's—and then launched into a bunch of stuff that made me wish I hadn't asked.

"Mark my words," she said, after saying a whole lot of them, "Maggie is special. She's the mother."

"*The* mother?"

"The mother."

Given that we live in a neighbourhood which is more or less over-run with kids of all ages, colours and volumes, this struck me as a tad woo-woo, even for Gran.

"Gran," I said, sitting down on the porch steps so she could comfortably tower over me, "what's so special about this mother?"

"She," Gran answered, with a sigh that indicated she didn't think much of my intellectual faculties, "doesn't have much choice."

"What's that supposed to mean?"

Gran shook her grey head, and her face wrinkled as she pursed her lips. "You think about it," she told me. "You're not always going to be this carefree. You have to *know* things."

That one caught me short. "Gran?"

"That's right," she said, pushing herself up out of her chair. "I won't be here forever, and when I'm gone, no one's going to do your thinking for you."

I remember thinking, at the time, that that would be a bit of a relief.

⁓ ◦⌒ ⌒

Asking Gran a question always involves a certain amount of humiliation, because to her, they all seem stupid. It's like she reads answers that are written across your forehead, only you're illiterate, even when she gives you the mirror. She'd spent the day working in the herb garden, and smelled of crushed bay leaves and smoke. But that aside, she was on her throne, and waiting with less patience than she usually did.

I used to think of the pipe she smoked as an affectation, a way of making her seem even more weird than she already was. I was younger then. Not even my memory can encompass that fact that she must have been younger as well; she never seemed to change. Even her clothing seemed to weather the passing of fad and style.

"All right, Gran," I told her, taking my seat on the stair, "I've been thinking."

"And?"

"I'm stupid."

She snorted, smoke coming out of her nostrils as if she were a wizened dragon. The ritual of emptying her pipe stilled her voice for a few minutes, which was its own kind of mercy. I don't smoke pipes, but I have a fondness for them anyway, probably because of her.

"I've talked to Maggie," I told her. I didn't tell her how *much* I'd been talking to Maggie; it wasn't her business.

But her eyes narrowed. "So what."

"She's not that fond of men at the moment, but it seems like she has a reason."

Gran snorted. "That's it?"

I shrugged. "She's got two kids."

"A boy and a girl."

"Pretty much."

"And a cat."

I'm not a cat person. "And a cat."

"Good. And?"

"A messy house. A better lawn. A job she hates just a little bit less than she'd hate welfare."

Gran inhaled. Exhaled. Frowned. "You're right," she said, spitting to the side. "You're stupid."

"I said that, didn't I?"

"Doesn't mean I can't."

My turn to shrug. "So what about her makes her *the* mother?"

"She didn't tell you?"

"I didn't exactly ask."

"But she didn't tell you?"

"No."

Tobacco ashes flew as she gestured. It was a pretty rude gesture for an old lady, and I dodged a few stray embers. "And you couldn't tell."

"Obviously."

She grabbed her cane, and I thought she might hit me with it. But she didn't. "Then maybe she doesn't know," she said. Using it, for a moment, to stand. It was the first time in my life I thought she looked old, and I didn't like it. "She's the mother," she said quietly, "because she was born to be the mother. It's a responsibility," she added, with a trace of sarcasm. "And a duty."

"Well, she's certainly had the kids."

"She *had* to. You ask her who the fathers were?"

"I got the impression she wasn't going to say."

"She can't."

"What?"

"She doesn't know." Not exactly the sort of thing you'd expect from your grandmother—at least not in that tone of voice. Tired voice, not judgmental. "She might think she does. She'd be wrong. If she'd never touched a man, she'd still have had those kids."

"She did say something about birth control. No, I'm not going to repeat it."

"She's angry about the kids?"

I shrugged. "She's angry about being alone with them, if I had to guess."

"Don't guess. It makes you sound—"

"Stupid. Yeah, I know." I chose the next words with care. She was still gripping the cane. "How did you know?"

"That's probably the first smart question you've asked all day."

Given that the rest of them had to do with lawn care, a thing she generally despised, this wasn't hard. "Does that mean you'll give me an answer?"

"I'm thinking about it."

I waited her out. Have I mentioned she loved to talk?

"I'm the crone," she said at last.

"And that makes me the maiden?" I couldn't keep the bitter sarcasm out of my voice.

"You?" Neither could she.

Having retreated back into the realm of idiocy, I waited, cheeks burning some. "I guess that's a no."

"Big damn no. You think I've taught you how to tend a garden all these years for nothing?"

No, because you're a sadist. Smart me, I didn't say it out loud. She rapped my knuckles anyway.

"I'm getting old," she continued.

I didn't point out that she'd *always* been old.

"And I'm getting tired." She sat down again. "And the damn pipe keeps going out."

"Gran—"

"There was another mother," she said at last. "And the maiden, which is definitely *not* you, so get that thought out of your head."

It wasn't in my head any more. "Another mother?"

"The mother," she told me quietly.

"What happened to her?" Because it was pretty clear that something had.

"She died."

Thanks, Gran. Guessed that. "When?"

"When I was younger."

"You weren't the crone then?"

"Damn well was."

"What *happened*?"

She shrugged. "War," she said at last, her eyes gone to blue. "She lost her son."

"Lost him?"

"He died."

"And she couldn't have another one?"

"No."

I frowned. "The kids are special, too?"

"The children are the mother's. They define her. She always has two."

"How did he die?"

"I told you. Pay attention. There was a war. He was in it. He didn't come back."

"And she died?"

Gran nodded quietly.

"Her daughter?"

And shrugged. "Her daughter buried her mother."

"That's it?"

"That's it."

"Then what—"

"It's been a long time," Gran continued, "since there *was* another mother." She got up again. "Better that I talk to her, since you're so useless."

"Gran, Maggie's—"

She rapped the porch with the cane tip. "You going to get out of my way, or am I going to have to go through you?"

I got out of her way, and trailed after her like a shadow. I *liked* Maggie. I didn't want to subject her to my grandmother without offering a little cowardly moral support.

⁓

Gran snorted at the grass. Emptied her pipe on it and shoved said pipe into her apron pocket. Then she marched up the walk, which was short, and knocked on the door with her cane. It opened. No one was behind it. I hate it when Gran does that. Then again, I hate it when she does anything that defies rational explanation.

She walked into the small vestibule. It was littered with the debris of two children; coats, boots, shoes, a smattering of dishevelled and empty clothing, a dirty stroller. "Margaret?" she shouted, standing in the center of the mess as if she owned it.

Maggie came out of the kitchen, frowning. Connell was on her hip. She saw me, and the frown sort of froze.

"This is my Gran," I told her.

And lifted. "I've heard a lot about you," she said, extending a hand. Her left hand; her right hand was full of baby, and she had nowhere to put him down. Mags is pretty practical.

Gran took it in that iron grip of hers, but instead of shaking it, she turned it up to the light, as if to inspect it. The frown that Maggie had surrendered, Gran picked up. "This won't do," the old woman said, in as stern a voice as she used on the racoon who had the temerity to inspect her garden.

"What?"

"What's this ring?"

"Detritus."

"Good. Take it off."

Maggie shot me an 'is she sane?' look. I shrugged.

"It's a wedding ring," Maggie told Gran.

"I *know* what it is. Why on earth are you wearing it?"

Maggie shrugged. I knew the shrug. It was nine tenths bitterness and one tenth pain, and I personally preferred the former.

"You aren't the wife," Gran said, in her most imperious voice. "You're the mother."

"Funny, that's what my ex said."

Gran ignored her. "This is the boy?" she asked. I started to say something smart, and thought better of it. At his age, it was hard to tell.

"This is my son, yes."

"And the girl?"

The 'is she sane' look grew a level in intensity. "My daughter is in the backyard digging her way to China."

Gran nodded, as if the answer made sense. Given that she'd raised me, it probably did.

"Well, he looks healthy enough." She pushed past Maggie, and Maggie looked at me. I shrugged. Gran made her way to the sliding doors of the kitchen and took a look out. "So does she."

"Thanks. I think."

"Give me the ring," Gran said.

"Yes she's sane." I added. "Mostly." I held out my arms for Connell, and Maggie slowly handed him to me. He was pretty substantial, and he was squirming, but he wasn't angry. Yet. Hands empty, she looked at my Gran, and then looked past her to me. She took off the wedding ring slowly, twisting it around her finger as she did.

Her expression made it clear that she was humouring the old lady for my sake, and I'd owe her. Given that I took care of her lawn, I figured we were even. Stupid me.

Gran took the ring and held it up to the kitchen light. Snorted, moved toward the sliding glass doors, and held it out to sunlight instead. She swore a lot. Closed her fingers around the ring, as if exposing it to light at all was a sin.

"What's wrong with the ring?" I asked.

She opened her fist.

And I saw it up close, for the first time. It looked different than it had when it had been a flash of gold on Maggie's finger. It was bumpy, but gleaming, more ivory than golden, and its pattern was a twisted braid.

"Not a braid," the old woman said, pursing her lips coolly. "A spiral."

"A . . . spiral?"

"This was fashioned," she continued coldly, "from a Unicorn horn."

Maggie stared at us both as if we were insane. But she didn't immediately reach out and grab Connell, so insanity of our kind wasn't immediately dangerous.

"It's a binding," Gran continued quietly. "And part of a binding spell. I'll take it to study, if you don't mind." It was like a request, but without the request part. She marched out of the kitchen, ring once again enclosed in her leathered fist.

When she'd also slammed the front door behind her, I looked at Mags. "Sorry," I said.

"That's lame," she replied. But she rubbed her finger thoughtfully, looking at the white band of skin that had lain beneath the ring for years. "She's a strange old woman," she added.

"Tell me about it."

⁓ ♋ ⁓

After the loss of the ring, things changed with Maggie. I didn't notice it all that much at first, which gave Gran several opportunities to wax eloquent about my intelligence. But shedding the ring, she seemed to shed some of her helpless, bitter anger. She wasn't as constantly tired. She even helped with the yardwork, although it took much longer with her help than without it, because Connell could crawl into everything, and Shanna insisted on helping too.

Connell discovered that dirt melted when you put it in your mouth. He wasn't impressed. Maggie picked him up with affectionate disdain, helped him clean out his mouth, and put him down again; he was already off on another spree of discovery.

She became happier, I think. Stronger.

And then, one day, when the Winter had come and everything was that white brown that snow in a city is, she invited my grandmother over. I came as well.

We sat down in the kitchen—all meetings of import were to be held there—around a pot of dark tea. Too bitter for me, it seemed perfect for Gran. Maggie herself hardly touched it.

She said, "I know I'm biased," which was usually the signal for some commentary about her children, "but sometimes it seems to me that my children are the most important thing in the world."

"It seems that way to all mothers," I said. "About their own children."

But Gran simply nodded. Quietly, even.

"Was that ring *really* made from a Unicorn's horn?"

"What do you think?"

She shrugged. "I think that once I was willing to let it go, I was happier. But there are a lot of men—and women—who could make money telling me that."

Gran nodded. "Too much money, if you ask me." Which, of course, no one had. Before she could get rolling, Maggie continued. She chose all her words carefully, and she didn't usually trouble herself that way.

"I feel," she continued softly, "as if, by protecting them and raising them, I'm somehow . . . preserving the future."

Again, not uncommon. But something about Mags was, so I didn't point it out.

"That I'm somehow helping other mothers, other sons, other daughters."

Gran nodded broadly, and even smiled.

"Which makes no sense to me," Maggie continued, dousing the smile before it had really started to take hold, "because it isn't as if other mothers aren't doing the same. Protecting the future." Smart girl, Mags. "And it isn't," she added, with just a hint of bitterness, "as if other children aren't dying as we sit here drinking tea."

"We aren't the arbiters of death," Gran said quietly.

"What in the hell are we?"

"You're the mother," Gran replied. "I'm the crone."

"And the crone is?"

"Knowledge. Experience. Wisdom, which usually follows. Not always," she added, sparing a casual glare for me.

"You said I was the mother."

"You are."

"For how long?"

"Good girl!"

Gran can be embarrassing at times.

"Who was the mother before me?"

The old woman's eyes darkened. "You're the first one in a long time."

"Why?"

She spit to the side. "If I had to guess," she said, with just a trace of fury, "I'd say those damn Unicorns have been up to no good. Again."

"You mean there were other mothers?"

"Like you, but not as strong. I should have known," she added. There is *nothing* worse than Gran when she's feeling guilty.

"What happened to the last one?"

"She failed."

"How?"

"Her son died."

Maggie closed her eyes.

"Wasn't her fault," Gran added. "But it doesn't matter. Her son died, and she died as well. Left a daughter. It should have passed on, then."

"It's like a public office?"

Gran shrugged. "Sort of. It should have passed on. Maybe it did. I'm not as sharp as I used to be."

"But you're older. Isn't wisdom—"

"Shut up." She lifted her cup, drained it, and thunked it back down on the table top. "Even the old get tired. Especially the old." She hesitated for just a moment.

I didn't like the sound of the silence.

"I'm better at hiding than I used to be," she finally said. "And I never answered your question."

"Hiding? From what?"

"You'll find out, girl. And that's a different question. You're the mother until your children are old enough to have children of their own."

"And then . . . my daughter?"

"Probably not. It doesn't pass down blood-lines. But when they are, you'll be free."

Maggie said, "You've never had children, have you?"

And Gran's voice was surprisingly bitter. "Oh, I've had 'em," she answered. "Outlived them all."

Maggie reached out and placed a hand over Gran's in something that was too visceral to be called sympathy. "When is it over, for you?"

"I get to choose," the old woman replied.

"And I don't."

"No. I often thought the mother got the rawest deal. No choice at all about having the children, only a choice about how they're raised. Raise 'em well," she added, "and the world changes."

Maggie looked openly sceptical. "The world?"

"There's a lot of difference between 1946 and 1966," the old woman replied softly. "And trust me, you wouldn't have liked living in either year."

"You're going to be with me for a while?"

"While you learn the ropes," Gran replied. "But don't be an idiot. Learn quickly." She got up and headed toward the front door.

Maggie's voice followed her. "If there's a mother, and a crone," she said, the growing distance forcing her to speak loudly and quickly, "what about a maiden?"

Gran's snort carried all the way back to the kitchen.

"She's a strange woman," Maggie said at last. "How old is she?"

I shrugged. "I asked her once."

"What'd she say?"

"She almost made me wash my mouth out with soap. It wasn't considered a *polite* question."

Mags laughed. I love it when she laughs.

"She'll probably answer that one later. She likes to parcel out information."

"Why?"

"Because she's sadistic."

~⌒~

Winter passed. Darkness made way for longer days and the snow melted.

Maggie started to garden, which scared me. Not only did she start, but she took to it with a passion that was only slightly scarier than the ferocity with which she watched out for her children.

Things *grew* when she touched them. Me? I'm no black thumb, but green isn't my colour either; it takes work. I envied Maggie, the way I envy someone with a natural singing voice. I would have put my foot down when she started collecting stray cats, but hey, it wasn't my house. And the kids seemed to like the cats—Connell even managed to survive pulling out a whisker or two from one of them.

But it wasn't until the height of Summer that Gran chose to answer the question about the maiden. She invited herself over to Maggie's. Apparently, all conversations of import were to be held at Maggie's. I think this is because Gran didn't particularly care to have children destroying the knick knacks in her house. Either that or because Gran's cats weren't as tolerant as Maggie's.

Tea was like ritual, although without the fuss. The pot sat in the centre of the table; Connell toddled his way around the chair, and Shanna drew pictures while laying flat out against ceramic tile. Unfortunately, some of those pictures tended to bleed off the page, so the floor was a bit more colourful than it had been when the previous owner had laid down said ceramic tiles.

"So," Gran said quietly. "You've started gardening."

Maggie's smile was calm and warm.

"And cat collecting. I'd advise you to take up a fondness for rabbits instead."

"Why?"

"Less of 'em. They're still work," she added. But she shrugged. "The kids are growing."

Maggie smiled fondly. She still looked like the same woman I'd first met—but not when she smiled. "I wanted to thank you both. But I also wanted to ask a question."

Gran snorted. She had her pipe in her hand, but she didn't light it. Mags would have thrown her out of the front door and watched to see how many times she bounced; she respected age and wisdom, but smoking around her children was a definite no-go. Gran seemed to expect this, and as she was in Mags' house, she obeyed the unspoken rules.

"You're the crone. I understand what you do."

"What?"

"You preserve wisdom," Maggie replied. "Collective wisdom. Maybe bitter wisdom."

"It's all bitter."

"Maybe. But necessary."

That got a 'good girl' out of the old lady.

"I'm the mother, and I understand—I think—what that means."

"Better harvests," Gran said.

Maggie raised a brow.

"It's true."

"Well," she said, looking doubtfully out at her garden, "we'll see." She picked up her cup, staring at the cooling tea. "What does the maiden do? Preserve our innocence?"

Gran snorted. "You've been reading those trashy novels again." It was a bit of a bone of contention between them.

Maggie chose to let the matter drop; she really *was* curious.

"Look," Gran said, with open disgust, "just how *innocent* do you think you were when you were a maiden?"

"Well," Maggie said, defensive in spite of her best intentions, "I wasn't *the* maiden now, was I?"

Gran laughed. "Good answer! No, you weren't. But I'm going to tell you that you're confusing innocence with inexperience."

"That's her way of saying stupidity," I added.

"Got that." She looked over at her daughter, who had finished her odd drawing and had started in on another piece of paper. Shanna was humming a song I tried very hard not to recognize. Because Gran didn't hold with television much, either.

"You think that the maiden is supposed to preserve stupidity?"

"*I* didn't use the word."

Gran snorted again. "Innocence implies guilt."

"Stupidity implies—"

"Not guilt," Gran snapped, before Maggie could get started. Watching the two of them, I could almost see a familial connection between them, and you know what? I almost got up and slunk out of the room. "Innocence is a Unicorn word. It's a defacement. It's a linguistic injustice, an act of defilement."

"Unicorns speak?"

Gran's laugh was dark and ugly. And unsettling. "You wore that ring for how many years, and you have to ask?"

Maggie's turn to get dark. "It didn't exactly whisper into my ear."

I *really* wanted to be anywhere else.

"It *did*. You just weren't listening. You want it back? I'll give it to you. You'll probably hear a lot more now."

Maggie's brows rose. "You didn't destroy it?"

Gran hesitated for just a second, and a shudder seemed to pass through her. "No."

"Why?"

"I'm no warrior," she replied.

"The maiden is a warrior?"

Gran was quiet for a long time. "At her best," she said at last, "she can be."

"And at her worst?"

"Lost."

"Was there a maiden, back when there was a mother?"

Gran said nothing at all for a long time. Silent Gran? Always made me nervous.

"Look, what *is* the maiden about?"

"Sex," Gran replied primly.

Maggie stared at her as if she'd started speaking in tongues.

One week later, round two.

"So, the maiden is about *sex*?"

"That's what I said."

"If she's about sex, she can hardly *be* a maiden."

Gran shook her head. "That's Unicorn talk," she said firmly.

"Will you *quit* that?"

"I could call it something else, but you probably don't want Shanna to repeat it at school."

Maggie hadn't asked for the ring back, and failed to mention it. Gran failed to offer. This was an armistice.

"The maiden has always been the most vulnerable of the three," Gran continued. "The hardest to find. The hardest to keep."

"Why?"

"Because."

"It's the sex."

"Something like that."

Maggie turned to me. "Your grandmother is driving me crazy." Unfair, trying to drag me into the discussion. "It's because of the sex, right? There aren't a lot of young women who don't. Have sex."

"It's because of the sex, but not in the way you think. You're thinking like a Unicorn," she added. So much for armistice.

"Look, what *are* Unicorns? I've seen a lot of pretty pictures, and I've read a lot of pretty books. I've done more internet research on that than I have on almost anything, and my saccharine levels are *never* going to be the same. For something malign, they seem to occupy a lot of young girls' minds."

"Not the practical ones," Gran snapped.

"Fine. Not the practical ones. Are we looking for a practical girl?"

Gran seemed to wither. "No," she said at last. "We're not. That's why it's so hard. To find her. To save her."

"She dies?"

"Not the way you or I do. But her gift is the easiest to lose. It gets passed on, but sometimes it's just the blink of an eye."

"Unicorns are usually associated with purity."

"What the hell is purity?" Gran snapped. "A bottled water slogan?"

⁓

Round three.

"Okay. If the maiden *isn't* defined by *not* having sex, and she isn't defined by purity—which," Mags added, holding a squirming

Connell while trying to get him to eat, "I'll agree is pretty nebulous, I have two questions."

"You've got a lot of questions. How, precisely, are you intending to pay for the answers?"

Maggie glared. It was a pretty glare. "By being the mother," she snapped.

Gran nodded, as if this was the only answer she expected. "What are your questions?"

"One: there are three. Maiden. Mother. Crone."

Gran nodded.

"You've been waiting for me."

Nodded again, but more wary this time.

"But we're only two. The third one must be important."

"She's important."

"But you weren't waiting for her."

Snorting, the old woman said, "I wasn't *exactly* waiting for you, either. I just knew you when I saw you."

"Fine. And the maiden?"

"You're not going to let go of this, are you?"

"No."

"Fine. Be like that. What's the other question."

"You haven't answered the first one yet."

"Never promised answers."

"She is *really* driving me crazy."

"Hah. You're getting there on your own."

"What is her role? Why is she important?"

"It's the sex," Gran said quietly. "And not the sex. It's not the act; it's the possibility inherent in the act."

Maggie looked pointedly down at Connell.

"The maiden never has children."

"Why?"

"Because children are the mother's. Try to pay attention."

"So she gets to have—"

Gran held up a hand. "She's important, because she's dreaming," she said quietly. "Dreams are fragile, and endless; they're also a tad self-centered. Have to be. Heroes dream. She's dreaming, and she can walk in any direction she wants. She has a freedom that neither you nor I have."

"You envy her?"

"You don't?"

"I've seen what happens to dreams," was the bitter reply. "Young girl dreams. You're right. I was stupid."

Gran's smile was bitter. Old. "I didn't say you were stupid," she said. She had, but I didn't point this out. "Or if I did, I didn't mean it." She sighed, and caressed the bowl of her pipe. "Sex is union," she said quietly. "When it's done right. Union of body. A glimpse of dream. It transfigures us."

"Sex is about babies."

"Wasn't always."

"Is now."

"Hah. You want my answer?"

Maggie shut up.

"Having sex doesn't destroy the maiden. Abstinence doesn't define her—*unless she lets it*. The maiden has freedom. But she doesn't see it yet. Maybe she will. More likely, she'll lose it; shackle it; accept what others tells her. By the time she wakes up, she's given over dreams to reality. She's become something solid, but she's not—"

"The maiden."

"Not anymore, no."

Maggie was thoughtful. "This is why you haven't looked for her."

"She's not entirely necessary," was the reluctant reply, "and she's much abused. Always. It's hard. To keep her. And it's damn painful to lose her," she added.

"How can you say she's not entirely necessary?"

"Sometimes dreams have edges. Sometimes they just cause pain."

"A world without dreaming—"

"There will *never* be a world without dreaming," Gran replied.

"Joan of Arc was a maiden?"

"Maybe. And look what happened."

"Buffy?"

"Buffy?"

"Television character," I told Gran. I started to explain, and she lifted a hand. "Maybe. First two seasons at any rate." Which *really* surprised me, given that Gran doesn't hold with television. "But she's *not* real. If she existed, she would be."

"So all we have to do is find—"

"We don't have to find anything." Gran stood up. End of conversation.

Question two was never asked.

Maggie's hands were on her hips. Unfortunately, no children were. This was her battle posture, and I didn't much like it. "Your grandmother drives me nuts."

"She has that effect on people."

"I thought wisdom was supposed to be soothing."

"Judge for yourself."

Maggie snorted. "We need to go on a Unicorn Hunt," she said at last.

Which more or less brings us full circle. "Why?"

"Because."

More argument, which I've already mentioned, followed by grim silence, which I may have failed to add.

"The ring," she said at last. "I would have held on to that ring forever. And it would have cost me my life. No, I'm not saying it would kill me—but look at me now. Look at me then. I'm *alive* now. I live in the present." She walked over to her computer and flipped up the lid. I suppose it won't come as a surprise to say Gran doesn't hold with computers much either, so I'm not real familiar with how they work.

"So you want revenge?"

Maggie was silent. For a minute. "I think this is the first time I've ever understood why your grandmother calls you stupid," she said in a flat voice.

"Ouch."

"Live with it." Maggie shouted a warning to Shanna, who seemed intent on turning two teetering chairs into a makeshift ladder. "I know the maiden is out there," she said at last.

"Pardon?"

"I *know* she's out there. I think she's close."

"How?"

"Because I feel younger than I have in years," she replied softly. "And I feel—right now—that I can do *anything*."

"You're the mother," I told her.

"Even the mother has to dream. Maybe especially the mother." She looked fondly at the head of her younger child. "Look at this." The computer was now flickering.

"Unicorn hunt."

"It's all garbage," she added. "I'm sure your Gran was right about that." Big concession. "But there's got to be a grain of truth in this somewhere. What if," she added, as her fingers added prints to the screen, directly across the face of a painted woman with a delicate, horned head in her lap, "it's true?"

"What's true?"

"Not that Unicorns are drawn to virgins," she said, "but that they're drawn to *maidens*."

"Which is usually the same thing."

"In Unicorn speak."

"Don't you start that too."

Maggie didn't seem to hear me. "If we go out on a Unicorn hunt," she continued, "we're bound to find the maiden."

"Okay. But."

"But?"

"What the hell does a Unicorn want with the maiden, anyway?"

"My guess? To kill her," she said softly.

"That's phallic."

"Idiot."

"And all that rot about Unicorn horns and healing?"

"I don't know. Maybe there's something in that. We can always find out." She paused. "But I'm guessing that Unicorns don't actually *look* like this either."

"They'd be pretty damn hard to miss."

So Maggie and I went over to Gran's house. Gran was waiting for us on her porch. Which is to say, she was sitting on it, her arms crossed, her expression pure vinegar.

"You know why we're here," Maggie said, without preamble.

"I might."

"We need your help."

Gran pushed herself out of her chair. "I don't have a lot of help to offer," she said at last. "You're going in search of the maiden."

"We're going in search of Unicorns," Maggie replied firmly. "And we're not certain that we'll be able to even *see* them."

"You might. She won't."

"I think you can see them well enough, if a glint of ring could tell you so much. We need to be able to *see* them."

"You won't like it," Gran said, as if that would make a difference.

"Doesn't matter. We'll live; we all do what we have to." She paused, and then added, "I'd like it if you kept an eye on the kids while we're out."

"That's your job."

"Yes. And I'd guess yours would be to find the maiden, which you *aren't* doing."

Gran relented so quickly it was pretty clear she'd already made her decision. "I'll go to your place," she said. "They won't be as safe here."

The tone of her voice made me wonder if I'd misjudged her reasons for keeping them out of her house in the first place. And I liked the older reasons better.

She gave us glasses. Sort of. Nothing you could wear on your face, though. She gave us some sort of sticky, foul-smelling ointment as well. "You might need it," she said. "But if you don't, don't waste it. Costs a fortune to make."

"Is that blood?"

Gran shrugged. The last thing she gave us, looped around fine, long strands of something that looked like hair, was Maggie's old ring.

Maggie looked at it, but she didn't touch it. "You carry it," she told me. I was looking at Gran.

"She's right. You carry it. It'll point you in the right direction."

"We can trust it?"

"To find a Unicorn? Yes. You can't use it against one, though. Don't even try. And if it talks? Don't listen."

"As if."

"There are a couple of other things I should have probably told you both. Maggie'll get a clue, once you've started. You might have trouble."

Great. "What?"

"You'll be walking old roads, if there's a Unicorn to be found."

"You're not talking about old city roads."

"Good girl."

"They're safe?"

"Not bloody likely."

"What does not safe mean?"

"You'll find out." She handed me the last item. It was a long dagger, slender and shiny. And not really legal, on account of the way it disappeared in the hand. "Concealed weapons," I told her, doubtfully.

"You take it, or you're not going."

"What am I supposed to do with it?"

"You'll figure it out. Oh, and one more thing."

"What?"

"You wait until the full moon. You hear me?"

"Yes, Gran."

~⌒~

Maggie was different, that night. Different in pretty much every way I could think of. Clothing was different. Hair was pulled right back off her face, and her skin seemed almost silver, like moonlight incarnate. Her eyes were clear and dark, and she didn't look afraid. Of anything.

The cars made their constant background purr, punctuated by honking. Gran cursed them roundly as she joined us in front of Maggie's house. "I'll stay until you get back," she told us firmly.

"You'd better," Maggie replied. But her tone of voice was strange as well.

Gran seemed smaller, thinner, than she usually did. "It's your time," she told Maggie, "not mine. But you're right—the maiden is out there. I can see her in your face."

Maggie didn't seem to hear. I took a good, hard look at Gran. "Don't light that," I told her, because she was fumbling with her pipe.

"I know, I know."

~⌒~

So, with a ring for a compass, and one that swayed every time there was the faintest hint of breeze, we began to walk down the street. Maggie decided—for reasons that aren't even clear to me now—that we had to walk in the *middle* of the damn road.

"You've got kids to think of," I told her. "What the hell is wrong with the sidewalk?"

She didn't answer. Then again, if I'd asked Gran that question, she'd have clipped me with her cane.

Instead, she walked. She didn't apparently look at the ring to see which direction we should be walking *in*, but she had me for that, and I was thankful for streetlights.

"Do you think your husband was a Unicorn? I mean, your ex?"

"No."

"But the ring—"

"No."

"But you think a Unicorn gave him the ring."

"Yes, I do."

Light dawned, in the figurative sense. "Because then you wouldn't know."

She nodded.

"And if you didn't know—"

"I couldn't find them."

"Why didn't they try that on Gran?"

"I don't think your Gran can do this," she said softly. "She's too far away from the maiden. And she *has* to be."

"Why?"

"Because of what she is. She can see the maiden in my face," she added softly. "But I would guess that *if* we manage to find the

Unicorn, and *if* the Unicorn is with the maiden, the maiden will see her in my face as well."

I thought about that for a long time. "My Gran does like you," I said.

"I know. She drives me crazy, but I like her too." She gave me an odd look, then. I didn't understand it. "She's tired." Maggie banked left. "But she's waited a long time, and I'm really grateful to her. She's the hardiest of the three of us," she added.

Looking at Maggie, I wasn't so sure.

I fingered the invisible knife, thought some more, and then asked Maggie, tentatively, if she wanted it.

Maggie's brows rose. "Me?"

"That would be no."

"Definite no."

"Why?"

"I'm the mother," she said quietly. "I don't think I could use it."

"Then I'll use it for you."

Maggie said nothing. After a while, I joined her in nothing, and we walked into the darkness.

⌒◡⌒

When the darkness changed, I can't be certain. But the streetlights vanished, and the moonlight grew more distinct. I could see stars, cold and clear, without the haze of light and pollution as a veil. Trees passed us by; they were tall, weeping willows, and beneath them, water pooled in still, clear mirrors. Everything about this road was beautiful. But you don't live long with Gran if you're an obvious sucker for beauty.

I followed Maggie. Maggie glanced occasionally at the ring, tilting her head with a vague look of disgust as she listened to it. I didn't hear anything. But it was clear that in this place, she could. I almost envied her the ability.

"We should have gone on the new moon," she said. Something about her voice made my hair stand on end. But she didn't dwell on the should have, and I was just as happy not to.

We made our way down a sloping hill, crushing flowers as we did; there wasn't any way to walk this place without leaving a mark. Maggie didn't seem to care, and because she didn't, I didn't. I never did like flowers much, anyway.

And I discovered, that night, that Unicorns run in packs. This goes against conventional wisdom, but then again, everything does. We stopped for a minute while we watched these creatures cavorting in the shadows. The shadows cast by one huge tree that seemed to go up forever. I thought that it must go down forever as well, but then again, Gran leaves the weeding to me, and I've learned to take roots personally.

I expected them to be beautiful. And they were. Breathtakingly beautiful, in the sense that I stopped breathing while watching them. Their white coats were gleaming, and they looked like some sort of cross between a deer and a horse. But their horns glittered, and it became clear after only a few minutes that they weren't exactly involved in a dance of joy.

They were fighting.

I don't think they noticed us at all. I really, really wanted to be unnoticed. But Maggie had other plans, and she didn't actually take the time to impart any of them to me. Instead, she ran the rest of the way down the hill, as if her feet were on fire.

As if, I thought suddenly, her children were in danger. This is the danger of putting the full moon, the old roads, and the mother together. I wouldn't have guessed it, but then again, Gran never called me the brightest star in the sky.

When she almost crashed into them, I was just a few feet behind her. Running down the damn slope had been effortless for her—but for me it was a constant battle not to wind up sliding down on my face. The ground here was treacherous; it whispered.

And the Unicorns? They screamed. In outrage. In fury. They reared up, muscles rippling on their hind legs, horns no longer turned in casual cruelty against each other, as they faced this unexpected intruder.

Maggie hardly seemed to notice.

But I knew that dying here was pretty much death. It didn't matter if we weren't in the city; it didn't matter if we weren't in reality. Had Gran told me that? I couldn't remember. I'd try later.

Gran's knife in hand, I leapt in after Maggie, moving faster than I'd ever moved in my life. A horn hit the blade, and the blade was no longer invisible.

I expected the impact to knock the weapon out of my hand; it's not as if I use weapons, much. But that didn't happen. Instead? The horn *gave*. The knife passed through it. The Unicorn's scream of rage gave way to a scream of what sounded—I swear—like mortified pain.

They had hooves, cloven hooves, and those should have been their weapon of choice. Would have done a damn sight more damage. But they didn't seem to clue in, and I wasn't about to tell them what to do.

I thought Maggie would; she's like my Gran that way. But even if we'd started out hunting Unicorns, they weren't on her radar at the moment. And I couldn't see what was, but I could guess.

I would have been half right.

The Unicorns drew back when I approached; the knife was literally glowing, and a faint trace of black ran down its edge. I thought it was blood, but the wrong colour. It probably was. Unicorn horns are tricky.

But they didn't approach us again, and no one was stupid enough to try the horn against the knife. I shadowed Maggie—literally. I knew that if I was too far away, they'd fall on her like jackals. Like really beautiful, really delicate, jackals.

She made her way to the tree they had been circling around, and I discovered a second thing about Unicorns. They can look an awful lot like men.

Or a man.

White haired, but youthful, tall, slender, garbed in something that would probably pass any fashion test an enterprising high-schooler would set—except for that horn. Middle of the forehead. Dead centre. Glistening as it drank moonlight.

Maggie was mad. Not angry, which I'm used to.

Mad mother? Not a good thing. I tried to call out to her. No, I *did*. But she was beyond listening.

And in a second, I was beyond trying. Her eyes were better than mine. If she was seeing with her eyes at all.

Because beyond the man, was a girl. Bruised eyes. Bruised lips. Skin the white that skin goes when fear has overtaken almost everything else. A lot of skin; exposed and framed by shredded fabric. Might have been a shirt, once. Or the top of a dress.

School-girl, I thought. Maybe. She seemed *so young* to me as I looked at her, I couldn't think straight. I had never been that young. Gran said I was born old.

Should've been a hint.

But Gran could have *told* me that Unicorns are rapists.

⁓ ᦆ ⁓

We split up the minute the Unicorn turned. His eyes were a startling shade of blue, clear and bright in the night sky. He looked beyond us, for just a moment; saw what must have been there—the gathering of his pack.

His hands fell away from the girl as he shoved her, hard, against tree-bark. Her hands gripped the tree as she tried to meld with it. Her eyes were dark, normal eyes. Her hair was dark and dishevelled.

He looked at Maggie.

He looked at me.

I held the dagger. I don't think I have ever wanted to kill. He looked at Maggie.

He looked at me.

I held the dagger. I don't think I have ever wanted to kill *anything* so badly in my life. He laughed. He could sense it.

But Maggie moved not toward him, but toward the girl. He wasn't her concern. No, I thought, he was mine. Mother creates life. Crone sees its end.

I'll stay until you get back.

I lunged with the dagger as he lunged with his horn. He narrowly avoided losing it, and I side-stepped. I'm not much of a fighter, but I was fast enough; it's kind of hard to really get into a tussle when your pants have dropped past your butt.

I wondered if this was what naked *men* actually looked like. Which was my stupid thought for the evening, and it almost cost me my arm.

The shadows were dancing at my back. The others were waiting. But they were a bit of a cowardly lot, when it came down to that; they knew what the knife could do, and they were willing to wait and see.

I could have despised them more if I tried really hard. But mostly, I was trying to stay alive.

Losing battle. What had my Gran said? She wasn't a warrior. I wasn't raised to be one either. His horn grazed my thigh, and the threads of my jeans unravelled at its touch, as if they were all trying to avoid the contact. I bled a bit.

He hit me again, and I bled more.

He wasn't laughing, but his eyes were glittering with rage. I had denied him something, and he intended to make me pay.

I would have died there.

I would have died had it not been for Maggie. At least I thought it was Maggie who came for me, Maggie who touched my shoulder, my wrist, my dagger arm.

But when Maggie took the dagger from my slowing hands, I knew I'd been wrong. Because Maggie was the mother, and she couldn't wield this knife.

The Unicorn's blue eyes widened, and he lost his form—which is to say, he reverted. It was certainly easier to look at him. Harder to look at the girl he'd had pinned to the tree a few wounds back.

She wasn't wearing much. But she didn't need to. She was utterly, completely beautiful in the stark night, and her expression was one that will haunt my nightmares for years.

She didn't speak a word.

Not a word of accusation. Not a word that spoke of betrayal. Nothing at all that made her seem like a wronged victim, or like any victim.

Crone sees life's end?

Not like *this*. She used the knife as if she'd been born with it in her hands. And he bled a lot; she wasn't kind. Or quick. Or even merciful.

But he was very much alone, in the end. Packs are like that.

❦

Later, I joined Maggie. Or Maggie joined us. The girl was holding the knife and her breasts rose and fell as lungs gave in to exertion, which was very distracting. Maggie had taken a sweater from her shoulders, leaving herself with a thin, black t-shirt. She put the sweater around the girl's shoulders in silence. Like a mother. Her hands were shaking.

They looked at each other, and then the girl looked down at the knife almost quizzically.

"It's yours," I told her.

"You're giving this to me?"

"No," I replied. "It was always yours."

She looked at it, and I handed her its sheath. She looked at that two. Her hands were shaking. "Did I kill him?"

I nodded.

"Good." And then her eyes started to film over. "You know, he said he loved me?"

I nodded quietly.

"And I believed him."

Before I could stop myself, I told her—in as gentle a voice as I could, "You had to."

"No, I didn't."

But she did. Because she was the maiden. I could see it in her clearly. Could see it; was horribly, selfishly glad that I would never be the maiden. I wasn't certain that she would stay that way, either.

"He was a Unicorn," I told her, after a pause.

"He was an asshole," she said, spitting. Like a cat.

"That too."

She gave me an odd look. "How did you know?"

"What?"

"That he was a Unicorn?"

"The horn was a dead giveaway."

"He wanted me because I was special." She was. I could see that.

"Yes," I told her, and I put an arm around her shoulder. "But he wanted to destroy what was special about you. Don't let him. Don't forget how to believe."

Maggie cleared her throat. "Your mother is probably worried about you," she said. In a mother's tone of voice. "And my kids are waiting for me. Why don't you come back to my place? You can phone her from there."

"I told her I was staying at a friend's house tonight," the girl said. She hesitated, and then added, "I'm Simone."

"I'm Irene," I told her, extending a hand. "And you can stay at Maggie's."

Maggie nodded quietly. She held out a hand, and the girl took it without hesitation. Good sign.

We made our way back to Maggie's house, but stopped at the foot of her walk. She looked at me, her eyes bright with moonlight. Simone was talking; she had started to talk when we had started to walk, and she hadn't stopped. She wasn't crying. She wasn't—at least to my eye—afraid. Rescue has its purpose.

"I think you should go in first," Maggie told me quietly.

I knew. I knew then.

"I'll be up; I think Simone and I have a lot to talk about." She hesitated, and then added, "We'll be waiting for you if you need company."

I nodded stiffly and made my way up the walk. Opened the door, which Gran hadn't bothered to lock. Very, very little can get past Gran when she's on the lookout.

She was in the kitchen, beside a pot of tea. She looked up as I entered, and the breath seemed to go out of her in a huff. As if she'd been holding it since we left.

"We found her," I told my Gran. "In time, I think."

"She's an idiot?"

I frowned, and Gran gave me a crooked smile. "You understand."

I nodded.

"Why it's hard to be the maiden."

And nodded again. "But Gran, I understand other things, too."

"Oh? That would be a change."

"I understand why it's hard to be the crone. To watch. To know and to have to sit back on your hands."

"Good." She rose, pipe in hand. "I'll be getting home, then."

"I'll go with you."

"I don't need company."

"I do."

She snorted. "You have company. Maiden and mother. I never thought—" She bit her lip. "I stopped hoping."

"You kept watch," I told her. "You remembered the old lore. You kept it for us." I offered her a hand, and she took it; her hand was shaking. Old, old hand.

"You'll be good at this," she said, as she rose. "But you take care of my garden, hear?"

"I'll take care of the garden," I told her. It was really hard. "And the house. And the lore."

"No television in my house."

"Yes, Gran."

"And none of that trashy garbage Maggie reads, either."

"Yes, Gran."

"And don't think too much."

I laughed. I walked her out of the house, and past Maggie, who stopped her and gave her a ferocious hug. No words, just a hug.

Gran snorted, and lit her pipe; Maggie, unaccompanied by her children, took it in stride.

And me? I waited. I bit my lip and I waited.

I walked Gran home. I took her up to the porch. I let her get comfortable in her chair. I even sat on the steps, because I wouldn't be sitting on them again anytime soon.

I don't know when she died. I know that she was talking; that she was telling me all the things that she thought I'd forget. That she *also* knew that I wouldn't be forgetting them, now.

Because I was the crone.

And she was finished. She could be tired. She could rest. She said as much, and then drifted off into silence, the way she sometimes did when she was satisfied with the state of her garden.

The silence lingered, grew louder, grew, at last, final.

And when it had gone on for long enough, I closed her eyes, took her pipe, and emptied it. I kissed her forehead. I would have asked her to hug me, but public displays of affection had always made her uncomfortable. I hugged her only afterward, because it wouldn't matter to her.

Then I made my way back to Maggie's house, carrying Gran's cane. The light was still on, and two thirds of my self were waiting for me to join them.

About the Authors

Kelley Armstrong is the author of the "Women of the Otherworld" paranormal suspense series, the "Darkest Powers" YA urban fantasy trilogy, and the Nadia Stafford crime series. She grew up in Ontario, Canada, where she still lives with her family. A former computer programmer, she's now escaped her corporate cubicle, and hopes never to return.

Patricia Briggs is the *New York Times* best-selling author of the Mercy Thompson series as well as many assorted other books. She lives in Montana with her husband and a menagerie of animals and kids in a house that resembles a zoo crossed with a library. The horses have to stay outside. And people wonder where the ideas for her stories come from.

The fourth book in Lillian Stewart Carl's Fairbairn/Cameron mystery series, *The Charm Stone*, appeared in November 2009, and the fifth, *The Blue Hackle*, is scheduled for November 2010. Her next short story (co-authored with Sylvia Kelso) will appear in *Love and Rockets* (December 2010). Eleven stories are collected in *Along the Rim of Time* and thirteen in *The Muse and Other Stories of History, Mystery, and Myth*. Most of her work, short stories as well as sixteen novels in different genres, is available in various electronic forms, including Fictionwise and Kindle. She is the co-editor (with John Helfers) of *The Vorkosigan Companion*, a non-fiction hardcover about the SF work of Lois McMaster Bujold. The book was nominated for a Hugo in 2009 and will soon appear in paperback.

Max Allan Collins has earned an unprecedented fifteen Private Eye Writers of America "Shamus" nominations, winning twice. His graphic novel *Road to Perdition* is the basis of the Academy Award-winning film starring Tom Hanks and Paul Newman, directed by Sam Mendes. An independent filmmaker in the Midwest, he has had half a dozen feature screenplays produced. His other credits include the *New York Times* bestsellers *Saving Private Ryan* and *American Gangster*. Both Spillane and Collins received the Private Eye Writers life achievement award, the Eye.

Carole Nelson Douglas's fifty-some multi-genre novels include mystery and suspense, science fiction, and high fantasy. Most recent is her Delilah Street, Paranormal Investigator noir urban fantasy series (*Silver Zombie*, etc.) The first writer with a female protagonist sleuthing in the Sherlock Holmes world, Carole's eight-book Irene Adler series debuted with the *New York Times* Notable Book of the Year, *Good Night, Mr. Holmes*. Her twenty-three-book Midnight Louie feline PI mystery series blends traditional "cozy" and classic "noir" elements to offer both satire and substance. Set in a slightly surreal Las Vegas, it features four human crime-solvers unknowingly aided by a "Sam Spade with hairballs," a big black alley cat whose first-person-feline narrations of his own investigations thread through the novels. Her numerous short stories include reprints in seven Year's Best Mystery anthologies, and her writing has won or been short-listed for more than fifty awards.

P. N. Elrod writes and edits, and is best known for *The Vampire Files*, where Bobbi Smythe hangs out with her undead boyfriend, vampire PI Jack Fleming. Elrod is a hopeless chocolate addict and cheerfully refuses all efforts at intervention. More about her toothy titles may be found at www.VampWriter.com.

Simon R. Green lives in the small country town of Bradford-on-Avon in England; the last Celtic town to fall to the invading Saxons in 504 AD. He is the *New York Times* best-selling author of the Nightside series (a private eye who operates in the Twilight Zone, solving cases of the weird and uncanny), and the Secret Histories series (the name's Bond, Shaman Bond). He also wrote the perennially in-print space opera series, the Deathstalker books. He appears in open air Shakespeare productions, rides motorbikes, and once had a near-death experience quite unlike anyone else's.

Nina Kiriki Hoffman has been writing science fiction and fantasy for more than twenty years and has sold more than 250 stories, plus novels and juvenile and media tie-in books. Her works have been finalists for the World Fantasy, Philip K. Dick, Sturgeon, and Endeavour awards. Her first novel, *The Thread That Binds the Bones*, won a Bram Stoker Award, and her short story "Trophy Wives" won a Nebula. Her middle school fantasy novel, *Thresholds*, will come out in 2010. Nina works does production work for *The Magazine of Fantasy & Science Fiction* and teaches short story writing through her local community college. She also works with teen writers. She lives in Eugene, Oregon, with several cats, a mannequin, and many strange toys.

Norman Partridge's compact thrill-a-minute style has been praised by Stephen King and Peter Straub, and his fiction has received three Bram Stokers and two IHG awards. His first short story appeared in the second issue of *Cemetery Dance*, and his debut novel, *Slippin' into Darkness*, was the first original novel published by *CD*. Partridge's chapbook *Spyder* was one of Subterranean Press's inaugural titles, while his World Fantasy-nominated collection *Bad Intentions* was the first hardcover in the Subterranean book line. Since then, Partridge has published pair of critically acclaimed suspense novels featuring ex-boxer Jack Baddalach for Berkley Prime Crime (*Saguaro Riptide* and *The Ten-Ounce Siesta*), comics for Mojo and DC, and a series novel (*The Crow: Wicked Prayer*) which was adapted for the screen. His award-winning collections include *Mr. Fox and Other Feral Tales* and *The Man with the Barbed-Wire Fists*. Partridge's latest novel, *Dark Harvest*, was chosen by *Publishers Weekly* as one of the 100 Best Books of 2006. A third-generation Californian, he lives in the San Francisco Bay Area with his wife, Canadian writer Tia V. Travis.

Anne Perry's publishing career began with *The Cater Street Hangman*. Published in 1979, the first book in the series featured the Victorian policeman Thomas Pitt and his well-born wife Charlotte. This is arguably the longest sustained crime series by a living writer. *Buckingham Palace Gardens*, the latest in the series, appeared on the *New York Times* best-seller list in April 2008. In 1990, Anne started a second series of detective novels with *The Face of a Stranger*. Set about thirty-five years earlier, they features the private detective William Monk and volatile nurse Hester Latterly. The most recent of these (fifteenth in the series) is *The Dark Assassin*, which appeared in the *New York Times* best-seller list. Anne won an Edgar award in 2000 with her short story "Heroes." The main character in the story features in an ambitious five-book series set during the First World War. The last of these was recently published in autumn 2007. None of her books has ever been out of print, and they have received critical acclaim and huge popular success: over twenty million copies of her books are in print worldwide. Her books have appeared on best-seller lists in a number of foreign countries, where she has also had excellent reviews. *The Times* selected her as one of the "100 Masters of Crime." Currently Anne is working on more titles in the Pitt and Monk series, and her next published novel will be a stand-alone epic set in the exotic and dangerous world of the Byzantine Empire.

Steve Perry has written scores of novels, animated teleplays, short stories, along with a couple of spec movie scripts. A number of his books have appeared on the *New York Times* best-seller list, and he is the co-author, with Michael Reaves, of the blockbuster Star Wars novel *Death Star*.

~~~

Melville Davisson Post (1869–1930) was a successful lawyer who turned to writing. He first gained fame with his three books of crime stories about Randolph Mason, a lawyer who used his knowledge to help criminals evade justice. Later, he combined elements of both the mystery and fantasy genres in the tales of Uncle Abner, a highly religious man who battled evil wherever it could be found, but primarily in the Virginia backwoods.

~~~

Laura Resnick is the author of dozens of short stories, as well as such fantasy novels as *Disappearing Nightly*, *In Legend Born*, *The Destroyer Goddess*, and *The White Dragon*, which made the "Year's Best" lists of *Publishers Weekly* and *Voya*. You can find her on the Web at www. LauraResnick.com.

~~~

Mike Resnick is, according to *Locus*, the all-time leading award winner, living or dead, for short science fiction. He has won five Hugos, plus other major awards in the USA, France, Japan, Spain, Croatia, and Poland, and has been nominated in England, Italy, and Australia. He is the author of sixty-one novels, 250 short stories, and two screenplays, and has edited more than forty anthologies. His work has been translated into twenty-six languages.

~~~

Michael A. Stackpole is an award-winning novelist, graphic novelist, screenwriter, podcaster, game and computer game designer best known for his *New York Times* best-selling novels *I, Jedi*, and *Rogue Squadron*. "If Vanity Doesn't Kill Me" is the second of seven Trick Malloy stories—most of which are available at his website: www.Stormwolf.com. Mike lives in the Phoenix area and enjoys both swing dancing and indoor soccer in his spare time.

Elizabeth A. Vaughan writes fantasy romance, and her most recent novel is *Destiny's Star*, part of the "Star Series" published by Berkley Sensation. Other Wan Sui Ye stories appear in *Furry Fantastic* and *A Girl's Guide to Guns and Monsters*. Currently she is owned by three incredibly spoiled cats and lives in the Northwest Territory, on the outskirts of the Black Swamp, along Mad Anthony's Trail on the banks of the Maumee River. You can learn more about her books at www.EAVWrites.com.

Kristine Kathryn Rusch is an award-winning mystery, romance, science fiction, and fantasy writer. She has written many novels under various names, including Kristine Grayson for romance, and Kris Nelscott for mystery. Her novels have made the best-seller lists even in London and have been published in fourteen countries and thirteen different languages. Her awards range from the Ellery Queen Readers Choice Award to the John W. Campbell Award. She is the only person in the history of the science fiction field to have won a Hugo award for editing and a Hugo award for fiction. Her short work has been reprinted in thirteen Year's Best collections.

In 2007, she became one of a handful of writers to twice win the Best Mystery Novel award given for the best mystery published in the Northwest (for her Kris Nelscott books). Her novella, "Diving into the Wreck," has won the prestigious international UPC award, given in Spain to the best science fiction novella in English, French, Spanish or Catalan. That novella also won the Asimov's Readers Choice award. She is the former editor of prestigious *The Magazine of Fantasy and Science Fiction*. Before that, she and Dean Wesley Smith started and ran Pulphouse Publishing, a science fiction and mystery press in Eugene. She lives and works on the Oregon Coast.

Michelle writes as both Michelle Sagara and Michelle West; she is also published as Michelle Sagara West. She lives in Toronto with her long-suffering husband and her two children, and to her regret has no dogs. Reading is one of her lifelong passions, and she is sometimes paid for her opinions about what she's read by the venerable *Magazine of Fantasy and Science Fiction*. No matter how many bookshelves she buys, there is Never Enough Shelf space. Ever.

About the Editor

Martin H. Greenberg is the CEP of Tekno Books and its predecessor companies, now the largest book developer of commercial fiction and nonfiction in the world, with over 2,300 published books that have been translated into 33 languages. He is the recipient of an unprecedented four Lifetime Achievement Awards in the Science Fiction, Mystery, and Supernatural Horror genres—the Milford Award in Science Fiction, the Solstice Award in Science Fiction, the Bram Stoker Award in Horror, and the Ellery Queen Award in Mystery—the only person in publishing history to have received all four awards.